continued . . .

"Fun, fast moving and introduces some wonderful new characters, along with having plenty of familiar faces."

—*Romantic Times*

"A laugh-out-loud series. Ms. Bartlett puts a different spin on the vampire romance. Fast paced with appealing characters you can fall in love with. It's like visiting old friends."

—*Night Owl Romance*

Real Vampires Live Large

"The return of ancient vampiress Glory surviving in a modern world is fun to follow as she struggles with her lover, a wannabe lover, vampire killers and Energy Vampires; all want a piece of her in differing ways. Fans of lighthearted paranormal romps will enjoy Gerry Bartlett's fun tale starring a heroine who has never forgiven Blade for biting her when she was bloated."

—*Midwest Book Review*

"Outstanding . . . equal parts humor and spice, with mystery and adventure tossed into the mix. Glory's world is a place I look forward to visiting again, the sooner the better."

—*Fresh Fiction*

"Gerry Bartlett has created a laugh-out-loud book that I couldn't put down. *Real Vampires Live Large* is a winner."

—*The Romance Readers Connection*

"Glory gives girl power a whole new meaning, especially in the undead way. What a fun read!"   —*All About Romance*

Real Vampires Have Curves

"A sharp, sassy, sexy read. Gerry Bartlett creates a vampire to die for in this sizzling new series."   —Kimberly Raye,
USA Today bestselling author of *Sucker for Love*

Real Vampires Hate Their Thighs

GERRY BARTLETT

BERKLEY BOOKS, NEW YORK

THE BERKLEY PUBLISHING GROUP
Published by the Penguin Group
Penguin Group (USA) Inc.
375 Hudson Street, New York, New York 10014, USA
Penguin Group (Canada), 90 Eglinton Avenue East, Suite 700, Toronto, Ontario M4P 2Y3, Canada
(a division of Pearson Penguin Canada Inc.)
Penguin Books Ltd., 80 Strand, London WC2R 0RL, England
Penguin Group Ireland, 25 St. Stephen's Green, Dublin 2, Ireland (a division of Penguin Books Ltd.)
Penguin Group (Australia), 250 Camberwell Road, Camberwell, Victoria 3124, Australia
(a division of Pearson Australia Group Pty. Ltd.)
Penguin Books India Pvt. Ltd., 11 Community Centre, Panchsheel Park, New Delhi—110 017, India
Penguin Group (NZ), 67 Apollo Drive, Rosedale, North Shore 0632, New Zealand
(a division of Pearson New Zealand Ltd.)
Penguin Books (South Africa) (Pty.) Ltd., 24 Sturdee Avenue, Rosebank, Johannesburg 2196,
South Africa

Penguin Books Ltd., Registered Offices: 80 Strand, London WC2R 0RL, England

This is an original publication of The Berkley Publishing Group.

This is a work of fiction. Names, characters, places, and incidents either are the product of the author's imagination or are used fictitiously, and any resemblance to actual persons, living or dead, business establishments, events, or locales is entirely coincidental. The publisher does not have any control over and does not assume any responsibility for author or third-party websites or their content.

PRINTING HISTORY
Berkley trade paperback edition / February 2010

Library of Congress Cataloging-in-Publication Data

Bartlett, Gerry.
    Real vampires hate their thighs / Gerry Bartlett.—Berkley Trade pbk. ed.
        p.   cm.
    ISBN 978-0-425-23223-1
    1. Vampires—Fiction.   2. Saint Clair, Glory (Fictitious character)—Fiction.   I. Title.
    PS3602.A83945R427 2010
    813'.6—dc22   2009044141

PRINTED IN THE UNITED STATES OF AMERICA

10   9   8   7   6   5   4   3   2   1

This book is dedicated to Kathy Bartlett,
who unselfishly gives her time to make sure sick
and abandoned animals find loving homes.
She and other volunteers like her have saved more of
our furry friends than I can count.
She also keeps her wicked stepmother's hair blond.
Thanks for being kind and *brilliant, Kathy.*

Acknowledgments

Thanks to my wonderful agent, Kimberly Whalen, who had faith in me and Glory's story from the very beginning. You rock, Kim. And I really appreciate my editor, Kate Seaver, and her instincts. She always spots what needs "tweaking" to make the book flow in the right direction. I've been blessed with a wonderful team at Berkley, including copy editor Mary Pell, who has been absolutely on point with her comments and "catches." Believe me, I know how lucky I am.

My fans are the best. On MySpace, I have a great group of friends whose words of encouragement mean everything to me. Thanks to Heather Weygandt, who started the wonderful MySpace.com/realvampswithcurves fan site. And to Danielle Garrett, who created the super realvampglorystclairfansite .weebly.com. Now Dani and Heather work together to keep it Google-worthy. Thanks so much, ladies! This just blows me away.

One

You know, there's something very unsexy about meeting your lover behind a Dumpster. But, hey, at least Gloriana St. Clair still had a lover to meet. There had been some nights recently when I'd been afraid I'd have to give celibacy another shot. You think a woman PMSing is bad? Try taking on a celibate vampire. But no worries. My guy was waiting just around the corner.

I adjusted my black "Cher in the eighties" wig, slung my purse over my shoulder and navigated the alley in my five-inch heels.

"Jeez, something reeks." Valdez, my bodyguard, sniffed.

"You got that right. Even ritzy hotels have bad garbage." I had a leash attached to him, but God forbid I actually tug on it. We gave the Dumpster a wide berth and walked right into a guy with a camera. Guys with cameras were the reason we were sneaking out the back door in the first place.

Camera Guy looked me over, trying to figure out if I was "Somebody." Then he eyed the dog on the end of the leash. Apparently even the canine failed the test.

"Forget it. I'm getting out of this pit and hitting the front door." The photographer snorted in disgust.

"Good idea. I heard Usher's coming down." I saw him sprint away and glanced down at Valdez. "Your disguise did the trick. Mine is pretty lame. Anyone can throw on a wig and sunglasses. But yours is the bomb."

"What'd I tell ya? I'm brilliant." Valdez grinned and practically dragged me to the street. *"Blade's here. He's got Flo and Richard with him."*

I still couldn't get used to my shape-shifting dog's new look. A Rottweiler. Cute, with his pink tongue and black mouth, but he looked a lot more dangerous than his usual curly coated Labradoodle self. Then I saw Blade, Jeremy Blade, my four-hundred-year-plus lover and the man who'd made me vampire all those centuries ago. Then he'd been known as Angus Jeremiah Campbell III, heir to Clan Campbell. With his father an immortal vamp too, though, it didn't look like he'd be laird anytime soon. Which was fine by me. It left him free to roam the world. Lately that had included following me to Austin and now this little trip to Los Angeles.

I stopped and checked him out. He always looked so good to me. Tall, buff and sexy as hell. But tonight he was in a Hollywood-style white silk shirt that made the most of his dark hair and eyes. Add expensive trousers with loafers and no socks and I wondered if some stylist had gotten hold of him.

Before I could ask, he had me in his arms and up against all that hard maleness. Yum. He tasted delicious, and I could feel his fangs when he kissed me. Great start to my evening.

"Nice to see you too, Jerry." I grinned up at him when he let me come up for air.

"You look very sexy. Forget going out. Let's go back to my hotel room, Gloriana." He obviously appreciated the effort I'd taken with my wardrobe choice.

When you've got too much in the caboose like I do, you learn to play up your assets. So I'd chosen a plunging neckline with blue sparkles that matched my eyes. Add a push-up bra and I guarantee male eyes never went below my personal equator. I'd put on a twirly skirt in black with some strappy black heels that were just made for dancing. So no hotel room. I wanted to hit some clubs.

"We're going out, Jerry. I'm sure Flo is with me on this." I pushed him toward the car he'd rented.

Do you wonder why we're not staying at the same hotel? Why we're sneaking around Dumpsters? Gee, nosey, aren't you? Okay, it's like this. I'm pretending to be engaged to a newly turned vampire, rock star Israel Caine. Since I'm indirectly responsible for his "condition," I'm mentoring him, helping him deal with the complications. Like no daytime gigs. You see where I'm going with this? So when the paparazzi, like that guy I just avoided by the Dumpster, kept seeing us together, they assumed we were an item. Ray (all his friends call him Ray) decided to go along with it, and next thing you know, we're pretending to be engaged.

Now, I know I should have called a halt to things, but, sue me, I kind of groove on the idea of the world thinking I'm a rock star's main squeeze. I mean, me, slightly chubby Glory St. Clair, who is nobody, living in the fast lane? I'm just the "barely making ends meet" owner of a vintage-clothing shop in Austin, Texas, and a sort-of ancient vampire, yet I'm engaged to a rock star. How cool is that?

And Ray is totally hot, sexy and when he sings . . . I was hooked on his music before he'd ever been dumped on me. Literally. Then he turned out to be a great guy and—would you believe it?—into me. I know, I thought I was dreaming. Sure, it's 90 percent gratitude for saving his life. Whatever.

It made Jerry superjealous. And that's not such a bad thing in a long-term relationship. Guys can get to taking you for granted after the first few centuries. Anyway, Ray's up for a Grammy. And the awards are in a week. So we're here in Hollywood. Israel Caine and Gloriana St. Clair, the happy couple. I promised Jerry I'd break up with Ray when we got back to Austin. After I get to wear the fabulous dress a designer is whipping up for me as we speak. For when we walk the red carpet. You see why I couldn't dump Ray just yet?

Now, can we get back to me sneaking out to meet Jerry?

Ray's at press briefings, or rehearsals or something. He doesn't need me so I arranged to go out, discreetly, of course. Ray knows I'm really with Jerry. No big deal, darn it. Except Ray *had* insisted on separate hotels so maybe he's a little jealous. Hmm.

My best friend, Flo, and her husband, Richard, came along on Jerry's chartered jet (yeah, Jerry's rich). Now I want to have fun. And not just one-on-one in a hotel room. We can do that, and have done that, many times, in Austin. All over the world, for that matter. And, after some dancing, I'm sure we'll do it again—I gave Jerry a hot look—and again.

"You sure you want to wait?" Jerry had read my mind and his own mental message promised all kinds of special services while his hand slid over my backside.

Valdez tugged on his leash and I snapped back to the here and now.

"Anticipation makes everything better." I grinned and patted Jerry's cheek. "Hi, guys. I love this car. You rented this, Jerry?" A vintage white Cadillac convertible with red leather interior sat at the curb. The top was down and three vampires lounged in the backseat. "Cool."

"Flo talked me into it. She said the Mercedes I was going for was stuffy." Jerry grinned. "She picked out the clothes too. What do you think?"

"I think Florence da Vinci should be on your payroll as your stylist." I ran my finger in between Jerry's button holes to the smooth skin of his chest. "You look unbelievably hot." I leaned in and ran my mouth along his jugular. "I'll show you how hot later. She tell you to go commando?" I felt Jerry swallow against my lips.

"Flo, you're hired."

"Of course I did. See, Jeremiah? You must always listen to me, *caro*." Flo jumped up on her knees. "Glory, that wig is not your color. You should have gone for a deep auburn."

"I had to take what I could get, Flo. Barry, Ray's publicist, brought it to me. Maybe you can find me something better for tomorrow night." I smiled at Richard, then at the man on Flo's other side. "Damian, didn't know you were coming."

"I decided you needed a guide. I know this area. You want to explore the vampire scene here? I'm your man. There's a club on Hollywood Boulevard you must go to." Damian Sabatini, Flo's brother, winked. "Jeremiah isn't crazy about the idea, but I say, what's the harm?"

"Too many vampires in one place is asking for trouble."

I slipped into the front passenger seat, laughing when the grumbling in the back started. Because there was nowhere else for Valdez to go. The front had a console and there was a seat belt law. So the three vamps in the backseat had to make room for my pooch.

I don't go anywhere without my dog slash bodyguard. Not my rule—Jerry's. Since he's paid for a succession of Valdezes for centuries, even when Jerry and I aren't a couple, I go along with it. It's a safety issue. Valdez makes me feel protected. A single girl can't be too careful, you know. And I've had some close calls lately. Not everyone loves me. Can you imagine that?

Jerry drove and Damian gave him directions. It was a cool, clear night and traffic was heavy but moving. Flo and I had fun spotting famous boutiques along Rodeo Drive. Many of them were open late and we promised ourselves a shopping trip another night. Not that I could afford anything in those shops, but I did have enough credit on one of my cards to splurge on something if we could find a resale shop.

When Jerry pulled up in front of an art gallery, Flo and I looked at each other.

"What's this? I thought we were going dancing." I leaned over the backseat. "Damian?"

"It's here. But in back. Behind the gallery. We'll enter through the alley." Damian told Jerry where to park and we were soon on the sidewalk.

There was plenty of people-watching here. Interesting. And not just humans in the swim. There were the usual Goths, vamp wannabees and tourists clicking away with their digital cameras. But there were other entities too. The real deal who looked more human than the humans. They exchanged knowing looks with us as we window-shopped various galleries and headed for a narrow gap between buildings. The fearful wouldn't have ventured down the dark walkway. We zipped along at vamp speed.

I was glad to be in the gloom and eager to see what a real vampire club looked like. I'd avoided them in the cities I'd been in before, not sure I'd be safe as a woman without a protector. Now, surrounded by Blade, Richard, Damian and Valdez, I figured that I had an army at my back. And, hey, Flo and I could kick butt ourselves.

The door in the alley was painted gray and had an old-fashioned hatch in it. Like a speakeasy I'd been to once, back in the roaring twenties. Damian dialed a number with his cell phone, proving that this was twenty-first-century stuff, and the hatch opened. A man's face appeared, his nose quivered, then he glanced at us before he nodded and threw open the door.

"Welcome." The man was dressed in L.A. evening wear. Expensive, casual and mostly black. He was tall, slim and vampire. "I'm afraid the shifter will have to wait outside unless he wishes to assume a more human form."

Not a conventionally handsome guy, but I wouldn't toss him out of my bed. Hey, figure of speech. I glanced at Jerry and smiled. Fortunately, he wasn't reading my mind; he was busy assessing the environment, checking for dangers, that kind of thing. Once a warrior, always a warrior.

"No, the shifter will wait out here." Jerry signaled Valdez, who grumbled, but settled next to the door outside.

Inside, there was music with a good beat, loud enough to encourage dancing, and a lighted floor crowded with couples. Some were same sex; some weren't. A bar in the corner was also crowded and I could see martini glasses being drained. Either they were selling synthetics or they had a supply of the real deal. My nose told me there was some fresh on hand and I was suddenly very thirsty. There was lots of chrome and glass and shiny gray walls that seemed to glow until the lights were dimmed as the music slowed. The effect was very urban chic, not the "dark, creepy crypt" thing that a mortal would expect from a vampire club.

Our greeter was still by Jerry's side. "I'll need a credit card from one of you to run a tab. There's a cover, plus if you want to use one of the donors, we have private booths. I can get you a menu if you're interested."

"We want to see what you've got." Damian handed him a Platinum Card.

The vamp smiled and showed fangs. "I'm Stephen, your host tonight. Let me know if you need something or someone you don't see on the menu." He snapped his fingers and a woman in a skimpy costume à la *Star Wars* handed each of us a laminated card. "And if you need an explanation of any of our choices, just ask your waitress. Let me lead you to a table." He took off across the crowded room and I, for one, wasn't going to let him out of my sight.

Wow! Talk about a menu. What was a "Train Wreck"? And what about a "Three Alarm"? Since my shop had been firebombed, I really didn't have the urge to check out anything to do with fire. Unless . . . three donors? Damian grinned and winked at me, obviously reading my mind. Hmm. Guess I was being too literal.

I did see that they sold fresh AB negative by the glass, hopefully from a blood bank somewhere. I'd sworn off feeding from humans. Stephen got us a round table near the dance floor and introduced Mandy, another barely dressed space cadet, as our waitress. Soon we each had a glass of our favorite blood type in front of us and I was ready to dance.

"Come on, Jerry. They're playing our song." I pulled him to his feet. I dropped my wig and sunglasses on the table.

"I don't think I've ever heard this song before."

I laughed. Of course he hadn't. Jerry's not exactly into rock bands. I stay very current. Because I believe in blending with my environment. As a rocker's girlfriend, I'd been really into this kind of music lately.

"Humor me, Jerry. Just stand there and look good and I'll dance around you." I leaned into him and gave him an encouraging kiss. That got him headed in the right direction and we were soon moving to the music.

When things slowed down and the lights dimmed to almost complete black except for the glowing pedestals under each table and the base of the bar, he pulled me into his arms. He'd taken some dance lessons not too long ago, but forget those. This was all about bodies and a rhythm that had more to do with sex than dancing. I held on to him and breathed in his yummy male essence. The music sped up, the lights got brighter and I'd just about decided that Jerry's hotel room was the right place for us after all when I felt a hand land on my back.

"Gloria Simmons! I swear to God, I never thought I'd see you here in L.A."

I turned, ready to deny the alias, though that had been the name I'd gone by in Vegas for almost two decades. But when I saw who it was, I forgot all about denials.

"Sheri!" I threw my arms around her neck. I'd had one good vampire friend in those days, and Sheri had been it. I'd told her I was leaving town and intended to keep in touch, but the e-mails had dwindled lately. "It's Glory St. Clair now. This is Jeremy Blade."

"Tell me this isn't the Scotsman you were pining for all those years." Sheri looked Jerry over from head to toe. "Girl, you were crazy for avoiding him."

"That's what I keep telling her." Jerry pulled both of us off the dance floor toward our table. "Gloria Simmons was your name in Las Vegas. Glory didn't really dance topless, did she, Sheri?"

Sheri winked at me. "Why wouldn't she? She's got the perfect equipment." She threw back her shoulders, stunning in a short red dress cut low in front. The clingy material made it clear her dancer's body was perfect. I'd always used tricks to make mine look good.

"Thanks, Sheri. It really is great to see you. Remember,

what happens in Vegas, stays in Vegas." I winked back at her and smiled at Jerry.

"I hear ya. But, Glory, honey, you should come back. I've got a part in the new vampire show. You'd love it. They want you to wear fake fangs, even troll through the casino in them." She laughed and tossed her dark hair. "They figure I'm one of their best erotic angels. 'Cause I wear my fangs everywhere I go."

"Sheri, you've got to meet my other friends." I didn't see Flo and Richard but Damian strolled up to the table, a full glass in his hand. "Damian, meet my old friend Sheri LaDouce. Sheri, this is Damian Sabatini."

"Honey, this year it's Sherry Landolt. You know how it is." She turned and got an eyeful of Damian. "Well, hello there."

In typical Damian fashion, he picked up her hand and pulled it to his lips. *"Bonjour, mademoiselle. Parlez-vous français?"*

"Mais oui." Sheri fluttered her eyelashes. "Let's cut the foreign stuff. Glory never could get her mouth around any of that. But it makes for wonderful pillow talk, don't you think, *cheri?"*

"Ah, I think we already speak the same language." Damian grinned at me. "I love your friend. Will you dance, Sheri?" He gestured at our waitress, pressed some bills in her hand and in moments, the lights dimmed again and there was another slow, sensual song playing.

"Oh, boy, I think I'm going to have my hands full, literally." Sheri laughed and let herself be pulled toward the dance floor. "Nice meeting you, Jeremy. See ya, Glory."

"Shouldn't you warn her about Damian?" Jerry looked like he wanted to go after the couple.

"Should I warn Damian about *her* is the question." I laughed and sat at the table. Damian's a Casanova type, but I knew Sheri was more than a match for him. "You should have seen her operate in Vegas. Sheri never has money problems because she always has a sugar daddy. Damian better get that Platinum Card ready. Before Sheri gets through with him, she'll have shopped Rodeo Drive from one end to the other, courtesy of his plastic."

"Good for her. He can afford it. Now, about that topless thing." Jerry stared at my cleavage. "I know you'd look good, Glory, but the thought—"

"Here's Flo and Richard. I wonder if they found out what a 'Train Wreck' is." I wasn't about to let Jerry know if I'd danced topless or not. I figure a little mystery in a relationship is a good thing.

"Glory, you'll never guess who we just met." Flo sat next to me.

"It's bogus. Don't get her stirred up about this nonsense." Richard sat and tapped his fingers on the table. He looked as handsome as Jerry did, but Richard is white blond and tanned with bright blue eyes. Obviously Flo had picked out his wardrobe too and he had a "Beverly Hills hottie" look to him that had other women in the room licking their lips. I'm sure Flo had been busy sending mental messages to those vamps to back off or die.

"You never know, Ricardo. It might be true. I owe it to my best friend to let her know, *amante*, that what she thought is impossible could be possible." Flo grabbed my arm.

"What are you talking about? What's impossible?" I winced. Flo's got a grip on her.

"There's a man here tonight. He's famous among the Los Angeles vampires. He claims he can make anyone, even vampires, lose weight." Flo frowned down at her thighs and I wanted to slap her. Excuse me? They were barely a six. What did she want? A four?

Wait. Had I heard her right? Not possible. Back in 1604 when Jerry had turned me vampire after I'd begged him to—so we could be together forever—I'd been "healthy." I mean, women who carried some extra weight back then were voluptuous and proud of it. So I didn't think ahead. If I'd known then what I know now, I'd have fasted a few days before the big turning. Lost ten pounds or so first. But, no, Glory was bloating, or at least that's my story and I'm sticking to it.

So I was stuck forever with hips that would have been great for delivering twelve-pound babies if I'd ever had that option. And thighs . . . Well, God knows if I were a Thanksgiving turkey, entire Pilgrim villages could have feasted on one of my thighs.

"Florence da Vinci. Are you telling me that there's a man here who says he can help a vampire lose weight?" I stood. Ready to ambush this guy and use every bit of my credit limit for a shot at skinny.

"Gloriana, stop this nonsense. You're perfect. Why would you want to lose weight?" Jerry stood beside me and patted my rump. Wrong move.

I turned slowly and looked him in the eye. He must have seen something there, because big, brave warrior Jerry actually backed up a step.

"Don't *ever* pat my butt in public again." I said this past the fangs that had shot down into my mouth like maybe I was thinking about ripping out Jerry's throat. Overreaction? Maybe. But, come on. Do you like having your fat ass patted in public? Why not just shine a spotlight on it? Or hang a sign? Hey, world, look at my lady's big butt. I just couldn't take it at that moment. Not when I suddenly, against all reason and rational thinking, had a glimmer of hope that maybe, just maybe, I might finally be able to do something about a problem that had weighed me down for centuries.

Two

"Where is he?" I reached for my vintage black satin bag and pulled out my lipstick, quickly slicking on a fresh coat. Then I checked my hair by feel. Damn, Jerry had flattened one side when he nuzzled my neck during our slow dance. I finger combed it and glanced at Flo.

"You look great. He's in one of the booths over by the exit. I'll show you." Flo frowned down at Richard's hand on her arm. "You're not thinking of stopping me, are you?"

"I didn't like his looks. I don't trust him." Richard exchanged stares with Jerry.

"You spent two minutes with the man. He was surrounded by beautiful women." Flo's smile was tight. "Beautiful, skinny bitches who got more than a casual glance from you, *caro*. If you don't want to sleep on the floor, I suggest you demonstrate your trust, eh?"

Richard backed up, his hands in the air. "Did I say I didn't trust you, my heart? It's the man I don't trust. I'm just suggesting to Blade that he go with Gloriana, see the man for himself. Assess the situation."

"Assess this, Richard." I got up in his face. "I can decide for myself who I trust or not." I whipped around when I heard a sound from Jerry. "You will *not* come with me. I know you don't get that this is important to me. Tough. I want to meet the guy. I'm *going* to meet the guy." Damn it, I was shaking and my stomach was in a knot. And it didn't take mind reading to know that Jerry thought this was a silly overreaction. Well, what did I expect? I took a breath and changed strategies.

"Jerry, lover, I know you appreciate my curves." I wrapped my arms around his waist and leaned against him. "That's one of the reasons I love you. You've always accepted me just as I am." I looked up and smiled, then kissed his strong chin. "But times have changed and thin is in. I want to see what this guy has to say. Humor me and stay here. Talk to Richard. Read the menu. Hey, check out the Train Wreck." I glanced at the curtained booths. "As long as it doesn't involve rescuing beautiful naked women from the caboose."

"The only caboose I'm interested in is yours, which is perfect, by the way." Jerry grinned and held me close, smart enough this time not to touch the caboose area. "Hurry, and you and I can play Train Wreck back at my hotel."

I kissed his smiling lips and patted his cheek. "It's a date. Flo, let's go. What's this guy's name anyway?"

Flo glanced at Jerry. "I'll tell you on the way. Come on. I think he was leaving and I don't want you to miss him." She grabbed my hand and dragged me across the room. "Richard, no beautiful naked women for you either, *amante*."

"You're more than enough woman for me, Florence." Richard's voice was amused as we left the men behind.

As soon as we were on the other side of the dance floor and the music was back to a loud rock song, I dragged Flo to a halt.

"Why didn't you want to tell me this guy's name in front of Jerry? What's up, Flo?" I studied my friend. She looked perfect as usual—red wrap dress and high, high heels that brought her up to my chin. Her dark hair was in a new tousled do that looked like the work of a high-priced L.A.

beautician. She glanced back at our table, but the crowds of paranormals at play blocked our view.

"He's a Scot. I think Jeremiah might know him. And not in a good way." Flo bit her bottom lip. New shade of lipstick. I was definitely going to have to find out the name. The red reminded me of—

"Wait a minute. You're not that big on history. At least not Scotland's, as far as I know. Unless he's an artist." I grabbed her arm. "Who is this guy? Did he say something to make you think he knows Jerry?"

"No, but I've heard this name before. You know I'm friends with Magdalena and Angus. They don't like the men of this—how they call it?—clan." Flo made a face. "Foolish feuds. But they've hated each other for centuries."

Angus and Mag, Jerry's parents. Angus likes me okay, but Mag hates me with a passion usually reserved for head lice and bad haircuts. I knew of only one clan that the Campbells had a real hate on for.

Damian walked up, Sheri by his side. "There you two are. Florence, I've been keeping Ian here like you asked, but he's ready to leave. Gloriana, you won't believe this guy. Actually claims he can make a vampire lose pounds and inches." Damian laughed and slung his arm around my waist. "Stay away from him. You don't need to do either." He slid a hand dangerously close to no-man-but-Jerry's-land, and I grabbed his fingers.

"Thanks, Damian, but I want to hear what he has to say anyway. Would you go get him and introduce us? Please?" I knew better than to take his flirting seriously, but I couldn't deny it felt good to have a handsome man making that kind of move on me.

"At your service, *cara*. Always. Remember that the next time Blade leaves the country." He winked, then disappeared into the crowd.

I sighed, then noticed Flo and Sheri checking each other out. "Sheri, this is Florence da Vinci Mainwaring, my best girlfriend in Austin. Flo, Sheri Landolt, my best girlfriend in Las Vegas."

"You're Damian's sister, right?" Sheri smiled and nodded. "Bet you've got some great stories about your brother."

"Pah, forget him. I want to hear about Las Vegas. Did you and Glory really dance topless?" Flo moved closer. "I would like to do that, but I'm so short, you see. Do you think they would have a place for me in the chorus?"

"Forget it, Flo. Your husband would have a fit if you danced like that for anyone but him. And, trust me, dancing in high heels while balancing a gigantic headdress night after night isn't as much fun as it sounds. Am I right, Sheri?"

Sheri said something to Flo about the killer heels while I zeroed in on Damian coming toward us, and the tall man walking beside him. Obviously this was the diet guru, though he looked more like a Viking warrior with his long blond hair, hawklike features and blue eyes. Damian said something and those brilliant blue eyes suddenly zeroed in on me. They were so penetrating that I threw up a shield to keep him from reading my thoughts. And my thoughts? Those naughty girls were stripping the finely tailored suit off his buff body and imagining him in a loincloth and at my mercy.

The men shouldered their way through the crowd toward us, leaving women and several men panting in their wake.

"I'd still like to try it at least once. If only to see the look on Ricardo's face." Flo laughed and turned to check out what I was staring at. "Hmm. *Molto bello.* Eh, Glory?"

"Uh." I couldn't drag myself back from the fantasy of peeking under the loincloth. "Oh, yeah."

Damian stopped in front of us and smiled. "Gloriana, allow me to introduce Ian MacDonald."

"Oh, shit." I clapped a hand over my mouth. But honestly, things had just gone to hell in a big way.

Ian laughed and held out his hand. "Well, that's a first. Good evening, Gloriana. What did I do to deserve such an enthusiastic greeting?"

I took his hand, drawn to the twinkle in his eyes and the flash of his white, white teeth. His grip was firm and too brief. I bit back a sigh.

"Sorry about that, Ian. It's just that you're a MacDonald and I'm here with a Campbell. Maybe you've heard of him. Angus Jeremiah Campbell III." I winced when Ian's face lost its charm and he spat something in what I figured was the old language. His hand went to his back in a gesture I knew well. Jerry did the same thing in certain situations. Reaching for his broadsword. Didn't have it on him, of course. Just a reflex. But I knew Jerry carried a knife hidden in his waistband under his shirt. Did Ian? I hoped I didn't have to find out.

"Relax, my friend. This is the twenty-first century. Surely old feuds can be forgotten." Damian clapped Ian on the shoulder and looked over the crowd, obviously checking to make sure Jerry wasn't within dagger-throwing range. Because, hello, Ian *had* produced one from somewhere. A sharp silver knife gleamed in his left hand.

"Where is he?" Ian's voice had gone from charming to stone cold.

I wanted to cry. My diet dreams were evaporating because of a damned centuries-old feud. No way. I stepped in front of Ian and put my hand on his forearm.

"He's not close by. I am. Talk to me. About this diet thing you've got going." I smiled and leaned in, flashing cleavage. "Look. I know your feud is important. It's a matter of honor, I'm sure." I felt the muscles clench under my fingertips and glanced at Flo and Sheri. "Campbells versus MacDonalds. It goes back a long way, a really long way. But a canny Scot knows when to put business first. Am I right?"

We all watched Ian visibly struggle to regain his sophisticated veneer. A really thin one, obviously. Because all it had taken was mention of his old enemy and he was right back in primitive killing-machine mode. Finally he slid the dagger out of sight and ran his long fingers through his hair.

"Sorry, ladies. I don't usually lose control like that. Of

course I'm interested in your business." He was still scanning the room, my cleavage obviously not tempting enough to keep his mind off his target. And I bet he'd noticed that I wasn't exactly sporting designer labels or wearing a load of diamonds like my buddy Flo. She waved her hand and her six-carat rock seemed to snap him back to attention. At least he looked at me when I squeezed his biceps.

"We understand, don't we, ladies? Who here hasn't had a hate on for someone?" I glanced at Sheri.

"No kidding. Glory, do you remember that freak who used to do our hair at the Grand? I swear, she just loved to bring tears to my eyes." Sheri snarled and we all saw that my beautiful friend had an edgy side. "I finally had enough of her trying to snatch me bald." She looked at Damian through her thick black lashes, obviously enhanced with some extensions. "Want to hear how I got even, big guy?"

"Of course, *cheri.*" Damian grinned, clearly liking his women with some bite. "Excuse us." He leaned down and whispered in my ear. "We'll stop and make sure Blade doesn't head this way, but don't linger, Glory. This man is dangerous. Be careful."

Ian smiled and slid his arm around my shoulders as soon as Damian disappeared into the crowd with Sheri. He'd obviously heard Damian's warning.

"Damian's right, Gloriana. I can be dangerous. But not to you and Florence. You came over here to ask me about my special products." He gestured toward one of the secluded booths. "Join me for a drink and I'll tell you all about them." He swept his eyes from my head down to my toes, lingering at the spots where I'd like to lose some inches. "Back when I was a lad, you would have been considered a handsome armful. But times change, don't they, lass? Bad for you, good for me and my business." He smiled sympathetically. "When were you turned?"

"Early sixteen hundreds." This man understood me like Jerry never had. I wanted to press my face to his strong chest and sob about all the times I'd felt bad about my size.

"Your figure was perfect then. Still is to an ancient vampire like me." He slid his hand from my shoulder down to my arm. He finally seemed to be giving my cleavage the attention it deserved. "But these modern times are different. I can tell from the way you're dressed that you're a woman who likes to stay current. Am I right?"

"Yes." I blinked before I let him whammy me right into one of those curtained booths and into something I might regret. This guy had some serious intuition. Or experience with women. Of course he did. It was his business to know what a woman wanted.

He turned to Florence. "I can't imagine, Florence, that you're serious about needing to lose weight. You're here to support your friend, of course."

Flo smiled, preening under his dazzling smile and obvious approval of her perfect figure. "I think Glory looks great. As you say. But she wants to be smaller. So I have to help my BFF." Flo ran her hands down the sides of her hips in her size-six designer dress that was obviously straight from a Rodeo Drive boutique. "I would like to lose just a few pounds. If I could choose where they would come from."

"Like the liposuction that mortals use." Ian shook his head. "Afraid I can't help you there. There's no predicting where the weight will come off. I say you should leave your body alone. What does your husband say?"

"Why, I wouldn't dream of asking him." Flo glanced at me. "We are still on our honeymoon. Now, after centuries of being on my own, I can't imagine asking Richard's permission for anything."

"Of course not." Ian winked at me. "But I'm sure a clever woman like yourself makes your Richard think he's in charge, eh, Florence?"

Flo smiled. "It's a game I play. I ask him for some things. If he really loves me, he must give me what I want. He always does. And it makes him think he's my lord and master." She shrugged, the gesture pure Italian. "So I do a little manipulation. It's a survival skill that has served me well for centuries. *Capisca?*"

"Sure, I get it. It's a fine art, one I admire in a master crafts-man or craftswoman." Ian moved a step closer to Florence.

Flo's eyes narrowed on Ian and she shook her head. "Why I tell you this? I think I'm not the only one who likes a little manipulation."

Ian just kept watching my friend while I tried not to screech at both of them to get back to what was important here, namely my hip measurement. Flo and Ian engaged in a stare-down until Flo suddenly nodded.

"So. We are here for my friend. Help her. Glory looks like she is ready to scream, she's so tired of waiting to find out if this diet thing is true or not."

Ian turned and grinned at me. "Relax, Glory. It's true and I think I can help you. Let me guess. You want to lose ten, maybe fifteen pounds. Is that right?"

For once I was speechless. I swayed toward him. My ulti-mate dream would be to lose twenty. So that people would come up to me and ask me if I'd been sick. Urge me to eat. Who knows? I might even discover cheekbones I never knew I had. You get my drift? I was jerked back from my fantasy by a hand on my other arm.

"This is good news. But we must go now, Glory. Jeremiah will be looking for you. You must meet with Ian later. When you are not with his enemy. *Sì?*" Flo smiled at Ian. "Is it re-ally possible? You're not playing with us, are you?"

"Oh, it's possible. Just not sure it's something I'm willing to do for a Campbell's woman." Ian frowned. "Why would I do one of those dung-eating sods a favor?"

That certainly snapped me out of my hero-worshipping trance. "You wouldn't be doing *him* a favor; you'd be doing it for *me*. I'm engaged to another man. Seriously. Read the tabloids if you don't believe me." I knew I wasn't mak-ing sense and took a breath. "Jerry's my sire. He made me vampire centuries ago. So I owe him, you know? But I'm engaged to Israel Caine, the rock star. We're out here in Los Angeles for the Grammys. Jerry followed us." I was shielding my thoughts with a block the size of the Great Wall of China. "I came to the club to be with my friends Flo, Damian and Richard. Israel's busy with Grammy stuff tonight or he'd be here."

"You're engaged to a mortal?" Ian stared at me, those sapphire eyes rightly very suspicious. He had up his own block and there was no reading his mind.

"Uh, no." I really shouldn't have been telling this, but I guessed Ian would find out if he was going to work with me. "Ray's a vampire." I saw a flare of surprise before Ian went back to suspicion again. "Seriously. He is. But that's a deep, dark secret. I know you won't tell anyone. Right?"

"I wouldn't be in business long if I didn't know how to keep a secret, Gloriana. As to whether I believe this . . ."

"Pick up a tabloid. Any of them. You'll see. I'm the big fat blueberry Ray's engaged to. They call me a blueberry because I had on this blue sweater the first time we were seen together and I've got these"—I looked down at my boobs and flushed— "well, you know. It's been a sensation for weeks. I even have a fan club. Other women of a certain size are rooting for me." I grabbed Ian's shirt, but his bodyguards—both vamps, but tall, tanned California-surfer types—moved in, obviously not too happy about my touching their boss with anything resembling aggression. He shook his head and they backed off without ripping out my throat. Whew. I carefully smoothed out his shirt.

"Sorry, Ian. Listen, though. I don't want my size to make me a tabloid headline. This weight-loss thing would be a dream come true. I'm not with Jerry, uh, Jeremiah Campbell, except when he commands my presence. You know, as my maker. Like he did tonight. Ray, Israel Caine, is my guy now." I gave Flo a warning look when she made a sound. "Please consider taking me on."

"Obviously we can't discuss anything here. Not with a Campbell close by. Men of that ilk would just as soon knife you in the back as not." Ian gestured and his two bodyguards flanked him.

I bit back my knee-jerk response, which was to defend Jerry's honor. Of course he wouldn't knife Ian in the back. But he would take great pleasure in killing a MacDonald. Or in trying to. God, I didn't want to see Jerry fight anyone, ever again. And this would be three against one unless Richard and Damian threw themselves into the fray. Of course Valdez was outside . . .

Forget it. No violence. I'd had enough of it lately, back in Austin, to realize it scared the hell out of me. Sorry if that disappoints you. Not all vampires are bloodthirsty. Well, okay, I'm thirsty for blood, just not for fighting, slashing and general mayhem.

"You're leaving?" I followed Ian and his men as they headed for the door.

"Yes, I have another engagement that I'm already late for." Ian handed me a card. "If you wish to hear more about my program, call me tomorrow night and we'll set up something. A private meeting. Without Campbell interference." He grabbed my shoulders and looked me in the eyes.

I shivered. This guy took intense to a whole new level. But if he could make me thin . . . "Sure, I can manage that. Like I said, Jerry doesn't own me. I'm an independent woman. This was a one-shot deal tonight."

"You said Israel Caine is a vampire. I'll want to verify that. Bring him when we meet." He grinned when I stiffened. "Don't worry. I know how to be discreet or I wouldn't have a business. And this procedure isn't cheap. I assume your fiancé will be willing to pay the freight?"

I determinedly kept from collapsing into a sobbing heap. "I'm sure we'll be able to work something out, though Ray is happy with my figure the way it is. *I'm* the one who wants to lose the weight." Money. Why hadn't I realized this wouldn't come cheap? And I sure wouldn't ask either guy in my life to pay for it. Damn, damn, damn. I bit back a question about payment plans.

"I'm sure you have great powers of persuasion, Gloriana. I'll be expecting to hear from you." I shivered when he slid a fingertip down my cheek. Then he gestured to his men and strode out the door.

I stood there and stared for a moment. Flo came up behind me.

"This isn't going to work, is it, *mia amica*?" She sighed.

"It's complicated, but I'm not giving up just yet." I straightened my spine. "Where are the guys?"

"They have a private booth and a thing on the menu called 'Las Vegas.' Shall we go see?" Flo tugged me toward a curtained area a few yards away.

Behind a black velvet curtain, Richard and Jerry were seated at a poker table. Each had a glass of dark red at their right hand, a thin cigar hanging out of their mouths and cards on the table in front of them. The stacks of chips showed that the play was about even. A scantily clad waitress hovered nearby to keep their glasses full and their ashtrays empty.

"Well, this is interesting. When does the floor show start?" I leaned over Jerry's shoulder and saw that he had a pair of nines and a pair of threes.

Richard laughed. "Glory, you should have blocked your thoughts. Now I'm folding. You win, Blade." Richard threw in his cards and turned to Flo. "Can we leave now? Are you both through with your diet wizard?"

"He was a phony, like you said, *amante*." Flo looked at me. "We waste no more time on such as that."

"Glad to hear it." Jerry raked in the poker chips. "Richard, you owe me big bucks here."

"Here's how I'll repay you. Flo and I are leaving and you and Glory can have this room to yourselves. We're taking KiKi with us." Richard smiled at the waitress and pressed what looked like a large bill in her hand. "No one will disturb you for the next hour. How's that for a payback?"

"Sounds like a plan." Jerry grinned at me. "I think I'm finally going to see how Glory danced in Vegas."

"You wish." I strolled around the room. Sure enough, there were some costumes on the shelves in one corner behind a screen. So role-playing was encouraged here. Well, that was something I could get into. There was also a small stereo and a selection of music that could work for a dance number. I peeked out from behind the screen. "Didn't you guys say you were leaving? Dim the lights on your way out." I grinned and winked at Flo. My friend had known just what to say to cover for me. I'd worry about diets and money tomorrow night. Tonight I was going to appreciate the guy who loved me as is, curves and all.

Jerry leaned back in his chair, the cigar stubbed out in an ashtray and carried off by KiKi. The stained glass lamp hanging over the table dimmed to cast a red glow, and Jerry looked handsome and mysterious in its light.

"Give me a minute to put on my costume, lover, and I'll dance for you." I gave him a finger wave, then disappeared behind the screen. The costumes were skimpy and sparkly. I chose one that had fishnet hose, a bikini bottom with gold spangles that hit halfway down my thighs and a bra top cut low enough to leave little to the imagination. Both bra and bikini were made of a sheer material guaranteed to make Jerry's eyes bug out.

I hit play on the stereo and picked up a black feather boa. When the music started, I eased one arm out from behind the screen and waved the feathers. Gradually, I revealed myself until I could strut around the table toward Jerry. His eyes weren't bugging out. They were narrowed. On me, on my costume. On the way I moved my hips as I walked in my high heels, while staying just out of his reach. Not that he was trying to grab me. Nope. He just stared, his mouth firm, his eyes dark. What was he thinking? That I was a lowborn slut like his mother had always said? I stumbled, then steadied.

Not thinking that way. I was a good dancer. I'd done what I'd had to do to earn a living. I'd been a product of my times. In 1604 I'd had no opportunity to be educated, to learn a trade, and I'd not had the luck to be born into a noble family. I'd been the widow of an actor when Jerry had met me. In the centuries since then I'd used my wits to survive and educate myself. I'd refused to depend on him or his money. Glory St. Clair, the original independent woman.

So I continued to dance, to strut my stuff. And I finally relaxed enough to let the music take me, and to just feel it and flow with it. I looked at Jerry again and his eyes were glowing. With desire. Ahh. So he did like what he saw. I ventured closer and trailed the feathers across his face. He reached for me and I danced out of the way.

I decided to up the stakes in this Vegas game and dropped the feathers on the table, then reached behind me for the bra clasp. When it came open, I slowly shimmied out of it and dropped it on the table. I saw Jerry lick his lips, his fangs glinting in the light. Ah.

I danced closer, then behind him, letting the tips of my breasts brush his soft hair. With a growl, he snatched me around the waist and lifted me into his arms. He stood there for a few endless seconds, a strong silent vampire with ravaging on his mind. I could see it, sense it and wanted it more than anything.

Then he raked the table clean with one arm, chips flying everywhere, his empty glass hitting against the wall. It landed on the carpet with a thump without breaking. He laid me gently on that table and stared down at me. The music still played, sensual, with a throbbing beat that echoed the pulsing going on inside both of us. I knew it because he let me read his mind. He pulled my hand to his chest and I felt the slow thrum of his heart. Very slow, but there, just as mine was. Then he slid my hand lower, to the heat and hardness of his cock, which was clearly aching with need . . . for me.

I took his other hand and put it to my breast. He covered it, my nipple tight against his palm. Then I pulled his hand down to where I needed to feel him inside me, and the pressure almost sent me over the brink before I'd even managed to wiggle out of my costume.

"Say something," I whispered.

"You rob me of speech." Jerry bent to take my breast into the heat of his mouth.

I wanted to ask what he meant. No speech. Good? Bad? What the hell? He was in "driving Glory insane" territory with his clever lips and tongue. And he was helping me get those bikini bottoms off without ripping the fishnets. I kicked off my high heels and concentrated on unbuttoning his shirt with shaking fingers. Loved the shirt or I'd have just ripped it off of him and tossed it aside. *Really* loved his chest, so manly, scarred from long-ago battles before he'd been turned vampire. No modern workouts for my guy. He'd earned his muscles the hard way, by wielding a broadsword taller than I am.

I knew every inch of him. I could, and had, traced this territory blindfolded more times than I could count, yet I never tired of exploring it. I went to work on his belt and trousers, and soon had him as naked as I was. I hoped to hell Richard had posted a Do Not Disturb sign on our love nest, because I'd hate to be interrupted just as Jerry began licking his way down my body to my favorite place for him to drink from me. Yep, there's a vein there at my inner thighs . . .

"Jerry, I love you." I had his hair in a grip that was probably painful, but he was bearing up. He had my legs over his shoulders and his eyes on the prize. "Drink from me."

He jerked me closer, his hands digging into my ass as he held me to him. "Gloriana, lass, you're beautiful. Just as you are. Never forget it." With a growl of pure predatory lust, he sank his fangs into the sweet spot. I flung myself into an orgasm that was of the "screaming like a banshee" variety. Lucky for both of us, banshees must be regulars at this club, because nobody came running in to check on us. Or, if they did, neither of us noticed.

Once he'd drunk his fill, Jerry eased me down and plunged

into me the old-fashioned way. Which was great for orgasm number two, or was it three? God, the man had a way about him. I was so busy kissing and biting him myself, I lost all claim to reason. I inhaled his sweet scent and sank my fangs into his jugular, drawing his life force into me as another orgasm roared through me. He held me close, the throb of his heartbeat echoed by my own as he waited for me to withdraw and lick the punctures closed. I held him tight, my body wrapped around him as we pulsed together. I felt powerful, energized and sexy as hell.

Oh, God, but he was still inside me, moving again now with a power no mortal could ever hope to match. He covered my mouth with his, his fangs lightly scraping across my lips as he tied my hands together with the feather boa. He shoved them over my head, then leaned down to draw one of my nipples into his mouth, using a stray feather to tease the other.

"Jerry!" I gasped, playing along even though I knew I could pull my hands apart without much effort.

"I want the truth now, Gloriana." He sat up, the strength of him throbbing inside me as he reached down to slide that feather down between us. "Did you or did you not dance topless in Las Vegas?"

"I—I don't remember." Truth. At this point, it was all I could do to remember my own name.

"Not an answer I'll accept, lass." He ran the feather down one of my thighs, then dropped it to pull me tighter against him. He slid out of me until he was a mere inch from leaving me altogether. "Yes? Or no?" He eased back inside but not nearly deep enough to satisfy me.

I raised my bound arms and leaned up to loop them around his neck. I ran the feathers close to his ears and grinned to see him give an involuntary shiver. Hah! Jerry doing anything involuntarily was a triumph as far as I was concerned.

"Are you jealous, Jeremiah?"

"I don't like the idea of strangers seeing you half-naked." He growled and kissed me like he was laying a claim.

I certainly couldn't complain about that. But we hadn't been together when I'd lived in Las Vegas. And I'm not the world's most talented dancer. At five feet five, I'm pretty short by Vegas standards too. So going topless was sometimes the only way I could get work. Jerry wasn't going to like it, but I wasn't going to lie to him about this anymore. I had other, more important secrets to keep.

I opened my mind and let him see my answer. He frowned. Then, instead of shoving off of me like I was afraid he would, he leaned down to kiss me with the finesse of a master craftsman. Which he was and is. I'm a sensual woman and I'm convinced that Jerry had seduced me into becoming vampire all those centuries ago. He's that good.

When he finally pulled back, he looked down, his face solemn. "I'm sorry, Glory, that you had to demean yourself in that way. I should have provided for your financial security better than that. I'm responsible—"

"Please don't start this again. I chose the vampire life. I get the consequences. I managed. Will always manage. And it wasn't demeaning. It was liberating." I reached up and smoothed the frown lines between his dark brows. "Can we drop it now? A few moments ago I was having a fine time. Even thinking about a big finish before someone else bursts in here and demands to use this room. What do you think, big guy? Got one more round in you?"

Jerry looked down at my breasts, obviously imagining them on parade. Of course he's proprietary. It's flattering, but has come between us before, when it gets to be too much for me. Right now, the issue would just have to be put aside. Jerry obviously decided he was able to do that. Because he lifted me into his lap, with us still connected, and let me feel just how big a finish he had in store for us.

"Damn you for being independent, woman." He pushed into me and I gasped. "Damn you for being prideful." He pushed into me again and my eyes crossed. "Damn you for being the only woman I can't ever seem to forget." He pushed into me once more and I arched my back and dug my fingernails into his shoulders. "And damn you for holding my heart in your contrary hands." He lifted me and sat me down on his shaft with such force that I screamed and we came together with a shudder that seemed to go on forever. When the tremors finally stopped, we leaned against each other and just held on.

"Viva Las Vegas," I whispered. I heard and felt Jerry's tired chuckle rumble through his chest against my cheek just before there was a knock outside the door.

Three

"*Glory, you've got to tell me what happened in there. Your mind has been closed as tight as a—*"

"Quit badgering me, Valdez. They had private booths. Blade and I had 'fun.' That's all. Do I need to draw you a picture?" I turned and saw that my bodyguard had shifted back into his usual Labradoodle form during the ride up in the elevator. "When we get into the suite, cool it. You know Ray and I are 'engaged' so we have to put on the lovey-dovey act. Do your thing and quit pouting about being left outside."

I was just glad we hadn't run into a MacDonald ambush once Jerry and I had left the club. But I guess Ian had really had an appointment. To keep up my charade as Ray's fiancée, Jerry'd dropped me off behind the hotel again. So now I was back there and about to enter rock-star world again. Trust me, it's not as glamorous as I'd once dreamed it would be. This week was all about work for Ray. He'd had a heck of a time setting up his interviews and rehearsals after dark. His new vampire status had done a number on his career.

I slid the key card into the lock and threw open the door. Usually I'd catch at least a few of his band members and their ladies hanging around, along with Ray's best friend and manager, Nathan Burke. Music always shook the walls, whether from the stereo system, the big-screen TV or, what was really cool, the guys jamming on their instruments.

Tonight it was quiet. Too quiet. The living room was empty. Well, except for the debris, evidence that mortals had enjoyed room service and the bar. The two bedroom doors, on either side of sliding glass doors leading out to the balcony, were closed. Ray and I shared one and Nathan slept in the other. Valdez would've made it a cozy threesome in ours if I'd let him. But I figured he could guard both of us quite well from a spot on the living room couch.

Blade signs V's paychecks. The only things I let my lover pick up the tab for are the bodyguard gig and our dates. We've had this arrangement for centuries and I've come to terms with it. I sure couldn't afford daylight protection and Valdez is way better than me burying myself in the dirt every day. Well, you get the picture.

I guess I'm lucky Jerry has this responsibility thing because he made me vampire. I'm pretty independent otherwise. So we compromised. Right now we're together, but there have been decades when we haven't been. The bodyguards made Jerry feel better about that. Keeping them in dog form is Jerry's way of making sure I didn't enjoy the bodyguard a bit too much. Yeah, he's the jealous type. Which is kind of cute, actually.

Seriously, though, if I decided to make love to every man in this hotel, I was free to do so, thank you very much. Unfortunately, until I spelled out for V that I wanted alone time with Ray, Valdez was going to, pardon the expression, dog us until we passed out at sunrise to make sure *all* we did was sleep in our bedroom.

I usually didn't have a problem with V's protectiveness. Vamps are dead all day, literally. The V-man kept out anyone who dared try to enter the bedroom while we're "asleep." The housekeepers knew that firsthand. Nathan had tipped them big to make sure they only made up the bedrooms after dark.

"Ray? Nathan?" I walked over to our bedroom. I always knocked as a courtesy even though I've seen Ray naked. It had been a pure pleasure and I wouldn't mind a replay. Not that we've been lovers, darn it. Okay, not really "darn it." When Jerry and I are together, like we are now, I'm true to him. But what woman with an ounce of hormones wouldn't be thrilled that a yummy guy like Ray had actually made some moves on her? I've resisted, even though he's tempting beyond belief.

As payback, because the mind-reading jerk knows how hot he is, Ray flaunts himself. He doesn't seem to have a self-conscious bone in his body. Not like me. I wear shapeless things to bed that hit me somewhere about midcalf. Not only to avoid stirring up stuff that I don't intend to act on, but if you don't got it, you don't flaunt it. Know what I mean?

Anyway, I knocked. Waited a beat, then turned the knob. I opened the door and came face-to-face with a woman I recognized immediately. I had her CDs at home. She was up for a Grammy, album of the year. And she was wearing one of Ray's T-shirts and nothing else.

I snarled. Yep, a primitive snarl that I barely kept my fangs out of. You should have seen that bimbo's face. She jumped back a full three feet, then landed on her skinny ass.

"What the hell's going on here?" I played the outraged fiancée to the hilt. Sure, this was a pretend engagement, but I doubt *she* knew that. I stomped into the room, Valdez on my heels. He got with the program, his growl raising the hair on my arms. I halted within scratching range of the woman's eyes and gave my sidekick an encouraging pat.

"I, uh, Ray, I mean . . ." She glanced at the rumpled sheets on the king-size bed. Big mistake.

I reached down and grabbed her by one of her twig arms. I could have snapped it between two fingers and actually thought about it. Not that I'm in love with Ray, though I'm really, really fond of him. But this betrayal hurt. Betrayal? Whoa. I didn't have the right to think like that. Still, this did feel like a cheap shot. I mean, what was he thinking, bringing a woman into *our* bed? At least I took my action off the premises.

I blinked back stupid tears and sniffed. Second big mistake. I got a whiff of human blood pumping through bimbo's veins and I was suddenly starved. Too bad her pale face made it clear she'd already donated tonight. Damn it. Ray'd had sex *and* dinner.

"Get out before I . . ." I lifted my fist, narrowly missing her surgically altered nose before I waved it at a pile of clothes by the bed. Tiny push-up bra that Victoria's Secret didn't even carry in *my* size, miniskirt that I couldn't have squeezed over even one of my thighs and a T-shirt that she'd obviously borrowed from a Chihuahua. Shit.

"Take your clothes and get the hell out of here." I heard my voice quiver and hated it. The shower went off. "Now." Okay, that was a hiss. Much better.

Little Miss Stick Figure got the message and hustled her butt like her feet were on fire. Valdez nipped at her heels in case she needed incentive. I slammed the door as soon as they both cleared it. I knew Valdez would keep her moving until she hit the hall. Then he'd come back to sit next to the door and listen in. Fine. But I didn't want or need his eyes on me during this showdown.

Ray came out with a towel around his lean middle. "Glory." He looked around, alarmed, like maybe he'd see a drained body on the floor. "Where's—"

I held up my hand. "Don't say her name. She's alive. No broken bones. Which is a miracle, come to think of it."

"Thanks." Ray sat on the foot of the bed. "Guess this wasn't such a hot idea."

"Ya think?" I paced the carpet in front of him and saw his nostrils flare. I really didn't have the right to say much of anything to him. Of course he smelled Blade on me and the evidence that I'd had recent sex. Lots of recent sex. And Ray had warned me not too long ago that he wasn't into celibacy.

Of course he wasn't. He was a virile man in his prime. And a newly made vampire with the libido to match. Since I wasn't going to scratch his itch, I'd known it was only a matter of time before he'd find someone who would.

"Well, go ahead. Ream me out. I didn't *plan* this, but that's no excuse." Ray ran another towel over his wet hair.

"I was rough on her. Blame it on the shock factor. But you certainly have the right . . ." I sat beside him, biting back the snarky comments I wanted to make. Did he have to pick someone so *thin*? His bedmate couldn't have been more different from me, even down to the dark hair and bikini wax. Oh, man, I so didn't want to go there.

He slid his hand over mine and squeezed. "Forgive me? I'm a stupid jerk. We should have taken this somewhere else. I'm really sorry if you were embarrassed."

I looked at him, all sincere apology and charm. I guess I'd always be attracted to him. He was handsome, built and had the kind of talent that sang to my soul if I let it. I'd been a fan even before he'd been tossed naked into my bed as a newly made vampire. The fact that now we were thrown together all the time had made it worse for a while, but I always went back to Blade in the end. So I knew it wasn't fair to expect Ray to just hang around in case I decided to drop Blade and pick up someone else.

"Not embarrassed so much as surprised. I threw a temper fit. Like a fiancée would under the circumstances."

"You didn't hurt her?"

I managed a shrug. "Not this time."

"Good. And there won't be a next time. Not here, anyway. DeeDee and I have a history. We're friends with benefits, I guess you could say. When we're not with someone else, we hook up." Ray dropped the hair towel into his lap.

"So how did you explain that you're engaged, but you're not 'with' someone?" I jumped up again. "Damn it, Ray, if this gets into the tabloids, I'll look like a fool and you'll look like a jerk." The tabloids already thought Ray was crazy for hanging out with a woman who wasn't model thin or famous in her own right. DeeDee was both. Damn. If I didn't quit grinding my teeth, I was going to loosen a fang.

Of course the tabloids figured I was springing the baby trap. What irony. "Made" vamps like me can't reproduce. Sigh.

"It won't get out. I told her you and I were breaking things off right after the Grammys. That's still what you plan, isn't it?" Ray stood and faced me. He knew the answer and was probably counting on it being the same. He didn't want this sham to go on any more than I did. He was grateful to me for mentoring him through his vamp adjustment period. Judging by what he'd just done, he was getting into the vampire groove now and wouldn't need my help much longer.

Besides, any vampire who thinks he wants to be hooked up to the same person for eternity needs to get a clue. Call me heartless, but *I* sure never thought it was a good idea or I would have caved and said the vows with Blade a long time ago. Even soul mates need a break once in a while.

"Relax, Ray. You're off the hook. After this awards show, when we get back to Austin, we'll announce irreconcilable differences and you can openly date whoever." I kicked off my high heels and sighed with relief. "You sure you can trust this lady? You did erase her memory, didn't you? Because unless she's anemic, I think the girl made a donation while she was satisfying your other urges."

Ray grinned. "Hell, yes, I fed from her. That part was almost better than the sex, if you want to know the truth."

I shook my head. Yep, Ray was definitely a full-fledged graduate vampire now. It was all about the blood. And when you got human blood and great sex at the same time? I sighed, remembering.

"Her memory, Ray."

"Yeah, yeah, I wiped her memory and the fang marks. All she'll remember is the great sex." He lost his smile. "Damn it, she *did* look pale. I tried to take it easy but it had been a while since I'd had fresh and it was so fine . . ." He gave me a worried look. "I might have taken too much. Think she'll be all right? Should I go up and check on her?"

"The way she ran out of here? I think she still had plenty of juice." I worked up a grin, trying really hard to act like I didn't give a damn. I turned away from him to pull off my earrings and drop them on the dresser. "Give her a call, though, if it'll make you feel better."

"Scared her, did you?" Ray got up and moved behind me to slide his arms around my waist. "Come on, Glory. Face facts. You've got Blade. I can smell him on you. And you have the look of a woman well loved. You've got to know it drives me crazy every time you come back after a night with him. I needed an outlet, you know? I was hurting."

"I'm sorry, Ray. I guess I can't blame you for wanting someone to, uh, take care of your needs." I covered his hands with mine.

"And DeeDee's all right. She won't tell a soul. That's why we hang out together. She's got the same issues with the gossip rags that I've got. Her room is two floors up. It was easy for her to sneak down here." He rested his chin on my shoulder.

"How convenient." I heard myself go snarky and took a breath. Stupid. Ray could screw every woman in Los Angeles for all I cared. "I didn't rip open her throat, but I put on a pretty scary show. Valdez too." I turned to face Ray.

"I'll just bet you did, vamp girl." Ray bumped against me, his hands on the dresser on either side of me so that I was trapped, or not. My choice. "I've seen you in action against some serious bad guys, remember? A mere mortal female wouldn't stand a chance."

"Exactly. I was actually holding back, but your 'friend' might not see it that way. So you may have to do some fast talking to get her to give you another shot." I smiled and caught a drop of water that slid down one of his lean cheeks. He was flaunting himself again, standing close in nothing but a towel. Ray was beautiful, from his broad shoulders to his narrow hips and everywhere in between. Thanks to a bitch who'd decided that turning him vampire would be the perfect payback for a man who'd loved playing in the sun, Ray would look like this forever—tanned, toned and 100 percent every woman's fantasy.

I licked my lips, a reflex I immediately regretted when Ray grinned and bumped against me again. I glanced down at the invitation under the towel and felt a flush warm my cheeks.

"I like you jealous. It's hot. And you'd better block your thoughts, Glory girl." His sapphire eyes sparkled. "You're looking like you want to take up where DeeDee left off."

"Get over yourself, Caine. I was playing a part earlier. Outraged fiancée. Now that we're alone, forget it." I put my hand on his bare chest and gave him a gentle shove to give me some space. "I've been more than satisfied tonight. Maybe you'd better see if DeeDee will give you another chance, though I wouldn't drink from her again. She needs some recovery time." I yawned and stretched. "I feel the sunrise coming, though."

"So do I and I don't do quickies. I like to take my time." He grinned, a wicked twinkle in his eyes. "I imagine I can talk DeeDee back into bed eventually. She and I have a really good time together. You and I could too if you just let me show you my moves." He slid one finger along my collarbone.

I smiled and grabbed his hand. "Give Blade some credit. I *am* a woman well loved. *Very* well loved." I yawned again. "Now I'm going to throw on my gown and crawl into bed. Would you let in Valdez? I want to say something to him before I conk out."

"Only to tell him to stay the hell in the living room during the day. He's supposed to guard the door, but I think he climbs in right between us as soon as we close our eyes. I swear these pillows smell like dog when I wake up. I haven't forgotten that he's really a man, you know." Ray walked over to the bedroom door.

"Hey, he's protecting both of us. Something happens during the day? We're golden. He'd die before he'd let harm come to either of us." I had to admit, I'd thought V was staying in the living room. Weird if he was actually in the bed with us. I didn't doubt that he could open and close doors, even in dog form. The shifter has some mad skills, not just shape-shifting either.

"Yeah, yeah. I get it. But he can do that job just as well outside the door as in." Ray threw open the bedroom door. "Okay, dog breath. Come in. I want to go over the rules with you."

"Listen, a-hole, you don't make the rules. Glory does. And next time you want some nookie, take it upstairs. Glory doesn't need to walk in on a scene like that, you hear me?" Valdez growled as he walked by Ray's knees.

"You're right about that anyway. I wasn't thinking." Ray dropped his towel, grabbed a pair of silk boxers and stepped into them.

"Not with the brain in your head anyway."

I left them bickering and headed for the bathroom where I'd hung my shapeless nightgown. I still had a queasy feeling in my stomach after realizing Ray had spent a night making love to another woman. And now I'd have to sleep on the same sheets. Yuck. And ouch. This was cruel and unusual. You know?

"My schedule's pretty full, Glory. Who is this guy anyway?" Ray polished off a bottle of CrimsonCrush, our latest find in the synthetic blood brands, while I paced the living room.

I was embarrassed to admit it, but if Ian wanted to meet Ray, then I was going to have to drag my "fiancé" along. A call to the diet guru to set up the meeting had made it clear: no rocker, no interest in helping a Campbell's woman. Damn.

"He's a vampire who has a special product I need. I really want to do this, Ray, but he won't deal with me unless he gets to meet you. He's a big fan." I glanced at my watch. I had a pretty full schedule too. First, I was meeting with designers who were making a dress for me to wear on the red carpet at the Grammys. I was nervous. This was a big deal and I wasn't a size zero.

Ray's publicist, Barry Donaldson, had arranged for me to be a guest judge for a segment on the design reality show *Designed to Kill*. The competitors would meet with me today to measure me and ask questions. All of this would be on camera, of course. If a vamp could dream, I would have been having nightmares about this. Imagine your measurements televised to millions. Somehow my waist, hip and thigh measurements were *not* going to be aired. Maybe there was a contract clause that Nathan could insist on. I looked around for Ray's best friend and business manager and saw him coming out of his bedroom.

"Nate, please, I need your help."

"Sure, Glory, but make it quick. I've got Grammy stuff to do tonight. They made an album of hits and Ray's duet with Sienna Star was on it. It's gone platinum and I want to make sure our cut of the money's right on it." Nathan was dressed in his usual Italian suit, silk tie and white shirt. Against his dark skin, it was a hot look and he usually had a beautiful woman on his arm. Oops, guess I got that right because here came one out of his bedroom, hopping on one foot while she stuck her other foot into a Louboutin pump. She grabbed Nathan's arm to steady herself, kissed his cheek, then headed out without waiting to be introduced to the rest of us.

Nate and Ray knocked fists while I just shook my head.

"Who was that? She was gorgeous." I really didn't have time for idle chitchat, but Nathan, who grinned and paced in front of the big-screen TV, was obviously bursting to share.

"Niki's the coordinator for the cable network we talked about, Ray. I may have a deal for you, if you're still interested in a music special." Nate grabbed a bottle of water. "Now, Glory, what did you need?"

"The designers are coming for this reality show. What rights do I have?" I hated how insecure I sounded. I mean, I'm a vampire. I could lay waste to the entire crew and just disappear and forget the whole thing. I glanced at Ray and Valdez when they both laughed.

"Hey! This isn't funny. I don't want to be made to look ridiculous. This will be seen by millions of people. And it's publicity for you, Israel Caine. Help me out here."

"Glory's right. And tearing out the throats of an entire cast and crew of a major cable network show would make headlines, but maybe not the kind you're looking for." Ray threw his arm around my shoulders.

Nathan looked alarmed. "Calm down, Glory. What's got you so worked up?"

"Look at me. These designers are going to come in and *measure* me. I don't want those numbers blasted over the TV. I'm not stupid. Ray's last hookup had a waist measurement smaller than that of my right thigh." Valdez and Ray nodded and I gave them both "Go to hell" mental messages.

"I'm sure that can't be right." Nate glanced at his friend, but Ray wisely kept his mouth shut.

"I know how these shows operate, Nate." I stopped just short of grabbing him by the lapels and shaking him. "Don't I have some kind of creative control?"

Nate frowned and moved back a step. "Barry's handling this. He didn't bring me a contract other than a standard release form. I never realized you'd have"—he looked me over—"issues."

"You look great. Worse comes to worst, you and Ray whammy everyone here and plant new numbers in their pointy heads. Give you a waist like Scarlett O'Hara's in Gone with the Wind *if that'll make you happy."* Valdez bumped against me.

"Get a clue, Valdez. Then the dresses won't fit." I looked longingly at the bedroom and wondered if I could just lock myself in. Valdez planted himself in the doorway.

"Caine, you've got to back up Glory on this. Stay here while this circus is going on. Make sure they treat her right."

"Sure, I'll do what I can, but I don't have all night. I've got rehearsals." Ray jumped back when I glared at him. "Hey, babe, I get it. This is for me. As long as it takes. I'm here. But it will all be on tape. That might be a problem."

"Fix it so there were technical difficulties. Use your vampire skills. Just don't kill anybody with them." Nathan glanced at his watch. "Hell, you two can work this out. And these shows are run by professionals. Just speak up, Glory. Let them know up front how you want it to be or threaten to walk. I'll deal with any legal fallout later if it comes to that."

"Those would be fun headlines: 'Thighs Matter. Grammy Gown Used as Awning after Glory Waddles Away in Outrage.'" I collapsed on the couch, ignoring Valdez, who'd buried his nose in a cushion to stifle his howls of laughter. Ray's snort turned into a cough when he saw my stare in his direction.

"As usual, you're too hard on yourself. Am I right, Ray?" Nate smiled and patted my shoulder.

Ray pulled himself together and nodded vigorously. "You're perfect, Glory. I've never seen you waddle." That gaffe earned him a gesture and sent Valdez into a roll across the floor.

Nate gave my bodyguard a hard look. "Seriously. These people want to make you look good so they can win. The prize is a contract for a clothing line. I personally can't wait to see the winning dress. I'm sure it'll make you look hot. One warning, though. Make sure you and Ray are aware when they're filming. There's nothing these shows like more than to catch you off guard. You and Ray need to be 100 percent together, if you know what I mean." Nate stared at Valdez. "And the dog needs to keep his trap shut."

"*Hey, I know how to do my thing in public.*" Valdez followed him to the door. "*You should have done yours. What kind of manager doesn't check the contracts? Glory should have had some say in how this was going down.*"

I heard the door close and sank down on the couch. Had

I even dressed right for this? I wore what I considered slimming black jeans and an Ed Hardy tee. I wanted to look like a rocker's woman. Not easy to do without a single piercing or tattoo. Been there, done that. Woke up after a day of healing sleep without either one. Bummer.

"You look great, Glory. And I'll do what I can to make sure they treat you right." Ray sat beside me, then jumped up and gathered the CrimsonCrush bottles and tossed them in the trash in our bathroom before closing the door. Housekeeping had been in during the day and cleaned the suite's living room, so we were ready when the knock came on the door.

When Barry ushered in a cast of thousands (okay, slight exaggeration), I wanted to retreat to that bathroom and never come out. Not that Barry would have hesitated to call in the Jaws of Life to pull me out of there. All of it sure to be caught on film.

First, we were introduced to Zia, a former model and hostess of the show. She was obviously a lot more than set decoration, though it didn't take mind reading to see that Ray was admiring her perfect body and gorgeous face. We were both blond and blue-eyed with a generous bustline. I liked to think she was me, only six inches taller, twenty pounds lighter and with the blessings of the gods as far as beauty was concerned. Okay, so she wasn't even close to being me.

"Listen, people, let's not waste Ray's valuable time." Of course she and Ray were already on a first-name basis. And my time? Not on her radar. She got us organized with the help of a pack of assistants and soon the contestants were firing questions at me.

Valdez managed to be an immediate hit with the cast and crew, posing shamelessly for the camera as they bickered the way they do on these reality shows. The three finalists, two guys and a girl, were really into winning.

"Glory, what's your favorite color?" Melanie asked. She looked like she belonged with Ray more than I did. I admired her dragon tattoos. She had a hard time focusing on me and kept glancing at Ray and licking her pierced lip with her pierced tongue.

"Red. And blue to go with my eyes, but I wear a lot of black. Because I think it's slimming." I ran my hands down my sides and hips in case the group missed the area I wanted to slim. We hadn't measured yet. I was sick with dread.

"Can we see your closet, Glory?" This from Butch, who wasn't, if you know what I mean.

"I didn't bring a lot with me." I glanced at Ray. The housekeepers had been allowed in to change the sheets fairly soon after sunset, so the bedroom was presentable. "Sure, come on."

This got everyone all excited and the gang trooped into the bedroom. My paltry offerings were brought out and examined.

"You seem to like short skirts and low-cut tops." Darren, the third finalist, was busy writing in a notebook. He seemed the most intense and had a no-nonsense vibe I liked.

"She's got great assets and knows how to use them." Ray pulled me close to his side. "Glory always looks good. She's an expert on fashion herself. You should see her store in Austin, Texas. Vintage Vamp's Emporium. If you're ever there, it's on Sixth Street, a cool area surrounded by clubs and other funky shops. A great place to hang out and buy vintage clothes."

I gave Ray a kiss on the cheek. Could I have asked for a better commercial? Valdez pushed between us and I reached down to pat him on the head. We were the picture of one big happy family.

Zia smiled and managed to pull Ray to her side. "And what would you like to see Glory wear, Israel Caine? This will be a big night for you." She went on and on about Ray's duet and the award he was up for. I could practically see his head grow three sizes.

Finally he had a chance to answer. "Like I said, Glory looks good in anything." He tucked me against him again.

"But I really like it when she wears stuff that's cut low in front." He grinned into the camera. "My girl's got great—"

"Ray!" I put my hand over his mouth. "I think we'd better let the contestants and the audience figure that one out for themselves." I felt him lick my palm and had to laugh. Zia's smile looked painted on when Ray pulled my hand away.

"I'm just sayin'. Anyone can see I'm a lucky man, darlin'.."

"Well, thanks." I kissed his cheek, then turned to the contestants. They were all writing in their notebooks. "Now, about the dress. I guess I should wear something long. But I'm anxious to see what you guys come up with." I smiled at them. "I want to look fabulous, of course." My smile froze when I saw a yellow measuring tape appear in each contestant's hand.

"Can we turn off the cameras for a moment?" Ray held up both hands, then pulled Zia to the side and began whispering to her. She frowned, but finally nodded.

"Okay, people, we're all going to wait in the living room while the contestants measure Glory in here. Off camera." There were gasps from the crowd. "Ray's going to give us an interview. We can use some of it for our promos for the show." There was some murmuring, but the room cleared while I shot Ray a grateful look. Valdez stayed behind, of course. I knew I wasn't going to be able to blast him out of there when I was surrounded by mortals he didn't know.

Melanie was first. She was brisk and efficient. I didn't even see the numbers she wrote in her little notebook, but she measured *everything*, even my wrists. At least she didn't gasp in horror but she did shake her head once and even clucked, I swear it. She caught herself and smiled, obviously remembering too late who was the judge here.

"You have tiny wrists." The suck-up smiled, her piercing clanking against her teeth. "Why no tats?"

"I'm allergic to the dyes." I'd prepared the story years ago. This wasn't the first time the question had come up. "Tried it once." I pointed to my bikini line. "You should see the scar. Never again."

"Too bad. Rockers dig tattoos." Melanie wrote something in her notebook.

I pulled a face. "Don't I know it. Ray's are awesome."

Melanie looked thoughtful as she slipped out of the bedroom and shut the door. I turned to Darren. "Are we done now? Can't you people just share the measurements?"

"No way." Darren smiled coldly. "You think that bitch would give me the correct ones? Right now she's copying the numbers and changing them in case I try to look at her notebook. She'll have the real ones stashed someplace safe." He whipped out his measuring tape, almost hitting me in the eye. "Hold still, now. I want to get this right. How high a heel can you walk in comfortably, Glory?"

"Four inch, five in a pinch. I get shoes?" I felt his knuckles brush my nipples and glanced up to catch a gleam in his eyes. Valdez growled and I nudged him with my foot.

"Of course you get shoes. What's your favorite brand? You'll also get an evening bag and jewelry for each outfit." He reached around me to pull the tape around my waist.

He was actually a nice-looking guy if you went for the grunge thing. He could use a haircut and shave, but the overall effect was nicely masculine. He also could have benefited from a gym membership. Of course his real appeal was the B positive thrumming through his veins. I slid my tongue over my fangs and ordered them to retreat. I'd had a bottle of synthetic earlier and wasn't really hungry. But then, fresh . . .

"Anything that looks hot and is perfect with the dress." I shook my head. "You guys have a real challenge. But I saw you studying my shoes in the closet. Get the right size and I'll be okay."

"There, all done." Darren looked down at Valdez, who growled again when the man brushed his hand down my hip. "I'll get you the best of everything, Glory. From your beautiful head down to your toes. Be sure to book a pedicure on the day of the event." He winked. "Go for a red polish. Now, guess I'll have to leave you with Butch. Sorry about that. See you in the living room." He took off, shutting the door behind him.

"Alone at last." Butch looked me over. "Please ignore that trash-talking idiot. Tell me what your dream dress would look like."

"Wouldn't that be cheating?" I held out my arms while Butch went to work getting a bust measurement.

"Not at all. Those idiots should have asked you the same thing." Butch was working on my waist now. I didn't dare look at the number. Some things you just don't want to know. "And just between us, I'm a stylist in my other life. Took care of Julia in her second trimester with the twins. Angelina too. By the time I dress you, no one will suspect a thing, sugar buns."

I looked down to where Valdez was struggling not to laugh out loud. As it was, he was turning into a wheezing, hacking, staggering dog that had Butch frowning at him.

"Is the dog okay?"

"This is what happens when he drinks out of the toilet." I grabbed his collar and pulled him toward the door. "He'll be okay. He just needs some air. Maybe Ray will shove him out on the balcony." I pushed him into the living room and shut the door. "There. Now, where were we?"

"I was about to measure your thighs. I don't suppose you'd drop those jeans. They're adding precious inches you can't afford, sweetie."

"No, I'm not dropping my pants. And, no, I'm not pregnant." I put my hands on my hips. "I'm not model thin like most of Ray's girlfriends, okay? But if you can come up with a design that can disguise my figure flaws, you'll be the winner. Are we clear?"

Butch grinned and put a finger over his lips. "Crystal, sugar buns. I know just what you need to wear to make you look fabulous." He quickly took a few more measurements, headed for the door and flung it open. "We'd better join the others before I get accused of conspiring with the judge."

Sure enough, all eyes were on us as we entered the room.

There were a few more questions, then Ray pleaded a full schedule and got them out of there. Zia was the last to leave, air-kissing Ray and ignoring me as she thanked him for the promo spots.

"That went pretty well." Ray shut the door behind the last of them.

"Yeah, there wasn't an unkind word about my figure issues. I imagine those comments will be in the behind-the-scenes shots they film while they cut yards and yards of fabric for my dress. Boy, won't that be a budget buster."

"Quit putting yourself down." Ray frowned.

I hugged him and kissed his cheek. "Thanks for taking care of the measurement thing. You're my hero. Always looking out for me."

"I try." He pulled me close and rested his chin on my head. "Valdez, quit growling."

"Are you really in a hurry? Because I still want to go see that guy . . ."

"Okay, I've got an hour to spare. Where do we meet him?"

"He has a place in Malibu." I had no idea how far away that was or how long it took to get there.

Ray frowned. "We'll never make it, unless . . ."

"Unless what?"

"What do you think, Glory? Ray wants you to shift with him and fly out there. It's the only way to fit it into his schedule. He's got rehearsal later." Valdez, who'd obviously been mind reading, frowned. *"I guess I could do the same. Not what Blade would like, but, hell, I've been shifting into other forms lately anyway. You're sure not going out there without me."*

"Is Valdez right, Ray? You want me to shift and fly out to Malibu with you? Are you sure we can find the place?" I hate shifting. It's a phobia I have. The whole process is creepy to me. I like my human form. It's comfortable, fits me like a glove, even if it is a little oversize. The bat or bird thing? Yuck.

"You got an address?" Ray held out his hand and I gave him Ian's card. "Yes, I know where this is. Pricy real estate.

Right on the beach. I can find it. But we need to get out there now. If Valdez thinks he needs to go, so be it. Is there something I should know about this deal that you're not telling me?"

I blocked my thoughts. Of course there was. Just about everything. I smiled. "Well, you'll love this. The MacDonalds and the Campbells are ancient enemies. They hate each other. That's why Ian needs to be sure I'm with you, not Blade."

"So I'll probably like this guy." Ray grinned and opened the door to the balcony. He looked at Nathan, who'd come back just as the TV crew had left. "You'll cover for us? Keep the gang away?"

"Sure. You do know how this freaks me out to watch you change, don't you, bro?" Nathan looked at me. "Glory, I thought you didn't like to do this. What does this guy have that motivates you so much?"

"Tell you later." I looked at my watch again and stepped onto the balcony. I steeled myself, feeling my nerves jumping as I tried to work up my courage. I really, really wanted to get skinny. Otherwise this was so not my thing.

"Bird or bat?" Valdez was still right beside me, his presence always a comfort. *"Stay close, Glory. We'll be right behind Ray. Got it?"*

"Yeah, I got it." Voice shaky, but I was determined.

"Bat, let's move." Then Ray *was* a bat, just like that.

I pictured the same change in myself and felt it shudder through me, the floor dropping below me as I soared into the air. I suppose it should be a cool experience to fly over Los Angeles at night like that. The lights of the city were beautiful when I dared glance down. But I was totally focused on not losing Ray. Not that he would have allowed that. He and Valdez flanked me, obviously taking care not to let me fly off on a tangent. In what seemed like hours but was probably only minutes, we were near the ocean and I could see it dark with a phosphorescent froth below us. The houses that lined the beach were massive and well lit.

Ray started down toward one that was on a cliff with a wooden stair that zigzagged down to the beach below. He landed on a wooden deck, changing back into his human form almost as soon as his feet hit. Valdez was back to Labradoodle form as well. They stared at me as I concentrated. I was relieved when I could shake out my hair, back to my Glory self with only a slight stumble. Maybe I was getting the hang of this.

"Man, what a rush." Ray was clearly jazzed by the whole flying-over-L.A. thing. "But if I hadn't spent a lot of time here, I sure could have gotten lost. Luckily I spotted some major highways and followed them."

"Move and you're dead, vampires." The voice that came out of the dark obviously meant business.

I didn't move an inch.

Four

"*Who says so?*" Valdez jumped in front of me. "*Damn it, Caine. We should have circled first. Landed farther down the beach.*"

"Shut up." A blond surfer, either one of the men from the club or his clone, stepped out of the darkness. Three more just like him soon had us surrounded. This time they wore wet suits. Like they'd actually been surfing instead of just body-guarding. Their hard stares made it clear they didn't welcome drop-in visitors who interrupted their playtime.

"Hate to admit it, but you're right, V." Ray moved up beside Valdez and snarled. "I've got the two on the right."

"Relax, gentlemen. My men are just doing their job. Of course you're welcome here, Mr. Caine." Ian strolled out onto the deck and the guards parted, though none of them smiled or relaxed. "Glory, I'm delighted you could make it. Sorry for the surly reception. My guests usually arrive at the front door."

I didn't see any weapons. But then, vamps don't usually use them anyway. The vampire males I know pride themselves on their hand-to-hand and their fang action. I grabbed Ray's arm. He was too new at the vamp game to be particularly good at either.

"Yes, well, Ray's a busy man. We're on a tight schedule and flew in." I really didn't like the vibe here, but forced a smile. "Israel Caine, Ian MacDonald."

"A pleasure." Ian held his hand out to Ray.

Ray just nodded. "Glory's also my mentor and she's taught me it's not wise to touch a newly met vampire." He slung his arm around my shoulders. "There are so many dirty tricks you guys enjoy playing."

"True enough." Ian laughed and glanced down at Valdez, who continued to snarl and looked like he wanted to rumble. "Glory, would you ask your shifter to stand down? I assume he's your bodyguard."

"Of course. Valdez, chill. You'll have to excuse him, but it's the wet suits. We had a bad experience recently in an Austin lake and neither of us is crazy about the water." I put my hand on Valdez's head. He growled and nipped at one of the surfer dude's knees when the guy moved in too close.

"I like to live by the ocean, but I promise I won't require you to get wet as part of my miracle cure." Ian waved his hand toward the open French door. "Please come inside. Let me tell you about my products. Show you what they can do."

"Cure?" Ray squeezed my shoulder. "Are you sick? Glory, what the hell is this guy selling?"

"Didn't your fiancée tell you why she brought you out here, Caine? I'm into helping people. Gloriana's not sick unless you consider that she's sick of the body she's been stuck with for four hundred plus years. Am I right, my dear?" Ian gave me a sympathetic look and I bit back an "Amen!"

"Well, yes." I looked everywhere but at Ray. This was absolutely humiliating, but I was bound and determined to at least hear what Ian had to say. "You have no idea what it's like, Ray, to never be able to change one thing about your size." I finally faced him and gripped his arm. "Seriously. I know you used to work out. Nathan spends hours in the gym. You guys probably made a conscious decision to get the bodies you wanted, then went for it."

"Sure. And it wasn't easy." Ray covered my hand with his.

"Baby, I never thought . . . What a trip. Of course this would drive you crazy." He pulled me close and rubbed my back. "Not that you're not great the way you are, but to never be able to change . . ." He hugged me, careful not to use his vamp strength and break a rib. "Darlin', that's just wrong."

I leaned against him until the urge to cry passed. Then I heard Ian clear his throat. Oh, yes, we were keeping the great man waiting. I stepped back.

"Thanks, Ray, for understanding. I really do want to finally lose a few pounds and keep them off."

"Yes! Something vampires have never been able to do, until now." Ian rubbed his hands together. "I've developed a revolutionary system that can melt the pounds away, even on an ancient vampire like Glory." Ian smiled, ignoring Valdez's chuff of disbelief.

I wanted to grab Ian and give him a soul kiss. Revolutionary. I'll say. Hope hit me right between the eyes and made the world go blurry. To finally, finally change the way I looked. This *had* to be too good to be true.

"Are you kidding me? Revolutionary sounds dangerous." Ray gave me the once-over. He started at the top of my head. Swell. I was sure my blond hair had been blown into a fright wig by the change for my bat flight. Then he checked out my snug jeans in a size twelve (oh, how I wished for a six!). Hmm. Back up north again, he lingered on my double Ds which I'd love to slip into a C cup. I could only imagine the joys of having to shop for new bras and to actually buy pretty, colorful ones. I grabbed Ray and squeezed his arm again.

"I'm immortal, remember? Unless this thing involves a stake, I should be able to handle it. And I want this, Ray. I've wanted it for over four hundred years." Here came the waterworks again. Stupid, but this was a big deal. The impossible dream. You know?

"I get that. And what's important to you, Glory girl, is important to me. Never met a woman who didn't hate something about her body. Even supermodels." He pulled me close again and kissed me on the lips, a sweet kiss. "If this is what you want, babe, and this guy has some magic formula that will get you there, I say go for it. Just be careful. I don't want to lose you. That's the bottom line for me."

Ian beamed. He was probably seeing a blank check and celebrity endorsements in his future.

I hugged Ray again, a tear slipping down my cheek. If there was one main difference between Blade, an ancient vampire, and Ray, a modern man, it was that Ray really seemed to get women and actually paid attention to what we want. I love Jerry, but he's still stuck back in the day when he had to be in protective mode all the time. Jerry figures he knows what we *should* want and that our basic needs and wants never change. You know: food, shelter, like that.

Sorry, but I've survived mostly on my own for centuries. I figure I've moved way beyond the basics. I may be foolish, but now I want what Jerry would consider the superficial—a flattering wardrobe, a car that starts when I need it and the occasional designer handbag. The best? To look cute in skinny jeans. Sue me, but this weight-loss thing *was* important, and Ray had just become one of my heroes. Again.

I leaned back. "I'm paying for this myself. I have credit cards. This is not going to be on you." I didn't need to look to know that Ian had sagged with disappointment.

"We'll discuss it later. I want to hear MacDonald's pitch." Ray kept me close by his side and glanced down. "Valdez, you put a hole in my pants and I guarantee you'll get no steak for a week."

"Glory's perfect. She doesn't need a diet." Valdez was obviously going to report this entire scene to Jerry as soon as he had a chance.

"I see you have a loyal guard." Ian smiled as he led the way into a massive den that could have been featured in a sophisticated design magazine. "But if I read him right, he's obviously in Campbell's employ, not Caine's."

I started to deny it, but my bigmouthed mutt beat me to the punch.

"Yeah, you read me right. I'm Campbell's man, MacDonald. As Glory's sire, he pays me to make sure she stays safe no matter how far south her love life goes." He gave Ray a doggy sneer. *"Glory's my number-one priority tonight and always. There'd better not be anything in this stuff you're selling that can hurt her."* Valdez stayed close to my side.

"I'd be a fool to hurt a client. Then I'd have to shut down a lucrative operation. Trust me, I help people. Sit and I'll show you." Ian gestured to a pair of cream leather sofas and picked up a remote. He waited until Ray and I were settled side by side, Valdez near my feet, before he hit a button that turned on a flat screen hanging on the wall above a natural stone fireplace.

The screen lit up with a picture of an unhappy woman who stood on his deck, the dark ocean behind her. She was about twenty pounds overweight, especially in the hip area, a pear shape.

"Hi. I'm Sarah Wainwright. I was turned vampire in 1786 and stuck with this pudgy body. Thanks to Ian Mac-Donald's magic formulas, I'm hoping I'll finally lose the extra weight I've carried around all these years." She frowned into the camera. "Are you freakin' kidding me? No way." She showed fangs and threw up her hands. "Back off. Touch me and die." She took a shuddering breath, her breasts heaving. "Of course I want to do the program." She sniffed and finally nodded. "Okay, okay, I'll take care of it myself." She jerked off her black hoodie and threw it toward the camera.

I looked at Ian. "What's that about?"

"I told her she had to strip off or people would think she was wearing padding for her 'before' pictures. She'd agreed to be on camera for a discount on the services. When I revealed this detail, obviously she didn't take it well." He smiled and shrugged. "They never do."

I shuddered as Sarah tugged down her elastic-waisted jeans after toeing off her clogs. I could so relate to her attitude. Surely I wouldn't have to do this. I had no interest in joining Ian's showcase of "success stories." Not even for a discount.

"Do we have to see this all the way through?" One glimpse of the cellulite on Sarah's thighs was enough for me. And now she was unbuttoning her white shirt. Valdez and Ray couldn't look away. I gave Ray an elbow and nudged the V-man with my foot.

"You want to see how the program works, don't you?" Ian raised an eyebrow when he saw Ray's grin. "Sarah's just one of many examples I could show you."

"Sure, but I don't want to be humiliated like this woman." I was relieved when she kept on her bra and panties.

"Relax, baby. You look a hell of a lot better than that chick naked." Ray nodded toward the screen. "See? She's flat-chested and all ass. You're much more . . ." He squeezed my waist. "Well-rounded."

"Got to agree with Caine. Put you up against that woman any day, Glory. But, whoa, check this out. Do you see what I see?" Valdez sat down with a thump.

I *was* checking it out. The date stamp indicated a two-week time lapse. Sarah had obviously lost all her excess baggage and just where she needed to. While she still wasn't exactly top-heavy, she was in proportion and looked amazing. Her stomach was flat and her ass taut. The bikini fit her like a second skin. But obviously Sarah wasn't content to strut her stuff in a swim suit. While we watched, she peeled it off and did a three-sixty for the camera. No doubt about it. Ian's program, whatever it was, had handed her a miracle cure. This was the same woman, just a lot less of her. She smiled into the camera.

"Ian, I can never thank you enough for the gift you gave me. I have more confidence, more energy and, even better, my vamp skills are off the charts." She showed off her fangs. "Honey, I don't know what's in this special brew you've cooked up, but I'm recommending it to every overweight vampire I know." She looked down and then up through her lashes.

A flushed Ian moved into camera range with a red silk robe. He wrapped Sarah in it and faced the camera.

"Thank you, Sarah, for that moving testimonial. Obviously my program has made *your* dreams come true."

"Not all of them, Ian baby." Sarah dropped the robe again and threw herself on the diet guru. "Let's celebrate."

"Obviously, Sarah, my elixirs have given you a tremendous amount of energy." Ian signaled frantically and two of his surfers pulled Sarah off him.

"Later, lover!" Sarah shouted as she was carried out of camera range.

Ian picked up the robe and tossed it aside, then cleared his throat as he buttoned his shirt.

"Sarah lost an incredible twenty-two pounds in just fourteen nights on my super-slimming weight-loss program." Ian smiled into the camera. "Following my simple plan and drinking my specially formulated, all-natural supplements, you too can finally achieve the ideal size you've always wanted. Visit my Web site or call my weight-loss hotline for details." The URL and eight-hundred number scrolled across the bottom of the screen before Ian turned off the TV.

"Wow." I gripped Ray's hand.

"Well, Glory, does this look like something you'd be interested in trying?"

Valdez and Ray stared at me, probably surprised I didn't immediately shout, "Yes." Which kind of pissed me off. What? Did I need to trim down so badly? Oh, who was I kidding? I'd done nothing but gripe about my weight since I'd met Valdez five years ago. And Ray knew how I felt too. Both men were way too smart to say a word, though. I took a breath and looked at Ian.

For a moment I wanted to bolt. Even if it meant shifting back into bat form, I wanted to get out of there. Smooth-talking, handsome-as-sin Ian MacDonald made me shiver. Why? I couldn't put my finger on it. Maybe it was the vacant-eyed surfer dudes scattered around the deck outside. Or the lavishly decorated den that, despite a roaring fire in the stone fireplace, still chilled me to the bone. Then there was the man himself with his video and obvious indifference to poor Sarah's humiliation when she'd exposed her cottage cheese thighs.

Of course I couldn't forget that he was Jerry's ancient enemy. I *had* paid attention to the "MacDonalds are demons from hell" stories I'd heard at Castle Campbell. But the Ian MacDonald waiting for my answer now was no kilt-wearing, broadsword-hacking demon. He had a Web site, cooked up magic formulas and had even managed to look cute when Sarah had embarrassed him with her gratitude.

I desperately wanted to be thin and had wanted that forever. That meant I was going to have to play Ian's game, his way. Too bad he had that last name. I'd just have to keep my eyes open. Of course Valdez was already on the case. I glanced down. V was practically quivering with animosity. Oookay.

"What's it going to cost me?" I flushed, not liking how that had come out. "I mean, obviously this elixir or whatever is a valuable commodity."

Valdez snorted and Ray reached for my hand again.

"I told you, babe. Let this be on me. Whatever makes you happy, makes me happy." Ray had the devoted fiancé act down pat.

"It's wonderful to see such a *committed* couple. So rare in the vampire world." Ian's smile seemed sincere, but I heard something in his voice . . .

I shot Ray a warning look. I'd blocked my thoughts from the get-go and assumed Ray had done the same. As far as Ian knew, Ray and I *were* a devoted couple. And my insistence on paying seemed silly under the circumstances. I decided I could settle this with my "fiancé" later.

"Well, if you insist, love." I leaned against Ray and smiled at Ian. "Ray's very generous. While the video was impressive, I really don't want to waste his money. So tell me more. Exactly what's involved here, Ian?"

"Ah, you're a practical woman. Admirable." Ian snapped his fingers and a slim woman in black running shorts and matching sports bra scurried into the room. She carried a tray loaded with bottles. It didn't take more than a few sec-

onds for me to pick up on the fact that the lady was mortal.
The bottles rattled as she set the tray on the wooden coffee
table in front of us. Then she stepped back, watching Ian
closely, her hands clasped behind her.

"This is Trina." Ian smiled at her and she visibly relaxed.
"Tell me, dear one, did you do your fifteen-mile run as I
instructed?"

"Yes, Master." She smiled and pushed her dark hair behind one ear. "I made it twenty, to please you."

"Excellent." Ian reached out his hand and she hurried to
take it. "And when was this?"

"I finished less than thirty minutes ago, then showered
and dried my hair." She pulled his hand to her stomach.
"*Have* I pleased you, Master?"

"Yes. Now this female vampire will drink from you. Make
it a pleasant experience for her. Do whatever she wishes." Ian
brushed his thumb across Trina's bare stomach when her
mouth tightened and it looked like she might protest. "This
will please me very much." He ran his thumb up to her
breast. "And later tonight I'll please *you*."

For a moment I thought I saw rebellion in Trina's dark
eyes, but she merely nodded.

"Of course, Master. Whatever you wish." She turned to
me. "You want to drink from me here? Or do you wish to be
private?"

"Wait just a minute." I glanced at Ray. He was fighting a
grin, like he could get into watching a little girl-on-girl action. I pinched his hard thigh. "First, I'm not into drinking
from mortals, thank you very much. And she brought in
bottles. I figured those contained your magic potion."

"Some of those bottles are supplements. I'll explain them
later. They're clearly labeled. Others are refreshments for Mr.
Caine to enjoy while he waits for us." Ian smiled. "My program
has several key components, Glory. One effective treatment is
to drink from a mortal who has just exercised vigorously." Ian
ran his hand down Trina's nonexistent hip.

"So I can't just drink something from a bottle?" I wasn't

sure I liked this, but, in a strange way, it made sense. Something to do with a revved-up metabolism, I guess.

"No, you must drink from the source and soon after that source"—he smiled as he stroked Trina's taut thigh—"has completed the exercise for the best effect." Ian stood and gestured for me to do the same. "Now, Glory, I'm going to weigh and measure you. After that, you'll drink from Trina. When you come back here tomorrow night, I'm willing to bet you'll be down at least two pounds. How does that sound?"

"Oh, come on, Ian. I thought you said this program was revolutionary. Any vampire knows you can drink from a mortal for special effects." I turned to Ray. "Remember, Ray? You can get high from a mortal who's just done drugs or is drunk. It's the same with a runner. The healing sleep wipes out any 'effects.' Always has." I stood and pulled Ray up with me, so disappointed I wanted to bawl like a baby. "I knew this was too good to be true. Let's go."

"Glory, wait. Hear me out." Ian was on his feet. He gestured at the bottles between us. "See those? *They* are the difference. My special formulas make it possible for the weight loss to stay off. Even after you sleep. I've spent decades in the lab perfecting these." He waved a hand toward the dark TV screen. "You saw Sarah. That kind of loss didn't happen overnight."

I slowly sat again. "No, I guess it couldn't have." I picked up one of the bottles. "What are you, some kind of scientist?"

"I've been many things in my over five hundred years. Even a medical doctor." Ian held out his hand. "Are you going to trust me on this?"

"Don't do it, Glory. This whole operation reeks. You'd be nuts to trust a MacDonald. When Blade hears about this—"

"Valdez, hush. Blade's old news. I'm with Ray now." I pretended not to notice Ian's intent gaze. "Give me a minute to wrap my brain around all this."

Ray put his arm around me. "Take your time, babe."

"Blade?" Ian sat across from us again.

"Jeremy Blade, Glory's former boyfriend. Valdez forgets who's buying his rib eyes these days." Ray gave V a warning look.

I hoped Ian bought that story. I tuned them out while I tried to think. *Down* two pounds in one night? Was it possible? But wait. Now he wanted to *weigh* me? No one, I mean no one, knew my weight. And he'd write it down where anyone could come across it. Those snoopy bastards from the tabloids, for example. I'd be like every other famous person with a weight issue, my number a headline on the front cover along with a picture of me with a really gross butt shot. Oh, God, could this possibly be worth it?

I wanted to fly the hell out of there. This was even worse than the measuring. But to actually lose two pounds after a day of healing sleep . . .

Valdez moved closer and bumped my knee. *"Seriously, Glo. Let's get the hell out of here. I'm getting bad vibes. Blade—"*

"He'll hate it, but won't be able to stop me. Don't mention him again." I grabbed Valdez's collar when he looked like he wanted to start something, like maybe "accidentally" knock over that tray of bottles. Of course if he really lunged at anything, I had zero chance of stopping him. I'm vamp strong, but he's in a category all by himself strengthwise.

And then there was Trina, who was checking out Ray and obviously wishing he was the one with the weight issue. Yeah, right. My "fiancé" had a single-digit percentage of body fat.

"Well, Glory, are you going to do this program or not? It's your call." Ray pulled out his wallet and extracted a black credit card that could have paid for a villa in the south of France and still not hit a limit. Ian played it cool, but I'm sure he wanted to snatch it and run up a big tab before Ray could put it out of sight again.

I sighed and stood. My jeans were cutting into my midsection despite the blessing of a little spandex. I pulled down my T-shirt but could still feel the muffin top bulging above the waistband. I walked over to Trina and sniffed. B positive, a nice healthy one too. And she was fresh from a shower that had involved a hint of lavender. Ian and Ray were both on their feet, watching me.

"Okay, but Ray, baby, you stay here. Valdez, you come with me for the weigh-in, but, I swear to God, if you look at my weight, I'll post a picture on the Internet of a Chihuahua having a bad hair day and claim it's your true form."

"Tough talk, Glory, but I'll do what I have to if this a-hole threatens your safety." Valdez stayed between Ian and me. *"Hear this, MacDonald. If any harm comes to Glory, you'll have every Campbell in Scotland on you like fleas on my ass."*

"I'm not afraid of the Campbells, but find that threat interesting. A sire isn't usually so involved with a vampire he's made and released, so to speak." Ian faced me. "Who do you belong to, Glory? Caine here? Or a Campbell?"

I felt my fangs fully extend and my face grow hot. "I don't belong to anyone, Ian. A Campbell made me, but we parted ways long ago." I snarled at Valdez. "The shifter oversteps and will hear about this later." I looked back at Ray and managed a smile. "My love life is my concern. Since Ray is willing to pay . . ."

"Say no more." Ian nodded and took Ray's credit card. "I admire independent women. Clearly you're one of them."

I stared at the MacDonald vampire. "I'm independent but not stupid and I do have powerful friends. So does Ray. This had better be on the up-and-up. And I *will* let the shifter do his thing if this 'treatment' is just a con."

Ray and Valdez were involved in a stare-down. "The shifter may not live that long. You keep popping off like that, fur face, and I'll see you replaced."

"Yeah?" Valdez glanced at me. *"That's not your call, Caine. Glory, care to straighten him out?"*

"Shut up, V. Right now you're hanging on by a thread." I wanted to get on with this. "Ian? Are we clear? This thing totally safe and on the up-and-up?"

"You saw the tape, Glory. And I could show you dozens more of my success stories if it would make you feel better.

Even introduce you to some of the vampires. But it would delay things. Maybe a week or more to get them here. If you wish to wait . . ." Ian smiled and toyed with the credit card, acting like he could care less if we proceeded or not.

A week. The Grammys would be over and I'd be on my way back to Texas. I really, really wanted to look good on the red carpet. The event would be televised. Millions would be watching, including Jerry's mum, who hates me and would be hoping I'd fall flat on my face. She cheered when Ray and I announced our fake engagement. Is still hoping I'll marry Ray and leave her precious son alone.

How cool to lose enough weight to freak out those designers on that reality show. They'd come for the fittings and their dresses would positively bag on me. They'd argue about who'd measured wrong. It would make for great TV and I'd just stand there, looking skinny and perfectly innocent in my new size-six body. Would that be mean of me? Maybe I was tired of being good old Glory.

"I don't want to wait. Let's do this." I looked at Ray and he winked.

"Fine. Follow me." Ian gestured at the coffee table. "There are several excellent bottles of mortal juice there, Mr. Caine, if you wish to indulge. As I said, they're clearly labeled for your enjoyment. I'll be back shortly. Glory and Trina will join us when they're done. This way, please, Glory."

I trailed Ian, my stomach doing a dip and roll that made me wonder if I *could* drink from Trina and keep it down. Valdez sulked by my side. We stepped into an office painted pale gray with a wall of windows overlooking the ocean. A chrome and glass desk held a computer and a setup that Ian made use of as he punched in numbers. Running Ray's card no doubt. His grin confirmed it. Well, that part was out of the way. I'd be sure we got a receipt. I just hoped I'd be able to pay the cost back before the turn of the *next* century.

Valdez stood, scowling, next to Trina, while Ian picked up a clipboard and led me to a doctor's scale in one corner of the room.

"I'll need your measurements too."

Valdez snorted. *"Four times in one night. That's some kind of record, Glory. Guess you've experienced your own personal hell tonight."*

"Yeah." I made a face at the tape in Ian's hand. "Reality show. Designers are making dresses for me to wear on the red carpet. Tonight they taped the first segment."

Ian kept smiling as he reached around me to measure my waist. "Won't they be surprised when they bring back those dresses and they're too big?"

I laughed, totally stoked by the whole idea. "That's exactly what I thought. They'll be back in four days for a fitting. Think that's enough time for them to see a difference?"

"You stick strictly to my program, the fast track, and I guarantee it." Ian reached around me to measure my breasts. His eyes gleamed as he sent me a mental message that made me blink.

Whoa. So Ian was a little tired of bony babes in running shorts. I filed that away. I figured I could be on the miracle cure of the ages and still have plenty upstairs. I glanced at Trina and then remembered Sarah in the video. I didn't want to end up flat-chested. And running shoes sure aren't my idea of a fashion statement.

"You can stop the program when you reach your ideal weight and size. You know what that is?" Ian led me to the scale.

I had forgotten to block my thoughts. So Mr. Nosy knew just what I'd been thinking. I glanced at Trina and Valdez. They both were very interested in what Ian and I were up to.

"Of course. I've had centuries to think about it. I want to fit into size-six jeans. I want to have the top to match, but still have nice cleavage." I flushed. Maybe that was too much information. Ian's gaze had gone hot and it swept over me.

"Step on the scale, Glory. Have you weighed before?"

I kicked off my shoes. "Yes, and I know my number. So I'll know if this scale is accurate." I stopped short. "Damn.

Maybe I should take off my jeans. I bet they're adding at least three pounds."

Ian grinned. "Go for it."

Valdez was beside me in a shot and growled at Ian. *"Over my dead body."*

I looked down at him. "That can be arranged."

Ian laughed. "Why don't we agree that I'll subtract three from whatever shows up on the scale?"

I could see Valdez wasn't budging. "Fine. Back to the door, V. I mean it." I watched until he was safely beside Trina again. "I guess we can't skip this part." I was avoiding the moment of truth. I knew my weight was too much for my five-foot-five-inch height. I'd studied the charts, read the articles, wailed about my fate for way too long.

"Not a chance." Ian smiled sympathetically. "Get it over with. It will only get better. When you see the number get smaller, you'll feel fantastic."

"Yeah, right. You promise no one else sees this? You did say you were a doctor with all that doctor-patient-confidentiality thing going on."

"Yes, yes, of course." Ian took my hand to help me step on the scale.

I whipped around. "Valdez, turn around. Face the door. I mean it. I don't want you even *looking* in this direction. Ian isn't going to hurt me. I'll yell if I need you."

"I don't like this." Valdez gave Ian one more growl and then did turn around, his tail going up to shoot a furry finger at the MacDonald.

"You too, Trina. This is none of your business."

"Oh, for God's sake." Trina looked like she wanted to say more, but a hard look from her "master" got her skinny butt moving and she faced the door in short order.

"Okay, let's do this." I stepped on the scale, wincing as Ian slid the metal weights up until he was satisfied. "Wait!" I blew out air, like that might make a pound difference.

Ian laughed and wrote down the number I knew too well. "Relax, Glory. You're overreacting. I've worked with vampires who had a lot more to lose than you have. By this time next week, you'll be in a size six or I'll give Caine his money back."

"Oh, my God!" I flung myself off the scale and into Ian's arms. Can you blame me? I'd just had a man promise me the moon. "That would be so incredible."

"*Yeah, incredible.*" Valdez was right beside me again. "*Let her go, MacDonald.*"

"Get back to the door!" I screeched, lunging to slide the weights back to zero. "Damn it, V, I told you to stay there."

"And, for the record, *she* was holding *me*, not the other way around." Ian laid his clipboard facedown and smiled at me. "Now, I'd better get back to Caine with a receipt for this. Glory, drink from Trina as soon as possible. The effects of her run will be wearing off in a few minutes. You don't want that to happen, do you?"

"No, of course not." I followed Ian to the door. I still felt funny drinking from a mortal, but if this is what it would take, and she *seemed* willing enough, I'd do it. I ignored Valdez's disapproving look. "Where . . . ?"

"Come with me. Guess the dog comes too. He doesn't seem to want you out of his sight." Trina gave Valdez a disdainful look. "Wise of you, mutt. I have a black belt."

"*What? Gucci?*" Valdez snarled and showed his impressive canines.

"You want to try me?" Trina struck a pose.

"Trina, get a clue. Valdez would be snacking on your foot before you got off kick one." I followed Trina into a bedroom. Oh, this was so not happening on a bed. "V? Sit outside the door. She's just a mortal. If I need you, I'll yell. You'll hear me and knock down the door. Think what fun that will be. Then you can tear Trina apart with my blessing."

"*Fine. I'll be waiting. Eagerly.*" Valdez plopped down on the Oriental rug in the hallway. "*And keep in mind that locks won't keep me out. I live to destroy—anyone who hurts my lady.*"

"Ooh, see me tremble." Trina shook her hands in the air.

I sent Valdez a message that said I agreed that Trina was an idiot and that I'd hurry, then slammed the door. There was a chair in the corner of the room next to a window with yet another breathtaking view of the ocean. No telling how many millions this house cost. Slimming down vampires obviously paid really well. The thought dampened my appetite. Then I saw Trina's open closet door. Size-zero jeans hung there. Zero. I'd never even bothered to dream about such a thing.

"Sit in the chair. Hand me your wrist." I pulled up a matching ottoman and sat on it.

"What? Not going to do a little more? Most of Ian's female vamps like turning this into fun and games." Trina touched my hair. "You're prettier than some clients. And you managed to get a man like Israel Caine to propose to you. I'm, um, intrigued." She slid her hand down to my shoulder. "Come on, Glory. At least take me at the neck. It's so much more intimate."

I breathed in a jolt of good-quality B positive. Then I shook my head. "I don't want to be intimate with you, Trina. I save that for the men I love. This is a business transaction, nothing more. And I really hate taking advantage of you this way. I meant it when I said I don't normally drink from mortals."

"I don't appeal to you at all?" Trina brushed against me, her nipples hard against my arm. "Don't tell me that in the hundreds of years you've been alive you've never experimented . . ."

I glanced at the door, sure Valdez was getting an earful with his supersonic hearing. "I'm not telling you anything." I pulled her wrist to my lips and hit the vein. The instant the rich blood filled my mouth, I was all about the feeding. I heard Trina moan, apparently enjoying the sensation. She even tried to reach for me again, but I didn't give a damn.

I was high on the taste and heat of the mortality surging into my body. It was so warm, made me feel so alive. It's the only time I really felt that way. And I'd missed it. Denied

myself the pleasure. And this time . . . Maybe Ian had something here. Because this experience . . . The energy was ex-
hilarating, beyond anything I'd ever felt before during
feeding. This was wow! Only the realization that Trina's
hand had crept onto my bra snapped me out of it.

I released her and reared back, plucking away that hand
and jumping to my feet. My whole body quivered. Oh, God.
I leaned over to make the room stop spinning. This feeling.
Like *I'd* run twenty miles, was still running. My heart
pounded and my legs ached. What a great feeling.

I struggled to catch my breath, my hands on my knees as
I glanced up and saw the ocean. One of Ian's surfers caught
a wave and rode it in. My adrenaline rush had to be similar.
I was soaring.

"Glory." Trina stood behind me, her warm hand on my
back. "Are you okay? Do I need to get Ian?" She rubbed my
shoulders, even leaned on me for a moment, her breath hot
as she kissed the back of my head. "That was incredible.
Please come to me again."

"I . . . I'm fine. Give me a moment." I finally straightened
and stepped away from her. "Thank you. For the donation. For
a mortal, you seem awfully at ease with our wacko world."

"I've always been into the paranormal. I just knew that
things like vampires had to be real." Her eyes were shining,
but her face was pale and she suddenly sat down on the foot
of the bed. "I'm hoping to become one of you. If I please the
master . . . You'll tell him, won't you? That I served you
well?" She put out a shaky hand.

"Sure, you were fantastic. Best feeding ever." Oh, great.
Now I had a serious case of the guilts. Had I taken too much?
I stepped closer to her, touched her cheek to see if she was
too cold, which would be a bad sign. She grabbed my hand
and sighed.

"I want to please you again, Glory."

Thank God, she was warm and I carefully extricated myself, relieved when she stood. I put up a hand when it looked
like she was going to hug me.

"Let's go. Ray's waiting. And Valdez, of course. Stay behind me. And, for God's sake, don't touch me in front of either of them. They wouldn't take it well."

Trina giggled. "Neither would Ian. Men. What do they know about pleasure? Next time, maybe . . . ?"

I shook my head but that didn't seem to faze her. I headed for the door. When I opened it, Valdez gave me a narrow-eyed look, like he was inspecting me for signs of debauchery. I just strutted past him. Because, boy, did I feel amazing. And, would you believe, lighter somehow. Seriously, I thought my jeans were already looser. Probably my imagination, but I was so going to find a scale when we got back to the hotel.

Ray and Ian were drinking from bottles of his "juice" when Trina and I got back to the living room. They jumped up when they saw us.

"You okay, Glory? You look . . . jazzed."

"I feel that way." I turned to Ian. "I don't know about weight loss, but the effects of feeding from her . . ."

"Quite a rush, isn't it?" Ian slung his arm around Trina. "She'll be here for you tomorrow. You must come every night around midnight. I'll make sure she's ready. There will be other things you'll have to do too. Not just this. I'll explain them tomorrow. For now, I have two bottles of other special products for you to take with you. Drink one before you sleep and one when you rise tomorrow. They're clearly marked. This is very important, Glory, if you want the effects of your feedings from Trina to last."

"Babe, we've got to go." Ray glanced at his watch. "I've got rehearsal and I'm not leaving you here."

"Right. I guess that means shifting again." I hated the thought but felt pumped enough that I figured I could do it easily.

"No need. I have a limo waiting to take you to the venue where Caine told me he's rehearsing, then it will take you on to the hotel, Glory. I hope that's satisfactory."

"Perfect." I smiled at Ian. Now I was really liking him, MacDonald or not. He'd been nice about the weigh-in. And

that feeding . . . Well, who knew? Shoot. Maybe I was high.
I smiled at Ray too. Even Valdez got a head pat. Nothing
could bring me down right now.

"See you tomorrow, Ian. It'll just be Valdez and me. Ray,
you don't have to come again. I know you're busy." I cud-
dled up to Ray. Part of the loving-engaged-couple thing, of
course.

Ray frowned. "We'll see. Now, let's hit the road. Forget
the Campbells, MacDonald. Take care of my girl or there
will be hell to pay from me. Are we clear?"

"Of course. I find all this protectiveness toward your fiancée quite admirable." Ian walked us to the stairs that led
down to the driveway and the waiting limousine. "And
think about that other product, Caine. It's a vampire's dream
come true."

We settled into the backseat of the limo, the glass up
and shielding us from the driver before I asked the burning
question.

"Okay, Ray, what's the other product Ian's trying to sell?"
Maybe my good feelings were wearing off, because now I
was a little tired. Running twenty miles will do that to you,
I guess.

"He says he's got something that can allow me to go out
in the sun." Ray stared into my eyes. "I'd see daylight again.
You know what that would mean to me, Glory?"

I grabbed his arm on one side and Valdez's fur on the
other. "I know that if it doesn't work and you try it, sweetheart, you're toast."

Five

"*You're* trusting him. Why shouldn't I?" Ray leaned back on the leather seat. "I want this. Ian says he can make it happen."

"I don't believe it. Not even the Energy Vampires have a formula for surviving daylight yet." I remembered the head of the vampire cult, famous for their Vampire Viagra, telling me that. (Yeah, go figure. Even vamps enjoy a boost in their sex lives.) "The only way to test a drug like that is to send a vampire into the sun. Who'd be crazy enough to try it out?"

"Ian says . . ." Ray shook his head. "Never mind. We're here. I've got to go. We'll talk about this later at the hotel." He leaned across me to look at Valdez. "Take care of my lady."

"Your *lady. Yeah, right. Don't let the act go to your head, Caine. And don't say I didn't warn you.*" Valdez lifted his chin. "*Blade's at the hotel waiting for her right now. When he hears where you took her tonight, the shit's goin' to hit the fan.*"

"Let it. Glory's going to do what she wants. Am I right, sweet thing?" Ray brushed his thumb across my cheek to my lips.

"Yes, you are." I held Ray's hand for a moment. "Promise me you won't do anything with Ian without discussing it with me first, Ray. Please?" I knew how much he missed the sun. He'd been a freak about his boat, his tropical island paradise, his beach. Even the fact that he'd now live forever hadn't come close to making up for the loss of those hours he'd spent in the sun. He was a "live for the moment" kind of guy. Forever didn't seem to matter that much to him.

"I'm not an idiot, Glory. You're still my vamp mentor, babe, but I don't dance to your tune." He leaned in and kissed my lips. "Still, I realize I owe you my life. Such as it is. See you later." He opened the door as soon as the limo stopped. "Say hi to Blade for me. The man doesn't pose a threat to me, Valdez. He's stuck in the past. Glory knows it and so do you. My lady's a 'now' kind of woman. When she gets her new look, she'll be ready for even more changes." He grinned, then slammed the door.

"Arrogant son of a bitch," Valdez muttered as the car pulled away from the curb.

I looked back and saw Ray surrounded by female fans and a few photographers. He was laughing and signing autographs, the picture of virile hot guy in worn jeans and leather jacket over a white T-shirt. I'd never seen Blade in that kind of outfit. Probably never would. Just like I'd never see Ray in a kilt. Though he had great legs . . .

"He shouldn't have gone without his bodyguards." I frowned as he disappeared from sight. "Some of his fans get aggressive."

"He's only a few steps from the auditorium entrance and he is *a freakin' vampire. But I guess he can't exactly show fang to his ador-ing public, now, can he?"* Valdez snorted. *"Call Brit and have her meet him there if you're so worried about him."*

Brittany was model gorgeous, had a killer body and the skills to match. Valdez had something going with the shifter who was one of Ray's paranormal bodyguards. Ray's mortal guards still hadn't figured out why Ray had added her to his security team, but they weren't complaining. She could twist any man around her well-manicured little finger, my V-man included.

"Good idea." I hit speed dial and soon had Brit headed to Ray's side.

"Don't worry about Caine. He can handle a few female fans gone wild." Valdez sat up when we got near the hotel.

"I'm more worried about this sunlight thing. I want Brit on Ray's tail his every waking moment. Get her alone and tell her that. If he tries to strike a deal with Ian to use this new potion, I want to know about it so I can try to head Ray off."

"So it's okay for you to drink whatever swill MacDonald's cooked up, but not for your buddy Ray?" Valdez nudged me with a paw. *"You see the problem with your logic? This Scot's got a hell of a lot more reason to do something nasty to you than to a world-famous rock star, Glory. You were made by a Campbell. That puts you solidly in the enemy camp in his book."*

"It's an ancient feud. Surely they've moved past it."

"You've been to Castle Campbell, heard the laird rant on the subject. These feuds never die. The one with the MacDonalds is particularly grim. Lots of murder and mayhem in the past. Google the two clans and see what you get. I think you'll find that Blade will have good reason to go nuts when he hears you've put your life in Ian's hands."

"That's overstating it, don't you think? I'm just trying to lose a few pounds. That's all." I frowned at the cloth bag in my lap with my two bottles of supplements. "Ray's deal is much more serious. He'd have to actually walk into the sun."

"Yeah, well, he'd have to stay awake to do that. Seems unlikely." Valdez showed his teeth. *"Once Blade hears the man's got you drinking God knows what and biting mortals, MacDonald won't live long enough to give Caine a glimmer of light."*

"You leave Jerry to me, V. I mean it. Not one word to him. I'll tell him about this when I'm ready." As the car pulled up in front of the hotel, I decided Ray was right about one thing. Blade's reaction to this deal with Ian would be important. If Jerry started issuing orders to me again like he'd done for centuries now . . . Well, it just wasn't going to work. And I was really tired of the same old arguments. You know?

With that depressing thought going round in my head, I walked into the hotel. We had to dodge only two paparazzi who snapped pictures of Valdez and me. I'd forgotten V's leash, which earned us frowns from some of the hotel guests and probably a headline about me and leash laws. I leaned down and grabbed his collar as we approached the front desk and the clerk behind the counter.

"You have a gym here, right?"

"Yes, of course, Ms. St. Clair. It's open twenty-four hours for your convenience. You may use your room key card to enter." The woman knew exactly who I was. Any consort of Israel Caine's could have walked an unleashed herd of rabid hyenas into the lobby and she wouldn't have cared. "Would you like for someone to show you where it is?"

"Is there a scale in there? I want to weigh myself." I smiled sheepishly and leaned in. "I've been dieting and I'm dying to know if I've lost any weight yet."

The clerk quickly hid her thrill at having something to sell to the tabloids. This was sure to hit newsstands soon. Which was fine by me. Better than the baby-trap stories.

"Of course we have scales, a state-of-the-art gym and even personal trainers available if you want one." She snapped her fingers and a bellman appeared at my elbow. "Fritz, escort Ms. St. Clair and her dog down to the gym, please."

"No trainer necessary and I forgot my key card." And my purse. I travel light when I change into a bat. I smiled. "I'm hoping someone upstairs will let me in after I weigh."

"No problem."

In less than a minute I had a new card and Fritz was leading us down a hall to the gym. Once I knew where to find the room with the scales, I quickly dismissed the bellman with a five-dollar bill I kept stashed in my pocket for emergencies.

"This is crazy. You really need to weigh now? You just left Ian's place. What's this going to prove?" Valdez slumped next to the

door in the spot where I pointed. *"Blade's going to be looking for you. He'll be on the roof right now."*

"This will just take a minute. Ian said I might have already lost a few pounds, and I feel lighter. I want to check it out." Jerry and I had set up this date before I'd met with the reality show people. I'd tried to estimate how my evening would go and picked a time, but I was cutting it close. Well, Jerry was used to me running late and this was important. I took a breath, closed the door with Valdez on the outside and looked around to make sure there weren't any security cameras recording this. Paranoid much? You bet. Then I stepped on the scale.

After adjusting the weights, I just stared. Subtracted the three for the jeans of course, then looked again. The scale didn't move. So this was it. My weight. I couldn't believe it. Two and a half pounds. I'd lost two and a half pounds. Just like that. I leaped off the scale, slammed the weights back to zero and then happy-danced around the room. I flung open the door and hugged a startled Valdez.

"I actually lost weight. And not a little like I might have done before when if I'd snacked on a mortal who'd taken a run, but two and a half pounds!" I hugged him again, then reached for the waistband of my jeans. Could I get a finger inside there? Yes! "Look! Can you believe it? This is insane."

"It's got to be a trick. Maybe the girl at the counter here at the hotel works for MacDonald. They set this up." Valdez obviously wasn't buying it. *"And you've got to see if it's still off in the evening when you wake up, remember?"*

I took a moment to think about that. Diabolical, but possible. Vampires are nothing if not devious. And Ian could be doing this to get a Campbell's woman to trust him for some reason. I didn't want to believe it. Or come down off this high.

"The supplements are supposed to keep the weight off while I sleep. But I'll keep an open mind. I'll get Nathan to send someone out to buy my own scale tomorrow to keep in the suite. Will that make you feel better?"

"It should make you *feel better. Now, let's head for the roof. I'll keep my mouth shut for a while, but if you don't tell Blade about MacDonald, I will."* Valdez gave me his best stare.

"Yeah, sure. You're right about stuff hitting the fan. Jerry will hate this and won't understand why it's such a big deal to me." Which was really a bummer. You'd like to think the most important man in your life would develop a little insight after four hundred years. "He's going to freak when he hears I spent the evening with a MacDonald." I heard a giggle come out of my mouth. I was that excited. "I tell you, V. If Ian's stuff works, there's no way in hell I'm giving it up."

Valdez followed me into the elevator. *"Then we'd better stop at the suite first. You could use a hairbrush and some lipstick before you see Blade."*

"Thanks, pal." I rubbed his head. "I'll do that. When talking doesn't work with Jerry, action usually does."

"I really don't want to hear this." Valdez watched me punch the button for our floor and bumped against me. *"Women."*

I just smiled and headed for the suite. I was going to change clothes too. Put on a clingy sweater in Jerry's favorite blue. I know how to turn my man into an obliging puddle of lust. But getting him to realize he was going to tolerate my trafficking with a MacDonald . . . Well, I didn't look forward to that argument. I definitely needed my war paint.

"You're late. I was just about to push my way into that room you share with Caine, Gloriana." Jerry pulled me into his arms as soon as I stepped onto the terrace of the rooftop restaurant. "I was getting worried."

"No need. I had that reality-show thing. Which took longer than I thought it would. Then we took a quick trip out to Malibu." I smiled and kissed Jerry's cheek. "The ocean is beautiful at night. We should go out there and have a romantic evening while we're here."

"I like the sound of that." He pulled me toward a table

set up near the brick wall surrounding the flat roof. The restaurant had closed for the night, but Jerry had probably bribed someone to light candles on the tables nearby and leave a stereo on with romantic music playing softly in the background. Bouquets of bloodred roses, my favorite, were scattered around the terrace. Their delicious scent perfumed the air, but I still detected the AB negative that filled the crystal wineglasses on one table. That had to have been strictly BYOB.

"This is wonderful. Very romantic." I smiled up at him as he held out a chair and I slipped into it, watching him as he gestured for Valdez to leave us alone. I got a significant look from my bodyguard before he disappeared into the open door to the restaurant. It closed softly behind him.

"I feel terribly underdressed. You look very handsome, Jeremiah." I leaned forward and took his hand as he sat across from me. I was telling the simple truth. He wore a soft sweater, probably cashmere, in a forest green that complemented his dark eyes and hair. It certainly hugged his broad shoulders nicely. He was much more strongly built than Ray, with a warrior's muscles. This warrior had been tested in battle before he'd been turned. Gulp. I suddenly remembered that some of those battles he'd told me about had been against Clan MacDonald.

"Florence has been shopping for me again. She insisted that Richard and I needed to update our wardrobes." Jerry shrugged and looked slightly embarrassed. "If it pleases you, then I'm okay with it."

I grinned and leaned across the table to kiss him thoroughly. I ran my hands over the soft wool, exploring those hard shoulders. Mmm. How could I ever be tempted by anyone else? He tasted clean and delicious and all mine. I sighed and leaned back. Was I stalling? Probably. No, definitely.

"Don't stop now." Jerry stood and walked around the table. "Come here and do that again."

"No, we need to talk." I hated to say it. Hated even more to follow through on it.

"Talk. Yes, I guess we should. Occasionally. It's what couples are supposed to do, Florence says. She's been watching some show on TV. She's got Richard promising to go to couples therapy if he doesn't 'open up' about his past." Jerry laughed. "Trust me. Flo doesn't want to hear about that man's past. He's killed more wrong-headed vampires than anyone I know."

I shuddered. I liked Richard. And my best friend loved him. I didn't want to picture him as a cold-blooded killer. "How does he decide who's 'wrong-headed'?"

"Ask him some night." Jerry pulled me up and into his arms. "I'm not getting involved in their love life. You wanted to talk. Let's stick to our own topics. What do you want to talk about? Why did you go to Malibu? Caine have business there?"

Uh-oh. Here it comes. I glanced toward the darkened restaurant, but Valdez was nowhere to be seen. Not that he'd help me. He would just make matters worse. Chime in that he'd warned me not to go out there. Blah, blah, blah.

"No, I had business out there. I went to see a man about a new product." I eased out of Jerry's arms and sat again. I took a sip of the synthetic, then set the glass down. Would this add more weight? Maybe I should only drink what Ian prescribed. I frowned and pushed it away.

"What's wrong? Is the synthetic off? That's the brand you like, the type." Jerry picked up the glass and sniffed, then took a sip. "Seems okay to me."

"No, it's fine. But I'm on a diet." I waited for his reaction. I didn't have long to wait.

He laughed. Yep, you heard me. A hearty, full-out, "isn't Glory a hoot" laugh. Oh, it was a real knee-slapper. The idea that a vampire would go on a diet. Because if it wasn't a joke, it was pathetic, right? I just waited it out. Until Jerry realized I wasn't smiling, just staring at him and still not sipping the expensive brew he'd poured for my enjoyment.

"All right. What's this, then? You seem serious. Haven't we been through this before?" He took my hand. "When you deny yourself nourishment, Gloriana, you become weak. It's dangerous." He lifted my hand to his lips and pressed a kiss to my palm. "I don't want you to risk it for a few measly ounces. Which, as I remember, is all this practice ever bought you."

Yes, I'd tried the starvation bit before. The first time had been before meeting his parents. Well, you try heading for Castle Campbell and facing a laird and his lady when you're nothing but a commoner. Back in those days stuff like that had mattered. And in Lady Campbell's tiny brain, believe me, it still did. The fact that I'd been an actress had also branded me a whore in her eyes. And then I'd refused to marry Jerry. Oh, yeah, I keep my scarlet *A* handy when I'm around Mag Campbell. I just paste it on my forehead to save her the trouble of screaming it in my face.

"I'm not starving myself, Jerry. This is different. I'm on a special program. I fed from a mortal earlier. A runner. You wouldn't believe the effect!" I squeezed his hand. "And I just weighed. I've already lost over two pounds!"

Jerry pulled me up and looked me over. He even turned me around and checked out my backside. "I can see that." He ran his hand down my rump. "Much as I love this curve, I know you fash yourself about it. So if this makes you happy, have at it."

I threw my arms around his neck and gave him a kiss guaranteed to melt his Prada belt buckle. But I carefully blocked my thoughts. The bad news was yet to come. I was going to have to spill the MacDonald beans before Valdez did. When I pulled back, we were both breathing hard.

"A runner, eh. Seems a simple concept. Who thought of it?" Jerry ran his hands down my back but kept me pressed against him.

"A vampire I met at the club last night. Damian introduced us. That's who Ray and I met out at Malibu." I pushed back, deciding I needed some space for this story.

"I thought I smelled another vampire." Jerry frowned and looked around the roof. "Guess it was his scent on you." He shook his head. "Tell me more. How is he going to keep this weight from disappearing after you sleep?"

"He has that all figured out. But, Jerry!" I grabbed his hand. "Drinking from the runner was incredible. Not only did I lose weight, but I felt powerful. And high on something."

"Endorphins." Jerry picked up his glass from the table and drank. "I've read about it. It's the endorphins mortals generate when they exercise. This seems like something we could do on our own." He grinned and set the glass down again. "You and I could chase down night runners in the park in Austin. I'd do it for the power and you'd do it for the"—he snagged me around the waist and jerked me to him again—"health benefits."

"I don't want to turn into a predator again. Like in the old days." I ran my hands up to his shoulders. "And I'd hate for you to lose weight. Seems that could happen too."

"True enough." He leaned down and nibbled my earlobe, causing me to shiver. "So we scratch that bit of foreplay. I'll just keep you company if you need to chase down a donor."

"Foreplay. Yes, all those endorphins *were* kind of a turn-on." I ran my fangs up his throat. Maybe if I gave Jerry a treat, he'd take the news about who I was dealing with better. But that was a pretty cowardly approach. And just putting off the inevitable. I had to have plenty of time to calm him down and make sure he wasn't going to interfere with this before the sun rose. The treat could come after the news. As a parting gift.

I sighed and pushed back again. "There's something else you need to know about this weight-loss thing."

"What?" Jerry took my hand and pulled me to the edge of the terrace. "Look at the city lights, Gloriana. I brought you up here because I did think this was a romantic setting."

"Oh, really?" I glanced at him. "Worried I'm with Ray too much?" I slipped my arm around his waist. He was so solid, so much more mine than Ray could ever be. How could I forget that?

"You *are* with him too much. This phony engagement guarantees it." He looked out at the city.

"You don't have to set up romantic evenings to keep me, Jerry. Ray talks a good game, but you and I have history." I leaned against him. "I love you. Ray knows that."

"He'd better. Because as soon as you're done playing his fiancée, you'd damn well better accept this, Gloriana." Jerry pulled a small box out of his pocket. A special blue one that I recognized instantly. Tiffany. Oh, God.

He popped it open and I gasped. I'm a pretty good judge of diamonds, being in the antique business and all. He'd managed to top Ray's offering by a good two carats. And, trust me, Ray's had been a very sizable ring. He'd insisted I needed one to fool the paparazzi. I'd always intended to give it back to him when we called off our charade.

"Jerry! It's—it's beautiful." I couldn't help myself. You knew I was going to have to try it on. Before I could touch it, though, Jerry pulled the ring out of the box and slipped that sparkler on my third finger, left hand. It fit perfectly.

"I know how you feel about marriage, Gloriana. But I'm tired of these games. When we leave Los Angeles, you will be my woman or we're done." Jerry sounded serious, but his eyes were warm, his hands firm as he gripped mine.

"That sounds like an ultimatum." I didn't pull back, though. It wasn't the ring that kept me close. It was the fact that Jerry knew everything about me, I mean *everything*, and yet he still wanted to claim me. He didn't care that his mother thought I wasn't good enough for the heir to Castle Campbell. He didn't care that my vampire skills were inadequate to say the least. He sure didn't care that my butt was too big or that I spent way too much time on my hair and makeup and not nearly enough on balancing my checkbook.

Jerry loved me, warts and all. And forgave me time and again when I did stupid things or said stupid things. And there had been plenty of those in four hundred plus years.

"I'm not forcing you to do something you don't want."
Jerry put my hands on his shoulders and pulled me close. "I
know you, Glory. You like your independence, but you also
need someone you can count on. Me. You've always had me,
haven't you?"

I flushed, trying desperately to ignore the way the moonlight flashed off the diamond in that gorgeous ring. "Yes,
I've always known you were there for me if I needed you.
Your choice, Jerry. Maybe you should cut me loose and see
how I do. Sink-or-swim time."

"But you'd still have Caine, wouldn't you, Gloriana? That
bastard would be happy to take my place." Jerry jerked me
closer. "Not going to happen. The time has passed to give
you up. I can't do it, damn it. I've tried. How many times?
Dozens, even more. But I couldn't. So I'd send you a bodyguard in the form of a dog. A Valdez. To make sure you were
kept safe. Because the thought of a world without you was
something I couldn't handle."

His eyes seared me and seemed to see into my soul. And I
could see into his. He was telling the truth, *his* truth. And
I couldn't imagine how on earth I'd deserved such devotion.
It stole my breath and stopped my heart. I knew I wasn't
worthy. That I was going to hurt him, *had* hurt him too
many times.

"Jeremiah!" Tears filled my eyes and I leaned my head
against his chest. I could hear the slow pump of his heart.
This was probably the longest speech I'd ever gotten from
him. And the most romantic. He was pulling out all the
stops. Because he wanted a commitment from me. And I was
about to ruin everything. I couldn't do it. No way was I telling him about MacDonald tonight. Valdez would just have
to deal with the delay.

I felt Jerry's hand on my back, gently touching me. He
was giving me time to think. Another unprecedented act.
The man had obviously been talking to someone on how to
proceed with our relationship. Flo? Richard? The former
priest had managed to get my friend to the altar and she'd

sworn never to marry. Richard must have some tricks up his sleeve.

Forget tricks. I had no doubt everything Jerry said came from his heart. My own was full. I was about to tell him how much this meant to me when there was a noise from the door into the restaurant.

"What the hell?" Jerry jerked away from me and ran toward the sound. He pulled open the door. Valdez was there, snarling as he faced off with two paparazzi, armed with cameras.

"Where is she? We heard Glory St. Clair was meeting another man here tonight. You the guy?"

I did the only thing I could do. I jumped off the roof. Good thing I was still feeling the effects of Trina's juice, because I managed to shift into bat form in midair. Nice. I swooped over the roof and landed in the shadows to watch Jerry handle the two men. He had them by the shirts and not too gently. In plain language he let them know he was waiting for someone and he didn't know who in the hell this St. Clair woman was, but she wasn't *his* woman.

Valdez made himself useful by tearing a hole in the seat of one of the men's pants. That seemed to cool off the Glory hunt even though they were sure that was Glory's dog trying to eat them alive. Both the guys, after a quick look to make sure there was no woman in sight, decided to head out. Jerry's shoe up their backsides sped them along.

"Glory?" Jerry turned around and spotted me as I left the shadows to soar above his head. "Well, would you look at you? Shifting like an old pro. That runner's donation must have really pumped you up."

"Sure did, boss. She tell you—" Valdez yelped when I landed on his head and dug in my claws. *"Okay, I get the message. I'm outta here again. Back to my guard post. You know where to find me."*

I released him and settled on the concrete next to the table, concentrated for a moment and was my old Glory self again. Jerry was right. Trina's donation had given me new confidence and the shifting had been easier than I could have imagined. The magic was wearing off, though, and I could feel the coming dawn in my bones. I wondered if I had time to run down and weigh again. Silly, but I was terrified that I felt the weight creeping back on.

I ran a hand through my hair, then surreptitiously stuck a finger in the waistband of my jeans. Yay! They still felt just the teeniest bit loose. But Jerry stood beside me again. I still wore his ring, but couldn't take it with me back to Ray's suite. The "engagement with Ray" charade had to go on until after the Grammy awards show. That was the deal I'd made with Ray. And it would give me some time to think. As Jerry had said, I'd avoided the commitment to him for all these years. And now I was lying to him by omission.

Well, I *would* tell him about MacDonald. But not now. Not when my heart was full and I wanted to hold him close and tell him how much his words earlier had meant to me.

"Hey, big guy. You really took care of those photographers." I looked up at him.

"I hate those creeps. They hound you. Then they use pictures that I swear they've altered on a computer. And the things they say . . ." Jerry pulled me into his arms. "I should have killed both of them."

"I'm not sure I would have stopped you. According to the tabloids I'm fat, a nobody and not good enough for Ray."

"Lying bastards." He pushed his hand into my hair and held my head until my lips were mere inches from his own. "But the worst for me is when they say you are carrying his child." He growled, his fangs glinting in the moonlight. "I would have given anything to have a child from you, Gloriana."

"Ah, Jerry." Stupid tears again. I never had a child, and after I was turned, never could have one. Jerry's only child had been sired by a true bitch. He loves his daughter, but he couldn't have said anything that would have meant more to me. I closed the distance between our mouths and kissed him, tasting him and letting his fangs scrape across my tongue. It didn't hurt, just added a sweet taste of what was to come.

Our mating was slow at first as Jerry pulled me down to a stack of cushions he'd obviously pulled from inside the restaurant. I sighed as he settled beside me and lifted my sweater, then pulled it up and off of me. The night air was cool but not cold and the stars were bright in the sky above us. I reached for his sweater and slid it off of him, eager to see that chest I loved so much. He was perfect in his imperfections. Maybe that was what he thought about me. At least that was what I hoped as he opened the clasp of my bra and tossed it aside, then went to work on my jeans.

We tasted and touched each other until we were naked and he was inside me. Then he stopped and gazed into my eyes again.

"I meant what I said, Gloriana. The time for these games is over. You must decide, lass, once and for all."

I reached up with a shaking hand to trace the contours of his face. Yes, our bodies were connected, but no more than our souls were. I could deny it a thousand times. And try to bury my feelings with a thousand other men. Yet I always came back to this one.

"Love me, Jeremiah. Take me and let me take you. I promise, I will—" I pulled his mouth to mine, suddenly terrified of saying the words that would bind me to him. Why? Mortals did it all the time. And thought nothing of casting off their bonds in divorce court. Immortals took their matings more seriously. I knew that. If Jerry and I made this commitment, I had a feeling he really would expect it to be the forever thing. I ran my hands down his back and opened my body to him, feeling the hard length of him surging inside me. I guess there was something wrong with me that forever scared me so much. That if I gave myself to Jerry in that way, I'd lose part of myself.

He lifted his head and frowned before he rolled so that I was on top of him. "I can feel your fears. Come, now, am I such an ogre that I would keep you from what you love?

Steal your freedom?" He lifted me off of him until we lay
side by side with the stars above us. "I guess Florence is
right. We should talk more. I don't tell you enough of what
I'm thinking. And you don't tell me why you run from me
every dozen years or so."

I turned on my side and put my hand on his chest. "It's
the truth, Jerry. I never expected you to be a chatterbox. But
I know how you are. Possessive and deeply loyal. That scares
me. What if my character isn't made of such, oh, such fine
qualities? I'm afraid I'll disappoint you."

"Hush, lass." Jerry pulled me on top of him again. "You've
never disappointed me. And you make me sound hard and
unyielding. I hope . . ." He closed his eyes and frowned. "No,
I must be honest. I *am* possessive. What's mine, I hold. Always have. It's what the Campbells do. I learned it at my
father's knee. And fought in many a battle to prove no one
can take what belongs to the Clan without regretting it." He
ran his hand down my back to the curve of my backside.

"Battles. Yes, you still bear the scars, from those you
fought before you were turned." I kissed a particularly jagged one on his left shoulder.

"That one a cowardly MacDonald gave me. It was an ambush. They'd stolen cattle from us." Jerry smiled. "They
came to regret it."

I quickly blocked my thoughts. "Surely all those old feuds
are ancient history now. Times have changed."

"Some things never do. My father called me just last
week. The MacDonald has been trying to claim some land
of ours. Using an ancient tax roll. Thieving bastard's still
at it. Too bad they were made vampire centuries ago. I'd
like to see that clan die out." Jerry shook his head. "But I'll
not let you shift the topic, lass. We were talking of our relationship." He grinned. "God help me, I can't believe I said
that."

"Neither can I." I laughed and rubbed against him. Lying
naked on top of him, I had no doubt that he could be easily
distracted. "Can we save that for another night? I love you,

Jeremiah. I love what you said to me tonight. That you care so deeply. Let me celebrate that. This moment. We'll look to the future later. I promise." I reached between us and touched him where he pressed hard against my thigh.

"I'll hold you to that." But his growl of hunger and his hand stroking my breast proved that my distraction had worked.

I moved down his body, kissing and tasting until he jerked me up to push into me again. So deep, he touched me just where I needed to feel him. The rhythm was right, the pace perfect. I couldn't give Trina's blood credit for my soaring orgasm. That was all Jerry's doing as he stroked me and brought me to fulfillment, just as I pushed him there. Time and time again I rose to meet him, finding the pinnacle of pleasure almost unbearable until I cried out to the night that I loved him.

He murmured the Gaelic words I'd learned meant the same, the words from his heart in the language of his birth. He swore he'd never said them to another woman the way he'd said them to me. And in that moment, lying sated under the stars, held close in his strong arms, I believed him. And believed I could never be so content with another man.

If only we could have stayed there, with Valdez keeping the world out. If only . . .

Six

I met Ray back in the suite just a few minutes before dawn.

"Did you tell Campbell about MacDonald?" Ray sat on the side of the bed and slipped off his loafers.

"No. The time wasn't right." I picked up a pad with the hotel logo and began to write a note for Nathan about the scale.

"You afraid of his reaction?" Ray got up to pull off his T-shirt. He tossed it on the closet floor.

"I'm not afraid. I just didn't want to get into it tonight. Jerry had arranged a romantic evening on the roof. I wasn't about to spoil it." I finished the note. "Where should I put this so I'll be sure Nate sees it tomorrow? I want a scale brought up to the suite and put in a private place so I can weigh myself every day."

"Good idea. I wouldn't trust MacDonald's scale either." Ray headed for the bathroom. "I'm going to shower. Put it on top of the TV remote. Nate starts every day with CNN and the stock market report."

"All right, then. I did weigh on the scale in the hotel gym when I got back and it agreed with Ian's scale. Two and a half pounds in one night, Ray!" I laughed. "But then I got paranoid and wondered if maybe Ian and the desk clerk could have worked together." I felt a flush heat my cheeks. "Stupid, but there you go."

"No, I see what you mean." Ray patted me on the shoulder. "You have a right to be suspicious. If Blade and MacDonald are old enemies, anything goes. You could be a pawn in a bigger game than you know, Glory. I say we're smart to be paranoid. That why you sent Brittany after me tonight?"

"You should always have a paranormal bodyguard with you, Ray. I've told you that before." I got up and kicked off my high heels. My feet were killing me. "Another vamp gets a whiff of you in L.A. and a turf war could start. We have no idea who's in charge here. I know the Austin scene pretty well, but we should probably ask Damian if there's someone we should be checking in with. Vamps are territorial. And they don't like newcomers making waves. We need to assure the powers that be that we're well behaved and find out the secret handshake around here."

"You're kidding. Sounds like organized crime or something."

"In a way." I limped toward the door to the living room. "Trust me, Ian's got permission to run his operation in Malibu from someone higher up. And if he goes after Blade, he'd better be careful or he'll have the big, bad vamps in L.A. after him in a big, bad way."

"Good to know." Ray watched me from the doorway. With his low-riding jeans, and barefoot, he was too sexy to ignore, but I made the effort. Valdez and Brittany were out on the balcony having a quiet conversation so we were alone for a change. "You looked really excited after drinking from Trina, Glory. Flushed, totally turned on. Must have been some experience."

"It was. I've never had a feeding like that. So I really wasn't surprised when it actually worked like Ian said it would." I looked down at the note. "This is silly. A waste of money. The hotel scales should be okay."

Ray walked over and put the note on top of the remote. "No, it's a good idea. We'll get the scale. For your peace of mind and to be sure we're getting our money's worth."

"About that. I'm paying. No discussion. I want to see the bill." I followed Ray into the bedroom.

Ray turned and smiled. "No, you don't, Glory girl. It's outrageous. I can afford it and you can't. You've saved my life more than once. Call it payback and that's that." He stepped closer and put his finger on my chin. "Get that mulish look off your pretty face. I'm not arguing. Dawn's coming. Put on a sexy nightgown and drink Ian's potion so we can go to bed."

Ray slipped past me, his chest brushing my arm. I did want to argue. But if the treatment was as expensive as he said, I probably *couldn't* afford it. I put my hand on his bare back.

"Thanks, Ray. This means a lot. I don't know how I'll ever repay you."

He turned and smiled. "Just be happy. If this deal with Ian works out, then maybe his daylight drug will too. That's what I'm hoping. Now, where's your tonic?"

"In the bag on the nightstand." I ignored Ray's daylight comment. I wasn't about to encourage that fantasy. I picked up the bag and pulled out the two bottles. One said drink before sleeping. The entire contents? Apparently. I twisted off the top and sniffed, then wrinkled my nose.

"What does it smell like? Not blood?"

"No, some kind of herbs. Or fruit. I don't know. Take a whiff." I held the bottle out to Ray.

"Mmm. Papaya with a hint of cinnamon maybe. Weird. I didn't think vamps like us could drink anything but blood." Ray took a sip. "Tasty. Too bad it's for weight loss. I could get into it."

"Hand it over." I grabbed the bottle and took a sip. "It's delicious." I waited to see if it agreed with me. Seriously, made vamps can't eat or drink anything except real or synthetic blood as far as I know. If we do hit food . . . ouch! I know, I've had a painful run-in with a bag of Cheetos. Delicious snacks, but not a great after-party, if you know what I mean.

So far my stomach didn't seem to mind the new concoction. So I kept sipping until I'd finished off the bottle. Okay, I was feeling fine. Maybe even better than fine. It was like I'd had another jolt from Trina's wrist. I waved Ray off to the shower and grabbed a nightgown from a drawer. Not sexy, no way. It was a pretty floral but my usual floor-length style and didn't allow Ray even a glimpse of my body. I settled on my side of the bed and closed my eyes. I felt the bed sag when Ray climbed in on his side.

"You okay?"

"Yes, just waiting for dawn. Stomach's fine, though I'm pretty revved up. Like after I drank from Trina. Ian's a genius, Ray, if this works. In my experience nothing outlives the healing sleep except for an alcoholic binge." I rolled over and stared at him. As usual, he'd come to bed in nothing but silk boxers. Tonight's were baby blue, like his eyes.

"Don't remind me." Ray winced and closed his eyes. "My one and only backslide with booze after turning vampire cured me of that addiction." He sighed. "I'd sure like to be able to enjoy a glass of my favorite Jack with the boys in the band now and then. I wonder if Ian's got a wonder drug for that."

"I'll ask him." I put my hand on his arm. "It's a lot safer dream than going out in the sun. Forget that one, Ray. It's suicide."

"Is it?" Ray's sapphire eyes swept over me, and I fiddled with the sheet. Nobody could do intense like Ray could. "You didn't think you could lose weight, but it's happening, Glory. Ian may just be proving to both of us that anything's possible." He leaned over and kissed me until I gently shoved him away.

"Not *anything*, Ray." I smiled and let him interpret that any way he wanted to.

"You guys set for the night?" Valdez was frowning from the

doorway. *"Brittany's going to keep me company for a while in the living room."*

"No problem. Try not to wake Nathan, though, V." I yawned and put my hand on Ray's chest. "'Night, Ray."

"Watch where you put that hand, Glory girl," Ray growled.

"Oops." I slid back to my own side, not sure what I'd done. I was a little loopy, to tell the truth. I felt dawn kick me in the teeth and I was out.

Monsters chased me through dark streets until I was cornered. Their giant teeth tore at my clothes, ripping them away from my body. No, not monsters. Men, with deliciously long fangs that teased every inch of my naked flesh. I writhed beneath them, begging them to take me. But they just played with me, spreading my legs, yet never entering me. There were three—no, four—of them. Blade came out of the darkness and hurled himself at the men, slashing at them with his broadsword. But he couldn't fight them all and he disappeared in a shower of red.

"No! Come back for me. Don't leave me here!"

"Glory! Wake up, Glory. What the hell?"

I felt hands on my back and struggled, fighting to keep from being taken. "I won't. You can't make me!" I pushed and was free. Eyes wide, I sat up and looked around for which way to run.

I was in bed, in the hotel. And Ray was across the room, rubbing the back of his head because I must have thrown him there, where he'd landed against a dresser. Valdez was showing all his teeth and looked like he was about to tear into Ray.

"No, stop! I don't—" I looked down and realized I was naked. I pulled up the sheet. "Valdez, don't hurt Ray. He didn't do anything."

"Then how do you explain what I just heard?" Valdez planted himself firmly between Ray and me, his teeth still showing and scary as hell. *"You were screaming for help, Glory."*

"I—I was having a nightmare." I shook my head. "Yes, I guess that was it. For the first time since I was turned vampire, I was having a nightmare."

"Damn, Glory. You scared the hell out of me." Ray stood, staying out of Valdez's reach. "Valdez, you heard her. She's okay. I was trying to wake her up."

"Why's she naked, I'd like to know."

"I didn't do it. When I woke up, she was like that. Screaming and crawling all over the bed. I guess she tore her gown off during the dream." Ray didn't smile. "I don't dream. I didn't think vamps ever dreamed."

"They don't. Never. Didn't you hear me? This is the first dream, bad or good, I've had in four hundred years!" I was shaking. I wanted to throw up, and vamps rarely do that either. We don't exactly fill our stomachs, you know. I pulled up the sheet and wiped my face. I'd been crying in my sleep and sweating too. The sheet was damp.

"It must have been Ian's brew. The herbs must've caused it." Ray walked into the bathroom and came out with a wet washcloth and a towel. "Wash your face. You look like hell."

"Gee, thanks. I feel like hell too."

"You drank MacDonald's shit last night and it did this to you?" Valdez paced around the bed. *"That settles it. You're not going back out there tonight. It's not worth it. We're telling Blade about this and we'll let him take care of MacDonald."*

"Sorry, bud, but you don't issue the orders around here." I tried to smile to take the sting out of that, but couldn't manage it. "I mean, I *am* going back out there. I *am* going to do this weight-loss thing. Now that I know what effect that particular potion has, I'll ask Ian if I can try another one." I saw the second bottle on the nightstand. "I'm supposed to drink this one now."

"Wait a minute. Let's smell it and see if it's the same thing." Ray opened it and sniffed. "No, smells completely different. This one is more like lemonade." He took a sip. "Tart but tasty. The man does know how to flavor his stuff. Are you sure you want this? That last brew really did a number on you."

"I wish you wouldn't." Valdez stared at me.

"I've got to, V. Ian said following the program is essential and I want to lose the weight." I held out my hand. "Besides, Ray paid a fortune for this deal. The least I can do is give it a shot."

"Hold it. Forget the money." Ray gave me a searching look. "You're pale. Maybe this isn't worth it."

Valdez nodded. *"All right, it's settled. Thanks, Caine, for backing me up."*

"I'm doing it. I don't care if the whole band and Nathan back you up, V. Now, give me the bottle, Ray." I held out my hand. Ray shrugged but passed it over. I ignored Valdez's muttered cursing and took a swallow, then made a face. "Not as good as the other one."

"How do you feel?" Valdez watched me closely.

"I'm okay." And I was. "Relax, V, Ray. So I had some bad dreams. That's not life threatening. I can deal with that kind of side effect. And maybe Ian can give me something else that won't affect me that way. I'll ask him when we go out there later." I looked down at myself covered only in a white sheet. "Now, would you guys leave and let me get dressed?"

"In a minute. I want to watch, Glory, while you finish the drink and then see if you're okay." Valdez jumped up on the foot of the bed. *"Caine, get dressed. You've got two reporters in the living room waiting to interview you for* Rolling Stone. *Nate set it up. He's out there too."*

"Damn, I forgot all about that." Ray pulled a pair of jeans out of the closet. "You sure you feel okay, babe?"

"Yes, I'm fine." I put my hand over my stomach. Okay, so there'd been a gurgle, but nothing major. "Go, knock their socks off. Downplay our engagement since it's temporary. Stick to your music if you can. Plug your new album. You know they're going to love it. Nate was going to have a piano brought up. Play a couple of the new tunes for them."

"I will." Ray pulled on a vintage Jim Morrison T-shirt I'd bought him for Hannakuh and stopped to kiss my cheek, ignoring Valdez's growl. "Thanks, Glory. Take care of yourself. V, maybe you should take Brittany with you when you go to MacDonald's later. I can do all right without a paranormal guard tonight since I'll be staying in the hotel."

"Maybe I will." Valdez swung back to look at me closely. *"You're making a face. Stomach pains? I swear to God—"*

"Just a twinge. Nothing like the time with the Cheetos. Calm down. I'm going to be fine. Go face the door when Ray leaves so I can grab some clothes and get a shower." I smiled at Ray. "Thanks, Ray. Maybe we will take Brittany. I want Ian to know we're not pushovers."

"Good. You need me, call my cell. Nothing is more important to me than you are, Glory." Ray stepped into the living room and closed the door.

"He does seem to care about you. I give him credit for that." Valdez ambled to the door and faced it.

"Yes, he does. Nice of you to admit it." I wrapped the sheet around me and grabbed some clothes before streaking to the bathroom. My stomach was in an uproar and I was afraid I was going to throw up. I heard the piano from the next room before I turned on the shower. Good. The more noise the better. Because I was about to toss my cookies or, more accurately, Ian's potion, and I didn't want Valdez to know and worry about it.

I leaned over the toilet and heaved. Oh, God. I hoped this didn't mean I was going to stop losing weight. I sank down on the bathroom floor and waited for the nausea to pass.

"I heard that, Glory. You going to be okay?"

"Yeah." I leaned against the tiled wall and took shallow breaths. Steam was filling the bathroom and I closed my eyes when I thought I was going to pass out. Sure I was going to be okay. If I didn't die first. I eyed the wooden handle of

Ray's hairbrush. Maybe I'd just fall on the pointy end and put myself out of this misery.

"Did you get the scale?" I practically attacked Nathan when I finally decided I'd live after all. The reporters had left and Ray had headed down to a conference room in the hotel to another interview. He'd taken his mortal bodyguards with him.

"Yes, and I compared it to the ones in the gym. They weigh the same." He gestured toward the powder room next to the suite entry. "It's in there. You said you didn't want an audience."

"Thanks. You're brilliant." I grabbed Nate and kissed him on the cheek. "But then, Harvard doesn't take dummies, does it?"

"Not without a rich daddy. Lucky for me, Pop's loaded." Nate grinned. "Now you going to tell me what this is about?"

"No." I ran into the powder room, slammed and locked the door. I was barefoot and had on the same outfit that I'd had on the night before, except for the color of the T-shirt—purely for weighing purposes, of course. I stepped on the scale. Hallelujah! Still down two and a half pounds. So the elixirs did work to counteract the healing sleep. Ian *was* a genius.

Well, sort of a genius. Surely he could make something that didn't make me so sick. I was still queasy, but determined to head back to Ian's in time to get there at midnight. I opened the bathroom door, almost tripping over Valdez.

"Your cell phone rang a moment ago." Nathan handed me my phone. "I answered it. The man left a message. A limo will pick you up in front of the hotel at eleven. What's that about?"

"I'm going back out to Malibu. Same place Ray and I went last night." I looked around. "Where's Brittany? Ray said we could take her with us."

"She'll be back in a minute. She wanted to shower and change." Nathan looked at Valdez. "I hope both shifters got some sleep last night. It's not a good idea for them to be on duty together. How can they be alert if they're on twenty-four seven?"

"*She*—we *slept. I told her to go to her room.*" Valdez grinned. "*But we got to talking and she fell asleep on the couch. Don't worry. We'll be in top form. Glory will be safe enough.*"

"Can you guarantee that?" Nathan frowned. "Oh, what the hell do I know? I'm a mere mortal in this paranormal zoo. You guys blow my mind. And Ray won't tell me anything. Flies off the balcony like it's no big deal and never tells me where he's going or who he's going to see. I'll bet Los Angeles is full of vampires who'd like a piece of Israel Caine. You guys better be careful." He slumped on the couch. "Now the stock market's so insane I've lost my faith in the mortal world too."

I sat next to him. "Relax, Nate. We're careful. I'll send Brittany down to be with Ray." My stomach gurgled and I put a hand over it. "V and I can handle Malibu on our own."

"*We won't be on our own.*" Valdez trotted over to the door. "*Reinforcements are arriving right now. Answer the door, Glory.*"

Sure enough, there was a knock. I looked through the peephole and saw Flo and Richard there. I flung open the door.

"What are you guys doing here?"

"Israel called us. Said you were fraternizing with a potentially badass vampire and might need some backup. Of course I knew who he was talking about. You went to see MacDonald, didn't you?" Flo had dressed in black leather for the occasion. I recognized the look as her "I'm going to kick some vampire butt" outfit. Tight leather pants and a form-fitting vest over a red satin blouse made her look taller than her five feet one. The colors set off her black hair and dark, flashing eyes perfectly. The pants were tucked into thigh-high boots with silver chain embellishments on the sides. The stiletto heels would make good weapons in an emergency. Which I hoped we didn't have.

Richard followed her inside. He was much more conservative in black jeans and a black cashmere pullover. But then, he fairly radiated lethal male power anyway. His pale eyes looked scary if you didn't know he adored his wife and would die for his friends. I was deeply grateful he counted me as one of them.

"Wow. This is a surprise. Ray didn't tell me." I hugged each of them in turn. "Thanks for coming. Sure I went to see him. I signed up for his weight-loss program."

Flo frowned. "I hope you're not sorry. I thought Ian Mac-Donald gave off a strange vibe when we met him. Handsome, of course."

"Yes, and I know what you mean. But I'm still determined to go out there again even if he does scare me a little."

"And some of the stuff he gave her made her sick. She had bad dreams too." Valdez bumped Flo and got an ear rub. He loves my ex-roomie.

"I don't like the sound of that." Richard looked grim. "What's this about dreams?"

"I *never* dream." Flo gave Valdez a final pat, then moved to my side. "What were they like? Sexy?"

"Parts were, but mostly violent, terrifying. And, yes, I did get sick. Ian had two potions. One to drink before I slept and one for when I woke tonight." I grabbed Flo's hand. "But, Flo, I lost two and a half pounds after one session! And they stayed off after a day of healing sleep!"

"You are kidding me!" Flo's eyes widened. She looked me up and down and turned me around. "I can see the difference. That is so worth it, Glory."

"I know! So you can see why I have to go out there again tonight. No matter what." I heard Valdez and Richard growl.

Nathan put some distance between himself and the other two men. "I think that's my cue to get the hell out of here. I'll go down to Brittany's room and tell her to stick with Ray tonight. And I'll do the same. He's got some important interviews lined up. Publicity for his new album." He stopped next to the door. "But, Glory, you call him if you need even more reinforcements. I know he and Brittany would want to be there."

"Thanks, Nate." I smiled gratefully. It was nice to have so many loyal friends.

Flo shook my arm. "Tell me more about this Ian's plan. What else did you do to lose so much weight so fast?"

"I drank from a mortal runner." I made a face. "You know how I am about taking advantage . . ."

"Don't be silly. I'm sure the mortal was honored to serve you." Florence figures anyone who isn't a vampire wishes he was one. A mortal is lucky to be a donor. Yeah, she's got something of a superiority complex, but I love her anyway.

"Well, yes, that's the way she saw it. Anyway, I'm to be there at midnight to drink from her again, right after she's done another run. That's when the feeding is most effective."

"Seems like you wouldn't have to depend on MacDonald for that." Richard shoved his hands in his pockets. "So why go out there again? Especially if he scares you."

"You know the effects of drinking won't last through a healing sleep. Not without the supplements Ian provides." I walked into the bedroom and brought out the two bottles. I still felt weak, which was weird. I mean, vamps are *never* weak. And just looking at the empties made my stomach roll again. "Here. Smell what was in these."

Richard moved closer and sniffed each of them. "Nothing unusual, but vamps don't ingest foreign substances at all. I certainly wouldn't take either of them again."

"I'm going to ask Ian if there's a different supplement I can take." I pointed to the one I'd just finished. "I couldn't keep that one down."

"Then it can't have helped you, *cara*." Flo patted my shoulder. "Do we fly out there?"

"No, Ian's sending a limo." I looked at my watch. "We should go down now. I'd better put on Valdez's leash."

"Gee, can't wait." Valdez sat patiently while I clipped it on his collar.

"Is that what you're going to wear, Glory? You know the

paparazzi will be out front waiting to take your picture. You have something cuter, no? This is too plain." Flo looked me over critically as she followed me into the bedroom where I was going to put on my shoes.

"I'm trying to wear clothes that weigh the same as the first night. For comparison." I looked in my closet. I did have some different jeans that would work. And a purple V-neck sweater that probably compared to a T-shirt. "All right. I'll change, but not into leather. That stuff probably weighs a ton."

"True, but is cute, no?"

"On you? You bet. When I'm a size six, I'll get some pants like that. Only red. I love red leather." I headed into the bathroom to slip into the clothes and to add a bit more blush. Couldn't use the mirror, no reflection. But I *felt* pale. All that throwing up. And I wasn't sure I wasn't going to do it again. I took a few shallow breaths until the nausea passed, then came out to sit on the side of the bed to slip on my heels.

"Much better." Flo sat next to me. "You're not losing this weight to please Israel, are you?"

"No, of course not. He's sweet about my size, even though the tabloids are positively gruesome to me. You know the headlines: 'Baby on Board? Caine Sings the Blues.'"

"*Bastardos!* I hope they have wives with elephant butts." Flo put her arm around me and squeezed.

"I'm losing the weight for me, Flo. Because I've always wanted to and couldn't. You know?"

"I know. I've heard you talk about it. Like me and my height. I am so short, people don't take me seriously. I am a, how you say, shrimp." She laughed. "But we are women who can take care of ourselves, no?"

"Yes, we can. And I'm going to do this. Even if I have to suffer a little bit." I bit back a moan when my stomach cramped. "Thanks for coming with me. It means a lot."

"No problem. Now, let's head out. I want to see this Malibu. Is the Pacific Ocean beautiful?"

"Very. Especially if you like the water." I walked behind her into the living room and grabbed my purse. "Ian's home is gorgeous. He has a fantastic view from every window. That's as close as I want to get to any ocean."

"The Pacific is beautiful." Richard handed Flo her tiny purse. "I'm surprised you've never seen it before, darling."

"So am I. Guess I'm just an East Coast, Mediterranean type of woman, eh, Ricardo?" She kissed his cheek as he opened the door into the hall. "Do we have a plan, gentlemen?" She looked at Valdez, who trotted in front of me.

"Sure. We watch Ian like a hawk. One wrong move from the MacDonald and we take him apart. That's my plan." Valdez looked back at me when I grabbed his tail. *"Ouch?"*

"Cool it, tough guy. I'll decide what a wrong move is. In your state of mind, Ian could scratch his chin and you'd take it as an offensive move."

Valdez chuckled and looked at Richard. *"It is. That's the old Prague maneuver. Am I right, Rich?"*

"Sure, seen it done a thousand times. Let it go and you're staring at the business end of a stake before you know it."

I punched the elevator call button. "Right. Keep amusing yourselves. But this is my deal. Screw it up and I'll never forgive you. Either of you. Florence, keep your man in line."

Flo pressed herself against Richard. "Ricardo, stay calm, let Glory enjoy Ian's magic. When she is a size six, you can tear him apart. *Sì*, Glory?" She grinned at me.

"Well, I wouldn't put it like that." The elevator arrived and Ray's former bedmate happened to be inside. Well, if that wasn't a kick in my size-twelve pants. I smiled and nodded and sent Flo a mental message. It had her narrowing her eyes and sending her own message that had the mortal female sweating and getting off at the first opportunity.

"Puttana!" Flo hissed after her when we were alone in the elevator again.

"What?" Richard had been humming under his breath, obviously not included in our mental messaging. "You know,

I've heard this name MacDonald before but can't place it. I'll have to ask Blade."

"Uh, don't do that. He's got a thing about the MacDonalds. Ever since they stole some of his cattle about five hundred years ago. Ancient history, and I want to enjoy this trip." I laughed while my stomach took a serious dive and I jabbed at the button for the lobby. "Trust me. Ian's not interested in cattle. So don't kill him, okay?"

"No promises. That scratching-the-chin thing is no joke. Especially if he's got his own security crew." Richard looked down at Valdez. "We need a signal. I say it's a foot jiggle. Left foot. Left front for you, V. That clear?"

"Got it. Then we strike." Valdez looked up at me. *"And don't get in our way if we do, Glory. It will be life or death or we wouldn't start the war."*

I swallowed as the elevator doors opened on the lobby. My stomach was rolling again and I had the feeling that everything was spiraling out of control. A camera flashed as we neared the waiting stretch limo and I heard a shouted question.

"Hey, Glory, when's the baby due?"

I kept my head down, but Valdez growled and apparently Flo shot the finger at the guy because there were more flashes and I could hear her shouting what sounded like dire threats in Italian. I grabbed Richard's arm so he wouldn't start something right there in front of the hotel. Yep, things were clearly going to hell in a handbasket. But I was going to lose this weight or die trying.

Seven

"**You** brought your friends with you, Glory." Ian smiled and bowed over Flo's hand. "But not Caine."

"Ray's really tied up with the Grammy promotional stuff, Ian." I smiled and swallowed the urge to heave all over Ian's leather loafers. "And would you believe Florence has never seen the Pacific Ocean? I knew you wouldn't mind if they rode out here with us. You remember Richard Mainwaring, Florence's husband. You met at the club."

The men nodded, obviously taking each other's measure again away from the excitement and noise of the vampire club. I shivered from the chill in the air. Or was it because I felt clammy and about to faint? I grabbed hold of Valdez's fur to steady myself.

"*Glory? What the hell?*" Valdez bumped me over to the leather couch and I fell onto it. "*MacDonald, do something. I think she's about to pass out.*"

I heard them all talking. Flo babbling in excited Italian, Richard's calm voice in the same language and Ian's cool hands on my face as he lifted my lids and looked into my eyes.

"Glory, how do you feel?"

"Like shit." I tried to sit up, but couldn't manage it. "That stuff you gave me to drink when I woke up"—I shuddered—"made me sick." I closed my eyes but the world kept spinning.

"Trina! Get in here!" Ian or somebody arranged me so I was lying back on the cool leather. Then I smelled Trina's warm wrist at my lips. My fangs came into play and that was all she wrote. I drank thirstily, as if I hadn't had a feeding in weeks. Finally, someone pulled her off me, or I'm pretty sure I would have drained her dry.

"Gee, that was intense." Trina sounded gleeful. "Master, did you see how I endured? I must have pleased you."

"Yes, now leave us. I'll reward you later." Ian actually sounded concerned, but not about Trina. She was merely a donor. He sat beside me again, rubbing my hands. "Glory, how do you feel now? Open your eyes."

I didn't want to. Not yet. I was savoring the rush again. Trina must have just completed a run and her adrenaline pulsed through me. I wanted to fly around the room or maybe jump somebody's bones. I inhaled Ian's scent and thought about what a good-looking man he was. And a friggin' genius. Hmm. If I didn't have an audience, I could open my legs and . . . Was I nuts? I finally sat up, pushing my hair out of my eyes.

"Glory! How do you feel?" Flo shoved Ian off the couch and sat beside me. "*Mio Dio*, you scared me."

"I feel great, Flo, seriously. Did you see her? Trina? She's the runner I told you about. I am *so* pumped." I grinned and slipped past Flo so I could jump up and stretch. Richard and Valdez watched me, waiting for me to collapse again.

"Hey, relax, guys. I'm fine. Just like last night, the feeding was fantastic." I turned to Ian. "But, sorry, those supplements have got to go. I can't handle them. Especially the one I drink when I wake up. Couldn't keep it down. It made me puke my guts up."

Ian frowned. "That's strange." He picked up a bottle from

the coffee table. "What about the first one you drank? Before you slept?"

"Gave me hideous nightmares." I shook my head. "Well, some of them were hideous. Parts were sexy." I winked at Flo. "To dream at all was so completely bizarre, but cool now that I think about it."

"Of course. Vampires don't dream. Not during the death sleep." Ian kept frowning. "Glory, you're having a very unusual reaction to my supplements. This simply doesn't happen."

Richard stepped in. "Oh, come on, MacDonald. I don't believe that for a minute. Did you hear what she said? Gloriana's reaction sounds like she was poisoned."

"Don't be ridiculous. I've treated dozens of vampires with these formulas. None of them have complained of these symptoms." Ian shook his head. "And I wouldn't experiment on Glory, not after Mr. Caine paid for the deluxe package. She's taking what all my top-drawer clients take when they want to lose weight. My reputation depends on getting excellent results."

"Then why don't you get some of those other special clients out here and let us interview them? I want to talk to vampires who have been through this. Check out your reputation." Richard glanced at me. "Did you bother to do that, Gloriana?"

"Well, no. But Ray and I saw a video. A success story." I gestured at the TV screen. "You should see the results Ian gets. And I didn't want to wait. I want to look good for the red carpet." I ignored Valdez's muttering. Nice to know he liked me the way I was, but I'd started this and I wanted to finish it.

"You know how vampires are. It's not like we publish a directory, Mainwaring. We fly under the radar. Change location, name, habits, constantly. As far as I know, and I told Glory this, none of the vampires have stayed close enough for her to meet them. But I could give you a few phone numbers that *might* still be good." Ian smiled, obviously convinced

Richard would drop this if he was charming enough. I knew better.

"And what would that prove?" Flo stayed close to my side. "Anyone can get on a phone and pretend to be a satisfied client. Am I right, *amante*?"

"Right, Florence." Richard looked approvingly at his wife. "Give me a copy of some of these videos. And I want names and addresses of your 'successes.' I'll check them out personally."

"Of course. Give me a few days—" Ian was suddenly jerked up by his custom-made Egyptian cotton shirt.

"*Now*, MacDonald. Or we take Gloriana out of here and report you to the vampire council of Los Angeles. You're obviously running a scam here. Unless you can prove us wrong." Richard released Ian but it was clear the war had started.

"Richard, Ian. I'm okay now. Seriously. I just want to know what I can use besides this particular wake-up drink. I can deal with the nightmares if I have to." I pushed between the two men. Valdez practically knocked me over, staying glued to my left hip.

"Richard, I appreciate what you're trying to do, but this is important to me. Back off." I sent Flo a mental message and she grabbed her husband's arm.

"Ricardo, you can't 'take' Glory anywhere." Flo looked me over. "But I don't like this sickness either, girlfriend. You're pale, not flushed like you should be after feeding. At least let Ricardo investigate."

"Sure, knock yourself out. But I'm going ahead with this." I sat on the couch again, still a little woozy, though I wasn't about to admit it. "What else have you got, Ian?"

"Are you sure you feel all right now, Glory?" Ian decided to ignore Richard for the moment and studied me.

"Yes, fine. Stomach's completely settled." I jumped up again and plastered on a smile. So what if the room tilted?

"Then come weigh in." He gestured toward his office. "I've got something else you can try. And I'll get copies of those records you want, Mainwaring."

When the whole gang acted like they were going to follow me into the office, I balked. "Hold it. It's a weigh-in. I don't need an escort." I put my hand on Flo's shoulder. "Flo, you get it, don't you? No one sees my weight." I felt a bump against my leg. Clearly I wasn't going in alone, not without World War III, and I didn't have the energy for that right now. "I'll let Valdez come, but even he looks away when I get on the scale."

"I'm going in the room, *mia amica*. I'll look away too." She stared hard at Ian. "But you're not going in there without me, not when you still feel funny from what this man gave you. Ricardo can wait out here." She glanced out at the deck, where there were more surfer bodyguards than before, this time half a dozen. "Humor us, Glory. You scared us when you got so sick."

"Okay, come on." So we trailed Ian into the office.

"There's the Pacific, Flo." Flo and I spent a few moments admiring the view from the windows while Ian rifled through files, pulled out a DVD and made copies of some papers.

His smile was strained as he picked up his clipboard and walked to the scale. "I think you'll be pleased, Glory. You've been with Trina twice now and you *did* take the supplements. We should see some good results."

"Wait. I threw up most of the second one. I don't see how it could have helped me." I sent Flo and Valdez mental messages and they both reluctantly faced the door.

Ian helped me step on the scale and I watched breathlessly as he slid the weights across the metal bar.

"Trust me, it did. You absorbed some of it into your bloodstream because look!" Ian wrote down the final number.

I squealed. Which brought Flo and Valdez running. I slammed back the weights, then grabbed both of them for a group hug.

"I've lost five pounds!"

"*Mio Dio!* I never heard of such a thing for a vampire." Flo wiped a tear from her eye. "But you scared me, Glory. I thought this man . . ." She shook her head. "Never mind. I'm happy for you."

"We'll check this out back at the hotel." Valdez was obviously Mr. Skeptic. *"But if you're happy, I'm happy. Now, let's get the hell out of here."*

"No, wait." I turned to Ian. "What else can I do to make sure the weight stays off? Barfing up my toenails doesn't seem like the way to go here. Surely there are other options."

Ian frowned when Valdez bumped against him. "I've got a few suggestions. Would you give me some space, shifter?"

"No." Valdez stayed put.

"Look, work with me here." I gave Valdez a nudge. "Back to the door. Ian didn't bring any of *his* bodyguards in here, did he? That's got to mean something."

"It means he's not scared of two women and a dog." Valdez growled. *"Big mistake, MacDonald."*

"Don't underestimate me, whatever you are. And I can get an army in here with a thought if I need to." Ian put out his hands and walked around me. "I have no desire to hurt you, Glory, no matter what your friends think. But maybe you need a refund. Some things are simply not worth the trouble."

"Now, Ian." I gave Valdez a "back off" look. "I'm sure we can work this out."

Flo looked from Ian to me. "Your jeans are baggy in the butt, *mia amica*! Feel!" She grabbed a handful of fabric.

I checked it out and, sure enough, she'd managed to get some material into her fist. I swayed and reached out for a handhold. I was dizzy again, but this time from shock.

"Glory!" Valdez let me grab him. *"What now?"*

"I'm okay. I just can't believe it!" I smiled and sniffled. "Ian, please, please, don't kick me out of the program. Just tell me what I can do besides drink that other potion. Or, if I have to, I'll deal with it. Even if I spend every evening hugging the toilet."

Ian patted my shoulder. "Let's try some other things first. Have you ever exercised?"

"What? Now you're talking nonsense. A vampire doesn't exercise." Flo exchanged glances with Valdez. "Why, Glory can already run and jump better than any mortal ever dreamed of doing. And lift a small car if she wants to."

"Doubt it." Valdez snorted. *"Okay, maybe one of those little electric Smart cars but not a—"*

"Quiet or you both can take this discussion outside in the hall. Are we clear?" I stared at them till I got two nods. Finally. I was desperate to hear an alternative. I'd lied when I'd offered to hug the toilet every night. Not going to happen.

"You need to rev your own metabolism. Exercise helps. Not just running, but lifting weights." Ian smiled. "And working out with a trainer on the areas where you want to get slim. Toning."

I felt my stomach roll and it wasn't the potion this time. Exercise. I'd always enjoyed the idea that while mere mortals toiled in gyms, I didn't have to. Sure I was stuck, but, hey, I was stuck! So there was absolutely no point in ever lifting a weight or stepping on a treadmill. And I'd seen those poor women sweating and panting. That equipment they used looked like it was meant to extract information from a reluctant informer.

"Seriously? You want me to work out? With a trainer?"

"They have them at the hotel." Valdez was being helpful for a change. He probably figured a little suffering in the gym was much safer than drinking unknown elixirs from a MacDonald.

"It's worth a try, Glory. Do it when you get back." Flo grabbed my arm and practically dragged me to the door. I let her because I was ready to go. "Richard is waiting and getting very impatient. You have the things he wanted, MacDonald?"

"Yes." Ian followed us to the door. "But look what's happened to Glory here. Five pounds in two nights. Sorry, Florence, but you've got plenty of proof right in front of you."

I kept my mouth shut. Yes, my jeans were loose. But I still couldn't believe they'd stay that way. I took a bottle of the bedtime supplement from Ian and promised to drink it before I went to sleep. Promised too to hook up with a trainer when we got back to the hotel and put in at least an hour of exercise before lights-out.

Richard studied the papers Ian handed him. "These men and women all seem to live pretty far away. No one is closer?"

"Not that I'm aware. But call them. Check. I'm sure you'll be satisfied that I'm not scamming anyone." Ian smiled at me. "Just helping vampire dreams come true."

"Dreams." I cradled the bottle against me. "I'd be thrilled to have dreams if they were pleasant ones. It would make me feel mortal again. Not like I'm dead to the world during the day."

"*Get a clue, Glory. A vampire* is *dead during daylight. That's why I'm around then. This dream stuff doesn't make sense. I've watched you lie there all day.*" Valdez looked at Flo and then Richard. "*You guys don't breathe, don't move, don't freakin'* live. *The miracle is the way you come to life as soon as the sun slips below the horizon.*"

Ian sighed. "A pity too. That's why I had to do something about it. So much wasted time."

"What the hell are you talking about?" Richard's gaze sharpened.

"A daylight drug, of course." Ian smiled at me. "I told Mr. Caine all about it. He's anxious to try it."

"Over my undead body." I got in Ian's face. "Don't you dare try one of your weirdo supplements on Ray, Ian." I *had* felt poisoned, but at least I'd been safely inside at night.

"Why, Glory, you were a believer a minute ago." Ian's attitude could only be called patronizing.

I was ready to smack him, but Richard got there first. He stepped between us.

"Does the Los Angeles Council know you're experimenting with this?" Richard's voice was hard.

"Experimenting? What makes you think it's not the real deal?" Ian didn't look a bit intimidated. He had guts. *I* sure wouldn't want to face off against Richard.

"I've had too much experience with daylight claims over the years." Richard didn't bother to mask his contempt.

"Those vampires duped into buying into those claims paid with their immortality, MacDonald. Why should we believe you?"

"Look." Ian picked up the remote and hit a button. The TV over the fireplace came to life and there he was on the big screen, standing under a cabana on the beach in front of his house. In broad daylight. The sun reflected off the water and Ian was wearing sunglasses.

Flo and I gasped and I fell onto the couch. No way. No vampire that I'd ever heard of had managed to stay out during the day. As Valdez had said, we couldn't even keep our eyes open.

"Good morning, vampire friends and colleagues." Ian on the television spoke. "Yes, you're seeing me out in broad daylight. I'm actually going to have to invest in some sunscreen." He laughed and held out his arms. He had on a blue and yellow Hawaiian-print short-sleeve shirt and looked like a sunburned tourist on an island vacation. "Can you believe it? After years of research, trial and a few regrettable errors . . ." He bowed his head as if for a moment of silent prayer.

"Well, I've done it. Created the miracle you've all been waiting for. With my special formula you too can experience the joys of watching the sun shine." He laughed again and turned to gaze out at the ocean sparkling in the sunlight. One of his surfers caught a wave and rode it in. "By God, I've missed this. But no more. Want to join me? Go to my Web site for details on how you too can be alive during the day again." He waved to the camera and the screen went dark.

Flo and I sighed and looked at each other.

Valdez and Richard looked at each other too, but cynicism was their expression of the evening.

"Nice use of Photoshop, MacDonald. Do it yourself or hire it done?" Richard pulled Flo to his side.

"It's not faked, Mainwaring. I can get you testimonials about it too." Ian just smiled. "Or you can wait and ask your friend Caine after he tries it. Notice I didn't let the sun's rays

hit me. They can still damage a vampire with fatal consequences. I'll warn Caine about that."

I jumped up and grabbed his arm. "I told you, Ian, leave
Ray alone. He's a new vampire. *My* new vampire. I don't
want him involved with something so dangerous."

"You can't tell a man what to do, Glory. And Caine's got
the money to pay. I told you, it's not experimental. It works.
He'll go for it. All he needs is a chance to think about it."
Ian winced when I dug my nails into his arm.

I didn't want to blow my chance to lose weight, but this
was important. "At least promise you won't go around me on
this. I have to be here when you make the deal with Ray.
Understand?"

"I understand that you'll try to talk him out of it." Ian
patted my hand. "Good luck. He's really keen on the idea."

"Let's get out of here, Glory." Valdez paced around us.
"You've told him what you think. Enough already."

"He's right about one thing, my friend." Flo looked up at
Richard. "You can't tell a man what to do. You can only let
him know how you feel and hope he respects that."

"Unfortunately, Florence is right." Richard glanced outside. "I'll see you all later. Now I'm going to follow up on
some things." He stuck the papers inside his waistband, covered them with his sweater and stepped out onto the deck.
The surfers there came to immediate attention. Richard
didn't spare them a glance, just shifted into bird form and
flew off.

"Well, there he goes." Flo smiled proudly. "He'll get to
the bottom of this." She turned to Ian. "So if you have any
secrets, MacDonald, be prepared to see them dragged out
and kicked around."

I followed Flo down to the limo, still clutching my bottle
of supplement. At least Ian hadn't asked for it back. But I'd
rather forget the whole weight-loss thing than stand by and
let Ray fry in a botched quest for sunshine.

That deal had to be bogus. And if it wasn't? No use for
me to daydream about it. It would cost the earth and be

available only to the elite, very rich vampires. That left me out. It was one thing to let Ray pay for weight loss. I was going to look good on his arm for the Grammys. The tabloids would have a field day when I showed up skinnier in my designer dress. The thought made me smile as we settled in the backseat, Valdez beside us.

"Why are you smiling, Glory? I don't trust this Ian Mac-Donald. I couldn't read his mind." Flo grabbed the bottle and unscrewed the cap. She sniffed. "Stuff smells good, though."

"So he blocks his thoughts." I snatched the potion back and carefully replaced the top. "You and Richard always do too. Does that make you villains?"

"No, just be careful around him." Flo shook her head. "I wonder . . . His weight-loss thing is working for you. Could Ian really have something that keeps a vampire awake during the day?"

"I don't know. But I do know the weight-loss thing isn't going like he promised. And fooling around with the sun can be fatal." I shuddered, imagining Ray taking a chance like that.

"Richard obviously doesn't believe it's possible." Flo sighed. "Let's move on. Tell me about your reality show. You met the designers?"

I filled her in and we spent the rest of the ride back to the hotel talking dresses and speculating about what they would look like. By the time we pulled up to the curb, Valdez had almost nodded off.

"If your dress is beautiful, maybe we can get the winning designer to make the bridesmaid dresses for my wedding." Flo frowned when Valdez groaned.

"I thought that was settled. I love the dresses you picked." And had spent many nights suffering through Flo's bride-zilla act as she'd planned her March wedding. I'd hoped this was a done deal. She and Richard had already gone through a ceremony, but Flo wanted a "real" wedding—translation: an enormous, expensive vampire blowout. Her brother Da-mian was hosting and had agreed that he would make sure

the event made a royal wedding look like it had been done
on a shoestring. As Flo's best friend and maid of honor, it
was my job just to be supportive no matter how crazy she
became.

"I'm just saying. If this winner can do better, it's something
to think about. I want my wedding to be perfect, no?" Flo
examined her nails, frowning at a chip in her red polish. "Now
I'm going to my hotel. I've booked a mani-pedi for two
o'clock. *Fantastico*, eh? Twenty-four-hour services here."

"Fantastic." I hugged her. "Thanks for going with me,
Flo. I hope I can get a trainer this late."

"Oh, I'm sure they'll hunt up someone. They're used to
musicians and funny hours." Flo looked me up and down.
"You feel okay? No more sickness?"

"No, I'm fine. Totally juiced up after Trina's donation." I
tapped on the window and told the driver to take Flo to her
hotel. "I know you drink from mortals all the time. I
shouldn't say this, but chase down a runner sometime. It's a
real rush."

"Ah, Glory, now you're talking like a true vampire." Flo
nodded approvingly. "And don't worry. I talk tough, but I'm
usually quite civilized. I only feed when I need to, and I'll
pick a nice, strong, very hunky male runner." She poked Valdez in the ribs when he grumbled. "I'm married, but I still
like to look, *signore*."

"Good night." I climbed out of the limo, then Valdez
hopped out, safely on his leash. Flashes let us know we were
documented coming back. I wanted to show them my baggy
pants, but decided it was too soon. Much better to wait for
the red carpet for the big reveal. We headed for the front
desk again, and the same clerk who was on duty.

"You said you had trainers available."

"Yes, Ms. St. Clair."

"Is it possible to get one now? I want to work out." I
leaned forward again and lowered my voice. "To speed up the
weight-loss process."

"Certainly. Let me check to see who's available." She

picked up the phone and made a call. "You're in luck. One of our best trainers will meet you in the gym in five minutes. You'll need to change into workout clothes, of course. Would you like me to call back and make it ten?"

"Uh, is the shopping arcade open? I didn't bring anything like that with me." Or own anything like that. Oh, I had some running shoes at home, designer ones that went with a cute outfit, but no serious workout clothes.

"All our shops are available twenty-four hours a day. What you're looking for is down the hall to the left. Have a nice night." We were hardly a step away when she was on the phone.

My supersharp hearing picked up on the fact that she was offering to split the take if the clerk in the shop would tell her what size I bought. It was almost enough to make me change my mind. But then I thought about the five pounds I'd already lost. I had to keep it off and keep going. Damn.

I dragged into the shop and found a smiling clerk eager to assist me. Yeah, right. I grabbed the cheapest running shoes, though they were still outrageous to a woman who liked the clearance rack at a discount store. Then I tried on shorts. Size large was too loose! I almost leaped over the clothes rack and hugged the clerk. That would have been an interesting factoid for the tabloids. The medium was tight and rode up between my cheeks, but no way was I buying the large now that I'd squeezed my butt into a medium.

I happily piled my medium shorts and large (not extra large!) top on the counter. I selected a pair of socks that, gulp, cost more than the purple purse I'd bought at an after-Christmas sale.

"Do you have a sports bra, Ms. St. Clair? If you're doing vigorous exercise, you really need one. You don't want to break down the breast tissue. It can cause sagging later in life." The clerk was happily clipping off tags.

Valdez choked back a laugh. Later in life? I was only four hundred and change. But I humored her, grabbing my choices, then going back into the fitting room and shoving my breasts into a binding thing that really should come with a warning label. Sorry, but the only thing breaking down my breast tissue was this horribly tight spandex band pressing my boobs flat. I'd decided to go ahead and get dressed in the whole outfit since I was running late. When I came out, Valdez rolled his eyes.

"Very cute, Ms. St. Clair. I'm sure Mr. Caine will love it." The clerk sighed. "He is so amazing. I have every CD he ever made." She pushed a sales slip to me. "Just sign here. It will all be charged to your room."

I glanced at the total and it was my turn to choke. I'd better look cute. I'd better look like a model for Miss Fitness America for that price. I didn't bother pulling out my own credit card. But I was going to have to settle up with Ray sometime. This wasn't fair to him, even if he was rolling in dough.

"Thanks for your help. I'll get someone to bring down an autographed advanced copy of Ray's new CD for you." I smiled, wishing I could ask for a discount. But that would be weird coming from Ray's fiancée. And would be reported to the tabloids. I couldn't start rumors that Ray was in financial trouble.

"Oh, my gosh! That is so nice of you." The woman had the grace to flush guiltily. Not that she wouldn't still leak my sizes to the press. But, hey, a medium and a large. I was rocking and rolling.

Valdez and I headed to the gym. As soon as we were alone, V stopped.

"What's wrong with you? You look funny."

I glanced down. "You're not supposed to be noticing stuff like that. But I've got on a sports bra. It smashes me flat and hurts like hell." I pulled at my shorts. "But as long as you're looking, check it out—my shorts are a medium."

"Should have gone with the large," he muttered.

"No way." I pulled open the gym door. "Hello? Anyone here?"

"Ms. St. Clair, Bill Black, at your service." The bronzed god flipped a switch, then stepped off a machine.

"Uh, hi. Call me Glory." I let go of Valdez's leash and pointed to a corner. "Sit."

"I understand you want to work out. Have you been doing any regular exercise?"

"Not really." I laughed nervously. Bill was looking me over from head to toe, walking around me like he was trying to decide what part he should start on. I barely resisted the urge to tug down those creeping shorts.

"Then we'll start slowly. Stretches first." He handed me a long lavender rubber band. "Put one end under your right foot and pull with your right hand. Straight out from your body. You won't be able to go—"

I'd pulled too hard and snapped the stupid thing. Bill's eyes were saucers.

"Oh, gosh, must be defective." And I must be an idiot. I couldn't use my vamp strength here. The point was to tone. How could I tone and not wreck the gym?

He picked up the rubber band and examined it. "First time that's ever happened. Well, reach up with both hands first. To the ceiling. Then bend over and see if you can touch your toes."

Sure. How about my knees? The bra was strangling me. I felt a warm hand on my back.

"A little farther now. You're not very flexible, are you?"

I bit back a comment about how none of the men in my life had ever made that complaint. No way was I going to flirt with this guy. Even though he smelled like a very nice and healthy A positive. We were at my shins now and Bill apparently figured this was as low as I could go.

"Now arch your back, like a cat doing a stretch. Roll your shoulders and then reach for the ceiling again." He stepped back and watched me through a series of what he called warm-ups.

Okay, I was warm. When were we going to work on my problem areas?

"Uh, Bill, I really want to reduce my hips and butt and trim my waist and tummy. How about we work on those first?" I got the look again. At least he hadn't whipped out a tape measure or tried to put me on the scale. I'd whammy him into submission before I let that happen.

"All right. You're the boss." He smiled. "Come over here to this machine. Sit here and put your feet in these stirrups." He adjusted my legs and I was soon in position like an astronaut ready for blastoff. "Now see if you can lift your legs. You should feel the burn on the back of your upper thighs."

I lifted. Nothing. Hell, I could no more *not* have vamp strength than I could *be* an astronaut.

"Guess you're stronger than you look, Glory. Kudos." Bill smiled and punched in a button. "Adding weight. Try that."

Same thing. Poor Bill kept adding and I kept lifting. He started sweating, like maybe he was going to hyperventilate. Uh-oh. I knew that look. My vamp reality had just hit his mortal reality. Believe me, they don't mix well. I looked into his eyes and put him to sleep.

"He was about to freak out, wasn't he?" Valdez trotted over to see what the machine said. *"You were lifting about two hundred pounds with your legs, Glo. Way to go."*

"Stupid, though. I can't tone squat. How do you tighten muscles when you can't use them?" I extricated myself from the machine. I hadn't even broken a sweat. Poor Bill was wringing wet. "How do I get this machine back to a reasonable weight for a woman who never exercises?"

Valdez told me what to do, then I suggested to Bill that he'd watched me struggle to do ten leg lifts. When I'd started whining, he'd called a halt. As soon as Valdez was back in the corner, I snapped Bill out of it.

"Thanks, Bill, I really couldn't do another one of those."

"Well, it is your first night. Now lie down on this mat and we'll work on your core."

"I have a core?" I looked down at my smashed boobs and tummy. Valdez was snorting again but I ignored him.

"Yes, those are the muscles that support your whole body. Strengthen those and you'll improve your posture, whittle your waist and flatten your stomach. Core strength is very important." Bill said this like he was delivering the commandments from the mountaintop.

"Fine, whatever." I lay back and Bill put his hand on my stomach. It was still sore from all that throwing up earlier. I hoped whatever we did wouldn't aggravate it. "What now?"

"Now you crunch."

"I couldn't. Really. Not even my favorite Cheetos." I batted my eyelashes. "I'm doing a liquid diet, Bill." I saw him frown. "Under a doctor's supervision, of course."

"Of course." He nodded, then smiled, showing perfect white teeth. "A crunch is an exercise, Glory. Let me show you." He got on the floor next to me, knees bent, chin tucked as he barely lifted his head and chest toward his really flat stomach.

"Okay, I can do that." Which I could. But it was harder and more painful than it looked. Which proved that vamp strength wasn't everything. We went through several other torturous floor exercises designed to tone my butt, thighs and stomach. I only had to whammy Bill two more times. First when I accidentally tossed the hand weights across the room and Valdez laughed out loud. Then when I popped another set of rubber bands. I had to hide those in the trash.

"We've done enough floor work for the first session. Maybe you can do a few more reps next time." Finally Bill gestured to a treadmill. "Why don't you jog for a while? You have jogged, haven't you? You've got the right shoes for it."

"Oh, sure," I lied, giving Valdez a look when he barked. Hey, I'd been in a few sprints lately, running for my life. Those had to count, right?

"This will burn calories and speed your metabolism." Bill helped me climb on the machine, then started fiddling with the settings. "Start walking, then we'll gradually increase the speed and the incline if you can handle it."

"Okay." Surely I couldn't mess this up. I had vamp speed

when I turned it on, but I could walk like a mortal. So I did, then I jogged. I was pathetically glad that I had on that vise of a sports bra. I didn't jiggle and, to my surprise, I actually broke a sweat.

Bill was beaming by the time he decided I'd had enough. "Time for cooldown." He handed me a bottle of water and waited for me to drink. "You must stay hydrated, Glory. This is very important."

"Yeah, sure. Stay here and let me weigh first, Bill. I want to see how I'm doing. No peeking." I carried the water bottle into the small room with the scales and shut the door. I fished an empty out of the trash and hid the full one inside, then stepped on board. Different clothes. Shoes, not barefoot. Skimpy shorts and tank, not jeans. All in all, maybe about the same. And . . . down five pounds. I leaned against the cool metal of the scale and just breathed. I hated working out. It seemed like a colossal waste of time. But if it kept this weight off . . .

I jumped off the scale, threw the weights back to zero and emerged waving my empty water bottle. "Still losing. I am so pumped."

"Same time tomorrow? Or do you want to schedule something during the day?" Bill had pulled out a BlackBerry.

"Same time. Days are with Ray—Israel Caine." I grinned. "I hope this isn't too hard on you, Bill. My weird schedule."

"No, not at all. I'm coaching a rock star. She's also a night owl." He looked at his watch. "In fact, I expect her any minute. Maybe you know her." He spoke the name and my smile froze.

Ray's friend with benefits. Had they hooked up again while I'd been out at Ian's? I wanted to hang around and sniff the skinny bitch for signs of Ray's DNA. Which made me a jealous hag. I had no right. I had Jerry, who might be calling me right now. I'd turned off my cell when we'd been at the beach. I had to get a grip. And I also had to figure out when I was going to tell Jerry about my dealings with Ian. Crap.

"Sure, it's really a pretty small world in rock-star land." I picked up Valdez's leash and the bag with my clothes along with my purse. "I'd rather you didn't tell her we worked out." I looked down at myself. "I know I'm not in shape like she is."

"You did fine. Especially for someone who isn't used to a regular routine." Bill flashed his white, white smile. "See you tomorrow. Don't worry. You can count on my discretion."

"Thanks." I glanced down at my purse. Did I tip him? Pay him? No, I guess this was another item that would be billed to Ray's room. Oh, well, I'd keep telling myself that Ray wanted to do this for me. He'd said so himself.

Valdez and I got on the elevator and rode it up to the suite. No sign of Ray or Nathan. I did have a message from Jerry, though. He wanted to meet. I couldn't avoid it any longer. I was going to have to tell him about my MacDonald connection. I called him back and we made plans to leave the hotel again. Valdez and I would do the disguise thing and exit via the Dumpster. Why not? I had a feeling my life was about to turn to garbage anyway.

Eight

I jumped in the shower and did my best to make myself irresistible. Not that it would do much good. Once Jerry heard the name MacDonald, how I looked wouldn't matter. Valdez did his doggie-disguise thing, this time as a standard poodle just because it amused him to mix it up. We ventured outside via the back door. My own disguise was little more than a silk scarf over my hair and sunglasses again.

Jerry met us on the other side of the Dumpster. "Valdez, you're not very threatening in that look."

"Sorry, boss, but I've got all my skills with me. Don't worry about that." Valdez leaped over a puddle of melted chocolate ice cream. It looked like a kid's party had been held in the hotel and the cleanup had been pretty sloppy. There were several cupcakes on the ground near the Dumpster and I saw Valdez look at them longingly. But he kept close beside me. We were both wired. We knew what was coming.

"Where are we going, Jerry? A club? Your hotel?" Which would be better? A public place where he'd have to control his rage or privacy where I could try to distract him by doing all the things I'd learned he liked after so many years together?

"How about a drive? We can take the convertible and drive along the Pacific Coast Highway. You said the coast was beautiful. We'll leave Valdez here." He gave Valdez a wave. "I can handle Gloriana's security on my own. Enjoy the night off."

"Thanks, boss, but maybe I should tag along. Glory—" Valdez snapped his mouth shut at a look from Jerry.

"Jerry, he's only doing his job. Quit looking at him like that." I smiled at V and sent him a mental message. I would be okay. Jerry would never hurt me. And I was surely better off without an audience anyway. "Get some sleep, Rafe. You've been on duty way too many nights without a lot of rest during the day. I know the suite's busy with Nathan in and out and the rest of the band looking for Ray at all hours."

"True enough. It's hell keeping everyone away from your bedroom. Nate's not a problem, but the band is. Those guys usually come by in the late afternoon ready to start the party or wanting to jam." Valdez shrugged one furry gray shoulder. *"Yeah, I could use some sleep. Maybe I'll find a real bed and stretch out."*

"You do that. Shift, enjoy a shower, do whatever you want. I'll bring her back right before dawn. Until then, you're on your own." Jerry put his hand at my waist and steered me toward the street.

"That was nice of you, Jerry." I smiled at him. "Rafe needs some real time off."

"I get that." Jerry pulled me closer, then stopped. "Hey, you *have* been losing weight!" He held me away from him.

I'd put on a black miniskirt and cardigan sweater, but I'd worn a red satin camisole under it and tucked it in. Tucking in is not a Glory thing. But the waistband on the skirt had actually been a little loose and I hadn't been able to resist. Now Jerry slipped the cardigan off my shoulders and looked me over, even turned me around.

"Look at you. Sexy and shrinking right before my eyes. I can't believe that vampire managed to do this for you."

Jerry toyed with the cami strap, his eyes dark and making promises.

"She worked at it too, boss. You wouldn't believe it, but Glory exercised." Valdez still lingered in the alley.

"Exercised." Jerry grinned. "I'd like to have seen that."

"No, you wouldn't. She's not exactly Olympic material." Valdez coughed and backed up a few steps. *"Oh, yeah, leaving now. No, I'm gone. See you much, much later, Glory. Good luck."* He turned tail and disappeared into the open back door of the hotel.

"Luck? Why do you need luck, Gloriana?" Jerry replaced the sweater on my shoulders and took my hand to lead me to his car. He helped me into the passenger seat with as much care as if I'd been a princess. Jerry always made me feel special.

"No reason. It was just a saying." I watched Jerry settle behind the wheel. "You sure you know how to get where we're going?"

"I have a portable GPS. This car is vintage, so I stopped and bought one. The salesman helped me program the thing to take us on a scenic drive. We'll end up at a place where we can have privacy and a beautiful view of the Pacific." He turned to me and smiled. "How does that sound?"

"Perfect." I relaxed as he started the car. Might as well. The drive would give me time to figure out exactly what I could say to keep Jerry from heading straight out to Ian's with a broadsword. Because, knowing my beloved, he'd packed one. The perks of chartering your own jet when you're traveling cross-country. I tied my scarf tight so the wind wouldn't whip my hair around my head as Jerry followed the voice on the GPS to the Pacific Coast Highway.

By the time he turned into a driveway that wandered up a hill, my nerves were shot. No amount of beautiful scenery could take my mind off the showdown to come. And if I kept stalling, Jerry was bound to find out from someone else. I felt sure Richard would tell him tomorrow night. Especially if he discovered that Jerry and Ian had a feud going.

Had I told Flo not to mention that to Richard? Damn. Surely she wouldn't . . . Who was I kidding? She'd fill Richard in on all the gory details if she thought it would help with his investigation. And he'd be on the Internet checking MacDonald out anyway even if Flo didn't say anything. What better reason would Ian have to poison me than that I'd been made by a Campbell vampire? Gee, now *I* was worried. No, Ian was a businessman. I was fine. Had lost five pounds. Not poisoned at all. Oh, hell. We were here. Wherever here was. Time for truth or consequences. Gulp.

Jerry pulled the car to a stop. We were on a cliff overlooking the ocean. The house behind us must have been built to fit perfectly on the spot. The stone and redwood structure hugged the terrain and had to have fabulous views from every window. It was dark and looked vacant.

"Who lives here?"

"No one right now. One of the Los Angeles vampires bought it as an investment. Then the market dipped. It's for sale and I have a key. We can go inside and look around." Jerry got out of the car. "What do you think? Is it romantic enough for you?"

"It's perfect." I walked over to the edge of a slate terrace and peered down to a beach far below. Steps had been carved into the side of the cliff. The waves drifted into a narrow beach and the wind had died down to a gentle breeze. I took off my scarf and brushed my hair back from my face. Then I felt Jerry's hand slide down my back.

"There's a heated pool. Want to go skinny dipping?" His voice was husky as he slid my sweater off my shoulders again.

"Why did you ask? Seems like you already know the answer." I reached back and unzipped my skirt, then stepped out of it. My black thong was looser than it used to be and I took a moment to savor the feeling. Then I turned and reached for Jerry's sweater, a yellow silk that had the look of Rodeo Drive. Flo had certainly had a ball with his credit card.

"I love this sweater on you. It looks great with your dark hair and eyes. But it has to come off." I threw it over to land on a chaise near the pool.

"Just like this bra. Red is definitely your color. And I like the way it pushes up your breasts and matches that silk thing you have on." Jerry leaned down to lick a path along the edge of the cami. "But they both have to come off right now." He made quick work of them.

I undid his belt and slid down his zipper. "Hmm. Are you sure you have time for a swim?" I held his hard length in my hand. "Seems you're ready to do a little something more." I shoved down his jeans.

"A little something?" Jerry grinned, tossed away my thong and swung me up into his arms.

I let my heels drop to the ground. "Okay, a big something. Don't get any of these clothes wet. I do have to go back to the hotel tonight. It's important."

"Why?" Jerry managed to kick off his pants.

"The weight-loss thing. I have to drink something special before I sleep." I made a face. "Sorry if that broke the mood."

Jerry ran his hand along my bottom. "Nothing could break this mood, sweetheart." He kissed me, slow and deep, then walked into the pool down some shallow steps until the water hit him midchest.

"The temperature's perfect." I slid against him to stand on my feet. I'm not a fan of water, especially lakes with creepy-crawly things in them. But here, in Jerry's arms, I felt safe.

"You make me hot, woman. I'm surprised the water's not boiling around us." He pulled my legs around his waist. I felt his hardness bump my stomach as he kissed me deeply, our tongues tangling together. Then he slid my legs over his shoulders.

"Don't let me drown!"

"No worries." He held one hand under my head and began to kiss a path up my inner thighs. My mind went blank and any pitiful swimming skills I had escaped me.

Forget that trainer's core. Jerry had found my real one. Like the core of a volcano, mine was deep inside me with a building pressure threatening to explode as he used his mouth on me. I felt the boiling, roiling, almost insanely explosive power shudder through me. My shudders made the water around us into wavelets but I just gripped Jerry's arms and reached for what I needed so desperately—release.

"Jerry, please. Come inside me. I . . ." I reached for him but he shook his head, refusing to stop his delicious torture. What was he waiting for? Tremors shook me. A California earthquake? No, this was the beginnings of my own impossibly delicious violent upheaval. Finally he let me slide down his body to rest my cheek on his shoulder.

"What was that about?" I panted harder than after that trek to nowhere on the treadmill. One of my wildly scattered thoughts was that I'd read somewhere that sex burned calories and revved metabolism. Maybe I should weigh again before dawn.

"Your pleasure." He smiled. "I know you well enough to realize I pleased you."

"I'm so pleased I'm limp. Wow." Thank God we were in the water because I couldn't have stood if my life depended on it.

"A day of vampire sleep should cure you, lass." He kissed my cheek. "Ready to see the inside of the house?"

"Not yet." I reached between us. "I have one more item on my agenda, Mr. Blade."

"Oh, you have an agenda, madam?"

"Yes, indeed." I guided him inside me, gasping as he penetrated my sensitive flesh. "Oh, God, that feels good."

"I didn't think you could—"

"Hush." I kissed his mouth shut. "I'm a vampire. I have superpowers, lover. Now, you know what to do. Do it. Until I scream and make waves and you can't hold back anymore and have to give me all you've got."

"A tall order." Jerry grinned and walked me over until I sat on the second step.

"I think you're up to it." I sighed and leaned back as he began to move. Pressure built inside me almost instantly. He gripped my buttocks and drove into me, his fangs glinting in the dim light. I offered my throat and he took me there, drinking for a moment, then pulling back, a strange look on his face. I didn't question him, just kissed him and held on to him as he pushed into me one last time, shuddering with his release. I screamed as pleasure rippled through me again, hoping there were no neighbors to report murder being committed on our hilltop.

We leaned against each other for a long moment. I knew the time for talking was overdue. I smoothed my hand up his back, then tugged on his wet hair.

"What?" He leaned back and looked down at me.

"You didn't drink from me like you usually do. What was wrong?"

He frowned. "You didn't taste the same. And, trust me, my love, I'd know your taste blindfolded in a room with a hundred other vampires."

"I believe that. Just like I'd know yours." My stomach lurched and I swallowed. I was *not* going to be sick again. No way. I just couldn't be. I gently pushed him away. "I'm sorry. I guess it's those supplements I've been drinking to lose weight. Now, let's go inside. I'd like to see the inside of the house."

"Okay. It's weird, though. Never thought I'd turn down a chance to drink from you. I'll be glad when this diet of yours is over and you're back to the Glory I know and love." He gave me a searching look, then pulled himself out of the pool. He walked over to a cabana and grabbed two white terry robes.

I couldn't look away. Jerry naked is art. Perfect male from dark wet hair, worn longish this week since apparently Flo had convinced him to skip a haircut, down to his muscular legs that looked so great in a kilt. And in between . . . I sighed. My warrior was back at poolside, reaching out a hand to pull me out and to wrap me in my own robe. I shivered as I stood next to him and tied the terry closed.

"Cold?" He picked up our clothes and held out his hand.

"Not really. It's a beautiful night." I stared at the ocean, then up at the stars. The moon was just a sliver this time of the month. But our vamp vision served us well along with the glow from the security lights at the edge of the terrace.

What was the deal with my strange taste? I must taste truly awful for Jerry to refuse to drink from me. It was usually our favorite finish to lovemaking. I hadn't tried to feed from him because of the stupid diet. And I'd missed the closeness of the act. Damn. I shook off the worry and grabbed his hand.

"Come on. This house looks fabulous from the outside." I walked with him toward the door. Forget the taste issue. That was nothing compared to the Ian issue. I felt disloyal working with a MacDonald. If Jerry laid down the law and forbid me to see Ian again, though . . . Well, I guess I'd leap over that Grand Canyon when I came to it.

"All right, I have the key here." He pulled out a key ring and went to work on the back door. Then he punched in a code on a pad inside. "Security code. Chip gave it to me. He's pretty trusting. Guess he's aware that another vampire would be a fool to cross a member of the ruling council here in L.A."

"A vampire named Chip. And he's on the Council?"

"Yes, Damian and I had drinks with some of the members last night. Some pretty powerful characters. They run a tight ship. I admire that. You don't want to cause trouble out here or you're staked."

I shivered. "That's drastic."

"Yes, it is. And it's why the Energy Vampires didn't set up shop here. They figured Austin was an easier territory to infiltrate." Jerry flipped a switch and we saw a beautiful sunken living room. The pale turquoise walls were hung with oil paintings of California landscapes. There was a natural stone fireplace similar to Ian's and a brown leather sectional couch that made you want to sink into it and enjoy the fire that came to life when Jerry flipped another switch.

"Nice." I approached the fire and held out my hands. I didn't want to talk about the Energy Vampires. We'd had run-ins with the bad guys in Austin and barely escaped with our lives. "I like this place. Beautiful art."

"Chip is a collector. Those paintings are worth a fortune. They don't necessarily come with the house. What do you think? Should I buy one? As a souvenir of our time here?" He smiled at me. "Which one is your favorite?"

What a question. Leave it to Jerry to go big. No little plastic "I heart L.A." key chain. I should pick out a favorite painting, one that would probably set Jerry back six figures, and he'd have *it* to remember our time in California. Oh, hell. Would he want to remember anything when he heard about Ian? I had to tell him. No way was I letting this go any further.

"Sit down, Jerry. We have to talk." I sat on the sofa.

"Again? We already talked this week. Florence said that was probably enough for a couple who'd been together as long as we have." Jerry faked a put-upon expression and sat close beside me. Maybe it was good that we wore our robes and nothing else. When he got ready to kill me, I could whip out a bare boob and distract him.

"Forget Flo and her TV talk show advice." I scooted over so I could face him. "This is serious. It's about who I went to see in Malibu."

"The diet guy. What about him?" Jerry moved his legs and his robe parted. He grinned when he saw me looking.

"Quit playing, Jerry. I mean it." I reached over and covered him. He was too quick for me and slapped his hand over mine, holding it down where he wanted it.

"I know you do. You're cute when you're serious." He had a twinkle in his eyes that I rarely got to see. Jerry teasing was a wonderful sight. He was clearly happy. With me.

And I was about to kill the joy. I gave in and increased the pressure of my fingers for a moment and leaned in to kiss his smile.

"I love you, Jerry. Remember that."

"Now you're scaring me, Gloriana. What the hell have you been up to?"

"The man I've been seeing. The man who has helped me lose an incredible five pounds." I couldn't help it. I had to stand and drop my robe. "Look. My butt is shrinking. It is, Jerry."

"I can see that, though it was fine the way it was. Now, finish, lass, before I go mad." But he did reach out and stroke his hand along the curve of my ass, as if testing the size of it. I sighed, then picked up my robe again.

He snatched it away with a grin. "No need to go crazy. Unless this is life or death, you can tell your tale as well naked as dressed. And"—he pulled me between his knees— "I'm sure I'll accept whatever 'news' this is much more happily with this view in front of me." He leaned forward and licked one of my nipples.

"Oh, God, Jerry, if only it were that simple." I pushed my fingers into his hair and held his head to my breast.

That got his attention. He looked up. "Glory?"

"Okay, here goes." I stepped back out of teeth-gnashing range. "The diet guru is Ian MacDonald."

Here it came. Gaelic. A string of what was surely profanity accompanied by Jerry jumping up and grabbing the only thing in the room that could stand in for a weapon. He brandished a silver candlestick, his face red, his eyes on fire. Finally, he took a calming breath, slammed the silver down on the tiled counter and faced me. I'd slipped on the robe again, figuring rightly that, naked or dressed, there was no way I could sex my way out of this.

"You've had truck with Ian MacDonald. Are you mad, woman?"

"No. He's been, uh, nice to me." I stayed standing. I wasn't about to let Jerry look down on me.

"And does he know you're *my* woman?" Jerry growled this, his fangs down, his eyes hard.

"I told him I'm with Ray. Just like the tabloids say. He seems to believe me." I reached out a shaking hand but thought better of touching him. "He knows you made me. But Ray went to Malibu with me. We played the devoted couple in front of Ian."

Jerry's mouth tightened. He hated the idea of my "devoted couple" act with Ray. He'd seen it for himself. Not good for his pride. And the reason he'd trotted out the giant ring the night before. I always wore Ray's ring in public those nights. It absolutely killed Jerry.

"And you think MacDonald bought your act."

"Sure. Ray paid for my treatment. He and Ray even talked about some other things, stuff Ray might try. Your name never came up." I had probably just said too much.

"You're a fool, Gloriana! He's using you to get to me." Jerry stalked to the window and looked out. "I wouldn't be surprised if he had you followed after you left there. I told you I smelled another vampire on the roof last night. If one of his spies saw us together, he knows you're mine."

"Stop saying that!" I stomped my bare foot. "I am not yours. Or Ray's or any man's." I knew I was getting off the subject but he'd just hit one of my hot buttons. "Damn it, Jerry, your attitude is not helping."

"Listen to yourself, Gloriana. You're spouting twenty-first-century women's lib idiocy and ignoring the fact that you've probably set me, yourself and even Caine up to be staked." Jerry threw off his robe and climbed into his clothes. "Get dressed. We need to get back to the hotel. I need backup and so do you."

"Jerry, you're overreacting. Ian's done nothing—"

"Hasn't he? Why the hell do you taste funny?" Jerry stopped to stare a hole in me. "Tell me more about his weight-loss thing. How does it work? You look pale. Why?"

"I'm a vampire. I'm always pale." I held on to the back of the couch, suddenly nauseated again. Damn.

"Don't play games with me, my girl." He strode over and

put his hands on my shoulders. "I want the truth. What's he doing to you?"

I shook my head. No way was I going to tell him anything else about the supplements and my reactions to them. That would just reinforce his opinion that I was on a suicide mission. I didn't believe it. Or maybe I didn't *want* to believe it. I just pulled on my clothes and walked in stony silence out to the car.

Jerry grabbed my arm as I was about to climb in. "Talk to me, Gloriana. I'm worried about you. This is dangerous. Don't you see that?"

"What I see is that you're all about an ancient feud. Do you even know Ian MacDonald?"

"Of course I do. We've fought many times. He hates me; I hate him. His family and mine are sworn enemies. He'd like nothing better than to cause me pain." Jerry ran his hand through his hair. "And hurting you would do that. More than you could ever know."

I felt my anger soften a little. "I believe that, Jerry. But believe this. I'm doing this diet thing. Can you try to be rational? Not make it all about you?" I opened the car door. "Let's go back. It's too close to dawn for either of us to think straight."

"That's not true. And *I'm* not the one being irrational." Jerry waited until I was settled, then slammed the car door. "I'm thinking that you're too damned concerned about how you'll look on Israel Caine's arm at the Grammys to think about anything else. So you'll risk whatever it takes to lose a few measly pounds. Well, I hope it's worth it, Gloriana, because, trust me, Ian MacDonald will make sure you pay well for your moment in the spotlight. I just hope it's not with your life."

I took a shaky breath and decided I couldn't respond to that or I'd burst into tears. Was I that shallow? That vain? And what was the freakin' deal about my tasting funny? We rode the miles back to the hotel in tense silence. By the time we got to the rear entrance, I wanted Jerry to say something, at least promise he wouldn't go after Ian until . . . Until what? After the Grammys so I could look good? Maybe I *was* that shallow and vain.

He helped me out of the car and walked me to the back door. It was just thirty minutes until the sun would come up and I was dragging. I'm sure Jerry was too, but you'd never know it to look at his firm step and squared shoulders. He was clearly so livid he was about to morph into a bat and screech, which, according to him, was a great way to blow off steam. I've never tried it myself or been tempted to.

"Wait, Gloriana." He stopped me at the back door with a hand on my arm.

I looked around, relieved that no paparazzi had staked out this area. "I'm sorry I didn't tell you sooner, Jerry. I knew you'd hate this, but *I'm* not feuding with the MacDonalds."

"Promise me you won't go out there again." His hands were on my shoulders now, his eyes boring into mine.

"I won't promise that. There are just a few more days until I never have to see Ian again. Give me that, Jerry." I looked away because there was so much I wasn't telling him. And he'd absolutely kill Valdez when he found out how those supplements had done a number on me.

"I assume you've taken Valdez with you to these meetings with MacDonald." His words hit me like ice chips.

Uh-oh. Was Jerry somehow reading my mind through my block? No, not possible. He just knew me too well. Obviously Rafe was already in deep guano.

"I swore him to secrecy. Sorry, Jer, but if he can't be loyal to me first, I won't have him around, period." I jerked back, taking Jerry by surprise. "You want me to go it alone? Fine."

"Hardheaded, impossible woman!" Jerry ran his hand through his hair, his go-to move when he was exasperated. If a vampire could age, he'd be bald by now. "Keep Valdez. I should send you more guards."

"No. Ray has another paranormal guard and I had Flo and

Richard with me tonight. I had backup out the yin-yang. Not that I needed it. Ian acted the perfect gentleman." I reached out to touch Jerry's cheek. His beard was rough, typical for this late at night. I moved closer. "I love that you're so concerned for me. Love that you want to see me safe. I'm not stupid, Jerry. I'm being very careful. Richard's investigating Ian. Talk to him tomorrow night. Maybe you can help him."

"Of course I can. I can help him send the worm to dust." Jerry jerked me to him and kissed me breathless. "God help me, I don't want to lose you, Gloriana. Why you persist in stepping into the lion's mouth, I don't know." He looked like he wanted to shake me. Instead he just shook his head. "Have a care." With that he turned on his heel and walked away.

"Well." I sighed and headed into the hotel. The ride up in the elevator was long enough for me to snap to the fact that all Jerry had promised was to stake Ian. Great. I stepped into the suite, greeted by Valdez back in his usual Labradoodle form.

"How'd he take it? You did tell him, didn't you?" He followed me to the bedroom door. *"Your hair's wet. Did he throw you into the ocean?"*

"I told him. My hair's wet from a nice swim *before* I told him." I kicked off my high heels. "Let's just say he didn't take it well. And the only reason you still have a job is because I threatened to go solo."

"Ouch."

I threw open the bedroom door. "Where's Ray?" I turned when I heard the hall door open.

"Here I am. Didn't think I'd get away before sunrise." He grinned and began unbuttoning his shirt. "Man, I'm beat." He stopped and studied me. "Whoa, what's wrong, sweet thing?"

I kept my mouth shut. Where to start? Ray reeked of sex. Okay, so he'd been getting some of his own. Not my business. I picked up the bottle of supplement I had to drink before bedtime and twisted off the cap.

"I told Jerry about Ian. He was pissed to say the least. Now I'm afraid to drink this, which will probably give me nightmares. So I'm not in a good mood. How was your night?"

"Not so great either." Ray sat on the side of the bed and watched me put down the supplement. "I admit you got me to thinking about the rush when I saw how you looked after you drank from Trina. So I arranged to hook up with DeeDee after she had a workout."

"Nice." I felt my lip curl and fought to suppress it. "Did you feel it? Was it the endorphin high you were looking for?" There. That actually sounded like casual interest as I took off my cardigan and hung it up.

"The feeding part was great. But then I realized something." Ray yawned and stretched, then dropped his shirt on the bed beside him.

"Oh, care to share your breakthrough?" I was *not* jealous. Seriously. How could I be? I'd just had my own hookup with a man I loved. Still, I really didn't want to hear this as I leaned over to set my shoes on the closet floor.

"Wait a minute." Ray stood and walked over to stand behind me. "Look at you. Ian's stuff really works. How much weight have you lost?"

I straightened and turned around, a flush heating my cheeks. "Five pounds."

"Hot damn!" Ray hugged me around the waist. "I can feel it! Now, that's what I'm talking about. This is so worth it."

Oh, yeah, Ray had paid what was probably more than the price of his luxury SUV for me to go down a dress size. I put some enthusiasm into hugging him back.

"Ray, I'll never be able to thank you properly for paying for this. I'm thrilled. No matter what Jerry says, Ian's a genius. Obviously his treatment is working!" I extricated myself and yawned. "I need to get into my nightgown. It's almost dawn."

"Right." Ray nodded to Valdez. "Leave us, fur face. I need to tell Glory something."

"I don't answer to you, Caine." Valdez stayed in the doorway.

"No, it's okay. See you tomorrow night." I waved him out and shut the door. "What's up, Ray?" I hoped this wasn't about that daylight drug.

"I'm sorry for throwing DeeDee in your face. I don't have feelings for her. I hope you know that." Ray approached me again and toyed with the strap on my camisole.

"Who or what you do on your own time is your business, Ray. I wouldn't dream of interfering." I gently removed his finger from under the strap.

"It's just that I realized tonight that what I did with her was meaningless. The only buzz I got was from her mortal juice." Ray's hand was back, this time at my waist. "Man, look at you. This skirt is loose." He pulled my camisole out of the waistband.

"So you're telling me sex with a mortal doesn't do it for you anymore?" I should have already disappeared into the bathroom, but I was kind of interested in this conversation. I'd had mortal lovers in the past, but it had been a long time ago. Frankly, I preferred vampire men myself. Especially when we could do the whole fang-banging thing too. It's like an extra orgasm. And I'd missed it tonight. Sigh.

"Yeah, I guess that's right. Of course I haven't had sex with a vampire. Yet." Ray leaned in and smelled my neck where my vein throbbed. "Mmm. I'd love to compare."

"I'll just bet you would. But it won't be with me. At least not tonight. The clock's ticking and it would have to be the quickest of quickies even if I was willing, which I'm not." I grinned and pushed him back. "But do me a favor."

"What?" Ray toed off his loafers and kicked them into the closet.

I held out my wrist. "Jerry said my blood tastes funny. Take a bite and see if he's right. I think maybe Ian's junk is doing more than making me lose weight. Richard mentioned poison."

"Holy shit, Glory!" Ray pulled my wrist to his mouth. Before I could say another word, he'd taken my vein. After only a moment, he pulled out and headed to the bathroom. I heard him spit into the sink and water running.

"What did it taste like?" I followed him and put my hand on his bare back while he rinsed out his mouth. He shuddered.

"I hate to tell you this, but Richard may be right." Ray turned to look at me, frown lines between his bright blue eyes. "Baby, if what's in your veins isn't poisoned, it's doing a hell of an imitation."

Nine

"I don't believe that for a minute, Ray." I'd dragged on my nightgown and was lying on my side of the bed. Ray settled next to me and stared at me worriedly.

"I'm not kidding you, Glory. You tasted toxic. You said Blade wouldn't even drink from you."

Tears filled my eyes and I swiped at them. "No, he wouldn't."

"Aw, honey, don't cry." Ray pulled me into his arms. "We'll worry about this when we wake up. You're not going to drink another supplement then, are you?"

"No." I sniffled. "Which means I'm not sure I'll keep off the weight I've lost." I wanted to wail. Had I suffered for nothing? My stomach ached from throwing up and from those damned crunches. And my legs! All that jogging and then wearing high heels for hours had taken a toll. At least when I woke up, I'd be good to go. I felt the dawn coming and gladly closed my eyes.

I hadn't confessed to Ray, though, that while he'd been in the bathroom brushing his teeth, I'd downed the nighttime supplement Ian had given me. Maybe it had been a stupid move, but it hadn't made me sick, just helped keep the weight off. And it allowed me to dream.

Maybe I'd have good dreams this time. When I was a little girl, I'd dreamed of knights and castles and a fairy-tale life. Jerry had made some of those dreams come true. Too bad he'd brought along wicked witches in the form of his mother and Mara, mother of his child and the woman who now wanted him for her second husband.

Mara danced around me. She had me tied to a stake in the public square. Mag, Jerry's mum, piled sticks around my feet.

"Ye'll burn for the witch ye are, ye whore."

I laughed and looked around. "Which am I, old woman, a witch or a whore?" I knew Jerry would ride in soon on his white horse and save me. He always did.

Mara carried a torch and set the branches alight. "There. Now you'll be all toasty. That's what you get for consorting with a MacDonald. Even I never sank so low. That's why Jeremiah loves *me* now. See the ring he gave me?" She waved a huge diamond in my face and screamed with laughter. Then she came at me with scissors, hacking away until I was bald. I could hear the sizzle as my blond curls fell into the flames.

"That should please ye, whore. Bet you lost a good pound with that haircut." Mag cackled and tossed another branch on the fire.

"Here they come, the MacDonalds and the Campbells! Hide!" Women screamed and ran when men in kilts rode into the square from opposite sides.

I heard the clash of swords and the squeal of wounded horses as the men fought. Wasn't anyone going to untie me? The flames were getting hotter and I could smell my feet burning. Ow. I hurt so bad.

"Jerry! Where are you?" I screamed.

"Leave her. She's a traitor to the clan." Jerry's voice, hard and cold. He rode past, his plaid flapping in the wind, and never bothered to look my way as I called his name over and over.

"She's mine now. I'll save you, Glory." Ray stopped his horse and jumped down, but his bucket was empty. He cursed and threw a white toweling robe on the blaze, then black satin jockey shorts. Stupid. The fire roared and got hotter.

He knelt in the dirt and picked up a guitar. "I'll sing to you, Glory. I wrote a new song in your memory. It's called 'Gone, Glory, Gone.' I'm going to put it on my new CD."

"Get me out of here! Ray, shut up and do something!" I staggered, suddenly free. Run. I had to run, but my feet hurt. I bumped into something hard and almost fell.

"Glory! What the hell?" Valdez grabbed me and pulled me into his arms. I pressed my face against his chest and held on.

"Feet hurt. Hot." I muttered it against him, feeling him move as he carried me away from the heat.

"I know. You got too damned near . . . Never mind. I've got you now." He laid me down gently.

Ah. Bed. I sighed and relaxed. Then I opened my eyes. He stood over me. The man Valdez, not the dog. Sunlight behind him made me blink. My vision blurred, then I realized this wasn't a dream anymore.

Valdez snatched up a pillow and held it in front of him. Oh, yeah. He'd told me he was usually naked when he shifted into his dog-body form for long periods of time.

"I'm awake and it's daytime."

"No shit, Sherlock. You made it halfway across the living room before I realized what the hell I was seeing. You were sleepwalking." Valdez lost the lopsided grin and dimples that always surprised me. Well, I'd actually only seen them once before. He had dimples on his cute butt too, but I wasn't supposed to remember that. "You had a near miss. I caught you just a few inches from stepping into sunlight."

"This isn't happening." I rubbed my eyes and tried to

focus. Impossible. I hadn't seen daylight in forever. Instead of being thrilled, I was suddenly terrified.

"Afraid it is." He stepped closer and frowned down at me. "You okay?"

"I don't know. I had another one of those nightmares." I tried to sit up, but my muscles screamed. "Oh, God, my stomach's killing me."

"More nausea?" He sat on the side of the bed, careful to keep that pillow in position. I wasn't so freaked-out that I didn't notice his great build. Bodyguard requirement. Along with his superpowers. The handsome face, dark hair and dark eyes were just perks. No wonder Brittany was all over him.

"Not nausea. Guess I didn't get enough healing vamp sleep to actually heal. I think I'm sore from my training session with Bill the pill." I yawned, exhausted. "How long before sunset?"

"About an hour. Are your feet okay? You said something about them being hot."

We both looked down at my bare feet. That was when I realized my long gown had ridden up to thigh high. Oops. I jerked it down.

"They're just sore from too much jogging and cute shoes." I sighed. "I'm lucky you were there to catch me before I got to the balcony. If I'd actually gotten in the sun . . ." I shuddered. "But that's why I have my trusty bodyguard." I smiled at Rafe. "You'll love this. I dreamed Mara and Mag burned me at the stake." I managed a chuckle. "Go figure."

"Sounds like a typical mortal nightmare. You and those two always manage to have heated words when you cross paths." Rafe grinned when I groaned, then he got serious again. "And your trusty bodyguard was asleep at the wheel to let you get as close as you did to that sunlight. I'm sorry, Glory. I'm going to be on high alert from now on. You look like hell, and that's a fact. I'm worried about you."

I put my hand on his. "Thanks, Rafe. I'm okay, just tired and feeling every muscle in my body for a change. Guess this is what four hundred plus feels like."

Rafe shook his head. "Doubt it. That would be much, much worse, I imagine. Now, close your eyes. Maybe you can catch some more z's. You obviously need them."

I glanced at Ray. He really was dead to the world. No movement at all. Pale. I laid my hand on his chest. Cool to the touch and no discernable heartbeat.

"You know Caine's going to freak when he realizes you saw daylight, don't you?"

"Don't you dare tell him, Rafe." I grabbed his arm. "He'll want to rush right out to Ian's place and buy a chance at it." I groaned because I'd felt that sudden movement in every abused muscle.

"Maybe you should let him." Rafe looked down to where I held on to him. "MacDonald's diet thing is working on *you*."

"True. But obviously there are side effects." I glanced at the open bedroom door. I could see the sunlight hitting the carpet in the suite's living room. "Besides, I have trust issues with Ian MacDonald. Blade tasted my blood last night and said there was something off about it. So I had Ray taste it too." I shuddered. "Rafe, Ray thinks Ian is poisoning me."

"That does it. The man is dead." Valdez jumped up, pillow forgotten.

My jaw dropped, then I forced myself to shut my eyes. I cleared my throat. "We'll discuss this when Ray and I get up at sunset. Guess you ought to shift back now."

"Relax, Glory. I'm decent."

More than decent. Oops. Didn't say that out loud, did I? No, thank God. I stole a peek. Yeah, his pillow was back in place.

"You did save my butt today, pal. I would have fried if I'd made it to the balcony." My throat suddenly clogged.

"Damn straight. That's why I changed, Glory." He reached out and touched my cheek. "You're not coming to harm on my watch, lady. And that's a promise."

I cleared my throat. "I know that. I've always known that. 'Thank you' seems pretty lame, but it's all I've got. Thanks,

Rafe." I sniffed, feeling weepy again. Like I had with Ray, the night before. I was blaming it on the diet stuff.

"You're welcome." He smiled, his dimples brief punctuation marks that vanished too soon. "I'll say it again: You never should have gotten so close to the balcony. I've gone soft or I'd have stopped you at the bedroom door."

I swept my eyes over him. Soft? Maybe the thick black hair that fell to his shoulders, but nothing else on this powerful man could ever be called soft. Tears filled my eyes. He'd risk everything for me without a second thought. I didn't deserve it.

"I never should have started this. I'm an idiot."

Valdez firmed his lips. "No, you're not. MacDonald's slick. He's obviously been running this con a long time. Just look at his video, Web site and fancy digs."

"Yeah." I sighed. "Tired. Sleep now." I closed my eyes. "Hey, V."

"What?"

I opened my eyes again and got a flash of his perfect dimpled buns. Sweet. I smiled. "It was nice to talk to you like this. Outside of my head for a change."

"Yeah, it was. See you later." He smiled and disappeared into the living room.

I snuggled next to Ray and realized that, aches and pains aside, I was incredibly lucky. I was literally surrounded by hot guys determined to protect me. No way did I deserve it, but I sure wasn't going to turn any of them away.

"Okay, Glory, it's time to figure out our next move." Ray pulled me down on the couch beside him.

I held back a scream when my sore thighs hit the seat. Valdez, safely back in Labradoodle guise, sat on the rug in front of us.

"The limo will be here to pick me up in about an hour. Ian will expect me to come out there to drink from Trina again."

"You're not going." Valdez glanced at the balcony.

"V's right. You want a runner, we can head out and find you one in a park or get someone coming out of a gym. If Ian's stuff is poisonous . . ." Ray picked up my hand. "How do you feel?"

"Achy. I didn't sleep well so I didn't heal." I tried to get comfortable but it wasn't happening. I'd already discovered that breathing hurt so forget that. And my feet! I was still barefoot, unable to deal with my high heels yet.

"One more night, guys. Then tomorrow I have my fitting for *Designed to Kill* and get to see my red-carpet dresses." I turned to Ray. "I have to finish what I started, Ray."

"No way. It's too dangerous."

"Caine's right. Forget it, Glory." Valdez moved closer. *"Those supplements . . ."*

"So I won't drink any more of the one that made me sick." I staggered to my feet and limped to the bathroom. Inside, with the door safely shut, I weighed again. Still down five pounds. All right. If I lost another two to three pounds tonight and then exercised, that should put me down to a size eight. I could be very happy in an eight. And if I drank my bedtime elixir, I could hold on to that size for another day, hopefully two. Long enough to make it to the red carpet. Maybe.

I threw open the bathroom door. "Come on, guys. No way is Ian poisoning me. Why do it gradually? And he's a businessman who wants your business, Ray. Hurting me would be stupid. Think about it."

"I am thinking about it." Ray jumped up and put his hands on my shoulders. "How do you explain your blood's weird flavor? And now you're creeping around like you can hardly walk."

"Because I'm sore from exercising. That's all. Happens to mortals all the time. So they say anyway. I hear them gripe about it in my shop all the time. Which reminds me. Lacy's having trouble with the new help we hired after Christmas. And we had a shoplifting incident that's costing me big bucks. I was on the phone with her for almost an hour." I tried to get away from Ray without making a big deal out of it. No go.

"Changing the subject? Not working. Lacy's handling the shop fine. Right?" Ray stared me down.

"Yes. But I do need to go back to Austin right after the Grammys." I realized I wasn't as eager to do that as I should be. It had been an adventure being out here as a rock star's fiancée. I'd be just plain Glory again in Texas. Well, plain Glory the vampire shop owner. I kept my hands on Ray's chest. Would he go back there with me? He seemed much more at home here and I knew it.

"About your blood, Glory. It was off last night." Ray glanced at Valdez. "Tasted toxic."

"It's that feud. Bet MacDonald knows she's still attached to a Campbell. Surprised he's being so subtle about it, though." Valdez paced the living room. *"It'll get Blade out there to him for a face-to-face. Maybe that's his plan."*

"There *is* no plan. I probably still had that other supplement in my system. The one that made me throw up." I held out my wrist. "Try again, Ray. Right now. See if it's better."

"Okay, but if it's not, you're done with this diet crap. No arguments." Ray pulled my wrist to his mouth and inhaled. "Smells good." He slid his hand down to my waist, then nuzzled my jugular. "Maybe I'll try it here. Closer to the big pump."

"Careful, Caine." Valdez pushed his nose between us.

"Leave him alone, V. I need to know the answer." I shoved my fingers into Ray's hair and felt his breath on my neck. "Go for it, Ray. But just a taste. Don't try to turn this into something, um—" I couldn't finish the thought because Ray had gone in and was taking what he wanted. At least this time he didn't jerk away and run to the sink. He eased out and licked his lips.

"Well?"

"Sweet as always, glorious woman." He kissed the spots

where his fangs had been and sealed them closed. "Guess you've recovered."

"See?" I put some space between us. "So why not go out to Ian's and get another round from Trina? And the bedtime supplement must be okay or I'd still taste weird."

"You're rationalizing, Glory. What did Blade tell you about MacDonald?" Valdez stood between me and the door to the hall. I had a feeling I'd have to go through him to leave.

"Of course, like you, Jerry thinks this is all a plot by Ian to get to him." I looked down at my now-loose black jeans. "Maybe, just maybe, I don't give a rat's hiney what Ian's motive is as long as I'm skinny by Grammy time."

"Caine, the Campbells and the MacDonalds have been feuding for centuries. Ian would think nothing of using a woman as a pawn in an effort to take down the enemy. Business comes second to a clan blood feud." Valdez obviously considered himself an expert on Scottish clan relations and warcraft.

"That settles it, then. You're not going out there, Glory." Ray frowned when his cell phone rang. He picked it up from the coffee table. "It's Nate. Hell, I'm late for a meeting." He answered the phone and walked out to the balcony. I heard him tell Nate he'd meet him downstairs in ten minutes before he shut the phone.

"Got to go." Ray looked great in a black silk shirt and black jeans. "Are we clear on your plans for the evening, Glory?"

I shook my head. "Don't worry, Ray. I'll be fine. I have another appointment later with Kill Bill the trainer. No date with Jerry that I know of. I don't think he's speaking to me." I followed Ray to the door. "Good luck with your meeting. This is about the TV special, isn't it?"

"Yes, it would be a great opportunity." Ray kissed my cheek. "Don't worry about Blade. Much as I'd like to see you free of the Scot, I figure he'll come around."

"He's probably with Richard, planning an attack on Mac-Donald." Valdez grinned like he wanted to be in on that session.

Ray looked me over. "I'm well aware that you haven't promised not to go to Ian's, Ms. Thing."

I flushed. "I have to go."

"No, you don't." Ray opened his cell and hit speed dial. "MacDonald? Israel Caine. Glory and I are swamped with this Grammy prep. Is there any way you can bring your program to us at the hotel tonight?" He listened and nodded. "Yeah, super. She'll be waiting. We've got a scale here. Thanks." He snapped the phone shut and looked at Valdez. "If you really think Ian's a danger, you'll need backup. I'll send Brittany to you. Think the two of you can handle Ian and Trina?"

"Guess we'll have to." Valdez was obviously not happy that I was continuing with the program, but it wasn't his call.

"Ray, thanks!" I threw my arms around his neck and started to kiss him on the cheek. Of course he turned his head so that smacker landed on his lips. He put his hand on the back of my head and made it a pretty good one. I wasn't going to push him away. I'm still a fangirl. Any woman who kissed Israel Caine would be, whether he was a rock star or not. Then we both staggered from a Valdez headbutt.

"Sorry, but aren't you running late for an important meeting, Caine?" Valdez didn't look sorry.

Ray grinned and slid his hands down my back. "No meeting's as important as this lady. Be careful, Glory. Want me to call Blade and get him over here for you?"

I blinked. Ray had just managed to surprise me. "Thanks, Ray. But I really don't want to spend an evening watching Scottish warriors face off." I walked with him out to the hall and hugged him one more time. "I know that took a lot. For you to offer to call Jerry. It means more than you know."

Ray smiled. "Purely selfish on my part. I had a fifty-fifty chance the MacDonald would win and I'd have Blade out of your life forever." He shrugged when his cell rang again. "All right, Nate, I'm coming. Glory, call me when Ian leaves. I want to know you're okay."

"Will do." I watched him head for the elevator. When it opened, Brittany stepped out. Reinforcements. Good. Would two shape-shifters be enough? I'd heard enough warnings about Ian to be nervous. So I called Flo and asked her to come too. She said Richard was still hunting down Ian's "success stories" and she was interested in checking out the shops in my hotel lobby so she'd be right over. Now I felt better. If Ian thought he could use me as a pawn in his feud against the Campbells, he'd have to go against me and my personal army first.

I limped back into the room and found Brittany and Valdez with their heads together.

"Caine handled that pretty well." Valdez said it grudgingly.

"You mean handled *me*. I called Flo. She's coming too. She doesn't think Richard's found any of Ian's former clients yet. Not that I'm surprised. Vamps move around a lot and stay off the grid." Since I wasn't going out, I might as well put on my workout clothes. I grabbed them, freshly laundered while I slept, headed for the bathroom and shut the door.

"Bet Ian brings those surfer a-holes with him too. Can't wait to throw some of them off the balcony." Valdez called through the door.

I crammed myself into the sports bra and tight shorts, then pulled on the tank top. I headed back out to sit on the bed to pull on my socks and shoes.

"Of course he will. I never go out to his house without *my* bodyguard. And toss as many as you like. They're vamps. They'll just turn into bats and fly right back in here, anxious to rip out your throat." I looked at him and at Brittany, standing in the bedroom doorway. "Seriously, guys, don't start trouble. Just finish it if they start something first. If I can go through with the weight-loss thing, I'm going to. Got it?"

"Sure." Brittany frowned when there was a knock on the door. "That can't be him already. It's too soon."

"Check it out. Don't let anyone in you don't know." Valdez was right behind her.

I groaned as I stood and followed them. I'd heard the

cliché, "No pain, no gain." Guess this was what it felt like. How did mortals stand working out if this was the result?

"It's Barry, Ray's publicist, and a group of people, two of them in snazzy workout clothes." Brittany grinned at me. "Sort of like yours, Glory. Should I let them in?"

"Why not?" I knew Barry was always looking for PR opportunities. I had a sinking feeling I knew what was coming. I tugged down my shorts, which were getting way too personal, and pasted on a smile.

"Glory, baby, look at you. It's true, then, you've been working out!" Barry rushed inside to give me air-kisses. "Let me introduce you to these people." He tossed me some names, which I immediately forgot, and offered bottles of water from the fridge at the bar all around.

I sank gratefully into a club chair while I waited for his pitch. And there had to be one.

"That's our spring 'Step into the Future' line you've got on, Ms. St. Clair. How do you like it?" One of the tanned and toned women spoke first. "Does it move the way you hoped?"

Does *it* move? I wish. Then I could lie back and let it do those torturous crunches. I merely nodded. "It's very comfortable." I leaned in, nodding toward where Barry was in deep conversation with the only other man in the group. "But this sports bra. Argh. It's a killer. Surely there's a way to keep me from bouncing around without mashing me flat."

The woman waved her hand. "Janet, take a note. You're absolutely right, Glory. May I call you Glory?" I nodded. "It's on our priority list. Naturally well-endowed women work out too, and they need support without pain, am I right?"

"Absolutely." I watched Janet scribble frantically. I had a feeling a new ad campaign had just been born, complete with tag line. "Support without pain. That's what I'm looking for."

"I'm afraid Barry didn't have time to fill you in on why we're here." Fake smile, fake smile.

"No, I didn't." Barry was suddenly at my side. "Glory, Fitzwell Fitness Wear would like to have you become a spokesperson. Do some ads for them. They'd follow you on your journey to hit the gym and lose a few inches where you need to." Barry smiled all around. "Not that Ray has a problem with her figure just the way it is, you understand, people. He's crazy about Glory. Would kill me if he thought I was criticizing her. Which I'm not." Barry turned red and grabbed a bottle of water.

I gave Barry a look that made him twist the top off and down half the contents. "Barry's right. Ray's always been very complimentary of my curves. This fitness kick I'm on is just for the Grammys. Since it's going to be on TV all over the world."

"Sure, Glory, I get it. But one of the tabloids printed an item about how you were hanging out at the hotel gym, dieting and stuff. And that you'd bought these new clothes in the lobby shop here in the hotel." Barry flushed and exchanged glances with the two women who wore outfits similar to mine. Of course theirs were obviously size small and their running shoes top of the line.

"Those tabloids. They bribe store clerks to spy on me." I made a face. "Disgusting, isn't it?"

All the mortals murmured sympathetically.

"No privacy when you're with a rock star." Barry put his hand on my shoulder. "But we might as well see if we could get a little publicity out of it."

"Relax, Barry. I totally get it." I stood, even though my muscles seized and I wanted to bend over and cry into my knee caps. "And I appreciate the offer and the opportunity." I smiled as everyone else stood. "But I just can't consider doing it. This is a temporary thing. Just until the Grammys. I've got less than a week and then I'm back to Texas and my sluggish existence. Honestly? I hate exercising." I looked down. "Love the clothes, though. Very cute."

"You'd get a free wardrobe, of course. We could take some photos here and then follow up later in Austin. Maybe you didn't have the right trainer. We could send you a member of our staff." The head honcho, the only woman in a business suit, really didn't want to let this go. "And someone to work with Mr. Caine too, if he's interested. Barry thought he might be willing to be included in some of the ads." Ah, now I knew why.

"Barry, may I speak to you in the bedroom?" I grabbed his arm and hustled him out of the living room.

The publicist looked down like he was surprised at my strength when I closed the bedroom door. "Gee, Glory, you *have* been working out."

"A little, but I'm not doing a commercial. Get rid of these people. Did you run this by Ray?"

"No, didn't have time." He tried to pull away, but finally gave up. "What's wrong with this gig? It's a reputable company. They'll pay you big bucks. You, not Ray. You could use the money, couldn't you?"

I couldn't argue about that. But I also knew that, once back in Austin, I'd be right back to my old size. So the slimming Glory campaign would be a bust. Unless . . .

"You think they'd be interested in just featuring a normal-size woman working out? One who never gets any smaller? Because I know I'm not going to stick with this program after we leave L.A., Barry." Oops. Or stick with Ray either, come to think about it. Well, there went the big bucks. There was no help for it. I was pulling the plug.

"They want a success story, Glory. Can't you trim down? For yourself, if not for Ray. It's the healthy thing to do." Barry smiled at me and used his free hand to pat me on the shoulder.

"I *am* healthy at my regular size, Barry. Sizes are just arbitrary numbers society has put on labels inside clothes to make most of us feel bad. I'm sorry I ever started this diet-and-exercise thing. My body hurts, I'm nauseated half the time and I can't sleep. For sure it stops when I say it does." I fought back my fangs. This was definitely one of my hot-button issues. Barry was just the messenger, but sometimes the messenger deserved to take the heat.

"Now, Glory. I didn't mean—" He winced and I realized I still held his arm.

I let him go and gave him some space. "Sorry, but screw their so-called success stories. I'm not doing it. And I'm staying in here until those people are gone. Get rid of them." I glared at him, opened the bedroom door and waited for him to scoot through it, then shut and locked it.

"Well, you told him." Valdez had watched all this from the foot of the bed.

"Yes, and now I feel bad. He was only doing his job." I peeked out of the bedroom door and saw Barry just disappearing into the hall. "Brittany, get Barry back in here, please."

"Sure, Glory." Brittany jerked open the door and returned with the alarmed publicist held in what resembled a headlock. We might have to whammy Barry. He'd obviously never dealt with such tough women before.

"Let him go, Brit." I led him to the couch. "Barry, I'm sorry. I know you were just trying to help me out."

"I was, Glory. You want me to get them back in here?" Barry pulled out his cell. "I could still make this happen."

"No, not that. But let me explain the real reason I couldn't do it." I settled beside him, barely stifling a groan.

"What?" Barry put the cell away. "You look serious. Not sick, are you? You've been moving funny. Like you're in pain."

"I am, but that's from working out. I think I did too much last night. Those trainers." I made a face.

Barry shook his head. "I know what you mean. I call mine Attila. She's a real bitch."

"There you go." I laughed. "But here's the scoop." I quit smiling. "Ray and I'll probably go our separate ways after the Grammys. He may not be coming back to Austin at all."

"No way! I thought—" Barry looked genuinely shocked.

"Well, I thought maybe he'd found the real deal this time."
He hugged me. "I'm sorry, Glory. You want me to punch
him out?"

"Why are you assuming *he's* dumping *me*?" I pushed back
and sighed. "I'm getting back with an old boyfriend." I felt
tears near the surface. Was this a lie or wishful thinking? I
had no idea. Or maybe I was getting way ahead of myself.
Saying it out loud was twisting my gut almost as badly as
Ian's potion had. Could I really just walk away from Ray?
He'd become so important to me, I couldn't imagine never
seeing him again.

I realized Barry was literally on the edge of his seat waiting for details. Well, I'd started this. I might as well finish
it. I could always change my mind later. Or not.

"You remember the pictures of Ray fighting Jeremy
Blade?"

"Of course I remember. That was a headline for days in all
the tabloids. *Star Snoops* ran the picture in color on the cover.
Surely you aren't choosing him over Ray." Barry grabbed my
hand. "If he's threatened you . . ."

"No, Jerry would never lay a hand on me or any woman.
He loves me. Has for years." Centuries actually, but who's
counting?

"And violent. I saw what he did to Ray, remember?"

"Well, Ray got his licks in too. Men will be men." I cleared
my throat. "It was nothing more than a pissing contest.
They're both territorial. Not a quality I appreciate in either
of them. But I'm telling you this so you can be ready. Maybe
you can do some damage control when Ray and I break up."

"Sure, I can do that. And I see why you don't want a
bunch of commitments as Ray's fiancée if the wedding's not
going to happen." Barry stood and paced the carpet. "Well,
hell. I had even more irons in the fire for you, Glory. You
were a publicist's dream whether you know it or not. You're
genuine. Relatable. I see a lot of Ray's fan mail and his approval rating went up among several key demographics since
you two hooked up."

"So glad I could help." I got up and walked Barry to the door. "But that's no reason to stay together and you know it."

"Of course not. I'm just saying." Barry smiled sadly. "Don't do anything hasty, Glory. Ray loves you. Oh, he may act like a dog now and then—it's that rock-star thing. Cut the boy some slack. He was single for a lot of years. It'll take a while for you to domesticate him."

"I told you. It's not Ray. It's me and the other guy. We have a lot of history that I can't just ignore. And this isn't to go public yet. I mean it, Barry. We've got the reality show and the Grammys to deal with first."

"No worries. My lips are sealed." Barry tapped his nose. "Besides, I'm not sure I'm buying this anyway. My bullshit meter's buzzing." Barry looked down when his cell vibrated. "And now so's my phone. Got to be those Fitzwell people. I know just who to steer them to. DeeDee's in the hotel. She'll be perfect."

"Sure. That's genius. She's the epitome of fitness."

Barry leaned down and kissed my cheek. "Hang in there with Ray, Glory. I've known him for years. He's a stand-up guy. And, honestly, he's never been as caught up in the rock-star hype as a lot of these yahoos are." Barry's phone buzzed again. "Okay, got to take this. Later, lady."

I watched him head out. He was talking on his cell before the hall door closed behind him.

"I liked what I was hearing from you." Valdez bumped against me gently. *"Blade's the one. About time."*

"Shut up, V." I felt like hell. So what if I'd made a mature decision. Putting it right out there for Barry so he could handle the inevitable fallout when Ray and I parted ways. Funny how maturity sucked.

Ten

"Okay, they're coming." Valdez faced the door, Brittany right beside him.

"Are you sure you want to go on with this, Glory?" Flo carefully put away the shoes she'd been showing me that she'd bought in the boutique downstairs.

"Of course I am. I've just got a few days until the red carpet." I sneezed and shrieked at the same time. Oh, God, that hurt. "I didn't go through all this to stop now."

"You sneezed. Vampires don't sneeze. Why?" Flo stared at me as if I'd sprouted a third eye.

"I don't know. Your perfume is tickling my nose. And when I sneeze . . ." I grabbed her arm. Another one was coming and, oh, help. I sneezed again.

"Why're you screaming when you sneeze?" Flo handed me a tissue from a box on the desk next to the wall.

"My stomach is killing me. I told you I did those crunches. That demon's spawn of a trainer made me do them." I blew my nose. "I didn't sleep well and didn't heal."

Flo narrowed her eyes. "You block your thoughts. What do you mean you didn't sleep well? The sun comes up, we die. We just *call* it sleep."

The knock on the door interrupted an interrogation I knew I'd have caved under. I wasn't sure I wanted Flo, and therefore Richard, to know I'd seen daylight. Vampires are funny creatures. Either one of them might have a secret craving for the sun and do something stupid about it if they knew. They'd seen Ian's video and seemed to scoff at it, but when they heard that I'd actually almost walked into daylight . . . Well, I didn't want to test either one of them. I was pretty sure stepping into the sun would have sent me up in flames.

I peeked through the spy hole and saw Ian, Trina and a pair of Ian's usual guards there. I threw open the door.

"Come in. I was just telling Flo how I was feeling."

Ian took my hand and looked into my eyes. "You don't look well. What is it, Glory?"

"My healing sleep didn't do the job. I'm sore from my training session last night." I smiled at Flo. "And now I'm suddenly allergic to my friend's perfume. I've been sneezing, which kills my stomach."

Trina linked her arm through mine and smiled. "That pain'll go away once you're used to regular exercise, Glory. Glad to see you're already in proper gear. You look great in those shorts."

I extricated myself and put a good foot between us. "Thanks. I've got a session scheduled with the trainer for after you guys leave." I winced. "Not that I'm looking forward to it. Sorry, Trina. That may be true for mortals, but vamps live in a different universe. I shouldn't be hurting at all tonight. This is freaking me out, Ian." I grabbed his arm. "Fix this."

"Your reactions to my regimen continue to puzzle me, Glory, but I've been working on the problem." He patted my hand and greeted Flo, who barely nodded. She'd obviously decided he was the enemy.

"Work fast." I pulled away from him, not willing to go all chummy, especially with Flo giving him the evil eye. "Oh, yeah, this is Brittany, Ian, another of my bodyguards. Seems only fair since you've brought two."

"Of course." Ian barely spared her a glance. Bodyguards were like furniture to him. "You're going to have to get used to exercise, Glory. Especially if you can't find a supplement that agrees with you. I've brought a different one for you to try when you wake up tomorrow night. It shouldn't make you sick and could even help you lose an extra pound or two."

"I'm all for that." I could hear Flo muttering something in Italian. "I'm okay, Flo, just sore."

"You're acting mortal, Glory my friend, sneezing and moaning about your stomach." Flo nodded dismissively at Trina. "We are vampire, *mia amica*. We *give* pain; we don't get it."

"She's right. This isn't how the program is supposed to work." Ian opened a black leather attaché case and pulled out two bottles. "So I've also made adjustments in the formula for your usual bedtime drink. I'm hoping those nightmares will go away. Then you should heal properly."

"Okay, I'll try it." I ignored Valdez's warning growl. "I guess now I just have to feed from Trina and we're done here."

"Not tonight." Ian put his hand on my shoulder. "I know you're anxious to speed along the process, so we're going to make tonight's treatment do double duty." He looked down because Valdez was all but sitting on his foot. The two surfers with Ian had moved in too. I felt like I was in a hunky man cave. Brittany kept hanging back, keeping an eye on the action.

"Back off, V. We're just talking here." I nudged him with my running shoe. "Seriously, I want to hear this."

"Yes, I'm sure you do. Because I think you'll lose at least five more pounds tonight if we do this my way." Ian grinned when Flo and I gasped.

"That would be incredible." I sneezed again when Flo came up behind me.

"You might get into that six before the Grammys after all, *mia amica*!" Flo patted my back when I sneezed once more and I grabbed my stomach. "Enough of this. I go wash off my perfume."

"No, don't bother, Florence. Glory's leaving." Ian held up his hand.

"*I don't think so.*" Valdez growled for good measure.

"The whole point was to stay in tonight, Ian. I have lots to do to get ready for the Grammys." I put my hand on Valdez's head to discourage him from starting something.

"Here's how it works, Glory." Trina pulled off her coat and I saw she had shorts and a tank underneath. I'd already noticed the running shoes on her feet. "You and I are going to run the twenty miles together. Then you come back here and take my blood. We'll both be revved so it'll really do you some good."

"Trina's right. We've done this before with great results. I know a twenty-mile sprint should be no big deal for you, Glory. A vampire can run all night if she wants to." Ian nodded toward Flo and smiled. "Though it's easier in the right shoes."

"I would fly before I would ruin my shoes, *signore*. A vamp would have to be *stupido* to stay on the ground." Flo flounced to a chair and sat, then seemed to remember that her best friend had spent centuries being afraid to shift and fly anywhere.

"Oh, no, Glory. I didn't mean . . . *Amica*, if you like to run, then run, of course."

"Thanks, Flo, but my feet are on fire and I feel like someone has ripped my intestines out through my belly button. This is a bad idea." I couldn't freakin' believe this. Twenty miles? And all it would take is one Glory sighting and I'd have a caravan of tabloid reporters on my tail waiting for me to fall on my face. Which was a distinct possibility right now.

"Now, Glory, surely you don't hurt that much. Let's start over. I don't understand why you didn't heal during your death sleep." Ian led me to the couch. "Sit. Let me examine you."

"Lift her shirt and die, *signore*." Flo was up again, had grabbed a pencil from the desk and had it aimed at Ian's heart.

His two bodyguards picked her up and plucked the pencil out of her hands before I could do more than wince. She screamed Italian invectives, but the men were obviously stronger than she was. Brittany piled on and one of them had to release Flo to deal with her. A lamp turned over and glass broke.

"Make them let her go, Ian. Flo, he's not going to lift my shirt, are you, Ian? He's just going to look into my eyes. Simple stuff. And he's a doctor, remember?"

Valdez snarled, torn between loyalty to me and staying close by my side, and watching Flo being manhandled without going to her defense. Clearly Brittany was holding her own with the other guard.

"Relax, Florence. Glory's right. I just want to get to the bottom of this problem she has." Ian lifted my wrist and took my pulse. "Set the woman down. If she comes at me again, you can stop her again."

"*Frattaglie*. Worthless pieces of shit. Apes!" Flo straightened her green silk blouse and checked her brown suede skirt for damage. "I kill them if they touch one hair on my head or on Glory's head, I tell you."

Brittany threw a few choice words at the man she'd managed to almost strip of his shirt. Then she tossed her hair and took her position next to the balcony doors again.

"Flo, honey, let Ian see if he can help me." I rolled my neck as he felt behind my ears, then he lifted my lids to look into my eyes.

"You look sleep deprived."

"I am. It's those nightmares. I had another one last night. I hope your new formula stops those." I sighed and looked down at Valdez. I sent him another silent message of thanks. I didn't doubt he'd saved my life when I almost walked into the sun.

"I have something that will make you feel better." Ian pulled a syringe out of his black bag.

"No way in hell." Valdez headbutted Ian's hand and the syringe went flying across the room. Brittany picked it up and put it out of sight. *"She can do twenty miles without that, can't you, Glory? I'll be right there with you, Brittany too. What about you, Flo?"*

"In these boots?" Flo looked down at her new Ralph Lauren leather high-heeled boots. I knew she'd never worn them before. "I don't think—" She and Valdez exchanged looks. "For my best friend? Of course." She frowned at Ian. "I *do* heal in my sleep. I get a blister? Poof, is gone the next evening when I wake."

I got to my feet. Apparently I had to prove to everyone that I was Wonder Woman. And I did want to lose more weight. If this would take off five pounds in one night, then I would do twenty miles on my knees if I had to. Even if the paparazzi were snapping pictures of the ordeal.

"Oh, Glory, you're just the bravest woman I know." Trina was all over me. Next thing I knew she was crumpled against the wall.

"Flo! What was that about?" I limped over to check on Trina's condition. She just grinned up at me and blew me a kiss.

"She had her hand on your ass. *Puttana!*" Flo got in Trina's face. "My friend doesn't go that way. If she did, it wouldn't be with a skinny bitch like you, you understand me? It would be with someone she loves." Flo grabbed me and kissed me on the lips. "So hands off!"

I leaned on Valdez as Trina got up and shot the finger at Flo. Well, that had been a cute little scene. And I didn't dare wipe off my mouth, though I had a feeling I was sporting Tahitian Sunrise on my lips now. Fine. Everyone kept saying I looked pale anyway.

"I have just one question. How are we going to get out of the hotel without being caught by the paparazzi?" I looked around. There were four women, three men and a dog in our party. We'd have as much luck sneaking out as a marching band playing "Hail to the Chief."

"There's a park down the street where you can start the run. Shift out of here. Trina can meet you there." Ian smiled and looked down at his Italian loafers. "Like Florence, I'm not dressed for a twenty-mile run and have no desire to join you. I'll wait for you here."

Well, that didn't exactly work for me. The idea that Ian would be left alone in our suite while we were all outside? No, not going to happen. Of course, a vampire can get in where he's not supposed to be without breaking a sweat anyway.

"I don't think so, Ian." I leaned against the door and looked at Flo, who was walking gingerly around the living room in her high-heeled boots. "Flo, honey, why don't you stay here too? Maybe you can ask Ian about his program and some of his former clients. Richard would like more information, wouldn't he?" Flo's look of relief was almost comical. Then I sneezed again, doubling over to scream into my T-shirt.

"Glory, are you sure you don't need me?" Flo patted my back while I struggled to stand upright again.

"I'm sure. Trina, you just run out the front door. No one's going to follow you. Let's shift out of here." I limped toward the balcony.

"Cool. I get to see you vamps shape-shift. I love that." Trina clapped her hands. "Go for it, Glory. What do you like to turn into?"

"Nothing." The way I felt, I wondered if I even *could* shift. Brittany threw open the French doors.

"*Mia amica*, are you sure you want to do this?" Flo rubbed what must be her lipstick from the corner of my mouth and gave Trina a superior look. "You don't look well."

"Sure. I'm okay. And I'll feel great after I feed from Trina. That really charges my battery." I enjoyed the cool breeze on my face and already felt marginally better. "I'm just down from not getting the rest I'm used to. It's a weird feeling.

But it's got to be temporary. And tomorrow night is my fitting." I sighed. "I called Zia and told her to warn the designers that I'd been losing weight. She laughed it off. Probably figured I'd only lost a pound or two."

"Wait till they see you, girlfriend. So skinny. They'll be blown away." Flo grinned. "This Zia, she is smart. Reality shows, they like the drama. Your designers will be going crazy trying to make the dresses fit."

I held on to the balcony railing, working up the courage to shift. "Guess this is worth it." The street was far below us and there was a beautiful sky above. A clear night, cool breeze and the lights of L.A. made me actually feel like flying for a change. It had to be better than standing on these aching feet. I leaned against Flo when she put her arm around me. "Of course it is. Totally."

Flo frowned. "I hope so." She hugged me. "Be careful. Brittany, Valdez, take care of her. Don't let her out of your sight."

"You bet." Valdez bumped my hip.

"Hey, we're two on two." Brittany checked out Ian's bodyguards. "No, make that two on zip. These guys are lame-ass losers."

"Oh? You want to go another round?" Surfer number one got in Brittany's face.

"Settle, children." Ian stood beside me, looking me over again. "You think you can shift, Glory?"

"I sure hope so. Just never has been my favorite thing to do. You guys go ahead. Valdez and I will be last." I saw Brittany and Ian's guards change and fly out following Ian's directions.

"We don't have to do this. Grab your sunglasses and a scarf and I'll do my Doberman thing. We'll go out the back." Valdez nudged me.

"No, I can do this." I closed my eyes, pictured a bat and flew out into the night sky. Valdez stayed by my side. I looked down and soon saw the park Ian had described. I actually felt better as the bat. Not so much stomach to ache.

Too bad I couldn't fly around here forever. I saw Trina jog out of the hotel entrance and down the street. I dive-bombed her just for the hell of it, enjoying her shrieks as I snatched at her hair. See? I'm not always sweet, easygoing Glory.

When Trina arrived at the park and the waiting guards, I landed on the ground next to her and concentrated on shifting back. For a moment, I stalled. Yep, there was a real scary hesitation. Maybe because I knew my stomach pain was waiting for me. That and my aching feet. But I finally got a grip on my reluctance and did the necessary.

"Ah, there you are. Hey, you attacked me." Trina laughed. "That was so cool." Obviously nothing fazed Trina. "And when you shifted . . . Man, you were just a blur and then off into the sky. Amazing!"

"Great, glad I could entertain you. Now, let's go."

"Stop! You're hurting. So you need to stretch." Trina got serious. She led me through a bunch of exercises that did work the kinks out of my knotted leg and thigh muscles. "We'll start slow and then you can put on some speed if you feel like it. I know you vamps—you can run really fast if you want to. I hope you won't just leave me in your dust, though. I hate it when vamps do that. It makes me feel so inadequate." She sighed. "I can't wait till Ian makes me a vampire."

I sat on a bench and patted the seat beside me. "Sit down for a minute, Trina. I want to talk to you."

"We really should go. We're already warmed up." She jogged in a small circle.

"We can get warm again. Sit." I pulled her down. "Now, listen. About becoming a vampire . . ."

"I know. It's so fantastic. Ian says you're over four hundred years old and look at you! You could pass for under twenty-one anywhere. I bet you're carded all the time in clubs."

I sighed. "Get a grip, Trina. They don't card anyone in a vampire club and I wouldn't bother going to a mortal one because I can't drink alcohol."

"No chocolate martinis? No lemon drops?" Trina smiled. "I may be a bit of a fitness freak, but I do like my cocktails."

"Forget cocktails. Alcohol and vampires don't mix." I shook my head. "Listen carefully now, Trina. Yes, I've lived that long and, no, I've never aged. I've never had children either. That part of you dies along with the rest of you when you're turned vampire. Ian explain that?"

"No." Trina got a thoughtful look. "But I probably wouldn't be a good mother anyway. I can't even keep a plant alive. And if I had kids first, then turned vampire, I'd either have to make them vampire too someday or watch them grow old and die. That would be a bummer, wouldn't it?"

Valdez snorted. Bummer. A word you'd use if your favorite TV program was preempted by a news break. Trina didn't have a clue how *permanent* this decision was.

Brittany was watching Ian's men, who were obviously too bored to pay attention to a conversation they'd probably heard a thousand times. How many of these mortals had Ian used? And how many had actually made it to immortality? A quick romp through Thing One's mind alarmed me. These mortals were disposable. Trina wasn't about to get to the exalted level of vampire. When she started slowing down on the track or became too whiny for Ian's taste, she'd be discarded, passed around among the guards at playtime, and they didn't care if she accidentally got drained dry.

Unfortunately, this was a common mind-set among old-school vamps. Damn. And here I thought Ian had evolved along with his love of technology.

No way could I yell, "Run!" right here in front of the guards. But, before I was done with this program, I was going to have to figure out how to get her away from Ian. I was afraid the good old whammy wasn't going to be enough. If Trina was a true vamp groupie, she'd just go home to an apartment painted black with the usual shrine to all things vampire and begin her obsession all over again. And Ian would know where to find her too.

"Trina, don't you like to eat?" I trotted out what I missed most about being mortal.

"I'm a vegan. Not much joy in eating anymore. I can't bring myself to eat anything with a face. And now I've read that even plants have feelings. Doesn't leave much that doesn't make me feel guilty." Trina got up again. "You won't talk me out of this, Glory. I'm determined." She started moving in that stupid circle again. "Come on. Get up. We need to get started. You're going to run like the wind."

"Yeah, well, I'm not even in breeze mode tonight, so let's just do what we need to, so I can get down to my ideal weight." I knew a dead end when I hit one. I groaned as I got up and started off after her. She'd picked a trail through the trees that was well lit. We were followed by our two men, one woman and a dog, a real pack.

She might be a dim bulb, but I had to admire Trina's stamina. She was in great shape for a mortal. She kept a steady pace and basically ran a marathon with me beside her. I never heard her complain. No, she just listened to *me* whine when we hit an artificial hill that some demon of design had decided would challenge the runners in this park. And we ran the five-mile course a total of four times. So I saw that hill four times. I hated it. Finally we were both panting and starting what Trina called cooldown. She'd obviously studied at the same school of torture that Bill the trainer had.

"Stretches and slow walking to finish this off, Glory. Then we can go back to the hotel." Trina was glowing with the effects of our run. She obviously loved this stuff. A real twisted sister.

"I've got an idea, Glory." Valdez was panting some himself, and he smelled like a wet fur rug.

"What?" I leaned over and held on to my quivering knees.

"We jog right into the lobby of the hotel. The paparazzi will love it. You out for a run surrounded by bodyguards. Maybe you even stop and give them a quote. Something to make them look forward to your appearance on the red carpet."

"Not a bad idea, V." Especially since I wasn't sure I had the energy to shift again. I straightened slowly. Thank God my stomach didn't hurt as badly as it had when we'd begun. Maybe because my feet had taken over first place in the pain game. Loved my new running shoes. They were cushiony, advertised as walking on pillows of air. Well, after twenty miles my pillows had gone flat and each step felt like the Devil himself was using a pitchfork on my soles.

"They'll take my picture. How do I look?"

"Like you've been working out." Trina brushed my hair out of my eyes. "Here." She pulled a hand towel off the belt holding her fanny pack at her waist. "Wipe off your face and get rid of the rest of the lipstick your friend planted on you." She grinned. "Now I have hope, sweetie. A little something goin' on there? Even I have to admit Flo's hot. Think she'll ever want to do Ian's program? Not that she needs it."

"Afraid not." I didn't bother denying anything. Whatever kept Trina off of me worked right now. I carefully blotted my face with the towel. "You got a hairbrush in there?"

"Of course. Here. Or do you want me to do it for you?" She playfully held it up.

"I can do it." I grabbed it and got to work. "Vamps always have to work without a mirror, you know. Another reason not to go there. You can't imagine what a horrible challenge it is."

"You aren't talking me out of this, Glory." Trina used the same towel on her face, inhaling my sweat in a way that made me want to hurl.

When I was satisfied that I'd done all I could do to make myself camera worthy, I handed the things back to Trina and we headed out. No leash for Valdez, but that was no big deal. As we got near the entrance to the hotel, I could see the usual limos and waiting taxis in line. Then the flashes started.

"It's Glory St. Clair! Glory, what's up?"

I stopped, my band of brothers and sisters right behind me. "I've been working out. I'm determined to look good for the red carpet. Be sure to look for me at the Grammys, fellas.

And watch for me on the reality show *Designed to Kill*." I named the network and the air times. "Big surprises coming and Israel Caine will be on there with me!" I nodded and we all moved out, as coordinated as a high school drill team.

Inside, I headed for the elevators but Trina stopped me. "Nope, let's go for broke. We take the stairs."

"The suite's on the twenty-third floor!" I wailed. Yep, wailed. What can I say? This was like the last straw. But Trina just smiled and pointed to her neck, then waved her wrist under my nose. Oh, yeah, the best was yet to come. I was going to lose big. And if we climbed those stairs . . .

So we climbed. Twenty-two freakin' flights. By ten I was ready to ride Valdez but realized that was cruelty to animals. Oh, yeah, right. He isn't an animal, not of the four-legged variety anyway. See? I wasn't even thinking straight at that point. I was crawling by the time we made it to the door of the suite. I handed my key card to Brittany and she let us in.

Flo and Ian were playing cards. Cards! I wanted to smack both of them.

"Feed me," I croaked. At least I'd quit sneezing. No energy for it.

"Shower first. You'll feel better and it'll work just as well." Ian was absolutely chirpy.

"Valdez, toss him off the balcony." I staggered toward my bathroom, but stopped and turned. "Flo, is Nathan here?"

"No, we're the only ones home." Flo gathered up some bills. Obviously they'd played for money.

"Trina, you can shower in the other bathroom. Put on one of the shirts in the closet there. Nathan won't notice. He has fifteen identical white button-downs."

"Thanks, Glory. I'll be sweet and clean for your feeding." Trina smirked at Flo. "Glory loves to take from me. It's very . . . erotic." She danced off toward the other bedroom accompanied by Flo's Italian curses. Danced. Like she hadn't just run twenty miles and walked up those flights of stairs.

"Are you all right, Glory?" Flo hurried to my side. "Yuck, you're sweating."

"Yeah, it was rough but I survived." I sniffed. "I'm disgusting. Finish your card game. See if you can win back the fee for my weight-loss program."

Ian moved into the doorway. "Not going to happen. I never bet that much." He touched my cheek. "Hurry up with that shower, Glory. You're very weak, aren't you?"

"Yes. If you hear a thump, Flo, come pick me up and wrap me in a towel. No one else sees my butt. Got it, pal?" I knew I sounded loopy, but couldn't seem to stop myself.

"Go, Glory. I'll take care of you." Flo pushed me toward the bathroom. "Call if you need me."

I shut myself inside the bathroom and stripped off my stinky clothes. Before I could think too much, I turned on the water and stepped into the shower. The hot water revived me enough to shampoo my hair and wash my body, but I got out quickly and pulled on one of the comfy robes the hotel provided.

I stopped with my hand on the bathroom door, reminded of the robes Jerry and I had worn at Chip's house. What was Jerry doing tonight? God, if he dropped by and found Ian . . . I picked my cell phone up out of the charger. No calls. That was either good news or bad. Good that Jerry hadn't left a message that he was on his way over. Bad that Jerry still wasn't speaking to me. One thing was clear. I needed to get MacDonald out of here as soon as possible.

I grabbed a towel and wrapped my wet hair in it, then headed to the bedroom but only made it as far as the bed. Exhaustion hit me right between the eyes. So . . . tired. A knock on the door interrupted the first sleep I'd had in what seemed like forever.

"What?" I opened one eye.

"It's me, Glory. I'm here for you," Trina sang as she opened the door. She wore one of Nathan's shirts and her shorts. "We've got to do the feeding now. Ian says the effects of our run are fading fast."

"Okay, come here and give me your wrist." I pushed myself up and shoved a pillow behind me.

Trina frowned as she was quickly stepped inside, Brittany on one side of her and Flo on the other. Obviously this wasn't going to be the fun and games the mortal had imagined.

"Sit on the side of the bed. Do not touch Glory." Flo pushed Trina down and then came around to sit on my other side.

"Hey, I'm a willing donor. I don't deserve to be treated this way." Trina looked from Flo to Brittany. "Glory, tell them. You and I get along fine. We don't need them around while we do this."

"That's okay, Trina. I'm fine with them here. Now, please your master and me, and be quiet. I need this." I took her wrist and inhaled the delicious scent of mortal blood thrumming under her warm skin. Then my fangs were in and I took her life force. I immediately knew this was something special. My heart raced and my toes curled. Not only curled, but my aching feet actually quit aching. Wow.

I drank greedily until Flo's hand squeezed my shoulder.

"Enough, Glory. I don't like this mortal, but you've had enough."

I pulled out and licked the punctures closed. Trina's eyes were shut and her face was deathly pale. What had I done?

"Trina?" I touched her cheek and her eyes popped open.

"I'm fine, Glory." She grinned. "I love it when you do that. Lose your mind. It's so . . . orgasmic. Is it like that for you?"

"Out! I do not have to listen to this." Flo jumped up and grabbed one of Trina's arms, then pushed her at Brittany. "Remove her." Flo turned her back on Trina's squeal of outrage as Brittany picked her up and hauled her to the door.

"Glory, don't let them treat me this way!"

Brittany clapped a hand over Trina's mouth and shut the door with her foot before I could answer.

"I don't care what this person does for you, Glory. Is better to take from a stranger than to have to deal with all this garbage. I should have let you drain her dry. We toss her skinny ass off the balcony. Eh?" Flo frowned when we heard one last Trina screech from the other side of the closed door.

"Oh, come on, Flo. You sound"—I bit back the word, but I was thinking jealous—"like you never had a mortal pet before. Didn't you once live with a group of vampires who kept mortals with them like that? I've heard your stories."

"Yes, and it never ends well." Flo sighed and settled back on the bed beside me. "They either want to be vampires or someone drinks too much and they end up dead. I'm over all that. It's better to hang out only with vampires. No complications like that *podista.*" She waved toward the living room and Trina.

There was a knock on the door. "Speaking of complications. Here's one. I'm sure that's Ian. Come in." I sat up straighter, making sure my robe was closed up to my neck.

"Glory, how are you feeling now?" He glanced at Flo, then came closer.

"Better. The feeding from Trina was fantastic. But the workout was brutal. She even made me climb the stairs!" I felt Flo's hand on my arm.

"She goes too far, Ian. You should fire her scrawny butt." Flo winced when I glared at her.

"She's just doing her job, Flo." I turned back to Ian. I knew he didn't "fire" mortals; he terminated them. "Don't fire her. She's great. Couldn't have done all that work without her encouragement."

"Get dressed and let's do your weigh-in, then. I know you're anxious to see the results." Ian and Flo exchanged looks. "As for Trina, I've sent her home. She won't be causing any more scenes. She needs to learn her place."

"Weigh in. I can't believe I almost forgot that part." I hopped out of bed. "I'll get dressed, but, Ian, I mean it. Trina's just enthusiastic about her job. I can deal with it. Don't hurt her." I really didn't want Ian to think it was time to get rid of Trina altogether.

"I apologize if I gave you the impression I was going to get rid of Trina." He smiled. "She needs to learn restraint,

but if you're happy, I'm happy." Ian gestured for Flo to pre-
cede him. "We'll wait for you in the living room."

"You're more forgiving than I would be, Glory. I just
hope this is worth it for you." Flo slid past Ian. "I'm glad I
was already a size I like when I was turned, *signore*. This
program of yours is very complicated."

"But are you totally satisfied with all aspects of the vampire life, my dear?" Ian closed the bedroom door but I could
still hear his smooth voice. "I have other products you might
be interested in, Florence. Products very easy to use but with
great potential for enhancing your pleasure. Let me tell you
about some of them."

I really didn't like the idea of Flo succumbing to one of
Ian's sales pitches. Did she crave sunlight? Was her current
favorite lipstick color a clue? Tahitian Sunrise, not Sunset.
And what other products did he offer? Flo's always really been into sex. If Ian had something comparable to the
Vampire Viagra that the Energy Vampires sold, she'd be all
over it.

Well, I couldn't worry about that now. Besides, Flo had a
strong husband to rein her in if necessary. Yeah, right. Richard would have as much luck reining in a herd of rampaging
were-hyenas during a full moon. Trust me, those guys will
not be herded. I was smiling as I checked out my closet and
decided to put on exactly the same outfit that I'd worn when
I'd first gone out to Ian's. It would be perfect for a weight
comparison. I didn't bother with shoes.

When I stepped into the living room, Flo was going over
a slick brochure. When she saw me, she quickly tucked it
into her purse. Hmm. So she was thinking about getting
into some of Ian's goodies. I wish I honestly believed they
were 100 percent safe. But the roller-coaster ride his supplements had taken me on didn't exactly inspire a testimonial,
and Flo knew that. Her decision. Still, I'd have felt better if
she'd tossed the brochure into the trash can.

"I'm ready. Let's do this." I gestured toward the powder
room where Nathan had set up my scale. It was going to be

a tight squeeze to get both Ian and me in there. No way was Valdez going to fit too. He wasn't going to like that.

Ian picked up his clipboard. "It's also time to measure you again." He looked in the bathroom. "After I weigh you, we can do that in the bedroom."

"Good idea." Actually, I couldn't wait to see how many inches I'd lost. My jeans now bagged in the seat, and the T-shirt was loose. Hell, even my bra cup didn't have overflow anymore. I was on cloud nine.

"You're not closing that bathroom door." Valdez stood in the doorway. *"No one will be able to see your freakin' weight, Glory. I'll stand guard out here, back to the scale. Will that work for you?"*

"Fine. Do what you have to, just don't look." I turned to Ian. "Okay, I'm ready." I stepped on the scale. I watched breathlessly as Ian adjusted the weights. It took so long I finally closed my eyes.

"Okay, you can look now."

"Oh, my God!" I jumped off the scale and straight into his arms. I planted a kiss on his lips that sent Valdez into a growling fit. Tough. I was grateful.

"Thanks, Glory." Ian set me down between him and my bodyguard. Brittany was now there too in case V needed backup.

I reached back and slipped the weights to zero, then wiped at my eyes. "I lost eight more pounds!" I leaned down and hugged Valdez next. "Can you believe it? That's a total of—" My mind went blank.

"Thirteen pounds." Ian wrote on his chart. "I think it's time you went shopping, Glory, for smaller sizes. Good thing Florence is here. She says she's an expert shopper."

"Glory, he's right. Your pants are falling off of you. Your butt's gone." Brittany hugged me next. "Flo, quit reading that stuff and come see. Glory's shrinking right before our eyes!"

I heard a squeal, then I was enveloped in a hug that made my lungs hurt. Trina's feeding had helped me a lot, but didn't have the power a healing sleep would have. I still felt my stomach muscles, and every step reminded me I had painful issues with my feet.

Ian smiled. "You've been an excellent client, Glory. Despite a few glitches, your weight loss has been truly remarkable. I should have asked you to do a video diary for me."

I shook my head. "No thanks, Ian. From what I saw of Sarah's, those things are, uh, a little too revealing."

He shrugged. "Too late for that now anyway. But look, I have a little gift for you. And you too, Florence." He walked over and pulled what seemed to be two thin white laptops out of his bag.

"What are these?" I took one and Flo the other.

"I don't like computers, Ian. Since Richard has learned to work with them, that's all he wants to do. Google, Google, Google." Flo made a face. "I hate this Google man."

I wasn't too excited about a computer either. I used one for my business. "Flo, Google's not a man; he's a search engine."

Flo gave me a blank look.

Ian grinned. "Just push the button and open it, Glory. You'll see, Florence. You'll love this."

I pushed a button and the thing popped open. It looked like a regular laptop but without the keyboard. "What is this?"

"Turn it on here." Ian pushed a red button. "Hold it up like this. Now look into it."

"Oh, wow!" It was like looking into a mirror. I showed it to Flo. "Check it out, Flo."

"It's me. *Che bella*, eh, Glory? Why didn't you tell me I have lipstick on my teeth?" She began scrubbing with her finger. "You made one of these for me?" She held it up and smiled. "I love it! How you do it?"

"It's basically a webcam with a high-resolution color monitor." Ian popped the other one open and handed it to me since clearly Flo wasn't letting go of the one she had. She'd pulled out her makeup bag and went to work on her eyeliner.

I smiled at my video and it smiled back. Cool. This was a serious breakthrough and I was temporarily mesmerized. I'd already realized Ian was brilliant, but he'd just moved up to idol status in my book. I tore myself away from myself and carefully closed the thing.

"This is an amazing gift. I don't get it, Ian. First all this personal attention and now this. What's up?"

"Come on, Glory. Mr. Caine paid for first-class service. That's what you're getting. I'd think you'd be used to it." Ian just kept smiling.

"Sure I am." Yeah, right. "But this"—I hugged my new toy—"is way more than service."

"I like you, Glory. And I figure your success is going to bring me more business when your vampire friends see you on TV at the Grammys. Consider this a thank-you gift." He nodded toward Flo, who'd moved on to renewing her lipstick. "My products are expensive and I cater to an affluent clientele. It's clear that's the kind of company you keep. Just spread the word that you were satisfied with my program and I'll be more than repaid for that bit of nonsense."

"You call this nonsense?" Flo finally shut her "mirror" gently. "It's *fantastico*! I must have at least two more. No, make that three. Can I order them in colors?" Flo's eyes glowed as she pulled out a credit card. "Please, *signore*, tell me you will sell me more."

Ian winked at me as if to say his marketing ploy was paying off already, then began to answer Flo's questions. After taking her order and measuring me (inches gone everywhere—wow!), he and his minions finally left and I went to put my "mirror" in a safe place. I also sighed with relief we'd made it through without Jerry showing up. Where was he, though? Plotting Ian's takedown? And was he staying away because he was too busy or still furious with me for consorting with his enemy?

I sat on the side of the bed and stuffed my poor feet into high heels, biting back a scream. I couldn't let Jerry kill Ian. Not after the MacDonald genius had helped me lose an incredible thirteen pounds! Too bad that once I got off Ian's stuff, those pounds would be right back where they thought they belonged.

Damn. Three days until the red carpet and the Grammys. I opened Ian's "mirror" and tried to see as much of myself as I could. God, I loved this new body. What if I wanted to keep it permanently? Yeah, right.

I looked at the bottles of supplements Ian had left for me. They scared the hell out of me. Exercise, dangerous nightmares, sleepwalking and who knew what effects from this new brew he'd given me to try. Could I abuse my body like that forever? And how much would a maintenance program cost me? I was an independent working girl who planned to break up with one rich man and had probably already burned her bridge with another one.

Oh, and if that Campbell guy managed to kill the MacDonald one? Then the vamp magic for weight loss would die with him. Now, there was a reason to end a feud if I ever heard one. I needed to call Jerry and do something to rebuild that bridge. But what? This was one problem that I was afraid even my sexiest moves couldn't fix.

Eleven

"I canceled my workout session with Bill. I decided I don't need it after that run with Trina." I headed for the elevators with Flo.

"So right, girlfriend. It was never a good idea. What's that kind of thing going to get you?" She punched the down button. "Pain, you said. Ian's program is working. That's all you need." She grinned. "I can't believe how much weight you lost so fast. We celebrate. Buy you something pretty. My treat."

The elevator doors opened and we both jumped back. Jerry and Richard stood there and neither of them wore happy faces.

"*Amante!*" Flo moved first, pulling Richard out of the elevator car and into the hallway. "What are you doing here?"

"I got your message. What the hell are you doing tackling Ian MacDonald on your own?" He looked up and down the hall like he was checking for lurking MacDonald guards to take down.

"We weren't on our own, eh, Valdez, Brittany?" Flo waved her hand at my two guards. "And, as you can see, we're perfectly fine. Glory had her treatment and we're on our way to shop. Look at her. Isn't she tiny?"

Richard did look but didn't seem overwhelmed.

"Forget shopping. We need to talk." Jerry took my arm and pulled me toward the suite.

"Isn't that my line?" I jerked free. "No need to get physical. Why don't we start over? You say, 'Hi, Glory. How are you?' I answer, 'Oh, I'll live. But, gee, Jerry, last time we saw each other you practically called me an idiot. Then you didn't bother to call, just showed up here and started throwing your muscle around. What's the deal?'"

"Sorry if you don't like my approach, Gloriana." Jerry glanced at Richard, who'd obviously sent him a mental warning that this approach wasn't too swift either.

I just stood there, tapping my aching toe and waiting for him to get a clue.

Flo studied her nails. "Is this going to take long? Glory needs to try on some things for her new little size." She grinned at me. "Major fun, eh, *mia amica*?"

"A lot more fun than standing here in the hall." I glanced at Valdez and Brittany, then back at Jerry. "Do I have to ask you again? Guess so. What's the deal, Jerry?"

"Okay, okay, look." He gently put his hand on my shoulder. "I'm worried about you. We have information on Mac-Donald that you should know. May we come in?"

"Now that you asked like a gentleman, sure. This had better be good, though. I've had a rough night." I used my key card and we all trooped back inside. Obviously shopping was out for now. And I really wanted to see what size I could fit into now. One look at Jerry's firm jaw and serious face, and I knew his information wasn't going to make me happy.

"What was rough about it?" Jerry was close beside me. "Did that bastard hurt you?"

"No, just made me exercise my butt off, literally." I turned around and showed him. "Totally worth it." I wanted to scream when he barely glanced at what I'd sweated so hard for. "Fine, so you don't care. Just sit. Tell us what you found out."

I collapsed in a chair on the opposite side of the room from Jerry. I didn't like his attitude. Maybe because I was afraid he was going to tell me something that would bring me down from my high. Can you blame me? Hey, I was feeling skinny and pumped from Trina's donation. It had been the best one yet, because we'd both done all that exercise. For a moment I toyed with the idea of getting my own mortal pet. If I could endure a run and stair climb with one every night, I could at least keep off a few pounds . . .

I realized everyone was staring at me. "What?"

"I asked you a question. Didn't you hear me?"

"No, guess I spaced. I'm still pretty jazzed. I've lost a total of thirteen pounds. Damn it, this time really look at me!" I stood and turned around, showing off the way my jeans bagged and almost slid off my hips. I even lifted my T-shirt so he could see my rib cage. Yep, my ribs were almost showing.

"Enough, Glory. Richard, look away." Flo waved at me to lower my shirt.

"Relax, darling. I know Glory is just a friend. This really is a remarkable loss in such a short time." Richard frowned. "But you know it can't last. Just like quick losses don't last for mortals. It's not safe either."

"I don't want to hear that!" I stomped my foot. Ouch.

"Whether you want to hear it or not, it's true." Jerry leaned forward. "Sit down and listen."

"I'll sit because my feet hurt. Not because you ordered me to." I sat. The guys sounded achingly like me talking to Trina earlier. She hadn't wanted to hear bad news either. Shit.

"I found some of Ian's success stories. Men and women who were on his supplements and did his program." Richard pulled a small notebook out of his shirt pocket. "Did Caine ever tell you what he paid for you to do this, Glory?"

"No, he just put it on a credit card." I heard Jerry and Valdez make a noise. "I offered to reimburse him! But he wouldn't allow it. Valdez, you were there. You heard it all. Ray said he just wanted me to be happy." I arched my brow at Jerry, like maybe this was more than *he'd* ever done. Which was a lie and mean-spirited but felt good anyway. "Besides, we'll be on TV worldwide at the Grammys. It's publicity. Ray can probably take the cost off his income tax."

"That'll be interesting for his accountant to deal with." Richard shook his head. "Anyway, it's ridiculously expensive. I know you couldn't afford it on your own, Gloriana."

"My business—"

"Is successful enough to support you and pay overhead with maybe a little left over." Richard smiled. "You forget. I helped you with your taxes for the shop last quarter."

"Oh, yeah." I've always worked for a living and never had much of a cushion. The fact that my ancient car had recently died meant that had to be my next big financial investment.

"Get to the point, *amante*." Flo pulled out Ian's brochure. "The man's a genius. You should see some of the things he advertises. I'm interested in trying some of them myself. Obviously he's not just, how you say it, blowing smoke. Look at our girlfriend Glory here."

"Hand that to me." Richard grabbed it. "He gave this to you, my heart?" Unspoken was a "How dare he?"

"Yes." Flo's eyes flashed. "And I can get another if I need it." She snatched it back. "Now, tell us what you have on him."

"Fine." Richard gave his wife a "we'll deal with this later" look. "His program costs a fortune. Then once clients are hooked, they have to buy his supplements or the weight comes right back on."

"I expected that. Just like a mortal weight-loss program." I got up and walked over to the couch. "Let me see the brochure, Flo. Does it say how much the supplements cost?" I quickly found the price list and gasped. No way could I handle it on my own. I used all my willpower to keep from ripping the paper to shreds.

"Was he telling the truth when he said I was the only one who had the weird reactions to the supplements?" I tossed the brochure back to Flo.

"Yes, none of them had a problem with them. Just the price. So now 90 percent of them, except for a few of the very rich, are back to their starting weight." Richard looked me over. "Ian's got some bitter enemies out there, Glory. He isn't exactly up front about the cost of the maintenance program."

"No, he wouldn't be. But it's pretty much the same way for mortals, isn't it? If you go on a special program, then go off, you usually gain what you've lost right back, sometimes even more. At least vamps can't do that." I was defending him. I could see Jerry struggling to keep his mouth shut. But to hear me back a MacDonald had to make him insane.

"Fine. So you're okay with the fact that you've been sucked into this, will look good for one event, then it's the old Glory, right back where you started." Richard turned the page in his notebook.

"I'm not okay. I'm just realistic. So far all this drama adds up to exactly zilch as far as I'm concerned. Time to go shopping, Flo." I turned to Jerry. "Unless Jerry's got something else. Surely you don't expect me to join in your feud because of my disappointment."

"I told you, I'm worried about you. And Richard asked me to come. So I came. Hear him out." Jerry crossed one leg over his knee and leaned back.

"We saw that video about Ian's sunlight drug. I tried to follow up on that too. To see if any vampires have tried it and lived to tell the tale."

Jerry and Flo leaned forward. Uh-oh. A lot of interest there. Well, why not? Maybe Ian could make it happen. But I doubted Jerry would ever be able to bring himself to trust a MacDonald's daylight drug even if a thousand vampires showed Jer their sunburns.

I glanced at Valdez. "Did you find any?"

"No. I took that to the Los Angeles Council. They were very interested in Ian's claims. They'll be calling on him to check it out." Richard narrowed his gaze on me. "Tell me about your nightmares, Gloriana. You're not sleeping when you should. That tells me you might actually wake up during daylight hours."

I waved my hand and kept the giant block to my thoughts

firmly in place. "Dreams, Richard. It's kind of cool, even when they're scary." I smiled at Jerry. "I dreamed your mother and Mara were burning me at the stake for being a witch. And you couldn't have cared less."

"Nonsense. I'll always care what happens to you, Gloriana, even when you're wrongheaded." Jerry looked at Valdez. "Does she move when she dreams?"

"I'm not in her bedroom, Blade. I stay out here, guarding the door." Valdez had effectively avoided the answer without telling an out-and-out lie.

"Ian said she was sleep deprived." Flo spoke up. "And during what he calls the 'death sleep,' she didn't heal like she was supposed to. What does that mean, Ricardo?"

"I don't know. But I don't like it." Richard frowned, pulled out a pen and wrote in his notebook. "How do you feel now, Gloriana?"

"I feel great. I fed from a mortal who ran twenty miles with me and then we both climbed twenty-two flights of stairs. I've lost all this weight and I'm skinny for the first time in my life. Why wouldn't I feel great? Now, can we forget the third degree? Flo and I are going shopping." I jumped up. If Jerry wasn't going to apologize or do something to show me he accepted my decisions, then I was out of here. Instead he just kept frowning at me, like he thought my baggy pants and loose T-shirt were evidence of my disloyalty.

"I'm with you, girlfriend. We'll be downstairs in the lobby shops, Ricardo. You can come with us or wait here or go do your investigating." Flo stopped in front of Richard, who'd jumped to his feet along with Jerry. She kissed his cheek. "Seriously, *amante*. We just spent the evening with Ian and his thugs and no one got hurt. Valdez and Brittany? Can you back me up on that?" Clearly Flo had decided to forget the incident with the pencil.

"I don't like the man. Just a gut feeling. And his bodyguards are stupid, but no one tried anything we couldn't handle." Valdez dropped his leash at my feet, obviously figuring if Flo was all right with the pencil incident, then he wasn't going

to mention it either. *"I'm watching her with MacDonald, boss. Brit's got you on speed dial if we run into a situation where we need you."*

"You call me immediately then." Jerry stepped closer and looked down at me. "Your face is thinner, Gloriana. You look tired. Let me taste your blood again."

"Fine. But Ray checked it when we woke up and it was okay." I held out my wrist. "See for yourself."

Jerry's eyes darkened, then he pressed his lips to my skin. Finally, he took a taste, the pressure lasting only a moment. He pulled back and licked his lips.

"No problem, you're fine. Better than." He leaned down as if he couldn't help himself and kissed me, then pulled me to him and held me tight as he delved deep and laid claim to my mouth.

I melted against him. I couldn't help myself either. This was Jerry, my Jerry, and I felt my usual response to his taste and his touch. Richard cleared his throat and we broke apart.

"I'll call you later." Jerry turned and followed Richard out the door.

I looked at Flo. "Well. I don't know whether he's still mad at me or not."

"Oh, he's still mad, but he'll get over it. Go fix your lipstick, then let's go shopping. I think you can fit into a six, girlfriend. See if you don't." Flo pulled out her own lipstick. "Richard's mad at me too. I have to work hard to bring him around because I want to buy something from Ian. The man's a magician, no? Look at you. And in just a few days."

By the time we'd hit the boutique in the lobby and I'd managed to squeeze into a size six (with spandex), I was calling Ian a freaking Houdini. I refused Flo's generous offer and made the clerk take my credit card instead of charging it to the room, coming up with a story about a surprise for Ray. Of course I figured my purchase was going to be leaked to the tabloids, but I'd love to see "Glory Wears Size Six" hit newsstands.

I told Flo good-bye, then headed upstairs. My cell phone rang just as I was hanging up my new pair of skinny jeans. Caller ID said it was Jerry. I took a breath and answered.

"Hi."

"Gloriana, I'm outside on your balcony. Will you let me in?"

"Sure." I closed the phone and headed out to see for myself. Brittany and Valdez were there. They'd just turned on the TV and hit the minibar for some snacks, but obviously they'd seen Jerry and were both waiting for their orders.

"You want to come in?" I opened the French door.

"Why don't you come somewhere with me?" Jerry signaled to Valdez. "We can leave the shifters here. I'll have you back before sunrise."

"Glory, you want to go or not?" Brittany was strictly on Ray's payroll. She didn't take orders from Jerry, just me or Ray.

"Sure, I'll be fine. You two enjoy an evening off." I glanced at the clock. "Actually we've only got about two hours. I'll be back." I looked up at Jerry. "I have to be. It's important."

"Right. Another of MacDonald's supplements." His mouth firmed.

"Not just that. I have the reality show people coming right after sundown. I've got to be up and ready to go as soon as I can." I smiled and touched his cheek. "That's part of why I did this. They're making my dress for the red carpet, remember?"

"How could I forget?" He turned his head and kissed my fingertips. "I don't want to argue with you. Let's go. Feel like shifting?"

"Sure. I'm still pumped from my feeding earlier. You should have seen me, Jerry. I was a real jock!" I laughed and held my arms out to the cool night air. "Where are we going?"

"Just follow me." He shifted into a beautiful black bird, waited for me to do the bird thing and then took off.

We flew out and over smaller buildings and the park

where Trina and I had run. We flew over streets with cars racing along under us. Finally we were in the hills above Los Angeles. Another empty house? Jerry's connections with the vampire council were paying off.

He landed on the balcony of the second floor, then swiftly changed back into his tall male form. I landed beside him and managed my own change with a speed that impressed us both.

"You're getting pretty good at that." He laughed and hugged me.

"I guess the more I do it, the more confidence I get." I turned and looked out at the lights of Los Angeles. "Oh, this is beautiful. Where are we?"

"Another of Chip's investments. We're in the Hollywood Hills. This one comes fully furnished. We're in the master bedroom." Jerry stepped inside.

"Right. Why do we always end up in bed together?" I heard the bitterness in my voice. Well, it was true. Was that all we had? Sex?

"So we won't this time." He held out his hands like he wouldn't dare touch me.

"You know what I mean. It's like we have to make a big deal out of just talking to each other. And when we do, it's a disaster. Like last night." I kept at least five feet between us. He looked too good to me and I couldn't blame it on Ian's supplement either. Jerry *always* looked good to me, damn it.

He frowned. "Yes, last night was pretty much a bad scene."

"Except for the sex."

"Right." He moved closer and smiled like he knew he could have me again with just a touch. "Because sex between us is always good."

"See? We're right back where we started." I walked around the king-size bed and kicked off my shoes because my feet hurt, no other reason. "I'm not doing this, Jerry."

"Fine. Go sit in that chair. Over there. Well away from

the bed." Jerry pointed to a pretty sitting area in front of a fireplace. It had another one of those automatic switches that he flipped and we had a beautiful fire going in moments. He sat in a chair across from me. "Let's talk about what you've been going through."

"You mean the weight-loss thing." I was sorry I hadn't had time to put on my new skinny jeans, but I did have on one of my new clingy sweaters, size medium, thank you very much. The deep rose vee showed off the edge of the C-cup bra I'd bought in hot pink with black lace trim. I absolutely loved it. Why had I turned down sex? I wanted Jerry to see this bra. All of it. Obviously I was certifiable. And, again, much as I'd like to, I couldn't blame my lust on Ian's program. Having Jerry near me always messed with my thought processes.

"Tell me how MacDonald's deal works. What the supplements have been doing to you."

So I told him. About the nausea. And the dreams. Not about the sleepwalking or the sunlight, of course. The fact that my healing sleep wasn't working seemed to worry him the most.

"And you say he's given you a new drug to drink when you wake up in the evening. You don't know how you'll react to it."

"No." And now I was worried. What if I got sick and then had to be on camera? This was a big deal. I'd get my first glimpse of what the designers had made for me and there'd be that fitting. At least a makeup artist would be on set if I looked like hell after hugging the toilet. Only three more days till the Grammys. I couldn't quit now but . . .

"Glory, is this really worth it?"

"Yes." I knew Jerry hated my one-word answers, but he might as well get used to it. Hey, it was what he usually gave me.

"I know I can't stop you, but I'm going to warn you about something." He got up, squatted in front of me and took my hands. "I told my father that the MacDonald heir is here. Da is on his way to help me take him down."

"No!" I jumped up. "You can't do that. An ambush? That's—that's cowardly. Not the Campbell way at all."

"When it comes to the MacDonalds there are no rules." Jerry grabbed my shoulders. "I've been trying to tell you. These men are the cowards. They'll lie and cheat and steal to get what they want. Ian knows you're a Campbell woman. Make no mistake about that. When Richard found out that no other vampire on MacDonald's weight-loss program got sick, I knew. This is his plan, Gloriana. He's hurting you to get to me. He's been trying to draw me out and it's working. But I'll not face him alone. I'll have the clan behind me."

"Jerry, stop! Don't do this. Call the laird back and tell him it was a mistake." I pulled my cell phone from my pocket. "Come on. I can't let you screw this up for me."

"Oh, right, for *you*." Jerry turned his back on me. "I should let him poison you, wait until you go to your big-deal event with your rock star and have your picture made for all the world to see. Then after you're dead and I'm mad with grief, *then* it's okay for me to take my men and drive MacDonald into the sea. Is that the way it should be?" He spun and grabbed me, his hands biting into my shoulders. "Is it?"

"Stop! Are you listening to yourself, Jerry? Since when does poison work on vampires? Besides, you tasted my blood earlier. You said it was fine. I'm not poisoned, am I?" I offered my neck. "Drink from me again. Take me to bed and let me show you how much energy I have tonight. I'm feeling, hell, alive! More alive than I've felt since the night you turned me. Ian's magic works, Jerry. Whether he's your ancient enemy or not doesn't matter to me."

"But it *does* matter to me, Gloriana. I can't be with a woman who doesn't understand that." Jerry released me and stepped back. "I never thought I'd finally have enough of you. But mayhap it's come to pass."

My heart fluttered, then seemed to stop. Was I crazy? What had I just done? I reached for him but he shook his head.

"Don't try to cozen me."

"I'm not." I was, but I'm not totally stupid. "Listen, Jerry. I get the feud thing. I do. I remember the stories your father told when I visited Castle Campbell. The MacDonalds did terrible things to members of your family."

"They did." Jerry nodded, his lips firm.

"And I'm sure the MacDonalds tell stories about the Campbells as well."

"All lies."

"No doubt." I could see logic wasn't going to work here. "This is the twenty-first century. Broadswords and cudgels are out; brains and computers are in. Can't you think of a way to take out Ian that's more subtle than a direct attack?" One that hopefully would take more than three days to plan. "You'd lose fewer men that way."

"Now you're making sense." Jerry actually stood still while I ran my hand up his arm. He wore a white silk shirt with full sleeves and a spread collar, a pirate's shirt. He'd tucked it into black jeans and left it unbuttoned just enough to make me want to finish the job.

"Use strategy, Jerry, not just brute strength. Ian's brilliant. You've got to give the man that much." I slid my hand inside the front of his shirt to tease his chest. "He's got all his inventions. He gave me a computer that works like a mirror. It's fantastic. Flo went nuts when he gave her one too."

"Yes, he's smart, too damned smart. He's fooled a lot of people with his tricks." Jerry looked down when he realized I'd released his buttons and pulled his shirt out of his pants.

"Including me, Jerry. Obviously. But I'm willing to go along with him because it suits my purposes. I've *used* him. So I'll look good for that big-deal event. That's all. And the rock star picked up the tab. So I've used him too. Naughty Glory." I pursed my lips into a pout. "But seems to me you like it when I'm naughty." Ah, he'd lost his frown, was softening toward me. I glanced down. Well, not all of him was going soft.

"Gloriana. You think I don't realize—"

"Hush." I took Jerry's hand and pulled it to the edge of my sweater. "Just look at the new bra I had to buy, Jerry. So pretty. They don't make this in my old bigger size."

"You *are* bad. You're trying to distract me with sex." He did push down my sweater, though, and looked his fill at the plunging bra. "I thought you weren't doing this."

"Maybe I changed my mind. Is it working?"

"Unfortunately. I can't remember why I was mad at you. I was planning to leave you here to find your way back by yourself. Or maybe send Valdez for you right before sunrise." He leaned down and pushed the bra down with his nose to trace my nipple with his fangs.

"That would be"—I gasped as he sucked it into the heat of his mouth—"mean."

He looked up, his eyes gleaming. "I felt at the time that you might deserve it. Loyalty to the clan is very important to a Campbell."

"I'm not a Campbell, Jerry." I rubbed my breasts against his bare chest to take the sting out of that reminder.

"You should be." He opened the bra and dropped it and the sweater on the floor. "Ah, they are smaller, but still very fine indeed, woman."

I unzipped his pants and wrapped my hands around his shaft. "Larger and always very fine indeed." I dropped to my knees and kissed every inch of him while he groaned my name and pushed his fingers into my hair. I took him into my mouth while I stroked his sacs. Finally I ran my fangs the length of him, resisting the urge to drink from the vein throbbing where his thighs met his trunk. I wanted that vein more than anything, but remembered that I had to keep this weight off. Damn. Were these sacrifices worth it?

He jerked me to my feet and swung me into his arms. He carried me to the rug in front of the fire, where he gently laid me down and peeled off my jeans.

"I shouldn't let you do this to me, lass."

"Am I doing it to you? I thought you were doing it to me." I reached for him. "It's a really bad idea. Totally doesn't solve the problem between us. But we have no willpower."

"Aye." He kissed me and ran his hands over my body. "Are you sure you feel all right? I wouldn't cause you pain."

"I feel fine except for an ache"—I took his hand and pressed it between my legs—"here. Ease me, Jeremiah Campbell."

"I'll do my best." He slid his fingers inside me, stroking me until my hips rose to meet his hand. Then he moved down to taste me, his lips and tongue working their magic as he found the place that always sent me over the edge too quickly. But I could go over the edge more than once, as he proved to me. He did drink from me there, settling in with his fangs and sending me mental messages of his love. He loved my taste, loved my ass, loved my, um, well, you get the idea. He's a guy.

Finally, he rolled me on top and lifted me to settle on him. I rode him and held his shoulders, his hands on my hips as we found our rhythm. He grinned and then stopped, just when I thought it was over for both of us.

"No, not yet." He stood while we were still connected, my legs linked around his waist to keep us together, and sat in the leather chair in front of the fire.

"I want to check out these new, smaller breasts. Sorry, Glory, but I miss the larger ones. They had more bounce, more"—he cupped them in his palms—"heft."

I feigned indignation and grabbed his ears to give them a twist. "You sound like you're describing a new broadsword, you awful man."

He grinned. "I love my broadsword. If it were a woman, I'd—" I kissed his mouth and began to move again. This position put a new pressure inside me and I quite liked it.

"Ah, Jerry." I leaned back, my hands on his shoulders again as I tried to keep it going. "I don't want to stop but

I—I . . ." Spasms shook me as the climax built and he grabbed my butt to hold me tight against him.

"God, Gloriana!"

I came apart then, calling his name.

We arrived back on the balcony with only minutes to spare before dawn. The suite was dark but I knew Valdez waited for me. I kissed Jerry good-bye, admonishing him to hurry back to his own hotel, then let myself in.

"I see you made up." It was Ray who spoke from the dark, not Valdez.

"Yes." I looked around. "Where's Valdez?"

"He and Brittany will be back in a few. I sent them down to have a decent breakfast. They can't operate full strength on just junk from the minibar." Ray stood and walked over to lock the French doors. "You smell like sex. Shit."

"Sorry, Ray. That's how Jerry and I make up." I slid past him and headed for the bedroom.

"Wait." Ray stopped me. "I'm not seeing DeeDee again."

"Your decision. Don't deprive yourself on my account." I realized that had come off pretty cold. "I mean, I'm sorry if you were disappointed in your deal with her. Mortal sex is pretty tame compared to the vampire kind." I smiled and knew Ray could see it in the dark. "We'll have to find you a vamp girlfriend."

"I'd hoped I'd found one." He moved closer. "Don't write me off yet, Glory. I can be patient. I'm even surprising my-self where you're concerned."

I shook my head. "Dawn's coming. I've got to drink Ian's stuff before I hit the sheets."

Ray followed me into the bedroom. "Brittany says you've lost thirteen pounds. Let me look at you."

I faced him when he turned on the bedroom light.

"Wow! Look at you. Sexy-peekaboo-bra thing going on there. No wonder you and Blade . . ." Ray shrugged. "Let me see your butt."

I turned around, gasping when I felt his hands cup my bottom. "Hey! Watch it."

"I'm watching it. You look fantastic." He turned me around and hugged me. "You're one hot mama. I can't wait to show you off on the red carpet."

"Aw, Ray, I don't know how to thank you. Richard said this was really, really expensive. And you never paused one second when—"

"Hush, Glory girl. I'd do anything for you. Got it?" Ray jerked off his shirt, stepped out of his jeans, then climbed into bed. As usual he was totally unconcerned that he wore only his underwear. "Now, drink your stuff and put on your gown. I feel daylight coming and you don't have a minute to spare."

I did what he said, but, for once, I didn't feel the sun in my bones. At all. Weird. I drank Ian's potion, brushed my teeth, even cleaned my face and tried some of the free hotel samples in the basket next to the sink. Finally I slipped on the gown I'd left hanging on a hook on the back of the bathroom door.

I heard the hall door open and close, then the TV go on. So that meant Valdez and Brittany were back from breakfast. There was a small window in the bathroom and I realized I could see light around the edges of the heavy curtains. Weird. Streetlights this high up?

I walked back into the bedroom and saw Ray dead to the world. Not moving. The death sleep, as Ian called it. And I was wide-awake. I went back to the window and lifted the curtain. The sun was coming up. I dropped the curtain and jumped back.

Holy shit. I was awake and it was daylight. What did this mean?

Twelve

"**Valdez**, come here!" I opened the door to the living room a crack. Of course Brittany heard me too. She was on her feet in a flash.

"What the hell?" She glanced at the morning light streaming in from the open curtains at the French doors.

"*Close the drapes!*" Valdez jumped off the couch. "*Hurry. Glory, get back in the bedroom.*" He ran to my side. "*You're wide-awake.*"

"No shit, Sherlock." I managed a smile. "Isn't that what you said to me yesterday?"

"*Yes. Now I'm wondering what the hell is going on.*" He glanced at the bed. Of course Ray hadn't moved.

"I don't know *what's* going on." I sat on the edge of the bed, my side, and looked at Ray again. "I should be out. Dead. Instead I'm talking to you. Still alive. Unless this is a dream." I held out my arm. "Pinch me. Hard. But not hard enough to leave a bruise in case I don't heal again. I've got that fitting tomorrow. I mean tonight. Guess my arms will show."

"*Lie back. You're babbling.*" Valdez gave me a gentle head-butt. "*I can't pinch you, Glory. Paws, not fingers, right now. I put on jeans before I shifted this time, though. In case I have to carry you back to bed later."* He shook his head. *"Figured it was better for our relationship to go for a little modesty."*

"Too bad." I was finally feeling the sun. "You'll tell me later if we really had this conversation. Right?" My eyelids started to droop.

"Maybe." He pushed his head under my hand. *"You're still warm, not cool like you should be. I don't like this one damned bit. I wonder what would have happened if you'd stepped into the sun out there."*

"Don't know. Might have fried." I yawned. "Tired. Hope . . . don't dream."

I was running. Down a beach. The water was a beautiful turquoise, but the sand felt hard under my feet, and hot. Ouch! I had to keep running, though. Couldn't rest because they were chasing me. The Campbells. They wore plaid and carried broadswords, old-fashioned cudgels and laptops. The laird screamed a battle cry, then threw a BlackBerry at me. It hit me between my shoulder blades. I staggered but didn't go down. Had to keep running.

"Traitor!" Mag suddenly appeared in front of me. She wore a beautiful gold dress and started posing for pictures. The paparazzi loved her and the flashes blinded me for a moment. Beside her, Mara, her breasts hanging out of a low-cut red dress, smirked at me. Mara's dress looked just like mine except hers was a size zero, mine a six. I'd never get that skinny.

Mag pointed at me. "Get away from here, bitch! Forget the red carpet. Israel Caine will take Mara to the ball."

"Ball? It's not a ball, old woman. You've been reading too many fairy tales. It's the Grammys. Ray's going to win an award. He's up for best vocal by a duo." I dodged a printer, then caught a broadsword that missed me by inches. I used it to slash a *G* in the front of Mara's dress.

"My beautiful dress. You ruined it. You jealous commoner! No handsome man would ever want to be seen with you on his arm." Mara sobbed and Mag patted her back.

"She's right, you know. You could weigh ninety-eight pounds and you wouldn't be thin enough for the tabloids, you chunky monkey." Mag screeched and ran, dragging Mara with her, when Ian MacDonald and his surfers scrambled out of the sand dunes and surrounded me. They faced off against the Campbells.

"Send out the Campbell heir." Ian held me against him. "We have his woman."

"Hah! That's not *my* woman. My woman has curves! That one is all sticks and stones." Jerry tossed a monitor at my face and it burned my cheek. "Keep her, MacDonald. Both of you can walk into the sun. It's what you deserve. Come on, Da. They're not worth the trouble."

"Jerry, wait!" I sat up. I held my hand to my throbbing cheek where I'd been hit.

"Damn it, Glory, I'm sorry. I didn't get to you soon enough." Valdez frowned down at me. "I never thought you'd get up again so soon."

"I—I got up again?"

"Afraid so. And I wasn't there for you. Brittany was on her way out the door and threatening to tell Ray you stayed awake past sunrise. I followed her into the hall, trying to talk her out of spilling the beans because I knew you wouldn't want him to know." Rafe sat next to me on the bed. "Just after I shut the door, I heard you scream. You'd walked into the living room and a ray of sunlight hit you. It burned your skin." He pulled my hand from my face. "Shit. Guess it's true what they say about vampires. I don't care what Mac-Donald claims—you guys can't handle the sun. That video was bogus."

I shuddered. If I'd made it all the way to the balcony . . .

"How does it look?" I gingerly touched my face. There was a raised blister more than an inch long and it hurt like hell. "It feels horrible. Bring me Ian's invention. I have to see."

"It'll heal, won't it?" He reluctantly got up and brought me the webcam. He did have on jeans, old worn ones that hugged his butt. No shirt or shoes, but I guess the fewer clothes the better when you're stuck in a dog body for hours on end.

"I sure as hell hope so." I grabbed the "mirror" but Rafe put his hand over mine.

"Don't look yet. Let it heal first. You've got to try to sleep again. I won't leave you for a minute this time. I'll stay right here on the floor next to the bed. You'll have to step on me to get out."

"That's not fair to you, Rafe." I teared up. This must be bad. "I'm looking anyway. I have to know." I turned on the device and peeked. Hideous. I had an ugly red streak down the left side of my face. Obviously the drapes had been open just an inch or two, but that had been enough to sear me. I probed the blistered skin carefully with a fingertip. How could I be seen on TV like this?

"Does it hurt?" He stood and walked into the bathroom, returning with a tube from the basket of freebies there.

"Like hell. I hope the TV show's makeup artist is genius enough to cover this if I don't heal in my sleep." I shuddered. "I've seen enough." I hit the off button and shut the webcam. "What's that?"

"Aloe. I figure if you're reacting like a mortal these days, might as well try a mortal treatment. Smear some on and see if that takes the sting out." He held it out to me.

"Thanks, Rafe. Will you do it for me?" I tried to think about the implications of what had just happened. I was staying awake during the day. Rafe thought Ian's video had been a fake, but MacDonald had warned us that direct rays of sunlight were dangerous. We could only *watch* the day from safely inside somewhere. Or, like Ian, from under a cabana.

Ray would love that. And now he'd get the scoop. Rafe was charming, but Brittany was bound to tell the man who signed her paychecks about my early-morning adventure. Well, why not? As long as Ray had guards to keep him from sleepwalking into a fiery death, he may as well try the daylight drug. But would it work like it should? My diet drug had proved to be unpredictable as hell.

Now I was mad. I didn't sign up for this. I was just supposed to lose some weight. Why was this other stuff happening?

Maybe I *should* encourage Jerry and the Campbells to wipe Ian MacDonald and his weird supplements off the face of the earth. If Valdez hadn't been here . . .

I shuddered again and closed my eyes. Rafe's fingers touched my skin as he gently rubbed the ointment on my face. I sighed and relaxed against my pillow.

"Does that help?" His deep voice reminded me that he was still in human form. He sounded slightly different, more growly, when he took on his dog persona.

"Yes, thanks." I opened my eyes and saw his concern. Funny how his warm brown eyes could be looking at me from the face of a dog or bat or whatever, yet I always saw the same intense loyalty and caring there. I reached for his hand and squeezed his strong fingers.

"Listen, Rafe, don't let this come between you and Brittany. She's just doing her job. I know where her loyalty has to lie."

"And she knows who I'm loyal to. Always." Rafe set the ointment on the bedside table. "Brit and I have different priorities. Our relationship amounts to nothing but some fun and games when we have the time, which is rarely." He shrugged, muscles rippling across his broad shoulders. "I let that relationship get in the way of my job and it almost cost you your life, Glory. Maybe you'd be better off with another bodyguard, someone who's more focused, more professional."

"I don't want anyone else." I sat up and slipped my hand

from his. "We've been through too much together. Besides, I don't see how you can take any blame here. You had no idea I was going to get up."

"Why not? You got up before. I knew that and should have been ready." He got up and paced restlessly around the room, shoving his hands into his pockets. Oops, shouldn't have done that. Those jeans were barely hanging on. I forced myself to concentrate on what he was saying.

"Instead I took advantage of Brit's night off. Invited her to hang out. If she hadn't been here with me, she wouldn't have seen you sleepwalking. Now you'll have to deal with Caine wanting to try MacDonald's daylight drug. Clearly I need to focus on what's important now. Brittany's a distraction I can't afford."

"It doesn't seem fair. You deserve a life too, you know." And I'm sure Brittany had been happy to hang out with this man who prowled around the room while I held my breath, hoping gravity would do a number on those worn jeans. Can you blame me?

He had the same handsome good looks of the Latin pop star who'd stopped by the suite one night. Put a guitar in Rafe's hands and he could take over the South American market.

I was pretty sure that when both guards knew their vampires truly slept like the undead, they shifted into whatever form they liked for their mutual satisfaction. The very thought made me sigh. I realized Rafe had stopped pacing and stared at me.

"What?"

"Sleepy yet?"

"No. And I want you to quit beating yourself up over what happened tonight. You have a tough job, Rafe. I'm sure you'll be glad when your contract is up and you can move on to something else." I smiled. "I'll never be able to thank you enough for the five years you've given me. I hope you know our friendship goes way beyond this bodyguard thing."

"Sure. It's been fun. And scary and, well, not dull anyway." He grinned, his dimples showing as he stopped by my side of the bed again. "With you I've always felt like the straight man in one of those stoner films. Can't wait to see what crazy thing you'll get us into next, Glory."

"Aw, come on, now. Surely I haven't been that bad." I hit his hard thigh.

"Not always. Lately you've been taking charge of your own life. Using your powers. Not letting guys like Blade or that boyfriend you had in Vegas take advantage of your good nature. High time, I'd say." He stared at me, not smiling. "You know what I mean?"

"Yes. Guess I'm finally figuring out who I am." I'd wasted a lot of years pretending I was a mortal who happened to have fangs and a liquid diet when I had the potential to be so much more. And a lot of years clinging to some old Glory ways that included dependency issues. Still had some of those. Which was why Jerry thought he needed to provide guys like Rafe for my protection. Lucky for me if today was an example.

Rafe stretched. "You need to sleep. And I wasn't kidding about being right here on the floor. It's no hardship for me. I'm used to it. I may even sleep myself knowing you can't get loose and do yourself any more harm." He walked over to the door and turned the lock. "I'm locking you in. I'll hear you if you somehow get off the foot of the bed or over Caine on the other side and try to make a break for it."

"Wow, you must really think I want to roam."

"I don't know what you want, Glory St. Clair. And that's a fact." His smile was a little off center, then—boom!—he turned back into Valdez the dog.

I pulled up the covers and snuggled down, desperate to sleep, to heal. Tomorrow night was going to be big for me. But I lay there for a long while listening to my bodyguard breathing on the floor beside me. The throbbing in my cheek reminded me why I needed him there. He did make me feel completely safe. I just wondered why Valdez had never shown up in my dreams. What did that mean?

• • •

I woke with a jolt and took stock. No aches, no pains. Hey, I actually felt like the old Glory. Refreshed. Full of energy. A quick look in the webcam assured me that my face had healed. Yes! I ran to weigh in and had kept the weight off. Even better.

I shampooed my hair again and blew it dry this time. I knew the stylist for the show would do more with it, but at least it would be ready for her to work with. I sniffed the new concoction Ian had left and decided not to chance it. Maybe after the crew from the show left.

Ray headed out soon after he got up. More rehearsals and an appearance on a talk show. It had been tough getting even one gig, when some of Ray's competition were doing them nonstop. Most of the shows taped during the day and Nathan had been getting flack from Barry over that problem. I'd had to listen to Ray's complaints while he got ready. I didn't mention the daylight drug. We were both in a hurry. That was my excuse anyway.

"They're here, Glory." Barry's assistant, Bethany, rushed in, bringing the hairstylist and makeup artist with her. "Thirty minutes, people. This is so exciting. Glory, wait till you see the designs! You'll freak."

"In a good way or bad, Beth?"

"I'll never tell." She giggled and rushed back out to the living room, slamming the bedroom door behind her.

I turned myself over to the two professionals, making excuses why I didn't want to look in the mirror when they were done. By the time I walked out to the living room, my stomach was knotted, but this time it was nerves and not from exercise.

My cell rang just as I was ready for the first fitting.

"Hello." I made a face at the exasperated producer who kept pointing to his watch.

"Glory, are you coming out here tonight or do you need for me to come to you again? Ian can't make it, but I can bring the supplements with me." Trina sounded her usual happy self. "I hope your friend Flo won't be there. She doesn't like me."

"Uh, I'm in the middle of something." I looked at the producer. "What time will we be finished here?"

"I have no idea, Ms. St. Clair." He looked significantly at my phone. "Depends on how many interruptions we have to endure."

"Come here and make it late. Do your run first. I can't go with you. Too much happening here. Make it about four thirty. Got to go." I hung up and realized I could actually afford to lose a few more pounds before the big night. Sweet. I heard the producer clear his throat. "I'm turning off my cell now." I smiled. "So sorry about that."

"Four thirty. Do you ever sleep?" The makeup artist brushed some powder on my chin and forehead. "Guess so. You're glowing." She smiled. "Glory's good to go."

"All right, people, let's roll."

Zia swept in and looked me over. "What's happened to you, Glory? Those are skinny jeans."

I laughed and felt my cheeks go warm. "I've been dieting, Zia."

"So you said. But you've lost so much so fast." Zia put her hand on my elbow and turned me around. "What's your secret?"

By the time I'd made a full circle, I realized they'd started filming. "I've been working really hard. And I've had a doctor's supervision."

"Oh, of course. There are many wonderful doctors in L.A., aren't there, Glory?" Zia would've raised her eyebrows but she'd obviously been freshly Botoxed. "I'm sure our audience would love for you to name names. He's obviously very . . . skilled." She was smirking.

"I told you it was a diet, Zia, no surgery involved. Isn't it time for me to see my dresses?" I looked longingly toward the hall where I knew they'd stashed the three designers.

"Cut. She's right. Let's set up for those shots." The director began issuing orders to rearrange the living room.

The plan was for me to look over each designer's offering, then try it on in the bedroom. I would emerge and there would be a fitting along with my overall impressions. It was decided that I would sit in a club chair in front of the balcony doors. Someone rolled in an empty rack to hang the dress and accessories on and naturally they brought in the dreaded mirror.

"Can I ask a favor?" I gestured for a producer to come over.

"What is it, Glory? Do you need a water?" The producer snapped his fingers and three assistants scurried to his side.

"No, no, it's just that I don't like the mirror."

"Why?" The producer looked puzzled. "Isn't it big enough?" He frowned at the group and they all groaned. "Where did you get this piece of crap?"

"No, not that. It's fine, but it seems so cliché, don't you see? I'd rather just look at the dress on the rack, try it on and feel it on me, then look into the camera and say what I think. Tomorrow night maybe we can bring Ray in to help with the final decision. I could do a kind of runway turn for him." I prayed Ray would do it. He'd been hungry for media exposure. Maybe this would help make up for those lost opportunities on the talk show circuit.

Zia was suddenly interested in me again.

"Israel Caine would help make the decision?" Her eyes lit up. "Do whatever she says, Lee."

"Lose the mirror. Hurry." The producer looked around to assure himself that everything was in place. "Okay, let's go."

"Melanie! You're up!" an assistant yelled.

Melanie came rushing in with a garment bag and a large tote. She hung up the bag, then started unloading a pair of shoes, an evening bag and jewelry. Finally, she unzipped the bag and pulled out the dress.

I sat back and stared. Okay. For starters it was blue. I love blue. Good choice. Low cut. Another smart decision. Some kind of sheer printed material filled in the space between the breasts and formed the long sleeves. Strange, but I could deal with it. Then there were the gold beaded and embroidered shoulder pads, perfect for a linebacker who liked bling on his uniform. Melanie had obviously been inspired by the recent Super Bowl.

She'd cinched in the waist with a wide belt with the buckle in the shape of a star. Okay, Ray is a star. Nice message but the belt was too big, of course. Gold stars marched down the front of the skirt to the hem. I figured this was designed to make me look taller and slimmer. I was going to try it on, obviously. But I wasn't sure about it. At all.

I smiled and commented on what I liked. Then Melanie carried it to the bedroom. An assistant helped me into it. It was too big everywhere. Yay! But that meant that my boobs were pretty well exposed and I had to go out for the cameras. Melanie started wringing her hands and muttering when I emerged.

"I'm sorry, Melanie, but I've been dieting. Obviously you're going to have to take it in a few inches." I hid a smile, not a bit sorry, as I held the front together enough for modesty.

The crew grinned when they realized they were going to have to bleep some of Melanie's comments.

"I can't believe you lost so much weight in four days. What kind of shit have you been smokin', lady?" She flushed when she remembered I was the judge. "Uh, I mean, you look great. Wish I could lose that fast." She whipped out a pin cushion and started pinning. "No problem, I can fix this." More muttering. "What do you think about the shoulder pads? I took a risk there."

"Yes, they're, uh, different." I reached up and felt them. They crunched. What had she stuffed them with? Foam peanuts?

Tears filled her eyes. "You hate them."

"I didn't say that. I think they probably make my waist look smaller. And Ray will appreciate the star motif." I winced when she jabbed me with a pin under one arm. "Uh, I'll be letting him help me decide the winner."

"Oh, wow, Israel Caine. Maybe I need more stars." Jab,

jab. Melanie wiped her eyes. "Does he like football? This was kind of an homage to the game." She pointed to the shoulders in case I didn't get it.

"Loves it. Never misses a game on TV. He and the band are addicted." I smiled into the camera, then realized how that could be taken out of context and show up on a tabloid cover. "To football. Sports of all kinds, but they love football. We had a great Super Bowl party back in Austin."

"Yeah, well, bigger shoulders and your waist will look freakin' *tiny* by comparison." Melanie held out the shoulders and squinted at me. "But might be too much."

"You're the designer." I had visions of having to turn sideways to get through doors. "Thanks, Melanie. Guess I'd better get out of this and see what Butch has come up with now. Good luck." I picked up the skirt.

"Wait!" Melanie darted around in front of me. "When the sleeves and bodice are tight, you'll see what I was trying to do with the sheer printed fabric." She sighed. "Oh well, just wait till tomorrow night. It'll be a surprise."

"Great. Can't wait." I walked carefully to the bedroom, pins stabbing me every step of the way. I did love the silver sandals that had a designer label and fit like a dream. The earrings and necklace were great too. I should have mentioned those things. Oh, well, I'd do better for designer number two on the accessories. I got back into my clothes, my wonderful size-six skinny jeans, and headed back to the club chair.

Butch came in next. He was practically skipping, he was so excited, and I suspected he was on something other than just adrenaline.

"Glory, oh, stand up, lady. Look at you. What have you done?" He turned me around so the camera could get a good shot. "You've been dieting, you bad girl. I'll have to take in this fabulous dress."

I couldn't stop grinning. "Afraid so. But this is a big event for me, Butch, so I've been working hard to get in shape."

"I can see that, girlfriend. So I won't mind taking a tuck here and there one little bit." He whipped the cover off his dress, then let me look my fill while he pulled out shoes, bag and accessories.

"Wow." I was almost speechless. Butch had chosen black for me, my favorite color when I'm trying to look skinny. Now that I was a six, I'd look positively waiflike in it. Hmm. Not a bad thought. This black dress was made of a sheer chiffon over nude lace that plunged front and back. The thin straps were rhinestone. Too bad the whole thing looked like a naughty nightie for a circus elephant. My new, slim body would be lost in the yards and yards of fabric.

"Black is good. I have a lot of black in my wardrobe." I turned. Uh-oh. My lack of enthusiasm had crushed his spirit. "Let me try it on. I want to feel how it moves."

"Thanks, Glory. Give it a chance. I believe it will make you feel like the beautiful woman you are." He carried the dress to the bedroom where he had a brief discussion with the assistant because apparently it was hard to tell the front from the back of his creation. I did like the way the dress felt. The fabric floated away from my body and rhinestone tassels dangled from the deep vee at the neckline and moved when I walked.

"Love the shoes." I stepped outside and walked over to the windows. They were rhinestone sandals. "And the bag." A vintage silver clutch that I would have liked to sell in my shop.

"But it's huge on you." He sniffled and wiped his eyes, then pulled out some jewelry. "I hope you like what I arranged for you to have from a famous Hollywood jeweler to go with the dress." Butch put a fabulous sapphire and diamond drop around my neck and matching sapphire earrings in my ears.

"Oh, wow!" I felt like a princess. I really, really wished for Ian's "mirror." "I'll definitely keep all this in mind. But, you're right—it's too big, Butch." I held the blousy fabric away from my body. "Uh, everywhere."

"I can take it in." He started rooting around in his bag.

"I'll be honest, Butch. I'm just not sure it's new. Something I haven't seen before."

"No!" He turned around, a giant pair of scissors in his hand, and aimed them straight at my heart.

A blur of fur flew through the air and knocked him on his butt. The scissors landed on the carpet a few feet away.

"Help!" Butch screamed when Valdez sat on his chest, growling and snapping an inch from his nose.

I held my breath, afraid my bodyguard was going to start asking questions. I grabbed the scissors.

"Butch, are you okay?" Stupid question. The designer sobbed and had covered his face with both hands. "Valdez, no!"

No one else in the room moved. Well, except for Zia, who'd hopped on the couch and had pushed three assistants in front of her like a human fence. She held two of them by their hair.

"This is why I have a cat, Glory." She wobbled and almost went over the back of the couch.

I ignored her and her poor assistants' screeches of pain and pulled on Valdez's collar, but he wasn't ready to move. "Animal instinct, Butch. Valdez must have thought you were threatening me with these scissors. What were you going to do with them?"

Butch finally peeked between two fingers. "Can't . . . breathe."

Of course no one else had the nerve to get near Valdez, not when he barked and snapped again, this time drawing blood when his teeth grazed Butch's fingers. I felt my fangs swell and had to fight the feeling. So not the time for that. Too bad Butch had a tasty type. *Down, Glory.*

"Oh, my God!" Butch wailed from behind his hands. "He's going to eat me."

"Someone call 911!" Zia clearly was antidog. "Or animal control."

I wanted to give her a look that should have melted the lacquer off her manicured nails but had to admit my guy was overreacting. Please. Butch as vampire slayer? I don't think so.

"Calm down, Zia. I'm handling this. Seriously, do not call anyone. Or this show will not go on." I swept the room with an icy stare and heard several cell phones snap shut. "Thank you." I turned back to my problem child. I'd already sent him a mental message to back off, which he'd ignored. Apparently he wanted his TV moment.

"Damn it, Valdez, get off of him!" I gave his collar a serious jerk.

"Ooo!" The crowd was impressed when V stepped back. Of course he just had to put his foot down where it would inflict maximum pain and Butch shrieked, rolling to his side and into the fetal position as soon as he was free.

"Butch, the scissors?" I finally noticed the red light that meant the camera was on. Of course this was too good to miss.

"C-c-culottes." Butch whimpered.

"What?" I shoved Valdez behind me and knelt beside the designer.

"I thought if I cut the skirt and t-t-turned it into culottes it would be f-f-fresh." Sob. "And added a belt." More sobbing.

"Culottes! Brilliant. Yes, I could go for those." I patted his shoulder and eventually got him up and on his feet. Camera still rolling. But someone would have to do some serious editing or this would end up a two-hour special instead of the usual hour show. It took two assistants to get Butch out to the hallway. Especially when he finally calmed down enough to ask for his scissors back. That request sent Valdez into another barking frenzy.

I passed them to a woman, obviously one of Zia's victims, whose ponytail looked a lot worse for wear. "Tell Butch to leave them at home when he comes back." I glanced at Valdez, who'd managed to keep one of Butch's shoes and was ripping the sole off of it. "Please tell Butch to send me a bill for a new pair of shoes." I grimaced for the ever-present camera. "Valdez is usually so well behaved. I'm thinking it must be something he ate." I frowned at V. "We've been spoiling him. Ordering from room service. He needs a more restricted diet."

"I'm thinking a muzzle." Zia eased behind the couch when Valdez growled. "Now, let's get a move on people. Where's the next victim—er, I mean designer?"

Darren strode in with his garment bag and a small suitcase. "You know, I'm kind of scared to come in here. Butch is out there crying and carrying on about how the dog ate his shoe and nearly took his arm off." He stopped dead when he saw me and frowned. "Whoa, Glory. Didn't anyone tell you you're not allowed to change during the production of this show?"

"No." I grinned because he looked so serious. "And, relax. Unless you plan to attack me, Valdez won't bother you."

He grinned back. "No, I'm not that stupid. I know who's doing the judging. You're looking great, by the way. But you just blew my design all to hell. I'm going to be up all night fixing this thing because the fit is very important." He sighed and hung up his bag. "Take a look."

I really wanted to like it because I liked Darren. But he'd picked red. Now, I love red. But it had two strikes against it. First, I'd had that nightmare and Mara and I'd both been in red dresses. Second, and the real reason not to pick red, it's a red carpet. Hello? I do not want to disappear into the carpet. Or worse, be just a shade off. You know? You have to be contrasting or complementing the carpet, not part of the stupid thing.

The dress was beautiful. Red silk, again cut low because Ray had made a big deal about showing off my assets. The shimmer and shine almost made up for the color choice. And the way the dress would hug my new smaller curves would be a thing of beauty. Too bad I simply couldn't see myself in that dress. I said nice things, though. Loved the shoes and bag he'd picked. And laughed when I found out that Butch wasn't the only one with the genuine jewels from a Hollywood jeweler. It was a deal with all the designers that they were on loan for the event.

Finally, we were done and the designers hurried back to their studio to do the alterations. The film crew was packing up when the curtains parted and a production assistant screamed.

"Who the hell is that and where did he come from?" The producer picked up a light stand like he was prepared to defend me from a cat burglar. "Why isn't the dog attacking him?"

"Relax, folks. This is a friend of ours. We have adjoining balconies." I walked over and smiled at a glowering Jerry. Valdez was right beside me as he'd been most of the night.

"I didn't think—"

"You're not paid to think, Daphne. Just finish packing and let's get out of here. We're already over budget with all this night shooting. No more overtime this month. Got it?" The producer shooed the group to the door. "Thanks, Ms. St. Clair. We'll see you tomorrow night for the big finish. Be sure Mr. Caine is here. Eight o'clock sharp."

"Right." I crossed my fingers. I'd have to make sure that happened. I hadn't even checked Ray's schedule yet. Finally the last of them left and I shut the door.

"Well, Jerry, that was a dramatic entrance. You scared that poor girl to death."

"Your cell phone was off." Jerry looked around. I had a feeling that any stray mortal would be sorry.

"Had no choice. We were filming." I sighed and sat again, then kicked off my shoes.

"Still hurting?" He squatted down and picked up my foot. "Need a foot rub?"

"I wouldn't turn one down. But I actually healed last night. I'm okay." I smiled when he massaged the ball of my foot. "Mmm, that's wonderful. Do the other one too."

"It's those damned high heels." He switched feet.

"Yes, but they're sexy, aren't they?" I wiggled my toes.

"Yes, but so are your bare feet." He dropped my foot and stood. "Are you seeing MacDonald tonight?"

So much for the niceties. "No, just his mortal. She should be here in"—I glanced at my watch—"about half an hour."

"Are you still drinking MacDonald's swill?" Jerry paced around the piano, then walked over to pull open the drapes.

"I drank the bedtime stuff, but not the new one he gave me for when I wake up. I was thinking of drinking it now."

He turned around and looked at me. "Don't. Brittany gave Flo that syringe that Ian tried to use on you last night. Richard's having it analyzed."

"I'm sure it's fine, Jerry." I slipped on my shoes and stood.

"You are? Why? Because everything he's given you has made you feel so fine?" Jerry frowned at me. "Richard took it to the Council here. They have excellent facilities on call and they're very interested now in MacDonald's operation."

"Just because he's a MacDonald . . ."

"He might have killed you, Glory. You have no idea what the syringe might have held."

"Are you listening to yourself, Jerry? If Ian wanted me dead, I'd be dead. Valdez knocked it out of his hand but, FYI, I wasn't going to let him give me a shot anyway." I sat down and stared at my bodyguard. "Appreciated the gesture, though."

"I should have killed him when I had the chance. All these reactions you've been having to his shit, it's only going one way, Glory. Maybe MacDonald wants your death to look like an accident. You're heading for suicide by sunlight, lady. You know it and I know it." Valdez looked up at me.

"What the hell do you mean?" Jerry sat beside me.

"Yes, I'd like to know the answer to that." Ray stood inside the hall door. "Brittany told me you've been waking up during the day. How is that happening, Glory?"

I looked from Jerry to Ray and back again. Obviously I was going to have to tell them both about my sleepwalking or whatever you wanted to call it. One of them was going to start his "Kill Ian" campaign and the other would rush out there and pay Ian a fortune for a chance at his own suicide by sunlight.

Oh, God, if ever there was a lose-lose situation, this was it.

Thirteen

"It has to do with the bedtime supplement I take, I guess."
I looked everywhere but at the men in my life. I was tired
and my feet still ached. Jerry and Ray had opened bottles of
synthetic blood. I'd turned it down. Trina was coming. The
fact that she'd been my only source for the last few days
made me feel rotten. I normally didn't drink from mortals,
even willing ones. And I still had the problem of saving her
from Ian. Treating mortals as disposable commodities didn't
necessarily make Ian any worse than most vampires, though.
Unfortunately.

"Glory, are you going to talk or do you want me to just
go on out there and see what MacDonald's selling?" Ray was
practically jumping out of his skin. Of course he was desperate to see the sun again. He'd only been a vampire for a few
months. Jerry and I had had centuries to get used to life after
dark.

"I wouldn't do that if I were you, Caine." Jerry sounded
like he was talking to an unruly schoolboy.

"I don't follow your orders, Blade." Ray pulled me up to
stand beside him. "And neither does Glory." He squeezed
my hand. "Look at her. Ian's formula works. She's lost the

weight she wanted in record time. I'd say he delivers on his promises."

Jerry gave Ray a condescending look. "There's a hell of a lot of difference between losing weight and walking into daylight. Valdez, tell us what Glory did yesterday afternoon."

Valdez risked his job by looking at me before he answered.

"Go ahead, V, tell him. Tell him *all* the stuff I did when I was supposed to be dead to the world." I held Ray's hand because Jerry looked as approachable as a thorny hedge.

"You know she was having those nightmares. They led to sleepwalking. The first night I caught her as she was heading into the living room, eyes closed, obviously out of it. I shifted and carried her back to bed. She didn't wake up until her head hit the pillow."

"You shifted." Jerry frowned.

"How else was he going to carry me, Jerry?" This pissed me off. "It's about time you got over this dog fetish you've had for centuries. If you don't trust me around hot guys, then tough." I smiled at Valdez. "Yes, my friend, you're hot. Don't pretend you don't know that, the way Brittany hangs around you."

"Can we get back to this sleepwalking?" Jerry looked like he wanted to smash the bottle he'd just drained over someone's head—there were several likely candidates, me included. Instead he set it on the bar, demonstrating admirable self-control.

"Yeah. I want to hear about yesterday. When Brittany saw you wide-awake after sunrise." Ray dropped my hand.

"I can tell this part. I *was* awake, you know." I cleared my throat, wishing I could drink something. No, couldn't do it, calories. So I faced the men, Jerry looking disapproving and Ray, eager, like I was about to launch into the tale of the century.

"I watched you lie down, Ray, then I headed into the bathroom to brush my teeth. I took my time until I noticed some light coming in around the curtains in the bathroom. I checked and saw you conked out per usual." I glanced at Valdez. "Rafe's right. When we're asleep during the day, we're as good as dead. First time I've seen that. Guess I never stuck around to watch you sleep before you made me vampire, Jerry." I shook my head. Stupid of me, to make the decision to become vamp without full disclosure. Hindsight. Not worth anything, was it?

"No, I wouldn't let you. We're too vulnerable then. And in those days I still slept in a coffin behind a locked door in a hidden room in the basement of our town house or a cave in the country. I didn't want to scare you away." He frowned when Ray made a noise. "You have something to say, Caine?"

"Sure, but not right now. I want to hear about Glory's experience." Ray sat on the opposite end of the couch from Jerry and leaned forward, his eyes on me. "So then what happened?"

"I realized I was wide-awake and the sun had already come up. That's when I signaled to Valdez in the living room."

"Why?" Jerry frowned at my bodyguard.

"To talk it over, I guess. Who else am I going to call? You?" I toed off my shoes again, stalked over to the club chair on the opposite side of the room and sat. "All my other friends are vampires. They'd be dead that time of day. Rafe wasn't. Of course neither was Brittany."

"Shape-shifters. Lucky bastards." Ray frowned at Valdez. "Glory, I'm thinking whatever Ian's giving you at bedtime must be like what he's developed to get vampires out during the day."

"*That's not all that happened, though.*" Valdez settled next to my chair. Like we'd drawn up sides. "*She eventually got drowsy and fell asleep. I waited a minute to be sure she was out, then went to talk to Brittany.*" He nodded toward Ray. "*I knew Glory didn't want Caine to know about this daylight thing and tried to talk Brit out of telling him about it until we knew more. I was coming in from the hall when I heard Glory scream.*"

"What?" Ray and Blade were both on their feet.

"Calm down. I'm here. I'm okay. Crisis averted. See?" I leaned back and crossed my legs, refusing to let them upset me.

"What crisis?" Jerry didn't sit down. Ray paced the carpet again, kicking my high heels out of the way.

"Hey! Watch the shoes!"

"Sorry. So what happened, Glory?" Ray finally stopped.

"I'll tell it." Valdez moved away from me. Like he wasn't going to use me for protection. *"She apparently had another nightmare right away and walked back into the living room. We'd shut the drapes when she stuck her head out the first time, but there was a sliver of sunlight. She stepped into it and burned her cheek."*

"Son of a bitch!" Jerry slammed a fist into the palm of his other hand. I had a feeling he was imagining Ian's face there.

Ray came up and put his hand under my chin to inspect my cheek. "Looks fine now. Makeup or did you heal?"

"I healed. Though Rafe put some mortal cream on my face too, as a precaution." I frowned at Ray. "Listen to me, Ray. I was burned by the sun. Do you see what this means?"

"Yeah. You can be awake, but you can't go out in it. He told me that when I went out to his place last night." Ray pulled me to my feet. "Did you see the video he has?"

"You went out there without backup?" I wanted to scream. He'd left both paranormal guards with me.

"I'm fine. I'm here, right?" He sneered at Jerry. "Blade's the one who's demonized MacDonald. The guy's not stupid; he's into this to make some cash. Killing off clients, especially someone high profile like me, would mean the end of his business." Ray smiled at me. "I told Nate where I was going. In case something did happen out there. But I didn't tell you, because I know you don't approve of this daylight deal. Imagine, Glory. I saw Ian on the beach in front of his house." Ray's eyes lit up and he hugged me. "I tell you, if I could do that, I could deal with this vampire thing."

"Get real, Caine. You're going to have to deal with this

vampire thing anyway." Jerry stalked over to the window and stared out at the night sky. "Seeing daylight is a foolish dream. You think all of us haven't had it at one time or another? I lost a good friend who tried for it. The Energy Vampires have been working on it for years and failed. It's a fairy tale that's cost more than one vampire his fortune and his life."

"This is the twenty-first century, Blade. You don't sleep in a coffin or a cave anymore. So maybe it's possible that MacDonald could have found a cure for the daylight problem." Ray let me go and actually had the stones to walk over to Jerry, close enough to get a face full of fist. "You're prejudiced against him because of his name, but that doesn't mean Ian isn't some kind of genius who could have figured this thing out."

Jerry smiled at Ray. That smile chilled me to my toes. "Fine. Rush out there and try MacDonald's daylight drug. The sooner the better. Good luck to you."

"Jerry!" I ran over to step between the two men. I knew an almost death threat when I heard one. "Ray, this daylight experiment will have to wait. We've already got more on our plate now than we can deal with. I'm afraid I committed you to something without asking about your schedule first. I need you to be here tomorrow night for the taping of the finale of *Designed to Kill*. It'll be great media exposure for you. So can you please, please, please help me pick a winning gown for the red carpet?"

"Of course he can. He's well qualified to judge a fashion show." Jerry stuck his hands in his pockets. To look at him, you'd think he could judge one too. Tonight he wore designer jeans that had been scrubbed and bleached to a fine, worn look. Obviously more of Flo's shopping handiwork because Jerry didn't have a clue about style. He was more about comfort and tradition. Not that he ever looked shabby.

Tonight even his T-shirt was trendy. It stretched over his broad shoulders, showing them off in fine form. He could have fit in with a rock band himself if I didn't know he had the musical ability of a lump of coal. The thought made me smile. Until I saw Ray's face flush and his muscles tense like he was about to lunge.

"Stop it, Jerry. I know you're trying to pick a fight and I won't have it." I turned to Ray. "What do you say, Ray? This will be great publicity. You can imagine how excited Zia was when I pitched the idea. Please tell me you can fit it into your schedule." I took his arm. "You know I value your opinion on what looks good on me." I sent Jerry a mental message to please cut me a break here. "You too, Jerry, but this is part of the Grammy thing. I'm sure you understand."

Jerry glowered, obviously not ready to concede anything.

"Sure, Glory, whatever makes you happy." Ray slid his arm around my waist. "We also need to remind the public that we're engaged. After the taping, you have to come with me to a couple of parties. The big-deal pre-Grammy blow-outs. One of them is thrown by my record label. It's a command performance." He shot Jerry a superior smirk. "The tabloids have noticed we haven't been seen together lately. Time to show them we're still hot and heavy before the awards show. That we can't keep our hands off of each other." He ran his hand down to pat my bottom.

I don't know who growled louder, Blade or Valdez. I eased Ray's hand back up to my waist. "Thanks, Ray. They had a mirror set up. Couldn't do that, could I? I had to distract the production crew so I offered you as a way to help make the decision." I looked at Jerry for signs he understood what I was up against here. Not a glimmer. He'd slipped on a mask of indifference. What? This time when Ray pulled me closer and nuzzled my neck, I didn't stop him.

"You can count on me, babe. Besides, I want to show off you and your new body. You look hot. I'm having a dress sent up from the boutique downstairs for the party tomorrow night. It'll work for the show too. The clerk there said you tried it on, but didn't buy it."

"Ray, you shouldn't do that." I'd tried on a ridiculously expensive cocktail dress for the hell of it, egged on by Flo. It was emerald green silk, short and flirty, with the kind of V-neck I loved and a belt to show off my new waistline.

"It's an investment, darlin'. It'll look great on the tabloid covers. When you wear it, they won't be able to say you're springing the baby trap." He kissed my cheek.

"No one reads that trash." Jerry strolled over to the couch and sat again. "Seems a waste of time to pretend to be lovers when Glory is dumping your sorry ass the day after the Grammys."

"Is she? You sure of that?" Ray picked up my left hand where I still wore his ring, the diamond flashing in the light.

"Millions do read the tabloids, Jerry, and it hurts me when I see those mean headlines." I smiled at Ray. "And, Ray, you know our plans."

A knock on the door was a welcome interruption. "That's got to be Trina."

Valdez loped to the door. *"Smells like her. Check through the peephole."*

I looked, then let her in. She was dressed in her usual running outfit.

"Seriously, Glory, don't you want to at least do the stairs?" She was panting. "I did them, but I can do a few more if you want to change. I bet it gives you another five pounds."

"Don't be ridiculous." Jerry shut the hall door behind her. "You're quite thin enough, Gloriana."

Ray stepped close to my other side. "Are you kidding me? If all she has to do is a few flights of stairs, why wouldn't she? Her big night's coming up. When is she going to be on TV all over the world again?" He looked down at my butt, then up at my face. "Five more pounds and you'll have the tabloids printing that mean Israel Caine has been starving you." He grinned and winked. "And your cheekbones! Baby, you're looking more like a supermodel every night."

Okay, I have to admit that would be a dream come true. "I'm doing it. Sit down, Trina. Ray, would you get her a bottle of water from the minibar? I'll be out in a minute." I headed for the bedroom to change.

"Gloriana, you're mad. You do realize this weight will come back when you're off whatever MacDonald's been giving you, don't you?" Jerry followed me into the bedroom and shut the door.

"Thanks for reminding me." I turned on him. "You don't think I'm haunted by that very thought? Hell, Jerry, for the first time in my life I feel thin! Like I have control over my body." I grabbed my shorts and T-shirt from the dresser. "What do you know about it? You've got all the muscles you'll ever need. And you don't have an ounce of fat on you. But I'm not like that." I jerked off my sweater and threw it on the bed.

"This is your fault, you know. I really didn't have a clue what I was getting into when I agreed to let you turn me. I'd have lost the weight first if I'd known." I unhooked my bra, ignoring Jerry's growl. Interest or indignation at the way my words had jabbed him? At the moment I didn't care. I picked the sports bra out of the drawer and slipped it over my breasts. Thank God it was looser now, only mildly viselike.

"I'm sorry if you're having regrets. But it's way too late for them. Besides, you know I've always thought your figure was perfect." Jerry moved close to run his thumb over one abused nipple. "Now, what the hell is that thing you're binding yourself with?" He tried to slip it up to look at my breasts again. "It's too tight."

"Oh, no, you don't. I'm going to exercise. It's a sports bra, keeps me from jiggling." I swatted away his hand and peeled off my skinny jeans. They were still tight and five fewer pounds would make them slide on easily. Oh, yeah.

"I like it when you jiggle." He sat on the side of the bed and watched me step into my shorts.

I'd just sat beside him to put on my socks and running shoes when his cell phone rang.

"Yes? What did you find out? Really? All right, I'll see what I can do. Thank you." He slapped the phone shut.

"Was that Richard?" I tied the first shoe.

"Yes."

"Well? Did he get the test results on the stuff in the syringe?" I stopped, scared to hear what he'd say.

"Yes, it was some kind of vitamin compound. Virtually harmless. Fact is, I don't know what the hell it would do for a vampire." Jerry frowned.

"See? I knew it!" I pulled on the other shoe and tied it. "Ian's a genius. He works with chemicals. Maybe vitamins would help us and we just don't know it. Your hatred for him is irrational, Jerry. It's based on an ancient feud that should have been settled a long time ago." I realized that had probably not been the smart thing to say.

"Gloriana, I don't appreciate that." Jerry followed me when I got up and walked to the door. "Our quarrel with the MacDonalds is based on wrongs they have done us that you know nothing about."

"Anything in the last century or two?" I held up my hand when I could tell he was probably going to start trotting out cattle-stealing misdemeanors. "No, forget I asked. Just tell me if you have one shred of proof that *this* MacDonald is the villain you claim?" I waited before I turned the knob. Ray and Valdez could probably hear through the door. Only mortal Trina would be unaware of our conversation.

"Not yet. But I want you to give me your bedtime supplement. The one that's causing your nightmares and sleep problems. Richard can have that analyzed as well." Jerry put his hands on either side of my head when I leaned against the door. "I'm convinced you could have died today, Gloriana, if I hadn't provided you with a daytime bodyguard."

I looked up at him, knowing what he said was true. I put my hands on his chest and felt the heartbeat that had been with me for so long. Slow but steady.

"I guess you're right, Jerry. No, I *know* you're right. But

I can't give you all of the supplement. Let me pour a small sample into an empty water bottle." I touched his frown. "I need to take it, Jer. Or I won't lose that last bit of weight."

"Damn it to hell, Gloriana. This is ridiculous."

"No, what you mean is *I* am ridiculous. I get that. You don't get *me*. Too bad. This is important to me. I'm doing it. Take it or leave it. Small sample. What's it going to be?"

"And if you try to walk into the sun again?" He grabbed my hand and scraped my palm with one fang. Blood welled up and he licked it clean. "You scare the hell out of me, woman."

"I'm sorry, Jerry, but Valdez is here to take care of me. Let him do his job." I felt the slide of his tongue again and fought the heat that pulsed deep inside me. Sorry, but I found it erotic as hell.

"Right. Shifting into human form. Carrying you to bed. You and Rafael are getting quite chummy, aren't you?"

"We have no choice. He's stuck with me. Now it's worse than ever since I might get up during the day. I'm sure he's exhausted." I made myself jerk my hand free. "I've got to go. Trina's waiting."

"And then you'll feed from her." Jerry followed me into the living room. "She's become your pet, then."

"Just temporarily. She's very generous." I smiled at her. She held one of Ray's new CDs and apparently he'd signed it for her. "When this is over, it's back to synthetics for me. You know that's what I do."

"I'm not sure I know what you do anymore, Gloriana." Jerry turned to Trina. "You have Glory's supplement for tonight?"

"Yes, it's right here." She looked at me, then, at my nod, handed him the bottle.

"I'll take just this much." Jerry poured about an inch into an empty water bottle and screwed on the cap. "Is that satisfactory, Gloriana?"

"Fine. Thanks, Jerry."

"Good night." With a nod, he walked out to the balcony, jammed the bottle into his jeans pocket, then shifted into bird form. He flew off without a sound.

"Wow. You really are popular, Glory." Trina giggled. "Thanks for the CD, Mr. Caine. It's awesome." She managed to cram it into her fanny pack. "Let's go, Glory. It's awfully late. You don't want to get caught by the sun."

"Hey, Trina." Ray approached her and took her arm. "Have you seen Ian outside during daylight hours?"

"What?" Her eyes were wide. "No way. He's a vampire. Creature of the night and all that. Why would he be out during the day? Seems like he'd go up in smoke or something." She giggled again. "But what do I know? You guys tell me. What would happen if you went out in the sun?" She looked from Ray to me.

"We're not sure. Stories are that we turn to ashes. That's all that's ever found of a staked vampire after his body is left out in the sun." I shook my head. "This is not a topic I want to get into. Ray, will you be here when I get back?"

"Sure, Glory. Too close to dawn for me to go anywhere else." He yawned. "I'm going to take a shower. Have fun, ladies."

I opened the hall door and Trina, Valdez and I headed to the elevators.

"I've got my second wind now. But let's just do fifteen or so. Why don't we get off at four and jog up the rest of the stairs?" Trina started stretching and made me do the same.

When we got off the elevator, the corridor was empty. We did a few more of Trina's warm-up exercises, then headed for the stairs.

"Ready?" Trina opened the door into the stairwell and Valdez bounded through. Then she slammed it with him on the stair side and pushed a dead bolt home while she and I were still in the hallway. Before I knew what she planned, I was staring at the pointy end of a short wooden stake, my back against the door.

"Trina? What the hell?" I heard a crash as Valdez hit the door and it vibrated between my shoulder blades.

"You manage to come through that door, dog, and you'll make this stake go right through Glory's heart!" Trina hissed at the door, then concentrated on me.

"Why?" I tried to grab her hand but that only got me a warning jab with the stake. "Why are you doing this?"

"You don't want me to be a vampire, you bitch. You tried to talk me out of it last night." She aimed it at my heart and I felt the sting as it pricked my skin through two layers of fabric.

"It's for your own good, Trina. You have no idea what you're getting into." I tried to catch her gaze so I could whammy her. Do some vamp mind control on her. No luck. She'd obviously spent enough time around Ian to know better than to look at me directly.

"It's my dream. And tonight I heard Ian tell his guards that he was never going to make it come true. He's already picking out a new mortal to serve him." Tears welled up but Trina ignored them. "I thought that meant he was going to finally make me a vampire but the guards laughed and said that they'd finally get to have me for their playmate."

"Maybe he meant as a new vampire." I saw the elevator open down the hall and a man step out.

"No, he didn't. The guard made it very clear that I'd be passed around, then drained and tossed in the ocean or wherever they put the trash." She shuddered and the stake sank deeper. "Mortals don't count for much with them. That's why I wanted to be a vampire." Her eyes were wild as she snarled in a good vamp imitation. "You told him, didn't you? That I wasn't worthy. This is all your fault. Die!" She raised her hand to take a good whack at me when she was grabbed from behind.

"Not going to happen." Rafe stripped the stake from her hand and wrapped his arms around her. "Glory, what do you want me to do with her?"

"Hold her still. I'm going to whammy her." I grabbed her

chin and looked deep into her eyes. "Trina, you're not going to remember this night except that you and I ran up the stairs and you fed me as usual. Nod if you understand me." I waited until I got that nod.

"Now, listen carefully. You're not ever going back to Ian's again because you're afraid of vampires now. They have sharp teeth and they hurt when they bite you."

"Hurt?" She shuddered in Rafe's arms.

"Yes. But forget that because those people were just pretending to be vampires. The fangs were fake and they just wanted to scare you." I obviously wasn't going to get my nightly feeding now. I'd just outsmarted myself. "It's all over. You don't know any real vampires. They're just make-believe creatures in comics and storybooks. You don't want to have anything to do with those scary characters anymore."

"Scary. Want to go home." Tears ran down her cheeks and she sniffled.

"That's right. You just came here to get a free copy of Israel Caine's new CD. You were lucky and he signed it for you. Now you can go home and take down all those vampire posters and put them in the trash. Good night, Trina." I nodded and Rafe released her.

"Night." She turned and walked away toward the elevator.

"Sorry about that, Glory. I failed you again." Rafe shook his head, his dark hair falling over his face.

"How on earth could you know she was going to pull a stunt like that?" I threw the dead bolt and jerked on the stairwell door. "I'm going to run up these damned stairs if it kills me, which it might. And your punishment is that you have to do it too." I looked down. "Barefoot. Come on."

"Thanks a lot." He grinned, those damned cute dimples showing. "I should do it in dog form."

"Oh, no, you don't. I won't have the strength to open the door when we get to the top. It's on you." I started off then, determined, since I wasn't going to have Trina waiting.

When we got to the twenty-third floor, I was huffing and puffing and Rafe did hold open the door and slide the key card for me when we got to the suite. It was close to dawn and I could hear the shower running. I pulled open the bag with my bottles of supplements inside. The bedtime bottle was empty. It didn't take a genius to know who had drained it.

I stomped into the bathroom and threw open the glass shower door. "Damn you for a thief, Israel Caine."

"Glory! So glad you could join me." Ray grinned and rinsed the last of the shampoo out of his hair. Of course he had no shame when it came to his naked body or his thievery.

I slammed my fist into his flat midsection. "Bastard. Idiot. Why did you do it?"

"Oof. Why do you think?" He turned off the water and stepped out of the shower, wrapping a towel around his middle.

"I can't believe, with the Grammys coming up and your big duet, you'd take a chance like this. What if you walk into the sun and get burned? Did you think about that?"

"You healed. So will I." He picked up another towel and dried his hair. Then he opened my webcam and got busy with a comb. "That Ian MacDonald is brilliant. I'm ordering several of these. Do they come in colors? I'd like black and silver for a bathroom I've got on the island."

I slammed it shut. "That's my mirror, you damned stupid son of a bitch. Ooo." I stomped my foot and words failed me. Then I found some more. "Did you even think about the fact that now I won't lose any more weight? How selfish can you get?"

"Obviously pretty selfish." Rafe stood in the doorway.

"Who the hell are you?" Ray jumped in front of me. "Glory?"

I sighed, just about ready to signal Rafe to take Ray down. What a pleasure to watch my bodyguard beat the living crap out of my "fiancé."

"This is Valdez in human form, Ray. He just saved my life for about the zillionth time."

"What?" Ray looked him up and down. "I see why Blade

doesn't want you like this, dog breath. Shift back or at least put on a shirt."

"I don't take orders from you, Caine. You need me in here, Glory?" Rafe leaned against the doorjamb, relaxed but obviously alert to whatever needed doing.

"Not now, but genius here took my supplement so he may be doing some strolling during the daylight hours. Whether you want to stop him from frying or not is on you." I smiled and stepped around Ray to head into the bedroom.

"Wait a minute. What do you mean he saved your life? What happened?" Ray followed me, not concerned that he was about to lose his towel.

"Trina brought a stake in her fanny pack. She decided I'd turned Ian against her." I rubbed the back of my neck, more tired than I'd ever felt. "Rafe got there in time to keep her from doing more than talk tough and poke me a few times."

"You realize you're bleeding?" Ray stepped close and touched my T-shirt.

I looked down and saw that he was right. Trina had stabbed a hole through my shirt and sports bra. I'd bled enough to stain them both. I pulled the fabric away from my breast and looked under it.

"Want me to check it for you?" Ray tried to put his arm around me.

"Not a chance." I used my arm to fend him off. "It's already stopped bleeding. Just stay out of my way, Ray. I'm still furious with you."

"Want me to put a hurt on him, Glory?" Rafe grinned from the doorway. "I've been itching to do that for more than a month."

"Listen, shifter, you're just an employee. I don't think—" Ray was suddenly up against the wall with an arm across his throat.

"Exactly, my man. You don't think. Respect the lady. And her wishes." Valdez glanced at me. "I've got Trina's stake in my pocket, Glory. Say the word and your problem's solved."

"Rafe, I know you're jacked up on adrenaline, but, for God's sake, calm down." I put my hand on his bare shoulder. For the first time I was seeing savage Rafael Valdez, the man who, yes, would die for me, but who would also happily jump into the fray against a dozen men if necessary for the pure joy of killing bad guys. Obviously he'd decided Ray was one.

"He's done this time and again, Glory. Taken advantage of your forgiving nature. And you let him get away with it." Rafe increased the pressure and I heard some cartilage snap.

"Damn it, Rafe, he's got to sing at the Grammys night after next. Don't you dare hurt him!" I punched his back. "You're way out of line. Ray's been generous, kind. Let him go. Now!"

"Oh, yeah, right. He's the big rock star. Of course you'll cut him all kinds of slack. Caine's right. I just work here." Rafe suddenly stepped back and walked to the doorway. "I'll be out here at my post, doing my job. Don't worry. I know my place." He slammed the door.

Ray coughed and rubbed his throat but didn't say anything.

I stared at the door. Well, that had been enlightening. If I didn't know better, I'd say Rafe had been jealous of Ray. No, impossible. He'd just been fed up with Ray's sometimes selfish, me-first attitude. I saw the empty supplement bottle on the dresser. I'd been just as fed up. Now I was worried. What if Ray did the sleepwalking thing? I wasn't sure Rafe would even bother to stop him if Ray headed for the sun. Damn.

"Are you okay?" Hell, I did care about Ray. And he'd been quiet too long.

"Yes, I'm fine." His voice was raspy.

"You just need to sleep it off." I hoped. What if that supplement kept him from healing? I blocked that thought.

"That damned bodyguard has got to go." He pulled open a drawer and dropped his towel to pull on his shorts. Business as usual.

"Don't worry. Rafe and I will both be out of your way once we're back in Austin." I didn't wait to see how Ray reacted to that. I just headed for the door. I stopped, my hand on the knob, and looked back. Ray was rubbing his throat again.

"You took a stupid risk drinking Ian's stuff tonight, Ray. I hope it doesn't mess you up." I sighed. "Now I'm going to weigh in and then see what I can do to make sure Valdez saves you if you take a walk in your sleep and head toward the balcony." I held up a hand when Ray started to say something. "Don't want to hear it. You're a damned thief. Go to bed. Or hell. Or wherever." I stomped out of the room.

As I headed to the powder room I ignored Valdez, who'd shifted back to dog form. Okay, down three more pounds. But what would the healing sleep do? Without my supplement the weight would probably come right back on. Damn.

Tough talk or not, I was sick with fear for Ray. What if he didn't heal and couldn't sing? Or got out on the balcony and fried? I walked back through the living room and saw Valdez sitting at the open drapes, staring out at the sky that was just beginning to lighten.

"You wouldn't let Ray get hurt, would you?"

"What do you think?" He looked over his shoulder at me.

"I think that if I order you to protect him, you will."

"Is that what you're doing?"

I walked over and jerked the drapes closed until there wasn't a speck of sky showing. "Yes. Do your job. Protect the vampires. Including Ray. For me, Rafe. I need him tomorrow night at the TV show. Okay?"

"Fine. Whatever you say, Glory." He walked over and leaped up on the couch. *"I hear and obey."*

I sighed and went to jump in the shower, still ignoring Ray, who was lying in bed staring at me. Of course he'd heard what I said to Rafe. But he knew better than to smile about it.

I felt like crap for all kinds of reasons. The coming dawn,

for one thing. That should be reassuring since it was familiar. But now it just scared me.

Rafe was disappointed in me. Somehow that had jumped into number-one position on the dread list, and I couldn't shrug it off. After I crawled into bed beside Ray, I turned my back on him. Whatever happened after the sun came up was out of my hands now. I had no idea what I'd wake up to.

Fourteen

"So how did it go?" I'd put off asking the question as long as I could stand it. Ray and I had been giving each other the silent treatment since we'd gotten up with the sunset. Like a stupid game of chicken. Of course you knew I was going to crack first. Now time was running out. I put the finishing touches on my hair and makeup, even though I figured the stylists for the show would do their thing too. They'd be at the door any minute. "Did you see the sun?"

"Ask your bodyguard. I don't remember what the hell happened and he's not talking. To me, anyway." Ray pulled on a black silk shirt and sat on the bed to slip on leather loafers.

"At least you healed. Voice sounds fine." I closed my "mirror" and stood. "Love the dress, Ray. Thanks." I didn't want to admit it felt a little snug. I'd weighed in. The three pounds hadn't stayed off and I'd gained one. I'd been afraid to try any of Ian's wake-up supplements in case they upset my stomach, but it had been tempting.

"You look great. Would you get the shifter in here and ask him what the hell happened last night? Before the show people arrive?" Ray got up and threw open the bedroom door. "Of course he acts like I'm invisible."

"Valdez, would you come in here? Please?" I sat down to buckle my silver sandals.

"Yes?" He appeared in the doorway.

"Did Ray get up during the day?"

"Yes." Valdez sat and just looked at me.

"Well? How about a few details? I don't remember a freakin' thing." Ray stepped into Valdez's space, which earned him a pretty serious snarl.

"Ray, get back here. I'll ask the questions. V, did Ray say anything? Did he wake up?"

"He didn't wake up. He did say something."

"Cut it out, V. Tell us what happened. All of it." This was getting ridiculous and Ray was losing his cool fast. I knew the TV folks were going to be here any second. I didn't need for them to arrive in the middle of a brawl that would be impossible to explain.

"Well, I heard Mr. Macho here crying in his sleep. Calling for his mommy or somebody. Then he staggers out of the bedroom, eyes closed. Guess that's why he doesn't remember. Had his Johnson in his hand. Begging somebody not to cut it off." Valdez nodded. *"Got issues there, buddy?"*

"Listen, you fur-faced freak, you don't know what the hell you're talking about." Ray glanced at me.

I knew his history and there'd been a bad scene once when some thugs had threatened him with castration. He'd obviously been reliving it. Valdez knew about it too and I was deeply ashamed of him for throwing it in Ray's face. I sent V a mental message but he ignored me, too intent on hitting Ray below the belt, literally.

"Did he get near the doors to the balcony? Did you have to pick him up and take him back to bed?" I put my hand on Ray's arm. I knew this was hard for him.

"No. He did some more carrying on, then he just fell down about halfway across the living room." Valdez shrugged. *"I*

dragged him back to bed, gave him a good headbutt and he man-aged to crawl in under the covers. Went dead after that and not another peep out of him." He snorted. *"Good thing. There's only so much of that I can stand."*

"Cool it, V." I hugged Ray. "I'm really sorry. At least you didn't have to remember your dream. I did remember mine." I leaned back and studied him.

He shook his head. "I'm okay, Glory. Your shifter's an ass-hole, but he's just telling it like he saw it, I guess." He frowned at Valdez. "He did get me out of the living room. If some of the guys from the band had come by and opened the drapes . . . Shit, I don't want to go there."

"See? Maybe not such an asshole after all." Valdez cocked his head. *"They're here. Out in the hall."* We all heard a knock on the door.

"Let 'em in, Glory." Ray rubbed his face. "The good news is I got up. But I'm thinking it probably takes several doses of that stuff to build it up in your system before you stay awake during the day. You didn't wake right away, did you?" He followed me to the door.

"No. Didn't want to either. The whole daylight thing scares the hell out of me." I stopped and faced Ray. "Smart vampires don't mess around with the sun."

"Well, maybe I'm stupid, but I want it. And I bet Ian's got this figured out. Your daylight gig was an accident. The real daylight drug is bound to be much stronger than what you took." Ray's eyes were shining with hope. "Don't you see, Glory? Forget the nightmares. Except as a clue that Ian's getting us back to being mortal again."

My stomach dropped like a rock. "Oh, Ray, that is so not happening. Ever." I laid my hand on his arm. There was another impatient knock on the door and I checked the peep-hole. Yep, the TV crew stood out there, anxious to get inside. I hesitated, knowing this was our last chance for a private word for hours.

"Ray, please think about this long and hard before you act

on it. And, remember, you said you'd tell me before you bought into the daylight deal with Ian."

"Did I?" Ray smiled and grabbed the doorknob. "I don't think so, Ms. Independent. But I do owe you an apology. I never should have taken your diet stuff. Not fair to you." He glanced at Valdez. "I deserved a nightmare and an ass whipping." He cleared his throat. "Now, let's do this."

Before I could respond to that, he opened the door and ushered in the crew, kissing Zia on the cheek and waving to the designers, who were relegated to the hall again.

The next hour went by in a blur as the crew set up the living room and we decided how this would go. Ray got makeup and I got a touch-up. Nathan popped in for a few minutes to change shirts and to meet Zia. There was some chemistry there and I had a feeling the two would be seeing each other again. They exchanged numbers, then Nathan left and filming started.

Zia did her usual intro. She played up Ray's involvement and made a big deal out of his Grammy nomination again. It was obvious that I was just a necessary evil.

Finally, an assistant brought Melanie in and sat her in the middle of the couch. I headed into the bedroom to change into her dress and accessories with the help of an assistant.

This time the dress fit perfectly and the horrible shoulders had been reduced to a manageable level. I actually liked the dress and wished I could have seen the thing in a full-length mirror. Made me wonder if a giant flat screen turned on its side and a webcam . . . Now I was thinking like Ian the inventor. Oh, well, the life of a vampire.

I walked out and saw Ray and Zia flanking Melanie. I did a turn in front of them, enjoying the way the blue skirt flared when I moved. The sheer fabric on the sleeves was now tight enough to show a blue, red and yellow dragon design, between my breasts too.

"Melanie, I just noticed what you were trying to do with

the sheer fabric." I looked up and grinned. "It looks like I have tattoos!"

"That's right, Glory. What do you think?" Melanie was all smiles.

"Let's hear from Israel Caine first, Melanie." Zia turned to Ray. "How do *you* like it, Ray?"

Ray stood and walked around me. "It's got a cool, edgy vibe. Love the tattoo thing going on." He winked at Melanie. "Glory's always wished she could get a tat, haven't you, baby?" We'd discussed my cover story. He smiled into the camera. "She's allergic to the dyes or she would." He traced a heart over the curve of my breast exposed by the plunging neckline. "She'd put my name right here, wouldn't you, Glory?"

I gave him a slow smile, well aware of the camera, then heard Valdez rumbling behind me. Tough. I'd warned him to be on his best behavior. Of course, I'd had ample proof that he was an unpredictable man under all that cute Labradoodle fur. So I grabbed Ray's hand and pulled it to my lips for a playful nip.

"Sure would, love. Don't you like the blue?"

"Matches your eyes, baby." Ray put his hands on my waist. "What's up with this belt?"

"Stars, Ray. Melanie was thinking of you when she made this belt." I frowned at Valdez when I heard a gagging noise.

"Piling it on a little thick, aren't you, Mel?" Ray laughed. "I like it, but we've got two more dresses to see. Let's move on. Good job, honey." He turned his famous smile on Melanie and I heard the clank as her pierced tongue fell out of her mouth and hit her pierced lip, another victim of Israel Caine's charm.

"Out you go, then, Melanie. Send in Darren next and Glory will change into his dress. You'll find out the winning design tomorrow night when you see what Glory is wearing when she appears on Israel Caine's arm at the Grammy awards show." Zia smiled as Ray settled on the couch again.

I really was fascinated by those sleeves. Tattoos! How cool was that? But I hurried back to the dressing room. I knew time was an issue. Ray had a schedule for us to follow that included stopping at several parties. I pulled off the dress and took the red one that was handed through the door. This time it fit perfectly so maybe it was just as well that I hadn't lost the three pounds the night before. I slipped on the shoes, which I loved, and the jewelry and walked out. I really felt like a princess in this one.

"Wow, Glory. That one is amazing." Ray jumped up and walked around me. "Really shows off your new body." He traced the low-cut bodice, then looked at Darren, who was sitting on the edge of his seat. "You were obviously listening to me on this."

"Yes, Mr. Caine. You were right. Glory's got the goods. She should show them off." Darren coughed when Ray flicked him with a look that should have drawn blood. Obviously Designer Boy had overstepped.

"This jewelry for sale?" Ray toyed with the diamond earrings in my ears. "They're perfect on you, Glory."

"Of course, Ray. I can put you in touch with the jeweler after the show." Zia smiled. "Now, Glory, why don't you tell me why you're frowning?"

"Well, I love the dress, the accessories and the way it fits, Darren. But I'm worried about the color. It's red."

"You said that was your favorite color." Darren jumped to his feet. He sat quickly when Valdez growled. Everyone in the room froze at that sound. They all remembered the Butch debacle.

"Yes, it is. But how is it going to look against a red carpet, Darren? What if it's the wrong shade of red? Or I just kind of disappear into the carpet? Do you see my concern?"

"Good points, Glory." Zia was thrilled at the controversy. "Well, Darren, what do you have to say to that?"

"I'm sorry, Glory." Tears filled his eyes, and he wiped them with his sleeve. "I guess I blew it."

"No, wait." Ray stopped looking down my front long

enough to join the conversation. "Didn't I tell you, Glory? This year is all about saving the environment and global warming. The carpet isn't going to be red. It's going to be green."

"Seriously?" I turned on him. "You didn't think to share that little bit of information with me until now?"

Zia had the same reaction. Her comments would have to be censored. "Why didn't someone notify us? I have a green dress for the stupid event. Now I'm back to square one. Of all the bleep, bleeping foul-ups." She took a shaky breath. "Okay, people, let's rewind." She smiled at Ray. "That's good drama. We'll just edit a little bit."

"Fine. I like the dress, Darren, and it's definitely still under consideration." I gave him a thumbs-up.

"Excellent." Zia clapped her hands. "Now it's Butch's turn. Ray, is the dog yours or Glory's?"

Ray frowned in Valdez's direction. "Oh, he's 100 percent Glory's animal. Why?"

Zia frowned. "He attacked one of the designers during the last shoot. It was, well, traumatic. Glory, that's not going to happen again, is it?"

I'd already noticed that the entire crew had given Valdez a wide berth since arriving. That had just made him grin and wag his tail. Yeah, Mr. Innocent. "It had better not. Butch won't be carrying scissors this time, will he?"

"No, no sharp objects at all. Guess the dog thought Butch was going to hurt Glory. Can you imagine? With such a huge prize at stake?" Zia laughed and touched Ray's hand, then she stood and straightened her purple knit micro-mini dress. Two inches shorter and it wouldn't have covered her butt at all. Trust me, Ray was noticing.

"Will someone assure Butch that the dog isn't going to attack him?" She smiled at me. "Glory, let's play it safe. Could you please put your dog in the bedroom for this part of the shoot? Butch has been under a doctor's care since that little dustup with your pooch last night. I think it would help if we didn't have to worry about a repeat."

I glanced at Valdez. He'd added a lolling tongue and a dumb look to his repertoire. He wasn't fooling me. If Butch or anyone on the crew—no, make that anyone in the *room*—even looked at me cross-eyed, he'd go for the jugular and not care who got it on film. I couldn't blame him. After what Trina had pulled, he was right to be cautious. Unfortunately, he'd be really happy if Ray gave him an excuse to go ballistic.

"Sure, Zia. Valdez can stay in the bedroom, but I have to leave the door ajar. He needs to know he's in on the action. Otherwise he'll just bark nonstop and spoil everything. He can get pretty noisy. You don't want to take that chance, do you?"

"No, of course not." Zia winced as she settled on the couch again and crossed her long legs. "Honey, have you considered obedience school? Or even, dare I say it, kenneling the creature when you travel?"

Valdez obviously decided to prove he didn't need to be shuttled off to some pet hotel or school for naughty dogs. He ran up to her, all wagging tail and lolling tongue. In an instant, the model jumped up on the coffee table, screaming at her assistants to "do something." One picked up a throw pillow, then screeched when Valdez knocked it out of her hands with his wagging tail. That sent the others scurrying into a huddle behind the cameraman. Zia was on her own.

"Zia, please. He's just trying to be friendly." I grabbed his collar to be on the safe side. "He's not growling, is he?" He also wasn't sitting. Instead he gazed at Zia adoringly before he "accidentally" bumped the table, sending her toppling over the edge.

"No!" She landed on the one assistant who'd been brave enough to venture out of the pack and come to her aid. That poor guy had obviously not expected to play cushion for her and they both fell on the floor in a tangle of arms and legs. I swear the air turned blue from Zia's curses. The camera caught it all, of course. There'd have to be a lot of bleeping.

"So sorry. Really. He's going straight into the bedroom. See?" I tugged on V's collar and pulled him out of the room.

"Bark and you're dead, mister." I glanced at the assistant assigned to help me with the wardrobe changes. Time for a mental message to my bodyguard. *"You think I don't know that table bump was deliberate? When I change clothes you'd damn well better turn your back. You're not checking out my underwear."*

He grinned and looked at me with such innocence I had to bite my lip to keep from laughing. When Zia had landed on that producer she'd shown the room her leopard print thong and her awesome butt. I stood and brushed my skirt, then walked carefully to the living room where order was being restored. Hair and makeup artists were hard at work on Zia, and Ray lounged on the couch trying not to laugh.

"Destroy that footage. If I see it on the Internet, I'll have the jobs of everyone in this room. Do you hear me, people?" Zia's face was red behind a cloud of powder and hair spray.

I'm sure the guests on the thirtieth floor had heard her. I kept my distance. "Uh, Zia, should I go change now?" My answer was a wave that I took as a yes.

I made sure Valdez faced the wall, then removed the dress that was my favorite so far and took the black chiffon that was thrust through the door. I looked it over. Butch had made it into culottes and added a belt. At least the tentlike creation no longer provided stadium seating. Now it just offered a cozy booth for two.

When I walked out this time, Butch sat on the sofa between Ray and Zia. He jumped when he saw me, clearly edgy and afraid my wild dog would come rampaging out with me. Zia had developed a tic, casting nervous glances at the bedroom door too. Swell, now I was an irresponsible pet owner. I decided to ease their minds and went back and shut the bedroom door. Valdez could hear through it and break it down if he thought I needed him. These people had been through enough. The tension in the room eased immediately.

Zia smiled. "Well, Glory, what do you think of the changes Butch incorporated into his design? He obviously had to do the most drastic alterations after your reaction last time." Zia was totally composed again, though I noticed she'd broken one heel and someone had used clear tape to keep it in place.

"Yes, he really listened to my concerns. This is 1000 percent better." I held out the flowing black pants. This was the kind of dress I would have killed for in a size twelve. It would have disguised my hips and made my waist look small by comparison.

"The black looks great on you, Glory. It shows off your pale skin. Love the low-cut front and back." Ray stood and walked around me. "Not sure about pants for such a big night."

"I like the pants. They're called culottes, Ray." I smiled at Butch. "I feel free in them. Like I don't have to be scared my skirt will blow up and show the world my underwear." Which, by the way, was a plain beige thong since I needed to do laundry. I'm sure Valdez would have been very disappointed if he'd managed to sneak a peek.

"I kept the dress loose too, Glory, and the belt adjustable." Butch flushed. "I know it won't happen, of course, but, if you did gain some weight, you could still wear this dress."

"I love that!" I looked at Zia. "He did a really good job of accessorizing too. The shoes and jewelry are perfect with this gown."

"Well, Butch, seems like you might have pulled off a miracle here. You were the underdog coming into tonight, but looks like you made the right changes to get back into the race. Of course we'll all have to wait to see what Glory is wearing at tomorrow night's Grammy awards show to see which one she picks as *her* winner."

Zia stood and faced the camera. "And of course our regular judges will decide, after that and after seeing the footage from these events, just who will go home and who the final two designers will be on *Designed to Kill.*"

"That's a wrap. Good job, people." The director signaled and the crew started packing up their gear.

"Thank you so much, Mr. Caine, Glory." Butch shook our

hands. "That dog's not around, is he?" Just then we heard a bark from behind the door. "I'm out of here!" He ran toward the hall.

Zia smiled and air-kissed Ray. "Me too! We'll have a camera crew at the, ha-ha, green carpet to see your pick, Glory. I'll conduct just a brief interview with both of you right on the spot. You've got to be there early, you know."

Ray and I looked at each other. The whole Grammy thing was one big logistical nightmare, starting with the fact that it was on the West Coast. At least in February sunset was still relatively early, but we'd be rushing to get there before Ray had to perform. Luckily his duet was slated to be late in the program and the award presented after that.

Ray just smiled and nodded. "Check with Nathan. I believe you have his number. Coordinate the time with him because I can't be late for my performance."

"No, no, of course not. I'll call Nathan in the morning." Zia finally remembered I was standing there.

"Oh, Glory, you get all three dresses, of course. They're yours now. Shoes and bags too. The vendors get rolling credits at the end of the segments, so they donated the accessories, except for the jewels, of course. Any hints for me on which dress you'll pick?"

"No, Ray and I'll talk it over. And I'd like to get my best friend's opinion if I have time." I shut up when I realized Zia wasn't listening. Free stuff—I couldn't argue with that.

She waved a hand and an assistant came out of the bedroom, Valdez racing out ahead of her. "Did you leave everything in Ms. St. Clair's closet?"

"Everything except these." The woman handed me three velvet bags. "Those are the jewels for each gown. They're marked so you'll know which one goes with which dress. Of course one of these bags is empty because you're wearing one set." She looked down at Valdez. "The dog was fine, just stayed by the door once you shut it." She glanced at Zia. "Don't know why he did those things out here. But then, animals sense—"

"Go on, Rita, help the others pack." Zia waved her away. "Ray, Glory, a courier from the jeweler will be at your hotel first thing the morning after the Grammys to pick up those bags. You know the jewelry is just on loan. Insured, of course. But we don't want to have to deal with any problems, now, do we?"

"They'll be fine, Zia. But tell him we'll leave them in the safe downstairs. I'll have instructions for the front desk. If I decide to buy anything, I'll be in touch with the jeweler personally later." Ray walked Zia to the door. She was limping because her heel wouldn't stay on. "We'll be sleeping in. Big night for me, win or lose. There are some after-parties."

"Of course. But I bet it's a win." Zia gasped when Valdez followed Ray to the door and gave her a toothy grin. "Bye, now." She ran out of the suite, finally jerking off her shoes when they slowed her down. The last of the TV crew with their equipment was right behind her.

"Glad that's over." I carried the jewelry into the bedroom. I'd have to hurry and change so we could leave. Valdez was going to have to stay here and I knew he wasn't going to like it. Too bad. No way was I taking a dog to a party. And I wasn't going to let him shift into human form either. Ray and I should be able to get along without extra protection. This whole paranoia thing was getting ridiculous. As far as I could see, no one in Los Angeles was out to get me. Not since Trina was safely whammied and taken care of.

When I stepped out of the bathroom in my green dress again, Valdez was waiting for me.

"If you don't want me to know your plans, Glory, you should block your thoughts."

"You're not going with us, V."

"Then take Brittany."

"Oh, right. There are already rumors that Ray's got something going on with his hot female bodyguard. So now we can add to the story that we're a threesome. I don't think so." Do you blame me? Even wearing a six, I felt like a bloating munchkin next to the tall beautiful Brit. For a moment I toyed with the idea of wearing a pair of the real diamond earrings. They were fabulous. But in the end, I chickened out and stuck with my fake diamond studs. The real jewels went into the safe in the closet.

"You think Caine can protect you?" Valdez wasn't giving up.

"From what?" I picked up my evening bag and my cell from its charger. I glanced at it. No missed calls. So Jerry hadn't bothered to check on me. I sighed, then stuck the phone inside my purse and headed for the living room. "You're being paranoid."

"Have you forgotten Trina?"

"She's been handled and is no longer a threat." I saw Ray on the phone and walked over to stare at the night sky. "Forget it, V. We'll have Ray's mortal bodyguards with us in case any of his fans get overly enthusiastic or the paparazzi bug us. That'll be enough."

"She's right. Limo's downstairs. The guys are waiting in the lobby. Let's go." Ray pulled on a charcoal gray Armani jacket over his silk shirt. He looked every bit the world-class rocker who made women melt and slip him their room keys. Don't laugh. There was a pile of them on the minibar.

"This is on you, Caine. Take care of our girl." Valdez followed us to the door.

"Our girl?" Ray put his hand on my waist. "Glory's a woman, more than capable of taking care of herself. Now you've got a night off, man. Spend it finding your own woman." He pushed me out into the hall and closed the door.

"Was that necessary?" I looked back.

"I thought so. You can't keep dragging him everywhere you go, Glory. I can take care of you tonight if there's anything that needs doing." He punched the button for the elevator. "Have I told you how incredible you look? The tabloids are going to go nuts."

"Thanks, Ray. But, sweetheart, I'm the vintage vamp here. *I'll* take care of *you*." I kissed his open mouth, then stepped into the elevator and hit the button for the lobby.

"Just when I think you can't get any sexier . . ." Ray pushed me against the back wall as the elevator doors slid shut. "So you're the alpha in this pack?"

I grinned up at him. "Is two a pack?" I ran my hands up his chest. "Don't wrinkle my dress, Ray."

"It'll be worth it." He leaned in and kissed a path along my jaw to a spot behind my ear, making me shiver.

"Probably." I sighed when he moved down to press his open mouth against the pulse in my neck. The elevator shuddered to a stop.

"Looks like we're interrupting something, DeeDee."

Ray didn't lift his head, just moved closer. I could see DeeDee, her expression never changing from neutral, like she'd caught two strangers making out.

"We'll wait for the next elevator." She shoved her date back and hit the button so the doors closed again.

I pushed Ray off of me. "Chicken. Couldn't you have at least said hi to your bed buddy?"

"I was busy. DeeDee knows the score." Ray shrugged, pulled down his jacket, then reached out to straighten my neckline that he'd managed to slip aside until it showed a trace of nipple. The elevator doors opened at the lobby.

"Here we go. Showtime." He grinned at me. "My life's in your hands."

"I know that. Believe me, I know that." I threw back my shoulders, on high alert. Between the two of us, I *was* the strong one here, the experienced vampire. Ray was a newbie, just coming into his skills. And his mortals would be useless if we ran across any paranormal threat. I actually felt a rush, though the odds of encountering a paranormal hit squad were slim to none. Okay, okay, that was a relief. I'm not an idiot.

We headed out of the main lobby entrance. Other celebrities were also taking off for a night out and the paparazzi were in a feeding frenzy. But they noticed me on Ray's arm and my new look.

"This way, Glory. What diet are you on?"

"Who did your lipo?"

"Did you lose the baby?"

The lipo question made me wonder if there had been a mole in the production staff of the TV show. The baby question was so crude and disgusting I sent the idiot a mental message that made him go pale and back away. After that, I refused to say a word as we hurried into the limo. Ray and I settled back, the two guards facing us as we drove to the first party.

Ray grabbed my hand. "Damned paparazzi. I'm sorry about that, Glory."

"Comes with the territory, I guess. Not your fault." I smiled at him, then leaned in to whisper in his ear. "I scared that one photographer. He's going somewhere so he can look and see if he's still got something between his legs."

Ray laughed. "Baby, I like the way you think."

"Yeah, I just wish I had the power to make stuff like that really happen." I eased my hand out of his and adjusted the silk wrap that matched my dress. "Tell me about this party we're going to."

"My record label's throwing this bash. I already had Nate spread the word that I'm on the wagon." Ray frowned and sat back. "Of course the execs were happy to hear that. Didn't know I had such an obvious problem."

I covered his hand where it rested on my thigh. "Just the insiders knew. Your fans didn't have a clue unless they believed some of the meaner tabloid stories." Ray had been on the brink of going into rehab for alcoholism when he'd been made vampire. It had been tough for him to realize his drinking days were over when he'd awakened to a liquid diet that wasn't his favorite Jack Daniel's. Bummer for him. Then to find out he couldn't see daylight again either . . . When you don't choose to become vampire, like I did, it can be a pretty depressing reality.

"Well, the upside is I've made the powers that be at the label very happy with my new sober work ethic. They really like my new tunes on the upcoming album. Now all I have to do is get them used to my crazy new work schedule. Of course I've always been pretty much a night owl. Never really appreciated the daylight before. But now . . . Hell, next time it'll be different." Ray turned his hand over and squeezed my fingers. "I'm not bugging you about this anymore. Or arguing about it tonight either. I'm sure it's not a bit sexy." He nodded toward the mortals who were both plugged into iPods to give us privacy. I didn't doubt they could still hear us, though.

"We can talk about this later." The limo was slowing and I could see another crowd gathered around a canopy in front of a restaurant. Our car was in a slow-moving line, until it was our turn and the guards jumped out first.

"Israel Caine!" Female screams made it clear that Ray still had plenty of female fans as a throng pushed against velvet ropes, and policemen kept the crowds back. Ray stopped and signed a few autographs, then waved at the crowd and escorted me inside. We left the bodyguards by the door and headed into the darkened restaurant that had apparently been totally taken over for the party. M.A.S. Records logos were everywhere, the bloodred letters on black background unmistakable, along with O.B.G. Sounds, the rock division that was Ray's label. One of the Grammy-nominated hits was loud and proud, played by a DJ. Scantily clad waitresses in tight white O.B.G. T-shirts, cut off to show their tiny waists, circulated, taking drink orders. Ray and I took our token glasses of sparkling water and pretended to sip.

We saw famous faces everywhere and Ray knew everyone. I was in fangirl heaven and had a hard time pretending to be cool. I wished Flo could have met the hunky country star we'd both drooled over in a video one night. Or the older man whose music we'd both had fun dancing to back in the sixties. I just hung on to Ray's arm and kept smiling. Then I caught a whiff of something I'd never expected to smell here. Vampire.

I looked around. No, not just one vampire, but several. Holy crap. I didn't feel menace, but that didn't mean Ray and I couldn't end up with our throats ripped out. We didn't know any of the Los Angeles vampires. I did have names I could throw around. Jerry, Richard and Damian had talked to the Council. Maybe they'd mentioned us. Let it be known we were in town and meant no harm. I gave Ray an elbow.

"What, baby? Let me introduce you to Celine." Ray pulled me forward. "Glory's a big fan. Has all of your CDs. We meant to make your show before you left Vegas."

"Ray's right. I just love you." I babbled and almost spilled water all over the famous singer. But I couldn't concentrate. I had to get Ray alone. I finally sent him a mental message.

"Ray, there are vampires here. Several. Sniff the air. See if you can pick them out."

Ray's eyes widened and he leaned in to kiss Celine's cheek. "Great to see you again. E-mail me your concert schedule and maybe we can connect." We watched her disappear into the crowd. "Well, she's not one."

I wanted to giggle hysterically. "I never thought she was." I felt a presence behind me and knew the vampires had found us.

"Come with me, please. There's someone who wants to meet you, Mr. Caine, Ms. St. Clair."

Ray and I turned and there stood a pair of vampires who could have been just your ordinary record executives. Hey, I challenge you to pick them out of a crowd in any boardroom. Thousand-dollar suits. Silk ties. White shirts and expensive haircuts. One even sported horn-rimmed glasses à la Clark Kent. The pair was completely nonthreatening if you weren't into mind reading. Unfortunately, Ray and I were able to get the mental message loud and clear. This wasn't an invitation we could turn down.

We were going to meet a big bad vampire whether we wanted to or not. Oh, yeah, and I was supposed to protect Ray. Uh-huh.

Fifteen

We followed the two vamps to the bar area of the restaurant where a blond man held court in a corner booth. It was obvious that bodyguards controlled who could and couldn't gain access to this section of the room. Our host had a beautiful woman on each side of him. He whispered in their ears and they quickly slid out of the booth and hurried off.

"Please, join me." He smiled and gestured, and two goblets of what smelled like a new and very excellent synthetic blood were set on the dark wood table on either side of him. "So glad to finally meet you, Caine. And the beautiful Gloriana."

Ray nodded and I was proud of him. Even though this was probably the man who held his recording contract, he wasn't about to shake hands with any vampire. We just stood there.

"Sit. Both of you." Now there was steel in his voice and the record execs were joined by two more muscular types.

"Sure." I smiled and slid in on one side of him. "I'm afraid I don't know your name. Ray?" I looked at him where he still stood, obviously reluctant to just cave to a command. "Sit, baby, let's get to know . . ."

"Chip Rollins. I own M.A.S. Records. Caine should know that." He smiled when Ray finally dropped into the booth on the other side.

"Sure, I know who runs the show at M.A.S. Nice to finally meet you. Didn't know you were"—Ray glanced around—"vampire."

"Of course not. Just like I didn't know until recently that one of my stars had joined the club. I call us Masters of the Night." Chip showed a hint of fang in his smile this time. "Has a nice ring to it, don't you think?"

"Much nicer than freak or bloodsucker. I'm sure you've been called that a time or two. I know I have." I smiled, picked up my glass and inhaled. "Mmm. This is something special, Mr. Rollins."

"Please, call me Chip. Only the best. That's my motto in all things." He glanced at Ray, who was obviously not a happy camper at being strong-armed away from the party. "My recording artists included, Ray. I won't talk business tonight, but we will talk soon."

"Great. Looking forward to it." Ray picked up his goblet and took a swallow. "This is good stuff. A club? Yeah, Glory said there might be a secret handshake." Ray smiled. "I draw the line at matching T-shirts."

Chip laughed. "So do I." He glanced at me. "You should teach your protégé to mask his thoughts better. Ray, I'm not insulted when you think I sound like a character from a comic book. Who do you think wrote those things back in the day?" He nodded toward the suit in the glasses, who took a bow. "I told Eric next time to make us the heroes. Vampires as superheroes. Why not?"

"Better than bloodsucking fiends, I guess." Ray smiled and let his fangs show.

I sent Ray a mental message to remember who signed his checks. His attitude was surly despite the smile. Guess he didn't like being surrounded by another vamp's bodyguards. Neither did I. Now I regretted refusing to bring Brittany along. She was worth two of these guys. I looked them over

again. Well, maybe not. Now, Valdez . . . Forget it. We were
on our own. And Chip wasn't about to harm one of his mon-
eymakers anyway. I smiled too, minus the fangs. I knew Ray
had just offered an insult to our host. Obviously we needed
more lessons in vampire etiquette.

"Ray's initiation into the club is a recent thing, Chip." I
toyed with my glass but didn't drink. Damn this diet. But
my dress was cutting into my middle already.

"Oh, I know that. I do my homework, Gloriana. I believe
that's your favorite, um, flavor. AB negative? You should try
it." Chip touched my hand and I shivered. "Or are you still
dieting?"

I set the glass down without tasting it. "You know a lot
about me, Chip."

"Of course I do. No vampire enters my territory without
being vetted." He turned to Ray. "I must say I was surprised
you and Gloriana went out to see MacDonald so soon after
arriving."

"Didn't realize we had to get permission. Oh, got to piss.
Do I have to raise my hand?" Ray looked like he was spoiling
for a fight.

One of Chip's men put his hand on Ray's shoulder and
Ray winced.

Chip laughed. "Point taken." He leaned forward and I
could see Ray doing his best not to show the slightest reaction to the implied threat as Chip invaded his space.

Sorry, but we could all feel Ray's fear. New vampire. Not
a chance he could mask his feelings that well. I gave in and
sipped the synthetic. God, it tasted great and gave me a jolt
of courage I needed.

"Listen to me, Ray. I get that you want to see daylight.
Hell, we all do." Chip looked down at his own hand, a nice
tan that had to have come from a spray. In fact, Chip could
have fit right in with Ian's surfer dudes. "We're investigating
MacDonald's claims. The Council here is on top of the situation. You'd be wise to wait for our findings. You don't want
to go off half-cocked, do you? And wind up toasted?"

"What the hell do you care what I do?" Ray wasn't going to back down. Dumbass.

I wanted to reach out to him. Do something. But Chip was between us and in Ray's face. And it was clear the man was giving Ray a chance to learn a lesson. I just hoped to hell Ray paid attention. I tried to send Ray a mental message but he wasn't receiving, totally focused on the man in front of him. Which was the first smart thing Ray'd done since we'd entered the bar.

"I care, Ray, because I own you. Ask your buddy Nathan Burke. He made you a sweet deal. A long-term deal. With more money than you can ever spend. Or at least it was until you became immortal. Don't throw that chance away." Chip picked up his glass and took a healthy swallow. "Forget this. Bring me the redhead. I'm going upstairs with her."

He nodded and one of his muscle men "helped" Ray out of the booth.

"Nobody owns me, Chip. I can buy my way out of your damned contract. There are other record companies." Ray held out his hand and I slid from the other side of the booth.

"Don't be an idiot, Ray. Who else is going to understand your special needs? Your weird recording and appearance schedule, for instance. When you can only go out after dark. And did I complain when you couldn't do all those promos on the talk shows?" Chip laughed and leaned back. "Hell, no. Because we're brothers in this fraternity. I also understand that in a few years you're going to have a little problem, bro."

"Oh, yeah? What? My voice will be golden forever." Ray picked up his goblet of synthetic, took a swallow, then slammed the glass on the table. I moved close to him and grabbed his hand. He had a wild look in his eyes and I worried he'd try something we'd both regret.

"Right. Sure, the voice will sing as sweet, but, Ray, you won't age. How long can you stay in the public eye and not have that noticed? Hair plugs and face-lifts can explain away only so much." Chip chuckled. "So you'll have to disappear. And maybe reemerge after a few decades with a new look and start a new career as somebody else. You may not get to sing in public at all the next go-round." He turned to the man in the glasses and said something in a foreign language. I had no idea which one.

"Ask Eric here. We started out together centuries ago in the Balkans. We've been everything from Dutch to Russians to whatever. Doctors, lawyers, Indian chiefs." He and Eric laughed. "Okay, the Indian thing was too much of a stretch to try. The last twenty years it's been L.A. and the music biz. That's got about another twenty years of shelf life, then it's on to something else and I'm a new person. Chip is no more." Chip smiled at me. "Smart vampires live forever. The others . . . ? Gloriana can tell you, we reinvent ourselves. Over and over and over again. Am I right, lady?"

"Ray knows that, Chip." I made myself smile too, though I didn't like Chip's attitude.

"Sure. Next life I'll grow a beard and run charters down in the islands."

"Night charters?" Chip didn't bother to hide his amusement.

I saw the truth hit Ray hard. Just one more nail in his vampire coffin. He'd had one after another since that night he'd been turned. His grip tightened until I had to bump him with my hip to remind him to ease up. He dropped my hand and leaned both fists on the table.

Chip's bodyguards quickly moved in but Chip held up a hand and they stopped just short of jerking Ray up and slamming him against a wall or tearing him apart. Violence fairly shimmered in the air and I wanted to run the hell out of there. I laid my hand on Ray's back and sent him frantic mental messages of caution.

"Thanks for laying it all out there, Chip. Makes it easier for me to make a decision about my future." Ray smiled tightly.

Chip drained his glass. "You've been given a fantastic

opportunity, Ray. I hope you have the balls to see this gig through." He turned to me. "Gloriana, you're his mentor. I think it's time you showed Ray some of the wonders of being vampire. And, lady, if you don't know what they are, I feel for you. I really do." He gestured and I knew we were free to go.

"Come on, Ray. Don't we have another party to hit?" I grabbed his arm when I was afraid Ray was about to take a parting shot.

"Just a minute, Glory. Now that I've got Chip here one-on-one and we're frat brothers, so to speak, I have a question for him." Ray gestured at the banner on the wall behind the booth. "What's with all the initials? What does M.A.S. and O.B.G. stand for? No one knows or will tell, anyway. Drives Nate and me crazy. Now that I'm one of your Masters of the Night," Ray said mockingly, "maybe you'll let me in on the secret."

"Ray! Chip doesn't have to tell you that." Especially since Ray hadn't exactly been Chip's buddy for the last few minutes.

"Relax, Gloriana. My vampire friends know and enjoy the irony. M.A.S. stands for Music At Stake, Ray." Chip nodded and one of his men pulled a small and lethal-looking stake out of his jacket pocket. "We're always vulnerable, aren't we?" He laughed. "Put it away, Danny. You're making our guests nervous."

Ray didn't acknowledge the truth of that, just shrugged. "Okay, so what about O.B.G. Sounds? That's my label."

"Yes. The one I use for my rockers." Chip winked at me. "I spent the sixties in England. Did some producing with Paul and the Fab Four before it was time to head to L.A. So O.B.G. is for Only Bloody Great Sounds. You're damned lucky I thought you were worth keeping under contract, Israel Caine. The way you were headed, the vampire deal and going on the wagon saved your career, my man."

"Yeah, got it." Ray nodded, clearly finally ready to get out of there.

"And don't put down the Masters of the Night thing. If you stick around L.A., you'll find there are some serious perks that go along with membership." Chip leaned back, his smile full of fang. "Does your buddy Nate know you're vampire?" He shook his head. "Of course he does. Rookies. Be careful who you let in on our secret, Ray. That's a lesson I learned the hard way a long time ago. Now, run along, enjoy the party and think about what I said. You have an amazing talent, man. And an opportunity to live forever. Don't blow it." He turned when the beautiful redhead approached his table. "Ah, dinner is served."

TWO hours later we were back at the hotel. Neither of us had been much in a party mood after the confrontation with Chip. We'd put in a token appearance at a big bash at a hotel ballroom for the Grammy nominees. There had been so many famous people there I'd gotten whiplash from gawking. Now we headed up to the suite. I'd called Flo from the limo and she was meeting me there to help me decide which dress to wear on the green carpet tomorrow night. I couldn't really get excited about it. Not with Ray in a funk.

"You're awfully quiet, Ray." I leaned against the elevator wall to take the pressure off my aching feet.

"I'm going to wake up Nate and ask him about my contract."

"It's pretty late." The doors opened and I pushed myself up and out to head down the hall.

"Tough." Ray pulled out the key card and opened the door when we got there. "I need some answers."

Valdez sat in front of the TV, his paw on the remote. He was fast, but not fast enough.

"Pay-per-view mud wrestling?" I looked at Ray.

"You're reimbursing me for that, asshole." Ray stalked over to Nathan's door.

"He's got company. She's noisy. That's why I had the TV on."

"Tough shit." Ray pounded on the door. "Nate, I need to talk to you. Now."

After a tense two minutes, Nate opened the door a crack. "Not a good time, bro."

Ray grabbed Nate's arm and jerked his best friend into the living room. His naked best friend.

"Ray!" I turned my back. Oh, boy. Nate's hours in the gym had sure paid off. There was a mirror across the room and I realized I still had an excellent view.

Ray glanced at me and handed Nate a throw pillow. "Cover yourself. Glory's getting off to this."

"Am not." I couldn't hide my grin, though, as I sat on the couch and kicked off my shoes.

"What the hell is this about?" Nate looked longingly back at his dark bedroom, then closed the door. "I'm kind of in the middle of something."

"Too damned bad." Ray frowned. "I met Chip Rollins tonight. We discussed my contract."

"Oh, yeah?" Nate picked up another pillow and covered his nicely toned tush.

"Yeah. Seems Chip *owns* me. His word. Why the hell would you make a deal like that for me, Nate?" Ray paced the floor. "And, news flash, Chip is a vampire."

"The hell you say." Nate fumbled his pillows for a breathless moment, then regained control. "No freakin' way."

"Ray!" I couldn't believe he'd just ignored Chip's warning. And if he didn't think Chip would read Nate's mind the next time they met, he was crazy. Ray had just put Nate in incredible danger. I didn't say anything else, though. One crisis at a time.

"I'm not Chip's property, Glory. Nate knows what I know." He frowned and shook his head. "But obviously that doesn't go both ways, does it, Nate?"

"I did the best I could for you, Ray." Nate dropped the back end pillow to put his hand on Ray's shoulder. "I was up against a wall. Your drinking was getting out of hand and everyone in the music business had heard the rumors. Sales were flat on your last album and reviewers called the work sloppy. The only hit to come out of the thing was the duet with Sienna Star, and that's because the woman's a perfectionist and you know it. That's why we're here at the Grammys this year."

Ray jerked away from Nate and strode over to the open doors at the balcony. "No one said anything to me about all this."

"Not that you remember anyway." Nate glanced back at me, then followed him to the doorway. "Ray, there *were* no other offers. You want to make records and, without a major label backing you, there's no distribution. Chip's got that all locked up. You have to work with him."

"Thanks a lot."

"No, man, this is good news. Don't you see? The Chipster will understand your condition. Am I right, Glory?" Nate looked to me to back him up.

I got up and walked to Ray's other side. "That's what Chip said, Ray."

"Yeah, right before he started issuing orders and making threats."

"Now, Ray, I don't think he exactly ordered you not to deal with MacDonald." Though I wished he had.

"He threatened you? And who's MacDonald?" Nate looked at me, then Ray.

"Never mind. Go back to your playmate. Screw your brains out." Ray frowned at me. "At least one of us is getting some. Aw, fuck it!" In a flash, he changed and flew off the balcony in bat form.

"Ray!" I screamed. "I've got to go after him."

"The hell you say." Valdez jumped in front of me. *"Not a chance."*

"He can't go out alone in that mood. He might do something crazy." I wiped at my wet cheeks. Stupid to cry for Ray. He was going to have to get over his disappointments. But if he was going out to MacDonald's, I was going with him.

"You're not going. Is Flo coming here?" Valdez bumped me back from the balcony railing.

"Yes, but what difference does that make? It'll be too late to follow Ray then. I have to go now or I'll lose his scent."

"Aw, shit. Stay here. Do not *leave."* And in a blur, Valdez shifted into a bat and flew off the balcony in the same direction Ray had taken.

"Wow. What was that about?" Nate gave up on modesty and gripped the railing to squint into the dark.

Good luck trying to see either Ray or Valdez. I had excellent vamp night vision and it was obvious to me that they were long out of sight. I just hoped Valdez caught up with Ray. I sighed and walked back to the couch.

"Ray wants to see daylight again. This vampire named MacDonald claims he has a magic formula that can make that possible. I'm afraid that's where Ray's going. To buy some of those drugs." I slumped in my seat and put my feet on the coffee table.

"That sounds dangerous." Nate was back in pillow mode and easing toward his bedroom. "You won't let Ray do anything stupid, will you, Glory?"

"I'm trying my best, Nate, but he's a man. Men do what they want. Am I right?" Just then I heard a woman speak Nate's name from the bedroom. "Go, your booty call is getting anxious. Oh, and I'm expecting company. So would you keep it down? I'd hate for Flo to be embarrassed." I said that with a straight face.

"Right. Sorry. I should have taken this downstairs to her room. There's still time . . ."

"No, carry on." I waved my hand, my voice rough with tears I struggled not to shed. I cleared my throat. "I'm just playing with you. We'll be in my bedroom. If we hear anything, we'll just turn the TV on loud."

Nate hurried out of the room and I gave in and actually shed a few tears. First for Ray because I felt like I'd failed him. Chip was right. A good mentor would have taught Ray to appreciate his new vampire powers, not obsess about what he couldn't have. And how about Valdez? I couldn't believe he'd taken off after Ray like that. He'd done it for me, because he sure didn't care if Ray flew into the sunrise or not. When the knock came at the door and I realized Flo had arrived, I blew my nose and forced a smile. I didn't want her walking in on this sobfest.

"What is this? Why are you sad?" Flo gave me a hug. "Where is your bodyguard? I don't think I ever see you by yourself."

"He went after Ray, who is upset and just took off. No guards, nothing." I took a shuddery breath. "Stupid idiot. I hope I never have to mentor another new vampire. They are nothing but trouble."

"You've got that right, girlfriend. I sure won't do it." Flo took my arm and pulled me to the bedroom. "Look at you. You bought the green dress after all? It looks great on you. And a six. You are so skinny!"

I couldn't believe I didn't care. Hadn't even weighed in for the last few hours. No point. The waistband was cutting into me and I couldn't wait to get out of this beautiful dress. Oh, God, I was *not* going to cry again. Wait. Really, I *wasn't* going to cry. Gee, maybe I was actually getting over my body image obsession.

"I didn't buy the dress. Ray bought it for me. To wear to the parties tonight. He was so proud of me." Oops. Another little crying jag. Stupid. I wiped my eyes and blew my nose.

Flo patted my shoulder. "He's smart. He knows you did this to look good for him. For tomorrow night. Now, show me these three dresses. Do you like them? Is one your favorite?"

"I like all three of them. Each one has something special about it." I pulled the first garment bag out of the closet. "And I didn't lose the weight for Ray; I lost it for myself. It made me feel great. For about five minutes anyway." I unzipped the bag. The first dress was the black one that would work even when I gained the weight back. Good thing.

"Pretty. Black is always elegant. Try it on." Flo got busy inspecting the shoes and purse while I pulled the jewelry out of the safe. "Oh, these are real. Can you keep them?"

"No, they're on loan. Ray talked about buying me something, but I won't let him." I sniffed and then decided enough of that. I glanced at the clock. The men had been gone less than an hour. How long did a temper tantrum take anyway? Had Valdez just trailed Ray or had he confronted him and tried to force him to come back? They both had been itching for a fight. Maybe they'd pounded each other and worked off some steam. Oops. More tears. No, not happening. I sucked it up and slipped into the black dress.

"Pants? The designer made you pants?" Flo walked around me. "Cute. But I don't think so. Not for such a big night. But that's just my opinion. What does Israel say?"

"He doesn't say. I haven't asked him yet. But his first reaction was just like yours. No pants." I loosened the belt. Oh, hell, I hadn't gone through all of this just to give up now. I needed one more night of skinny and I didn't have a nighttime supplement. Ian might have called and I'd turned off my cell at the parties. And Jerry. Had he tried to call me? I'd been so wrapped up in the Ray drama, I hadn't given a thought to what was going on with the Campbell Clan. I grabbed my purse and turned on my cell. One message.

"Gloriana, this is Ian MacDonald. Trina didn't show up tonight but I've got another mortal I can send you. Call me and let me know when you want your nighttime supplement." I closed the phone.

Flo pursed her lips. "Are you going to call him back? What happened to that bitch who wanted you? Now she doesn't show up?"

"She tried to kill me. I had to take care of her." I sat on the side of the bed, then jumped up. Couldn't wrinkle the dress. "Unzip me."

"Wait a minute. She tried to kill you?" Flo unzipped the dress. "I hope you ripped out her throat."

"No, just did the whammy on her. She's over the whole

vampire obsession. Thinks we're a figment of her imagination." I stepped out of the dress and hung it up. Did I want to do one more treatment or not? I'd try on the next dress and see how it fit, then decide.

"You are too good to her." Flo unzipped the next garment bag. "I like blue. But the colors and fabrics are strange together."

"Wait till you see it on. Ray liked this one. It's different." I slipped my arms into the sheer sleeves and let Flo zip me up. I did love the tattoo thing. This time I could use Ian's webcam to at least see some of the effect. Cool. But maybe not what I wanted on the green carpet.

"I see what you mean. There are designs on the material." Flo walked around me. "I like the shoulders. Pretty beading."

"See? I look like I have tattoos. But it feels snug." Snug? I had a vise around my waist. "Does it look too tight?"

"Do you want to have tattoos? Oh, yes, Israel has them. On him they're sexy." Flo stepped back and studied me. "It *is* a little clingy in the middle. You can't gain another ounce, girlfriend. I hate for you to drink Ian's stuff, but maybe you should."

"Well, let me try on the red dress. I guess it really is my favorite." I let her unzip me and carefully hung up the blue dress. Good thing I didn't have to breathe because it had not been an option in that dress.

Flo opened the last bag. "Oh, yes! Now, this is a well-made dress! It reminds me of a couture piece I once bought in Paris."

"It does look like a classic, doesn't it? I guess that's why I'm drawn to it. You know how I am about vintage stuff." I slipped into the dress, loving the feel of the silk. "Well, are you going to zip me up?"

"I'm trying, but don't think I can." Flo tugged. "Sorry, Glory, but there is more you than there is dress. Have you weighed tonight?"

"No. I was afraid to." I picked up the webcam and looked at the front of the dress. I loved the way the dress plunged.

And the color was perfect with my skin and hair. The jewelry, shoes, everything about the outfit made me look like the lady I'd always yearned to be when I'd first met Jerry way back when. Oh, crap. Was that what this was all about?

Yeah, probably was. I wanted to walk down that carpet on Ray's arm and look like a first-class lady. The kind any man would be proud to be seen with. Maybe have Jerry get jealous and his mother finally admit that I wasn't the lowborn whore she'd always called me. In this dress, I could greet the queen and not be ashamed. I saw the sheen of tears in my eyes and ordered myself to dry up. Enough of dreams and looking back. This wasn't going to happen without drastic action.

"Suck it in, Glory. I think I can force it." Flo pulled on the fabric.

"No, don't! It might tear." I stroked the skirt and realized I had no choice if I wanted to wear this dress. And I *really* wanted to wear this one. "I'm calling Ian." I picked up the phone.

"Are you sure?" Flo put her hand on mine. "You know I have no problem with you drinking from some mortal. All for it. But his special stuff." She made a face. "If it makes you do strange things, like walk around and get in the sun. *Mia amica*, it's too dangerous."

"It's the last time, Flo. And I've got Valdez to keep me from walking into the sun." I glanced at the closed bedroom door. Not back yet. I hoped I had Valdez. What if he and Ray landed at MacDonald's stronghold and got into it with the guards? A dozen scenarios flashed through my mind, all of them ending badly. No, couldn't happen.

"Anyway, I'm resigned. After this, I have to just let nature take its course. Which means it's back to the old Glory size and shape."

"No more of Ian's drinks?" Flo tried on a pair of the diamond earrings and studied herself in the webcam. "If it's money that's stopping you, I can always help you out." She looked at me, her eyes shining. "You know that, don't you? If this is something you truly want."

"Thanks, dear friend." I hugged her. "Your money is better spent on those earrings for yourself. Or make Richard buy them for you. They look great on you. Valentine's Day is coming up. The name of the jeweler is on the box." I sighed. "Now, let me call Ian. While I'm at it, I'm going to ask if he's seen Ray. Or Jerry, for that matter."

"Jeremiah?" Flo stopped in the act of trying on a necklace. "Why would he go to see Ian?"

"To kill him. And he'd take the entire Campbell Clan with him. Remember the feud?"

"The laird's in town?" Flo dropped the necklace and jumped up. "This is not good. I must take Richard and leave here. We should go back to Austin. Or maybe take a little honeymoon trip to Tahiti."

"Why?" If I didn't know better, I'd think Flo was actually scared of something.

"Well, in a stupid fit of honesty and wanting to have open communication, I told Richard about a little affair I had once." Flo took off the diamond earrings and spat a few Italian words as she paced the bedroom floor. "Damn those TV talk shows. I should not listen to them."

"And am I right in thinking the laird, the laird of Clan Campbell, was the man you played footsie with?" I had to smile. So Mag, the very superior witch of the castle, had been betrayed by her beloved husband. This was too sweet.

"More than our feet were playing, Glory. And it was long ago. My name was totally different then. I can't even remember for sure what I called myself." Flo helped me pull off the red dress and hang it up.

"So why would Richard care about it?"

"Because I made the mistake of saying I'd had a grand passion for Angus. That he had been the only man to ever really satisfy me before Richard came along." Flo opened her purse and pulled out her lipstick. "Not true, of course. But

I was telling a story, enjoying the way Richard was getting jealous. You know?"

I knew Flo and her little dramas. I could imagine that she had embellished the hell out of the thing. By the time she'd gotten through telling the tale, she and Angus had worked their way through a plaid version of the Kama Sutra, accompanied by bagpipes. No wonder she didn't want Richard to meet him. Well acquainted with Flo and her appetites, Richard would want to make sure Angus knew that his wife was off the market, permanently. And the Angus I remembered didn't like to be *told* anything.

"Does Mag know about this affair?"

Flo jumped and smeared her lipstick. "Of course not! We are dear friends. It would be like if I had a little fling with your Jeremiah." She got up and grabbed my hand. "Which I have not. I swear on the blessed Virgin that I have not, Glory." She crossed herself for good measure and looked skyward.

"Magdalena cannot know. The only reason Angus and I got together was that he and his wife were taking a break. They hadn't lived together for, oh, decades then. And Angus was so charming." Flo got a faraway look in her eyes. "I tell you, Glory, if Jeremiah is anything like his father? *Mio Dio*, what a lover." She sighed. "But I moved on and now my Ricardo is everything to me."

I couldn't imagine the stern Scot Angus Campbell I knew, who made sure the women in his Clan were "protected" just like they'd always been in the Middle Ages, as a wild man in bed, but I just smiled and nodded. Hey, Jerry certainly drove me wild and had that protective gene too.

"Richard and Angus can't come within shouting distance of each other. You understand?"

"Sure. So I guess that means you'll be leaving L.A. as soon as possible."

"Right. Richard has been telling me he needs to get back to Austin for some business of his mother's. So I guess that means no honeymoon right now." Flo tapped her chin. "I know. I'll tell Richard you need us to hurry back to help with some crisis at your little shop. You have one, don't you? You usually do." She smiled, like this was a good thing.

"Well, sure. So glad I could help. I just had to fire one of my weekend night clerks. You can go work for me. How's that?" I grinned, knowing that Florence da Vinci Mainwaring had never clerked in a store a day in her life.

"I'll do it. Even if I have to"—she shuddered—"make change."

"Great. Take off. Tell Richard I begged you to help me. Pack and arrange to ship your clothes home. You and Rich can shift out of here right after sunset tomorrow. Sorry you'll miss the Grammys, though. Ray got you seats in the balcony, first row."

"Now I'm sad and upset. I'll watch you on TV. Everyone in your shop will watch with me." Flo hugged me. "You really are my best friend. But I must save my marriage. If the whole Clan is here with Angus, Richard might get hurt if he tries to start something. I can't let that happen."

"Of course not. So go. I'll call Ian and see if he's got someone to send me." I sat on the bed.

"Will you be all right? When will Valdez be back?" Flo paused in the doorway.

"Any minute, I'm sure. Head out. I'm fine." I waved her out and hit speed dial for Ian. I heard the hall door close just as Ian picked up.

"Gloriana, I was hoping to hear from you. I took the liberty of going ahead and sending someone to you. He should be there momentarily."

"Thanks, Ian. I'm cutting it pretty close to dawn." I glanced at the clock. "Uh, have you seen Ray tonight?"

"Yes, he just left here. We had a nice talk. And I sold him a new supplement to try." Ian chuckled. "Relax, Glory. I can practically hear you grinding your teeth through the phone. Ray's being cautious. I told him to wait until after his awards show to try it."

"Well, that's just swell of you, Ian. Thanks a lot." I shut

the phone before I could say more. When there was a knock on the hall door, I threw a robe on over my underwear and went to answer it. I looked through the peephole and saw a tall handsome man standing there. Oh, yeah, Ian had said the mortal he had sent was a "he." Hmm.

I heard a moan from Nathan's bedroom. Okay. Still action going on in there, apparently. And now I had my own boy toy. My game was definitely not anything Nate and his playmate would imagine playing.

A mere mortal? Sure, I could handle him. I'd just have to make certain this guy didn't come with a stake in his pocket. I threw open the door and looked him over. Cute. So the search wouldn't be a hardship. At all.

Sixteen

His name was Bart. Short for Bartholomew. He was out of breath from running up twenty-two flights of stairs per Ian's instructions. He glowed with good health and reeked of AB negative. I was beginning to wonder if every vampire in town had a Glory dossier. I might as well put up a Facebook page with my favorite things and be done with it. Bonus points for Bart. He was about to jump out of his gel-pumped running shoes he was so eager to do whatever my little fangs desired. Another vamp groupie.

"Let's keep this simple, Bart. Just sit next to me on the couch and hand me your wrist." I kept one eye on the balcony and one on Nate's bedroom door. I was about to take my donor into my bedroom, when he stepped a little too close and eyed my cleavage. No, we'd stay out here.

If Ray's buddy and his date came out and caught me with my fangs down, I'd just whammy the woman and be done with it. Nate had seen it all before and it grossed him out unless he thought it was vamp foreplay and he was the player who was finally going to get into my bed. Long story.

"Please, Ms. St. Clair, if you'd just take me at the neck, I'd be really, really grateful. Or I could make you feel good, if you know what I mean." Bart ventured a hand toward where my robe had slipped open over my knees.

I froze him with a look that said "stop" and made sure my robe covered me down to my ankles. "I already feel just fine, thank you, Bart. I'm sure Ian explained that you're just a donor here. I have a man in my life, a fiancé, who gives me everything I need in that other department." Had Ian been pimping as well as providing his other services? Jeez.

"Okay, I get it." Bart managed to look suitably crushed, but he still wasn't giving up on the neck thing. He ripped his tank top off over his head and tossed it on the floor.

Wow. First Nate, now Bart. I was getting a clinic on how a buff male bod should look. Not that Jerry and Ray weren't built. They were. But neither had been fanatics about working out in their mortal lives. And Valdez . . . The times I'd seen him in the altogether had been brief and I'd tried not to stare because it would have been violating some kind of friendship thing. If there was a next time, though, I was going to have to do the full tour. I shook off the thought and focused.

"What the hell are you doing, Bart?"

"Nothing you don't want, Ms. St. Clair. Ian says I'm your very favorite blood type. Is he right?" Bart stared at me with green eyes the color of old money. His dark hair was cut short and he either shaved his chest or didn't grow hair anywhere but on his head. Oops, I was checking out his body again.

"Ian's right. So what?" I picked up his wrist and inhaled. Oh, man, but I loved his type. My fangs zipped into position.

"I'm doing you a favor, aren't I? Why not hold me close and hit me in the jugular?" Bart smiled, an even dimmer bulb than Trina had been.

Didn't these mortals have anything more in their lives than an obsession with vampires? I read Bart's mind—except for an interest in what I might or might not be wearing under my terry robe, apparently not.

"Listen, Bart. I've had a rough night. Sorry if this isn't the joyride you fantasized about, but I'm hoping Ian compensates you well for this. Now, let's get this over with. Where's my supplement?"

"I'll tell you if you'll kiss me first and let me feel your fangs with my tongue." Bart leaned toward me, mouth open like a trout going for the goodies on the end of a hook.

That did it. I used the whammy, then checked the backpack Bart had worn in to the suite and pulled out the distinctive bottle of my supplement. I set it on the coffee table, then turned to fish face.

"Now, Bart, you're going to give me your wrist. Feel lucky I didn't rip out your throat for being so insolent to a badass vampire. Now, snap out of it." I kept my face stern as he blinked, then shook his head.

"I'm sorry, Ms. St. Clair. Please don't tell the master that I spoke to you like that." He held out his arm, his hand shaking.

"It's our little secret, Bart. But I want to warn you." I held his wrist and showed him that my fangs were full out. "Vampires come in all shapes and sizes and we may not *look* dangerous, but we always are. I could have taken offense just now. And, if my fiancé had heard you . . ." I faked a shudder. "He'd have tossed you right off that balcony."

"I—I didn't think . . ." He glanced at the balcony, suddenly pale. "You won't say anything to him, will you?"

"Not if you just hush and let me get on with this." I pulled his wrist to my lips.

"Y-yes, ma'am." He closed his eyes when I sank my teeth into the sweet spot and drew. "Oh, my God, but this is the good part. Uh, excuse me. I'll shut up now."

I wasn't about to stop what I was doing to chitchat. I enjoyed the rush. I'd forgotten to weigh myself before Bart had arrived, but I knew my target weight for tomorrow night. If this and the supplement got me there, then the red dress should fit perfectly. After that, it was home to Austin and back to the old Glory.

I felt the surge that told me I'd probably had enough and pulled out, licking the punctures closed and patting Bart on the shoulder. He didn't open his eyes and I leaned closer, touching his cheek to make sure I hadn't accidentally taken too much.

"What's this? Are you picking up mortals and bringing them home with you now, Gloriana?"

"Knew she was a whore. Look at him, almost naked. Bet it isn't just his blood she enjoyed. What did I tell you, son?"

"Hush, Ma. Da, let Glory explain."

I looked up and saw Jerry and his parents on the balcony. Oh, boy. My warning to Bart could not have been more timely. Mag looked like a thirtysomething schoolmistress with her stern mouth and sharp features. Her green and black wrap dress and high heels, though, could have come straight out of the pages of a glossy fashion magazine.

Angus, the laird of Clan Campbell, was a slightly shorter and sturdier version of Jerry with the same dark hair and dark eyes. Father and son could have passed for brothers. But that was the way of the Campbell men, turned vampire when they hit the age of thirty. Both of them wore dark cotton shirts and jeans but Jerry's were obviously Rodeo Drive and hugged his butt, while Angus could have benefited from a tighter fit.

Shouldn't have noticed that. Not with the hard stares I was getting from two out of three on the balcony. Of course my Jerry still defended me and tried to look calm and unconcerned, even though he probably didn't like the scene they'd stumbled upon any more than his parents did.

I stood and jerked Bart to his feet. He quickly recovered, his eyes bugging out when he saw the group on the balcony. That convinced me he'd been faking weakness to try to get some sympathy from me and maybe a little mouth-to-mouth.

"My donor was just leaving." I handed Bart his shirt and backpack, dragged him to the door and shoved him out into the hall. "Tell Ian thanks. You were fine. No complaints."

"Sure. Bye."

I slammed the door and locked it, then glanced at Nate's

closed bedroom door. "There are two mortals in there. Maybe this isn't a good time or place for this, uh, meeting."

"It'll have to do, lass. We need to know more about Ian MacDonald and apparently you've been consorting with him and his minions." Angus nodded toward the hall door. "That mortal bein' one of them if I read him aright."

"He's harmless. A blood donor, nothing more. Ian has several on his payroll." I gestured toward my bedroom. Of course Angus had read Bart's mind. They all had. And Mag knew I hadn't been whoring with the idiot. I gave her a cool look.

"Let's go into my bedroom. At least we won't be in danger of anyone walking in on us. Jerry?" I held my hand out to him.

"Thank you, Gloriana. I'm sorry we had to drop in on you like this, but my parents were in a hurry to get this thing with MacDonald going." Jerry took my hand and dropped a kiss on my lips. "Are you all right? You look flushed."

"Sure, I'm just a little high. Ian's donors come after exercising. It gives you a rush. Something to do with endorphins." I glanced at Jerry's mother. "You should try it sometime, Mag. Since you make a habit of drinking from mortals anyway. As you know, it's not my usual thing." I grabbed my supplement and led the way into the bedroom. Once there with the door safely closed, I pointed to the two chairs grouped around a table in the corner.

"I wouldn't bring a strange mortal into my home, Gloriana. It's irresponsible." Mag looked at the king-size bed and sniffed. "This is the room you share with that Israel Caine, isn't it?" She smiled at Jerry. "I hear you're engaged to him."

"It's a sham, Ma. I told you that." Jerry looked everywhere but at the bed.

"She wears his ring." Mag nodded toward my left hand.

"Window dressing. We had a Grammy thing tonight." I pulled it off and set it on the dresser. "Now, please, Angus, Mag, won't you sit?" I'd just about quit calling them lord and lady over a century ago. It didn't seem to win me any points and Jerry had said it was okay to drop the titles. Being in America had given us both a new perspective on the whole royalty issue. The fact that it bugged the hell out of Mag when I didn't bother to give her the proper "respect" just sweetened the deal.

Angus and Mag sat. Jerry gestured that I should sit beside him on the bed facing them. Well, why not? Guess Jerry had decided he was going to make the bed *his* turf now. So I sat, well aware that I was at a disadvantage in my robe and not much else. But the looks on their faces didn't give me time for a wardrobe change.

"What do you want to know?" I'd be cooperative for Jerry's sake, but I wasn't about to offer information they didn't ask for.

"Any idea how many men MacDonald has?" Angus leaned forward.

"The most I've seen is six bodyguards. They all look like surfers." I saw a puzzled frown on both Mag's and Angus's faces. "Tanned, blond, built. Like they spent a lot of time in the sun in their mortal lives. Anyway, they hang out on the beach in front of Ian's house. They're all vampires. I don't believe I saw a single shifter or other kind of paranormal in his crew. But he may have some as day guards. Just like I do." Which reminded me that Valdez wasn't back. I threw up a block. Oops. Too late. Jerry gave me a narrow-eyed look but, with his parents there, I knew the questions would come later.

"Any other security?" Jerry pulled a knife from the scabbard on his belt and toyed with it. "Did you see any weapons?"

"What? You think he would display stakes or something?" I shook my head. "Honestly, you guys need to rethink this. Ian is all about the future. He's computerized, on the Web. He's not going to worry about the Campbells. He's too busy trying to figure out how to stay awake during the day."

"The hell you say." Angus glanced at his wife. "Only a fool would believe in such a claim."

"Maybe so, Angus, but I've seen a video. I'm not sure it's not some kind of fabrication, but Ray—Israel Caine, the vampire I'm mentoring—believes in it so strongly he's willing to try Ian's special supplements." I sighed, leaned on Jerry a minute and felt his arm go around me. "I'm afraid he'll go up in flames, but Ian swears his stuff works. That he's been out during the day himself and lived to tell the tale."

"Nonsense. Vampires out in daylight? It's a fantasy we've all had, to see the sun again, but know better than to believe in. Especially coming from the likes of a MacDonald." Mag jumped up. "Angus, maybe we won't have to risk an attack. Bide your time and this MacDonald will destroy himself."

"It's possible, Ma." Jerry squeezed my shoulders. "Valdez tells me that Glory has been taking Ian's potions and has actually been awake during the day already. Haven't you, Glory?"

"Yes." I said it in a small voice, not sure I wanted to be Exhibit A with Mag and Angus staring a hole in me. I had a vivid memory of being burned at the stake as a witch. Not a dream, a nightmare. Never really happened.

Mag approached me and I stood, not willing to be loomed over by her.

"You saw it. You saw the sun?"

"I was afraid to actually look at it directly, Mag. But I did see the light from it around the curtains. I was awake after sunrise. The sunshine burned me when I stepped into it." I met her gaze. "It was strange and, I admit, awesome. I never thought it could happen again. That I'd see daylight."

"Liar!" Mag slapped me across my face, rocking me back.

I balled up my fist and landed a good one right on her pointy chin, relishing her screech of outrage. Jerry threw himself between us. Was he protecting her or me?

"You bitch! I will never let you hit me again. You even haunt my nightmares!" I dove for her, but Jerry grabbed me around the waist.

Angus grabbed Mag's arm, obviously stunned into silence.

"Filthy whore! Lowborn slut! Jeremiah never should have brought you into our home." Mag held her jaw and sobbed.

"That's enough, Ma!" Jerry held me against his chest when I tried to go after her again. "Calm down, Gloriana."

"She started it, Jerry. I wasn't lying and you know it." I shoved back and stomped to the far side of the bed, still pumped. I hoped Mag came after me again. I wanted to pound her into the carpet. Hit her until she wept and begged my forgiveness and admitted I was good enough for Jerry. I felt my nails digging into my palms and took a calming breath.

"Mother, listen to me!" Jerry grabbed his mother's shoulders, pushing her away from me when she started forward again. "Glory tells the truth. Valdez was there. He saved her from more harm."

"More's the pity." Mag snarled. "They are probably lovers, Jeremiah. The shifter would say anything for her. When are you going to realize what this woman is?" She turned to Angus. "We're wasting our time here. Let's go."

"Yes, it's best you leave. I'll see you at the hotel later." Jerry exchanged looks with his father before his parents stalked from the bedroom.

"Yes, get out, Mag. I'll be happy if I never see you again." I followed them to the bedroom door. Mag just sniffed, like she couldn't be bothered to reply to the ravings of a commoner. I collapsed on the bed when Jerry closed the bedroom door again. Damn. I guess I'd never be a lady. But then, who'd thrown the first punch? Not me. Not very ladylike of Mag, was it?

"I'm sorry about that. My mother—"

"Your mother hates me. Nothing new there." I rubbed my throbbing cheek, coming down off my high with a vengeance. "She still packs a wallop."

"You scared the hell out of her." Jerry sat beside me and gathered me in his arms.

"Scared? Mag Campbell?" I laughed and leaned against Jerry.

"Think about it, Glory. If the MacDonalds have the secret to staying awake during the day, we're lost. We'd have to hire an army of shifters to protect us." Jerry rested his chin on my hair. "And, sorry, but I've yet to meet one I totally trust. Including your current Valdez."

That got me. I didn't, or actually couldn't, say anything. Because I knew what was coming. Where was my trusty bodyguard right now? The man who was never to leave my side under any circumstances? Oh, yeah. Off chasing after my fake fiancé. And it was close to dawn. If Valdez didn't make it back by then, where did that leave me? We both heard the hall door open and close and we jumped up.

"Who?" I sniffed the air. "Brittany." I smiled. "She can watch over me during the day if Valdez doesn't get back."

"Back from where, Glory?" Jerry lifted my chin until I stared into his eyes. "You know damned good and well he has strict orders not to leave you alone. Not unless I'm with you. Yet I found you with a strange mortal, unguarded."

"The mortal was clearly harmless. And Valdez followed Ray for me. I was desperate, Jerry. Ray was upset, bound and determined to go out to Ian's place to see about the daylight thing. I was going to follow him myself but Valdez forbade it."

"Of course he did. You shouldn't be so foolish. Never should have gone out there in the first place. As I've told you more than once."

"Yes, yes, I know." I held up a hand to forestall another lecture. I'd had enough of them. "Just spare me, okay?" I opened the bedroom door. Brittany stood on the balcony. She turned when she saw Jerry and me in the doorway.

"Where's Rafe?"

"He should be back any minute. He followed Ray tonight. Since you weren't here." I frowned at her. "Where were you anyway?"

"Mr. Caine told me to take the night off. So I did." Brittany crossed her arms over her ample chest. "Unlike Rafe, I do try to maintain a decent life away from the job." She cocked her head. "They're coming, both of them." She stepped back. "Good thing too. You've only got about a half hour till dawn."

I looked at Jerry. "That means you'd better go." Too much to hope that I could get him out of there before Valdez and Ray dropped out of the sky.

"Not a chance." He smiled grimly. "Not before I have a word with, um, Rafe."

Too late anyway. First one bat, then another landed on the balcony. One morphed into a man, the other into a Labradoodle dog.

"I see you entertained while I was gone, Glory." Ray scowled and strode into the living room. He pulled a small bottle from his pants pocket and set it on the bar.

"It wasn't exactly entertaining. Jerry and his parents dropped by for some information about Ian." I gasped when Jerry squeezed my waist. Oops, maybe I wasn't supposed to tell that. "You're not the only one who wants to see the sun, you know." I looked back at Jerry. Had that been a nice save or what?

"Give me a break. I know about your feud, Blade." Ray sat in a chair and kicked off his shoes. "So your parents are in town. The head of the Clan. I'd better let Ian know to run for his life or call up his own clan and prepare for battle."

Jerry crossed the room in a blur of motion and had Ray up by his shirt in an instant. "You'll do no such thing."

"Hands off, Blade." Brittany held a stake against Jerry's back, right where it could go through to his heart. "Mr. Caine pays me to keep him safe. If I have to turn you to dust, that's what I'll do."

"*Brit, put that damned thing down.*" Valdez stood next to her, every sharp tooth in his mouth showing and he was clearly poised to spring. "*I don't want this to get ugly, but I'll tear off your arm if I have to.*"

"Stop it, all of you." I tried to push myself between Ray and Jerry. Not happening now that Ray had both hands wrapped around Jerry's neck and was doing his best to break it. Jerry's face was turning red but he couldn't move. Not with a stake pressed against him.

"I'm not backing off, Rafe. You put one claw on me and Blade's gone." Brittany's hand stayed steady and she didn't once look at Valdez. "Mr. Caine, say the word and I'll do it."

Ray glanced at me. I could see his mind working. Yep, this was his chance to get rid of his rival. I let Ray see that if he ordered Blade killed, he'd lose any hope of being with me. That I'd be out of his life forever. Not that I really believed that was a deal breaker. But I had to give it a shot.

"Jerry, let him go. You can talk this out like reasonable men." I tried again to get between them, jerking on Jerry's arm.

"Ray, tell Brit to put down the stake." I hit Ray's back. No answer. Reasonable? Forget it. These were two damned stubborn men hell-bent on killing each other.

I couldn't believe what happened next. Blame it on the weight-loss gig or emotional overload. I have no idea. But next thing I knew, I was on the floor sobbing my heart out. Yep, big boo hoos. Loud and obnoxious enough to bring Nathan to his bedroom door to peek out. What he saw sent him right back inside, and we all heard his lock click. Where was strong, self-reliant Glory now? Guess when both the men I loved were at risk, all my tough talk was just that. I tried to stop crying, but obviously Mag's slap had jarred something loose in my tiny brain and I was stuck in "poor me" mode.

Jerry swore bitterly and released Ray. Ray let his hands slide off of Jerry's neck. He nodded to Brittany and she lowered the stake. Valdez didn't move, still not convinced the action wouldn't escalate again.

I just kept crying. I couldn't see any way out of this mess. Of course Ray wanted Ian to live. The man was a friggin' genius who might be able to give vampires sunlight someday. Even the Neanderthal-throwback Campbells probably wanted to see the light for themselves. And of course Jerry wanted to kill Ian. It was as natural as breathing for a Campbell to hate a MacDonald. Rational thought didn't enter into the equation.

Jerry knelt on one side of me and Ray on the other.

"Gloriana. Stop yer bawling, lass. The she-shifter didn't stake me." Jerry tried to pull me into his arms, but I shook my head and held him off.

"Glory, baby, come on, now. We stopped fighting. See?" Ray rubbed my back until I raised my head and iced him with a look that made him snatch his hand away.

"*Get away from her, both of you. She's finally had enough.*" Valdez pushed between the two of them. "*Come on, Glory. Get up and sit on the couch. Your eyes are red and your nose is running. One of you get her a box of tissues.*"

I sniffled and leaned on my bodyguard to get up. Seemed I'd accidentally restored some sort of order. Of course, I'd lost points on the "strong, independent Glory" scale. But at least the two men in my life had quit trying to kill each other and Brittany had put that horrible stake out of sight. I waved away any other offers of help and settled on the couch, accepting tissues from Brittany and wiping my eyes and nose.

"Please, both of you, get away from me and sit over there." I gestured at the chairs on the other side of the room, frowning away first Jerry's, then Ray's, attempt to sit beside me on the couch. "Not you either, Rafe. I've had it with all of you." I sniffed, then gave Brittany a hard look. "Not too fond of you either, Brit. You carry a stake? Would you use it on me if Ray asked you to?"

"Not answering that." Brit held up her hand and glanced at Valdez. "But I'm hired to do a job. Mr. Caine's a vampire who might be attacked by another vampire. I have to carry a stake. Blade, you put Rafe at a hell of a disadvantage requiring that dog body. I guess you know that." She focused on Jerry. "It's absurd, if you ask me. Either you trust your woman or you don't. And if you don't, why the hell are you paying the freight for a full-time bodyguard?" With that, she stepped out on the balcony and shut the door.

"Good point, Blade. Something I've said to Glory more than once." Ray leaned back in one of the club chairs and smiled. "Time to face facts. The way you've been treating this woman is criminal. No wonder she's leaning toward cutting you loose."

"Ray, shut up," I said this calmly when I wanted to smack that stupid smile right off his handsome face. "Jerry, which way I lean is not the point. And Brittany was way out of line. My relationship with either one of you is not up for discussion. I'm worried about Ian MacDonald and this feud with the Campbells."

"Don't worry about that, Gloriana. It'll be over soon enough." Jerry frowned at Ray. "And how I treat my woman is none of your damned business, Caine. I've managed to keep her for over four hundred years. You've known her less than one. Don't think that makes you an expert on what she wants or needs."

"Jerry, stop! The feud won't be over. There are MacDonalds all over the world. There will be retaliations just like there always are. You simply cannot attack Ian MacDonald." Now I was pissed. Mr. Expert on Glory didn't have a freakin' clue. "And you haven't 'kept' me for four hundred years. Seems like we're off as much as we're on."

"Oh, really?" Ray's eyes gleamed and he leaned forward. "Now I get the Valdez deal. Blade needs to keep tabs on you, Glory. In case you get away from him again."

I could see Jerry's steam rising, fists clenching, jaw like iron. "Can we get back to this Ian MacDonald thing?"

Jerry reluctantly gave up trying to stare a hole in Ray and turned to me. "What about him? You described his pitiful defense. I've got more men and the element of surprise. Tomorrow night will be the end of that worthless sod." He whipped around and glared at Ray. "And you will not warn him. I'll make sure of that if I have to lock you in a lead-lined coffin until after the battle is over."

"Oh, I'm so scared." Ray laughed.

Fool. Didn't he realize that Jerry could do just that? But

maybe I hadn't told Ray we were vulnerable to the lead-lined thing. Yep. Vamps can't get out through lead, no matter how much strength we've got. Forget the myths about silver. It's lead that stymies us. But never mind that. I needed to convince Jerry that Ian had to live.

"I heard your mother tonight, Jerry. I'll bet both your parents want to see the sun again." I leaned forward. So what if my robe gapped open to flash some boob? I carry my own weapons and know how to use them. Remember, I had three virile men in the room.

"Yes, of course they would. What vampire wouldn't? They're a little more ancient than I am. The three of us are over five hundred years old." Jerry sneered at Ray. "All of it spent in the dark. Best get used to it, Caine. The rest of us have. Instead of chasing silly dreams."

"You think they're silly dreams?" Ray smiled slowly. "Ask me about that after the Grammys. I've got a potion here that Ian says will keep me awake during the day. Hell, Glory's already seen daylight, haven't you, babe?"

"Yes, but it was an accident. Ian's claims of having a formula that could help vampires see the day, Jerry, may be true." I couldn't sit still a moment longer. I got up and walked around the coffee table to pick up the small bottle Ray had brought from Ian's. "I don't know exactly what this will do for Ray." I turned to him. "And I hope like hell you'll be careful with it. But it's a beginning, Jerry. Ian's on to something. He's not the worthless sod you take him for."

Jerry actually looked thoughtful.

"She's right, Blade. I told you she stayed awake after the sun came up. Wide-awake, not just sleepwalking." Valdez nodded toward Ray. *"Of course she got burned when the sunlight hit her."*

"Yeah, so far it's just looking at sunlight, not actually letting it touch you. But Ian said he's working on a special sunscreen. He's tried it on himself, but, like Glory, suffered painful burns." Ray jumped up. "Seriously, Glory. I'm not stupid or suicidal. I just want to see some daylight. I'm going to try this, see if I can stay awake first. That's a big freakin' deal, don't you think?"

"Yes, I do. Just be careful. It would be so easy to get carried away." I waved toward the balcony. "You be sure Brittany is there to take care of you. To keep you from forgetting what you are."

"Yeah, right. A Master of the Night." Ray laughed and sat again. "That Chip Rollins. He's a jerk, but he got me to thinking anyway. Even with your watchdog here tailing me, it was cool flying back and forth to Malibu while mortals were fighting traffic down below me."

"Yes, Valdez and I need to discuss that later. But you met Chip?" Jerry was up and pacing the way he did when he had a lot on his mind.

"At the party tonight. He owns Ray's recording company. I didn't tell him I'd been to two of his houses." I smiled at Ray. "Chip's into real estate. Jerry showed me two of Chip's fabulous houses he's got for sale. One near the beach and one in the Hollywood Hills."

Ray frowned, quickly figuring out why Jerry had taken me to a vacant house. "Interesting. Guess if I decide to stay in town, I'll know who to call for a place to live."

"You really think MacDonald will make this drug for vampires safe to use?" Jerry stopped next to me, his hand on my shoulder.

"I don't know. But, Jerry, he's not plotting ways to kill Campbells. He's a businessman. If you guys are on his radar at all, it's because he knows the Campbells are rich. You're his kind of clients. He'd like nothing more than to sell you some product. He sure wouldn't let an ancient feud stand in the way of making a profit."

"You don't know that for sure, Gloriana." Jerry started pacing again. "Da is hot to go after Ian. He's the MacDonald heir, you know."

"With vampires that doesn't mean a lot, us being immortal and all. I'm sure Ian's not worrying about leading his clan someday." I paced right along with Jerry. "Think, Jerry. If you were right and Ian knew all along that you and I were together, then he willingly let me have the diet stuff anyway. And it didn't kill me. It worked. Made me lose an incredible amount of weight in time for the Grammys just like I wanted." I glanced at Ray. "Because Ray paid him big bucks."

"Send me the bill, Caine." Jerry stopped and pulled me tight against him. "You've given me plenty to think about, Gloriana."

"You want the bill, you got it." Ray stood and yawned. "Now you'd better get the hell out of here. Dawn's only minutes away."

"Less than that, boss." Valdez walked over to the balcony and tapped it with his paw. Brittany opened the door. *"I don't think you can make it back to your hotel in time."*

"Stay here. We're dead after dawn anyway." I looked at Ray.

"No way in hell." He headed into the bedroom, pulling off his shirt as he went.

"Come on, Ray. What can it hurt?" I followed him.

"I'd rather not, Gloriana. Maybe there's a vacancy in the hotel." Jerry stayed right behind me.

"You don't have time to check in and arrange that. Besides, I know for a fact the place is booked solid. I heard the desk clerk on the phone when we walked through the lobby tonight." I sighed when Ray dropped his pants.

Jerry growled as I knew he would. "What the hell is he doing?"

"Means nothing, Jerry. Ignore him. I do." I slid my hand down Jerry's chest.

"Fine." Jerry smiled and unbuttoned his shirt, flinging it on the chair behind him. Then he deliberately pulled off his belt and set his knife and scabbard on the nightstand. When he went to work on his jeans, Ray growled.

"What the hell are *you* doing?"

"Getting ready for bed." Jerry grinned, dropped his jeans on the floor and stepped out of them.

Wow, did I ever have a view. Two hunky men standing on either side of a king-size bed in nothing but their underwear. Jerry favored briefs and had worn black stretchy ones that left nothing to the imagination. Not that I needed one. I'd seen his stuff thousands of times. Yeah.

"Glory, your mouth is open. Want us to go head-to-head?" Ray grinned. "Or will your old man there be exposing his shortcomings?"

"By God!" Jerry roared.

"Ray, behave. I'm sleeping in the middle. Vampires have to stick together and this is an emergency. No one will be naked."

I grabbed my gown from a drawer and ran into the bathroom.

The silence coming from the bedroom was deafening. I quickly brushed my teeth, washed my face, then decided to slap on some makeup again since I was sleeping with two hot guys. I emerged in my floor-length, totally unsexy gown and saw Ray in his usual spot on the bed. Jerry stood on the other side, glaring at Ray.

"This is not going to work, Gloriana." Jerry snarled when Ray patted the spot next to him.

"Cuddle up next to me, baby." Ray grinned at Jerry. "Blade, why don't you just lay on the floor. Dead men don't care where they lie, do they?"

"Now, Ray, be nice. Jerry can sleep on my other side." I picked up my bottle of supplement and opened it.

"What the hell is that you're drinking?" Jerry made a grab for it.

I skipped out of reach. "I have to lose the pounds I gained yesterday. This will take care of it. Don't mess with me, Jerry. This is important. I know which dress I want to wear and I won't fit into it otherwise." I quickly drained the bottle.

"Valdez!" Jerry shouted and I jumped.

"*Sir?*" Valdez appeared in the open doorway.

"I want this door locked. But if Gloriana somehow does

her day walking and gets out of here, make sure she doesn't harm herself. Got it?"

"Got it." Valdez looked at me. *"Did you drink some more of Ian's shit?"*

"Yes. And don't give me a hard time about it. It's too late. Done deal. Now, do as Jerry said. I'm counting on you. And I'll take care of the door." I walked over and shut the door myself, then turned the lock.

I didn't feel the dawn coming but I could tell that both men were just about out for the count. So I pretended that I was conking out too. I yawned and stretched, gratified that both watched my chest rise and fall. Then I crawled into bed, leaving a few inches between me and Ray. Jerry climbed in beside me, making a big deal out of taking me in his arms. In moments, both he and Ray were goners.

I slipped out of Jerry's arms and lay there, staring at the ceiling and waiting for Ian's death sleep to come. I'd left the bathroom door open and could see the lightening sky around the edges of the curtains again. Magic. This time I was going to appreciate it. I crept out of bed, though I could have ridden an elephant out of there with accompanying trumpets and the guys wouldn't have heard it. I walked into the bathroom and carefully raised the edge of the curtain.

There it was. The pinks, pale blues and yellows of the dawn. For the first time in over four hundred years I saw the beginning of a new day. I leaned against the marble counter and wept. Silly, but I cried for my lost mortality. I'd given up so many things for love. For the first time I realized I might be able to get at least one of them back.

Seventeen

I woke up before sunset. I knew it in my bones. Cool. Even more cool was lying there, the filling in a man sandwich. I could reach out and touch a perfect male chest on either side of me. First, out of loyalty and, yeah, love, I rolled over to study Jerry. Dark stubble that he'd shave as soon as he had a chance covered his firm jaw and, even in sleep, he never seemed fully relaxed. He had long lashes. Nice. His great broad chest with its well-earned scars from so very long ago tapered down to a flat stomach that he certainly didn't shave like my earlier donor had.

None of us had pulled up the covers. Probably a case of dueling egos with the men and I'd just forgotten. We don't get cold when we sleep. We just die. I shuddered, suddenly freaked-out at the thought. Stupid, I knew it, but the fact that I could lay my cheek against Jerry's chest and hear absolutely nothing disturbed me. A sure cure for that was to continue my tour south, to where his briefs bulged. No morning or, in our case, evening erection for a vamp. Nope, just the usual at-ease position. Which was impressive enough. Now down to his muscular legs, so very fine and strong. I smiled and leaned down to kiss his shoulder, then turned to my other side.

Ray. He was as still as Jerry. And I loved him too. When had that happened? Didn't matter. It did matter that, when he'd tossed in the fact that he was thinking of staying in L.A., my heart had rolled over. Yep, it had really hurt.

I shook off my emotional confusion and focused on the physical. Ray had a nice body. *Okay, be honest, Glory.* Ray had a great body. Which was a miracle considering his hard-drinking lifestyle before he'd been turned. But he'd hit the gym often enough with his buddy Nate to be trim with naturally broad shoulders and flat abs. He had evening stubble too. Both my guys were dark. Though when Ray opened his eyes they'd be that bright blue that sent his fans into orgasms.

Ray had an arrow of hair pointing straight down to his trademark black silk boxers. They hid the package I knew was inside. I didn't need to see it. He'd flaunted it often enough. In a comparison, I'd say the men were about equal in the size department. I'd never given Ray a chance to demonstrate his prowess. I sighed, sure I'd missed the boat now. He'd move here, I'd go back to Austin and our fake engagement would be called off as planned.

I collapsed back on the pillow and boldly put a hand on each man's chest, imagining what it would be like to have them both doing whatever I wanted to please me. I laughed. Impossible. Neither one was into sharing. There'd be a dead vampire on one side of the bed before *I* got any attention.

"Glory? Are you awake?" Valdez from outside the door.

I crawled out of bed. A glance at the digital clock beside the bed showed me I probably still had some time before sunset. I unlocked the door and opened it.

"Yep. What's up?" I saw Valdez with Nate hovering anxiously behind him.

"Is everyone okay in there?" Nate looked around me. "Oh, my God! How did you manage that?" He grinned. "Or is one of them dead permanently?" He stopped smiling. "It had better not be Ray."

"No, they're both fine. We called a truce. Nothing happens while we sleep, remember?" I glanced at the closed drapes. Brittany sat on the couch. She nodded at me but didn't say anything. I had a feeling we weren't exactly friends. Well, what did I do? Oh, yeah, made Valdez my slave, I guess. Ouch.

"That was quite a scene I almost walked in on last night. I hope you guys worked things out." Nate shook his head. "The people from *Designed to Kill* have called six times already. They've got the hair and makeup people waiting in the lobby for the signal to come up and start on you, Glory. You and Ray are going to be cutting it close." He glanced at the drapes. "Hey, the sun's not down yet. What the hell?"

"I took something and woke up early. Wait right here." I ran into the powder room and weighed. Yes. The red dress would fit. "Okay, I'll jump in the shower and wash my hair. The guys should wake up in about ten minutes. As soon as the sun hits the horizon, call the TV people and have them come up."

"*I think I should go with you to the Grammys, Glory.*" Valdez glanced at Brittany. "*In human form. To keep an eye on things. Brittany can stay with Ray when he's backstage.*"

"Do you have something to wear?" I guess I owed this to Rafe. And if Jerry had a problem with it, he'd just have to get over it. Brittany was right. This wasn't fair to me. Hey, where was the trust? It was nice having a bodyguard, but when I got home to Austin, I was going to learn to live without one and Rafe was going to have to go job hunting.

"Yes, I had Brit buy me something in the shops downstairs. I'll be okay." He nodded toward the bedroom. "You should clear it with Blade first."

"No. Just do it. Brit, go get his stuff. V, you can shower and change in Nate's room. Is that okay with you, Nate?" I could see Ray's friend and manager was ready to go in a sharp-looking Armani suit with his usual white shirt and gray silk tie.

"Yeah, sure. I've got the two tickets Flo and Richard were going to use. Brit and Valdez can have them to get in and sit up there in the balcony." Nate pulled the tickets out of his jacket pocket and handed them to Brittany. "Now, get in that shower, Glory. Clock's ticking."

"Right." I grabbed underwear and my robe and jumped in the shower. I was excited. I'd been looking forward to this night for ages and I was going to wear *the* most glorious dress. My picture would be in the tabloids and they couldn't possibly say anything nasty about me for once. By the time I rinsed out the shampoo, I was so happy I was humming one of Ray's tunes.

Then the glass door opened and I wasn't alone. Jerry, naked and reaching for me.

"This isn't a good idea, Jer." I ran my hands over his chest, then looked behind him. Thank God, I didn't see Ray getting ready to lunge with a stake in his hand.

"Don't worry. Your fiancé is in the living room talking to his manager. There are television people there too. I'm supposed to be ducking out through the bathroom window." Jerry leaned down to lick my breast.

"Which is what you're going to do." I enjoyed the sensation of his mouth on my nipple for a breathless moment, then reluctantly pushed him away. "I can't do this now." I reached behind me and turned off the water. "The crew from the show is waiting."

"Let them wait." Jerry slid his hands down my back to grab my ass. "Spread your legs, lass, and let me inside."

"Jerry!" I gasped as he lifted me until my back hit the tile wall. I closed my eyes as he pushed into me, taking me hard and fast, possessing me. My eyes popped open. Bastard. What had happened to foreplay? He stared into my eyes, his gaze fierce and determined as he held me.

"I'll not come for you, damn you." I raked his shoulders with my nails.

"Aye, ye will." He bent his head and teased the vein in my neck, breathing on it, then lightly stroking it with his fangs. All the while he kept up his rhythm, deeper and faster.

"You're jealous, aren't you? Of Ray?" I pushed my hands into his hair and tugged.

"Damned right, I am." He finally eased back and began to kiss my breasts like he regretted the rough approach. Too late. "I made you, lass. I won't share you again," he murmured as he ran his hands over my body, trying to coax a response from me.

"Not your call." I could see that bathroom window where I'd cried for the dawn and all the pieces of my mortality I'd left behind. Jerry had selfishly taken those from me. For a moment I hated him. I'd been so young, so blinded by lust and a grand passion that I hadn't realized what I'd be giving up. He'd known but had wanted me with him. Forever. The consequences to me be damned.

Enough. I used my vamp strength to shove him off of me and down to his knees. The look on his face would have been funny if I hadn't been so near tears.

"Gloriana! What—"

"Beg me for it, Jeremiah." I kept my hands hard on his shoulders. "You want it so damned badly. By God, beg me for it." I leaned against the tile, my head thrown back to expose my throat, my legs still wide. "Say the words. 'Please, Gloriana, please let me inside you.'"

"Are you mad?" His eyes were cold as they raked up my body.

"Mad as hell." I pushed him away. "Forget it. But this is why I never married you, Jeremiah Campbell. Why I didn't take your ring." I was suddenly sick of this. It was so late in the game. I brushed the wet strands of hair from my face. "I've got to go. This isn't the time or place for this."

He stood and put his hands on the wall on either side of my head. "Oh, no. Spit it out. You've run me a merry chase for over four hundred years. I deserve the truth. You say you love me."

"I do. That's the problem and what got me into this in the first place. I gave up my mortality for you, Jerry." I put my hand over his heart, that heart that died every sunrise. "You *took* my mortality. I've been mad about it ever since."

"Angry? All this time? But you knew . . ." Jerry looked honestly confused.

"It's complicated. I need time to sort it out."

"Damn it, Gloriana, you've had four hundred years!"

There was a loud knock on the door. "Glory! Quit listening to that radio and come out of there. The TV people need to get started on you." Ray pounded on the door again.

"Coming."

"Shit! We're not done, Gloriana." Jerry frowned and opened the shower stall door. He grabbed his clothes.

"I'm afraid we are." I threw open the window and watched Jerry turn into a bat and fly into the night. I slipped on a terry robe before hurrying to the bathroom door that Jerry must have locked.

"Glory, are you all right? You were in there quite a while." Ray pulled me into his arms. I could tell he was worried. He looked around the bathroom in case Jerry still lurked somewhere, but Ray couldn't miss the open window.

"I'm fine. Sorry to keep everyone waiting." I grabbed a towel for my wet hair. "Let's get started." I could see a crowd behind him in the bedroom. A frowning Rafe in trousers and no shirt, Nate, Brittany and the reality show hair and makeup crew, all craning their necks to see what was up.

"Ray, don't you need to get a shower too? We've got to get moving." Might as well let the prep begin. But, after that scene with Jerry, not even the fact that my perfect red dress zipped up easily could bring my excitement back. Damn.

"Glory, what made you decide to pick Darren's design as the winner of the green-carpet challenge?" Zia held the microphone in front of me. She looked stunning in a cream silk one-shoulder dress that hit her midthigh.

"I loved the details and the way it fit, Zia. It had a retro look that appealed to me too. Ray and I both agreed that the color was perfect with my hair and skin tone." I smiled as Ray slid his arm around my waist.

"She looks great, doesn't she, Zia?" Ray kissed my cheek, totally convincing as my adoring fiancé. "I'm buying her these earrings. They're perfect on her."

"Well, I know Beaman's of Hollywood, jeweler to the stars, will be happy to hear that, Ray. Now, I know you're in a hurry to get inside." Zia managed to wedge herself between Ray and me. "For your Grammy-nominated duet with Sienna Star. We're all going to be rooting for you to win that category."

"Thanks, Zia. Now we've got to go." Ray pulled me away and down the green carpet that was almost deserted except for the excited fans that still lined the roped-off area outside. They'd screamed and shouted his name when we'd arrived in our limo. The paparazzi had gone crazy too. I'd heard whispered speculation about the new bodyguard in our retinue.

Rafe looked sharp in his dark suit with white silk shirt open at the neck. With his steady gaze and no-nonsense attitude, he fit right in with the other hot guys working the crowd. When one middle-aged groupie had tried to launch herself across the ropes into Ray's arms, Rafe had simply picked up the screaming woman and gently set her back behind the barrier.

Brittany was kept busy working the other side of the walkway. She managed to look sexy and professional in a black silk jumpsuit unbuttoned just far enough to be interesting.

"Glory!" I turned. Paparazzi? No, the group of women looked angry.

"Sellout!"

"Quit starving yourself!" This last was accompanied by a blueberry pie thrown by a woman with a strong right arm.

Only Rafe's quick reflexes kept me from getting it in my face. Of course I dodged too, relieved when not one blue drop splattered my skirt. Zia's Manolos weren't so lucky and we could hear her curses echoing down the corridor as we rushed into the building.

"That was close." Ray looked me over. "You okay?"

"Fine. Rafe?" I looked behind me before the door swished closed.

"Never better." He grinned and licked whipped cream off his fingers. "Guess that was the California branch of what used to be your fan club, Glory. Not exactly happy about your diet, are they? But damn, the ladies can cook."

Ray laughed. "Did you hear Zia? Hope that wasn't going out live."

"No, they've learned to delay her broadcasts." I sighed. The Glory St. Clair MySpace fan club, the Blueberries, had been so great, cheering me on because a woman with curves had hooked a rock star. If the women had just waited a week, they'd see me back in my old body. Back in Austin without my rocker too. Damn. I refused to cry and ruin my makeup. I dredged up a smile and put my hand on Ray's sleeve.

"You heading straight backstage, Ray?"

"Yeah, I'm sure Sienna's chewing the scenery by now. I should have been back there and changed ten minutes ago." Ray whispered, even though we were still in the lobby. The program, televised around the world, had already started, and an usher had quickly made it clear we'd have to wait for a commercial break before we could go to our seats.

"You'll be great. Break a leg or knock 'em dead or whatever they say at times like these." I smiled at him.

"Thanks, Glory." He dropped a kiss on my lips and looked at Brittany. "Let's go." They dashed off to a side door that led backstage.

"Commercial break, folks." The usher looked at our tickets, directing Rafe up a flight of stairs while I got star treatment and his arm to go right down to one of the first rows.

Wow. It paid to be with one of the Grammy nominees. I

loved it and felt great in my red dress. I even got a whispered compliment from one of the stars next to me. Cool. The show started again with songs sung by famous recording artists up for Grammys in different categories and more awards were given out.

Then it was time for Ray and Sienna's duet. The auditorium went dark until there was a single spotlight on the grand piano. Ray sat there in a tux and white shirt, open at the throat. My heart skipped a beat, he looked so gorgeous and so lonely. He started to play the haunting melody I'd heard hundreds of times. He and Sienna had practiced together in Austin before we'd ever arrived in L.A.

Then Sienna strolled up to the piano in a hot pink minidress that matched a stripe in her short spiky hair and she started to sing. She sang of missed chances and how she'd lost her love. Ray sang with her, a counterpoint. How he'd wanted to try again. But she said no. They harmonized, then went off on their own riffs. It was beautiful and sad and when it ended, you could have heard a sigh or a sniffle, it was that quiet.

The applause rolled up from the floor all the way to the balcony. Sienna grinned and pulled Ray up from the piano bench. She hugged him, then they both took a bow and hurried off the stage. No time for more. The show was on a schedule.

I sat back, relieved that it was over and that it had been so glorious. Wow. I felt a hand touch mine and looked over to take whispered compliments from artists nearby who I'd admired for years. Double wow. A few minutes later, Ray, now changed back into the black silk suit and black shirt he'd worn in to the awards show, slid into his seat. I leaned over and kissed his cheek.

"You were awesome." I held on to his hand. "I never heard you sing like that before. With your whole heart."

"Thanks, babe." He smiled. "Guess I had nothing to lose." He looked around, answered some hand signals from some people around him, nodded to others. The smile became a grin. He was beginning to believe he *had* done well and could relax. I could see it.

We sat back then and enjoyed the show until it was time for the award for best performance by a group or duo. Ray's category. Sienna and her date, a new guy I'd met just a few times, sat just behind us. She put her hand on Ray's shoulder when they read the nominees. Their names got a lot of loud applause and whistles, so they were a popular choice.

"And the winner is, Israel Caine and Sienna Star for—" The rest was drowned out by a roar of applause.

Ray grabbed me and gave me a big kiss, then turned around and hugged Sienna. They jumped into the aisle and headed toward the stage to the whoops and hollers of their friends and fellow nominees. Both of them had such joyful grins, I felt myself tear up. Ray held his Grammy for a moment, then handed it to Sienna.

"I want to thank my lady, Glory St. Clair, for literally saving my life. I wouldn't be standing here today if it wasn't for her. I love you, babe." He blew me a kiss and I wiped my eyes and blew one back. "Also, thanks to Chip Rollins and O.B.G. Sounds for keeping the faith." He winked at me, then turned the mike over to Sienna. She thanked a long list of people until music drowned her out.

A few minutes later, Ray was back in his seat with a Grammy in his lap. "Check it out," he whispered, then handed it over.

I fondled it, though it was just a piece of metal and wood to me. What mattered was what Ray had told millions of people tonight.

"It's amazing, Ray." I handed it back. "I already knew you were a star. This is just concrete proof."

It seemed to take forever, but finally the last award was handed out and the show was over. Ray and Sienna were surrounded and congratulated. Several of the well-wishers wanted to talk future deals. Nate worked his way forward from where he had been sitting and passed out business cards. Seemed like Chip might have some competition if it came to contract talks again.

"Okay, woman, I think we can get out of here now." Ray slung his arm around my shoulder.

"Are we going to Chip's party?" The vampire had made sure we knew he was holding a special celebration for his winners. Ray wasn't the only one of his stars to cop a Grammy tonight. There had been three others. As far as I knew Ray was the only vampire among them.

"I let him know I was skipping out. He gave me a key to the Masters' Club. That's the private vamp club here. Why don't we go check it out?" He was leaning close and said this into my ear. "You're supposed to be teaching me the joys of my condition, remember?"

"I guess I owe you something after that tribute from the podium." I couldn't help it. I pulled his face down and gave him a kiss. He quickly turned it into something special. When I heard someone clearing his throat, I pulled back. Valdez, with Brittany beside him, stood in the aisle waiting for us.

"Where to?" Rafe didn't show by his expression what he thought of the kiss, just followed us up the aisle of the rapidly clearing building. "Fred called. The limo's in front."

"Good. We're heading to a new club. I've got the address right here." Ray handed a card to Rafe. "Give this to Fred." Outside, Ray followed me into the back of the limo while Brittany and Rafe were told to squeeze into the front with Fred.

"Alone at last. Where were we?" Ray pulled me into his arms.

"On our way to a club. I was thanking you a minute ago. Don't take it as a green light, Ray." I smiled and patted his chest. "That was a wonderful thing you said up there. My friends will be amazed."

"I meant it. I've never forgotten how you took me on after Lucky turned me. You kept me from losing my mind and my life." Ray kept his arm around me. "I didn't want to be a vampire, you know that. But I'm stuck. Chip's right. Time to make the best of it. I'm staying in L.A. and keeping an eye on Ian's experiments. I'm going to plug into the vampire scene and get in good with Chip's crowd. He's got power and not just in the music biz." Ray played with one of the curls the hairdresser had left to fall next to my cheeks. The rest of my hair was in a twist at the back of my head. It exposed my neck and let the fabulous earrings and diamond necklace I wore show off to advantage.

"I'm glad to hear you making plans like that, Ray." I shivered when his fingers brushed down my jaw to my neck. "But I'll miss you. Unfortunately, I've always known Austin is too far from your usual scene to stay your home base."

"Oh, I could make it work if I thought you really wanted me there." Ray leaned down and put his lips against the vein throbbing at my neck.

God, but these vampire men and their moves. Of course it didn't take them long to figure out how erotic it was to have a man play around with your life force. I shifted in the leather seat and ordered my body to quit reacting. So what if I'd sort of had sex with Blade just hours before? If Ray had figured that out, he'd just take it as a challenge. He eased his hand along my knee and up my thigh. Somehow my silk dress worked its way even higher.

"You do need to be here. Chip's a good connection for you. He obviously can show you aspects of the vamp life that I don't have a clue about. I've never been into the power and, uh, the high life the way he is." I worked hard to keep my voice steady, but it wasn't easy with Mr. Magic Fingers such a busy boy.

I didn't want Ray to get away with touching my breast. It was wrong. I wasn't going to make love with him. It would send the wrong message. I was leaving and he was staying. I'd push him away in a moment, but, oh, when he slipped aside a bodice so well made it hadn't required a bra, it felt so, um, good. He had a light touch. Not mean and rough against a tile wall.

My eyes popped open. When had I closed them? Ray's head was bent over my breast and he'd worked the dress down. He was about to draw my nipple into his mouth if I didn't stop him. I slid my hands into his hair and helped him along instead. Why the hell not?

"Glory," he whispered just before he pulled it into the warmth of his mouth. He traced the lacy edge of my thong and slipped a finger inside. Of course I was wet. This man could always make me want him. I'd like to blame Ian's supplement, which revved my libido along with my metabolism, but it was more than physical this time.

Israel Caine had stood onstage and told millions of people all over the world that I'd saved his life and that he loved me. *Loved* me. I pulled him with me, to lie on top of me as I fell back on the leather seat.

"Ray." My hands were in his hair again as I brought his mouth to mine. "Kiss me, Ray." I wanted to taste him and memorize his flavor. It would be a long time, maybe never, before I'd see him again. He licked his tongue into my mouth and I raked it with my fangs. His finger probed me and I knew he felt my desire as I moaned and arched against his hand.

The car stopped and the intercom came to life. "Mr. Caine, we're here."

"Tell him to drive around the block," a shameless slut named Glory whispered.

"Just once?" He smiled against my mouth and added a second finger inside me.

"Twenty times." Then I laughed and sat up, forcing him to roll off of me and almost hit the floor. "Oops. Guess that was a close call."

"No way. We're going around the block." Ray reached for the switch to call the driver.

"No, we're not. I'm not doing this in a backseat of a rented limo." I pulled up my bodice and straightened my skirt. "Let's go check out this club." I put my hand on his flushed cheek. "It'll be fun."

"I know something else that'll be fun. In bed back at the hotel." Ray slid his hand up under my skirt again.

"Nope. We're here. Let's go." I plucked out his hand and shook my head. "Not happening."

"Oh, man, I thought I finally got you with that big speech tonight." Ray reached for the door handle.

"Was that all that dramatic declaration was? A way to get into my panties?" I slapped at his arm. "And here I was full of warm fuzzy feelings and you were just being a conniving jackass."

"They're such pretty panties." Ray grabbed my hand and pulled it against his swollen crotch. "And the way you've been leading me around by my cock made me desperate. Whatever works, darlin', whatever works."

The car door opened and Ray hopped out like nothing had happened. I climbed out after him, swishing my skirt and taking his arm. Two could play at that game. And that was all it had to be. A game. He was the great Grammy-winning Israel Caine, and I was ordinary shopgirl Glory St. Clair. I needed to keep that in mind. Too bad my heart didn't seem to be getting the message. And Ray forgot that I was a mind reader. All that tough talk had been so much b.s. He did have some genuine feelings for me behind that smart talk and playful attitude. But I'd rejected him one too many times. So he was being cautious. I couldn't blame him. If I truly wanted him, I was going to have to send a clear signal with no last-minute rejection. I just wished like hell I knew what to do about that.

He said something to Brittany and she laughed and stayed with the limo. Rafe ignored him and followed us inside what looked like an upscale office building. The doorman stood under a red awning and watched as Ray used a key card to enter. Soon we were in an elevator and headed for the pent-house.

"Why is Brittany still downstairs?" I decided we needed to talk. Anything to keep Rafe from examining my wrinkled dress too closely. Fortunately, it had come with a matching wrap and I held it over my bodice where one of the ruffles had come loose.

"She's guarding my Grammy. I'd hate for some obsessed fan to get hold of it." Ray grinned. "I've got three more of them at home, but this one's special. Everyone had written me off. This signals a big comeback."

"Right. That's what Chip said." I stepped out of the elevator as soon as it stopped. "Nice place." An understatement. The luxurious bar was made of zebra wood and curved around one side of the room. There were walls of sliding glass doors that opened onto terraces. Tables were scattered over the darkened room and wine-colored leather banquettes made for cozy corners where couples lounged over goblets of red. I sniffed. There were mortals and vampires here. Shifters too. Maybe some other paranormals. I'd have to ask Valdez if he could identify some of the others.

The music was heavy on the bass and conducive to slow dancing. Some couples were taking advantage. Just like at the other vamp club, some were heterosexual, some were same sex. All were very friendly to each other.

"Good evening. Mr. Caine. Congratulations on your win. I'm Dom, your host. Mr. Rollins phoned and said you might be joining us." The tall man wore a tux and black tie with his snowy shirt.

"Thanks, Dom." Ray looked around. "Can we get a table? You can put our bodyguard at the bar."

"Certainly, Mr. Caine, this way." Dom directed Rafe to a spot at the bar, then led us to a table near the terrace. We had a great view of the city lights. Ray held my chair, then ordered us drinks of fresh in my favorite flavor.

"I assume you're off the diet now, aren't you, Glory?"

"Might as well. I'm not taking any more of Ian's supplement." I inhaled when the goblet was placed in front of me. I looked up at the young waiter. "Your source?"

"Blood bank, ma'am. We're very careful here."

"Thank you. That's all I ask."

The waiter nodded and stepped away.

"Very smooth, Glory. I wouldn't have thought to ask. What could be wrong with it?" Ray sipped his drink. "This is good."

"Hey, I'm still your mentor, you know. Remember it could be tainted with alcohol or drugs. We've been through that scene and I know you don't want someone else's hangover." I glanced around again. "I'm sure the Council approved this place. So we can relax here and drink freely. Kind of like a health inspection for vamps. That's a perk of having an organization in town. That's why Damian's trying to do it in Austin."

"Right. But I need to ask Ian if he's got a supplement that'll let me have a glass of Jack once in a while." Ray laughed. "Hey, it's as important to me as your diet is to you." He frowned. "Shit, I guess I *am* an alcoholic."

"See? One of the blessings of being made vampire. It cured you of that." I sipped my drink. "Another caution. Always smell the blood you're taking for disease too, Ray. Don't know if your life out here is going to include hunting mortals. I hope not. I don't recommend it. Too dangerous. For the mortal and for you."

"Yeah, unless someone like Ian sends you an offering. Didn't see you turning that down." Ray sipped his drink. "This beats the hell out of most synthetics. I'll have to see how to hook up with a blood bank. That's the way to go."

"Expensive, but you're probably right. I'll stick with my synthetics from now on." I looked around and spotted a few attractive female mortals in the crowd giving Ray the eye. "Just play it safe, Ray. You may find some mortals served to you on a platter, so to speak. Vamp groupies. Just be careful. If something smells off to you, pass. If they've got a disease, you can pick it up, at least for a while. You'll heal, but sometimes it can be a painful process."

"Weird. You mean I could take on someone's, I don't know, butt boils and end up with them?"

I laughed. "Please don't make me picture that." I sipped my drink and felt the pressure increase at my waistline.

"This is good. I'll miss this dress. But it was fun while it lasted."

"You were the most beautiful woman there tonight." Ray reached for my hand. "I was proud to be seen with you. I arranged for a DVD of the TV show to be sent to our suite. When I thanked you, I saw them flash your picture on the big screen. You were glowing, you know." He squeezed my fingers.

"Damn, Ray. I was so in the moment, I didn't even look." I blinked back stupid tears. "Thanks."

He pulled my fingers to his lips and nibbled them. "You sure you don't want to stay here in L.A. and keep me company? Hell, I need your guidance. I might end up with butt boils or cock rot."

I laughed and slipped my hand from his. "If you pick up a case of either of those, you deserve to suffer. E-mail me pictures." I shook my head. "I appreciate the offer, Ray, but you know I've got a store in Austin. People depend on me there."

"Lacy would love to run it for you. Turn it over to her and start one here. Have you had a chance to check out the vintage-clothing scene? Sienna tells me it's cool." Ray picked up his glass again.

"I know. I talked to her about it. She's found some great buys. The dress she wore tonight was sixties haute couture." I could see that I'd just lost Ray's attention. "What are you looking at?"

"I think I just spotted my first vampire call girl." Ray nodded toward the bar and a woman talking to Valdez.

"You think?" I examined the redhead with legs a mile long and creamy skin. In a way she reminded me of Mara, except this woman was less evil witch and more Miss Congeniality. She leaned toward Valdez and flashed him some impressive cleavage before they both laughed at something she said. Hmm.

"Well, she just slid a business card across the bar to him. Her number." Ray glanced at me. "Maybe she's not for hire. Maybe she's just into old Rafe. He's a decent-looking guy."

"Yeah, he is." I picked up my goblet again. "Good to know you can find a call girl here. You need to get laid. That much is obvious. And by a vampire. Since your try with mortal DeeDee was such a disappointment."

"Don't remind me. She's called me twice, wanting to know what's up with us. Told her you and I were making up. Now we're the real deal. That's why I ignored her in the elevator. Had to keep on message." Ray slid close on the leather banquette. "Come on, Glory. Stay here, make it real. We have fun together. Like right now. Fly with me to the beach. We can stop at Ian's, pick up two bottles of the daylight thing and see the sun rise together. How does that sound?" He picked up my hand and stroked his fangs across my palm.

Truth? It sounded wonderful. I was so tempted I almost jumped up and ran out to the terrace.

"I can't stay. And I can't make it real. But I could use some fun." I took a breath. "Ray, I saw the sun rise this morning."

"Oh, God." He groaned and leaned his head on my hand. "Tell me about it." He looked up and waited. "Every detail."

"It was amazing. The colors. I'd forgotten. You have any idea how long it's been for me?" I blinked and had to stop while I gathered myself. "Anyway, I knew enough not to let the sun touch me, but I looked out the window and saw the sun come up. Birds chirped and the sky gradually lightened. You and Blade were lying there on the bed. No heartbeat, no movement. Dead. And I was, well, alive. It was incredible."

"Shit! Let's go!" Ray jumped up and pulled me toward the terrace.

I stopped and looked back. Valdez was on his feet and tossing a few bills on our table. I nodded once, then did the bat thing. Why not? I wanted to go. Ray wanted me with him. This was a once-in-a-lifetime opportunity and I wasn't going to miss out.

Eighteen

"How long does this last, Ian?" Now that I had this tiny bottle in my hand, I was having second thoughts. Nothing Ian had given me so far had acted like it was supposed to. And it didn't help that Ray was practically jumping out of his skin and talking about lying on the beach under some cabana and watching the sun come up over the ocean. Yeah, right. And what if this wore off and we died right there in the sand? Was Rafe going to cover us with a tarp or something and stand guard until sunset?

"That's hard to say, Glory." Ian smiled. "It varies. You're smaller than Ray. The same dosage might last a little longer with you than him."

"See, Ray? It's unpredictable. Think this through." I held on to his arm. Valdez was behind us and staying silent. I liked him better as a dog. Then I couldn't see the stony disapproval on his handsome face. Or the lethal glances he divided equally between Ian and Ray.

"It won't last all day?" Ray uncapped his bottle and sniffed. "What's in this stuff?"

"Not one dose anyway. And the formula's my secret. So's the diet one." Ian smiled at me. "You look great, Glory. You want to keep this up, we can work something out. Make a special deal. Recruit new clients and I'll give you the supplement for free."

My breath stalled. Forever a size six?

"That's a hell of an offer." Ray grinned. "She's gorgeous, isn't she?"

"She certainly is. One of my best success stories."

"Too bad you don't have a video." Ray obviously had visions of me in a bikini.

No way. Even at a six, my thighs weren't anywhere near camera ready.

"Oh, but I do." Ian picked up a remote. "Put this together from surveillance footage." The screen lit up. "Before." There I was, stuffed into my size-twelve jeans and T-shirt playing cool rocker chick as I stood next to Ray on Ian's deck.

"Nothing wrong with that, babe." Ray squeezed my waist. "Nobody fills out a T-shirt like my woman."

"Thanks, Ray." But when I saw the "after" picture, obviously taken just minutes ago, I had to sigh. My beautiful dress. Like a flame. Thanks to Darren's genius design, my waist looked impossibly small. And my hips! Even my face looked thinner. Yep, I had cheekbones.

"Very dramatic. What do you say, Glory? Want to keep it up?" Ian froze the picture. To tease me, I guess.

"No thanks, not interested. I'd have to chase down runners every night and I don't like taking advantage of mortals. Then there's the fact that your supplements do weird things to me, like wake me up and give me nightmares."

"True. Your reactions intrigue me." Ian picked up my wrist and inhaled. "I'd like to draw a blood sample if you don't mind. To analyze this. It might help me make my products more effective."

"Rather not." I snatched my hand away. Ian was a scientist. And I knew he was only trying to help vamps realize a dream. But it was all about the money. He wasn't exactly handing out daylight to the average working vamp, was he? And the diet thing had a high price too. I didn't want to become one of his lab rats. Next thing you knew I'd be calling him "master" and making house calls. No thanks.

"Your decision, of course. But if you change your mind . . ." He looked out toward the deck. "I think we've got company. I've been expecting this. Your boyfriend and his family have arrived, Glory."

"Ray is my boyfriend." I slid my arm around his waist. "I don't know what you're talking about." I'd really hoped I'd talked Jerry into stalling his father, maybe even getting him to head back to Scotland.

"I'm not a fool. I've known since the first night that you and Jeremiah Campbell are together." Ian smiled. "Surprised you share the same woman, Ray." He shrugged. "But obviously Glory is something special."

Ray and Valdez both made ominous sounds.

"I think that was a compliment, guys. To me anyway. Please don't start something." I looked out the glass toward the beach. Hell, there was an army. No, make that two armies facing each other. One looked like the guys were ready for a remake of *Beach Blanket Bingo*. The other? The warrior gang from *300*. What woman wouldn't be happy to share a towel or a plaid with any one of the buff hunks doing the staredown out there? "I think Ian's already got his hands full."

"Nothing I can't handle. But looks like the fangs are about to start ripping and tearing." Ian was surprisingly calm considering he was the prize in this blood war.

"Ian, do something. They'll kill each other." I stepped out of his reach when I realized I would make an excellent hostage in a negotiation. The laird might not care, but Jerry would feel obligated to take me into account.

"That would be entertaining." Ian glanced at Ray. He knew Ray wasn't going to harm him. Ray was all about the formulas. No Ian, no daylight. In a fight, I had no doubt where Ray would line up.

"Rafe, back off." Because Valdez looked ready to take on Ian. Not a good idea. When it came to vampire against shifter? I'd always assumed vamps would come out the winner and that's what Jerry claimed. I really didn't want to see that tested.

"Shall we join the party?" Ian nodded toward the terrace. "There seems to be a standoff and the laird is calling for me. I'd hate to disappoint him."

I looked around for something to use as a weapon. I'd like to threaten Ian and make him avoid a showdown. Didn't he have a tunnel or some way he could disappear and avoid what was sure to be a bloodbath? But I'd told Jerry that Ian didn't display stakes and it was the truth. He didn't have so much as a toothpick lying around that could be used against him. Even the fire in the fireplace was done with fake logs. I did manage to slip a small Murano glass sculpture into the folds of my skirts. The dolphin's snout wasn't much of a weapon, but it might slow somebody down for a moment or two.

"Maybe you should fly out the back, Ian. Set up shop somewhere else." Ray slipped his bottle into his pocket. "I don't know how tough your guys are, but those Highlanders look like mean sons of bitches."

"Of course they are, Ray. 'Tis my heritage too." Ian smiled, showing impressive fangs. "We pride ourselves on being mean sons of bitches." He cocked his head toward the beach. "Angus has a way with words. He's describing my mother's character now. Thinks that will bring me to the sand." He shook his head.

"Won't it?" I knew how these Scots were about the women in their families. I wasn't even technically part of Jerry's and look what he'd done for me. I heard a particularly ugly word shouted down below and winced. Now Ian was bound to charge down those stairs.

"Relax, Glory. You look worried about your Campbell lover." He smiled at Ray. "Or friend or whatever. Angus is wasting his breath. My mum *is* a slut. I quit defending her so-called honor centuries ago." He winked. "Ray, you'd love my baby sister LeeAnn. She's a fiery redhead. God knows who her father is. Da sure doesn't." He laughed bitterly.

"You see why I can't concern myself with matters of clan loyalty? It's a joke."

He held up a hand. "Now, that was a low blow. There was never a MacDonald man who didn't have a cock less than . . ." Ian grinned at me. "Sorry you and I never hooked up, Glory. You could see what I mean." He nodded. "I've heard enough of Campbell's rants. I'm going out. Are you coming with me?"

"Wait." I stared at him. I'd known too many proud Highlanders and there was something off here. "Cut the crap, Ian. I'm not buying this 'I don't care about the feud' line. How do you really feel about it?" I gripped his arm and took a chance. I stared directly into his eyes.

"You sure you want to know?" He covered my hand with his and I felt Ray and Rafe move closer. I gestured them back with my other hand.

"Yes." I didn't blink. "Men have died on both sides, haven't they? Don't you want it to end?"

"Hell yes! I hate this. I've lost two brothers to it. More cousins than I can count." He still didn't look away. "The lairds are stubborn bastards and immortal, damn them. They won't quit. It's endless and mindless. So I left." He ran his hand through his hair, a gesture very like Jerry's when he was upset. "Yet here they are. Bloody hell. Why won't they leave me be?"

I looked into his mind and saw the truth, amazed that Ian let me see it. So much pain. There'd been a child lost too, but he wouldn't speak of it. I nodded.

"All right. Let's see if we can fix this." I turned and walked boldly out to the terrace at Ian's side. I had an idea and gripped the small bottle in one of my fists, the dolphin still hidden in the other.

Angus stopped raving as soon as he saw our group step to the edge of the terrace. Jerry stood next to him. No sign of Mag, but that didn't surprise me. Angus would have ordered her to stay behind. War was man's work in his universe.

"MacDonald. Come down here and fight me like a man." Angus stepped away from the pack and glared up at Ian.

"Why?" Ian leaned against the railing. "I have no quarrel with you, Campbell."

"You're the son of a whore. I spit on the name MacDonald." Angus spit in the sand and stomped the spot for good measure.

Ian laughed. Angus charged then, headed straight for the stairs. Jerry jumped in front of his father, but was knocked flat by a swing of a beefy fist. The surfers moved into action, but stopped at a word from Ian.

"Let him come." Ian jumped to the top of the stairs. "Have at me, Campbell. I can take whatever you think you've got. But this will solve nothing."

"No!" I leaped in front of Ian, my red dress flowing around me like a bloodred cape. I barely made it before Angus bellowed and stopped right in front of me.

"Out of the way, Gloriana!" Angus's face was red and his fangs looked huge. Fortunately, he was just enough of a gentleman to hesitate using his fist on me.

"No! Listen to me." I could see Jerry behind his father, poised to grab his shoulders and try to jerk him back down the stairs. "Leave him for a moment, Jerry. Just listen, Angus."

"Why the hell should I? I've got a coffin all ready. I'm taking the MacDonald heir back to Scotland. We'll see what his father thinks when we send word we've got his boy set to stake." Angus laughed. "Finally, we'll have this settled in our favor."

"Don't be daft. Next it'll be one of your bairns 'napped and staked and then you'll have to retaliate. Hasn't that been the way of it for centuries?" Ian shook his head. "You and my father are fools, stuck in a time when action substituted for brains."

"I don't have to listen to this." Angus reached for me.

"Touch her and I won't hesitate to hurt you, Da." Jerry had his hands on his father's neck.

"You won't have to. I'm taking care of any one of you who lays a hand on the lady." Valdez had ripped a leg off a table and held the jagged piece of wood in his hand as he leaped into position next to me. "Now, listen to what she has to say or die."

"Shit, Valdez, way to go." Ray shouldered past Ian to flank my other side. "You heard the man. Let her say her piece."

I took a shaky breath and prayed this would work. "Okay, now listen. I have a bottle of Ian's daylight formula here." I held it up. "Angus, you'd like to see the sun, wouldn't you?"

"I don't believe in that nonsense." Angus didn't take his eyes off the makeshift stake in Rafe's hands.

"Believe it. I told you. It works. Want to see the sun again?" I waved it under his nose. "You could try it this very day."

"And trust a MacDonald? I'd have to be mad." He finally glanced at me.

"He sold the bottle to *me*, Angus. Had no idea a Campbell might taste it. It's safe. You could see the sun rise." I reached out and brushed his cheek, so much like his son's, with the back of my fist. I looked past him and gazed into Jerry's dark eyes. "It's beautiful, Angus. The break of day. Can you re-member it? The cool quiet as the earth turns and the sun begins to peek above the horizon?"

Angus cleared his throat. "It's been too long, lass. Ye ken I've not seen it in centuries. And even then I was apt to play all night and sleep well into the day."

"So this would be a new and wondrous experience." I grabbed his hand, jabbing it with the dolphin before tossing it impatiently aside to press the bottle into it. "Just imagine, Angus. Ian can make that happen. Is working on making it possible for vampires to actually walk in the sun without burning."

"True. It's still a work in progress." Ian nodded. "Right now all I can promise is a view of the day from safely inside, where the sun's rays can't harm you."

"What's to keep us from taking your formula, making this stuff ourselves and then staking you anyway?" Angus clutched the bottle and stared at Ian like he was primed to do just that.

"I have my formulas right up here." Ian pointed to his

head. "Nowhere else. I die and all my work goes with me. Do you really want to lose that opportunity, Campbell?"

"Not sure I believe it anyway. But can't deny the MacDs are a wily bunch or we would have finished this feud in our favor centuries ago." Angus looked down at the bottle again, then at Jerry. "You trust what Gloriana says? Enough to take this potion with her?"

Jerry narrowed his eyes on Ian. "Gloriana's word I don't doubt for a second. But Ian's swill? Glory, it did strange things to you. Remember?"

"Jerry, please. This is different. I know you must be as sick of this feud as Ian is. Prove to your father that this works and maybe . . ." I wondered if I was wasting my breath, but Angus still stared down at the bottle in his hand. Maybe not.

"The secret to seeing daylight. Mag and I talked of this after Gloriana told us what happened to her. I agree a business-man is unlikely to poison a paying customer. Is there another untainted bottle handy, lass? One this MacDonald intended to sell ye?" Angus thrust his bottle into Jerry's hand.

I turned to Ray. "Give me your bottle, Ray. I'm sure Ian will give you another one."

"Of course." Ian smiled. "And, Campbell, I guarantee you and your son will be back with your checkbooks once you've proof for yourself that the potion works. Of course I take all major credit cards. Price list is on my Web site."

"Web sites. Credit cards. Seems the MacDonalds have gone soft in the new century." Angus toyed with the handle of a dagger stuck in his belt. "Jeremiah, you don't have to do this. We can still finish things here and now."

Two of Ian's guards, who'd been in the shadows, suddenly moved in behind Ian. They looked ready to leap into action. I wondered if this was all about to go to hell in a hurry.

"Soft?" Ian laughed and gestured. More guards appeared on the roof. "You're outnumbered two to one. But I'll not take anything for granted. I know Highlanders."

Angus never blinked. "Aye. That you should."

"No, Da. I'll go with Gloriana and try the drug. If I see

daylight, then we'll know *this* MacDonald is worth more alive than dead." Jerry held out his hand to me. "Is that what you wish, Gloriana?"

"If it will keep you all from killing each other." I glanced at Ray, then stepped toward Jerry. "Rafe's coming too."

Angus frowned. "All right, MacDonald. But if this doesn't work, you know I'll be back. And I'll no waste time blatherin' either."

"I make no claim I can't back up with facts." Ian stuck his hands in his pockets and smiled.

Angus swept his clansmen with a stare. "I have said how it will be. MacDonald, your men will not follow them. Agreed?"

"Agreed. Jeremiah, enjoy the sunrise. Glory, sorry you'll have to endure with a Campbell for company." Ian lost his smile and waved his men off until they moved enough to give the Campbells room to retreat.

"Glory, you don't have to do this." Ray held my arm.

"Caine's right. You don't owe the Campbells this." Rafe glared at Angus. "Glory shouldn't be dragged into the middle of your damned feud."

"I put myself here. And I may not owe the Campbells anything, but I don't want anyone to get hurt if it can be avoided. Are you with me, Rafe?" The fact that I was surrounded by a Campbell army had obviously freaked out both Ray and Rafe. "Ray, I'll be okay. You say you believe in this daylight drug. So believe that. You know Jerry has never hurt me."

"Maybe not, but I don't know that about his father." Ray acted like he wanted to follow us down to the sand.

"Stay where you are, Caine. I can take care of Gloriana." Jerry held on to my hand, his stern face still in warrior mode and not giving me much reassurance that I wasn't about to be in the middle of a vamp tug-of-war. "My father would never harm her. Rafe, are you coming or not?"

"I'm with Glory all the way." Rafe kept his makeshift stake firmly in hand, sticking close behind me.

"Very well." Angus raked the group, both camps, with another hard stare. "We'll stay here to be sure you're not followed. Jeremiah, you know where to go. I'll meet you back at the hotel right after sunset."

"Ray, I'll see you back at our hotel then too." I saw that his face was beyond grim. "I'll be okay. Jerry, let me go." I looked down until he dropped my hand, then I moved closer to Ray.

"Be careful, Glory." Ray pulled me to him for a quick kiss.

"No problem." I eased back and took his bottle of daylight drug, handing it to Jerry. He stuck both bottles into his sporran. Jerry started to say something, then just firmed his lips. I stared at him, looking my fill. At least the clan hadn't broken out the bagpipes, but they looked mighty fine in their plaids. My heart twisted and I wished . . . I started to brush past him, but he grabbed my arm.

"Gloriana, thank you for this."

"Glad to help." I smoothed my skirt. No comment on my dress?

"You look beautiful tonight." Jerry had obviously read my thoughts. Which made the compliment too late and not worth a damn.

"Thank you." I headed down the stairs behind Angus, Rafe at my back.

"Stay close to Jeremiah. He'll show you where to go." Once we hit the sand, Angus stepped aside and clasped Jerry's hand. "Godspeed, son." Jerry nodded, then shifted into bat form and flew inland.

Rafe and I shifted and followed him. It soon became obvious that Jerry was taking no chances that anyone might have decided to pursue us. He led us on a long and winding tour of the coast before we landed on the deck of a beach house not very far from Ian's place. Jerry used a key he pulled from his sporran, then punched in a security code.

"Another of Chip's properties?" I shook out my skirt as I stepped inside the well-furnished living room.

"Yes. The man is heavily invested in real estate. Da's men scouted the area around MacDonald's home, then I arranged to rent this place for a week so we'd have somewhere to bring the wounded after the battle." Jerry sighed. "Thank God it hasn't come to that. Yet."

"I hope it never does." I could feel the dawn coming and saw Jerry yawn. "Ready to try Ian's daylight drug?"

"You sure it's not poison, Glory? I haven't forgotten how some of MacDonald's brew tainted your blood."

"Only for a short time. And that was his weight-loss stuff. This is totally different. Remember, I've seen the dawn since then. And awakened before sunset. As far as I know, vamps can't *be* poisoned. Why would I lie about that, Jerry?" I smiled. "Seeing a sunrise is a miracle that I hope we can share together."

"Valdez, I guess you're the one who will have to go tell my parents if Glory and I both expire after we drink this. I don't envy you the task." Jerry dug the bottles out of his sporran and held them up to the lightening sky. We'd stepped outside and stood on a deck overlooking the Pacific. It was a beautiful, quiet night, with waves coming ashore just yards away on a sandy beach.

"Then you'd better both live through this, because you don't pay me enough to face Mag Campbell with that kind of news. Come in here, both of you, before the sun catches you." Rafe went into the large house and shut the French doors after we were safely inside.

"She'd be thrilled if *I* finally went up in smoke." I took my bottle and twisted off the cap. It smelled different from the other drugs I'd had from Ian. Still fruity but very subtle. I watched Jerry sniff it suspiciously.

"Ignore her, Glory. I'll tell you why Ma's like that with you if we stay awake long enough." Jerry finally looked up. "Guess we'd better drink." It was perilously close to dawn, and I'm sure he felt the heaviness of it as much as I did. "To miracles." He held his bottle out toward mine.

I saw all kinds of hidden meanings in his eyes but was too tired to figure them out right then.

"Miracles." I smiled, we clinked bottles, then both drank.

"Mmm. Bit of a treat to taste something besides blood, you know." His eyes opened wide. "Well, well. How are you feeling, Gloriana?"

"Great! Awake actually." I turned to Rafe. "Look out and see if the sun's coming up yet."

Rafe walked over and peeked, then looked at his watch. "Just about. There are sheers behind these drapes. Both of you step way back in the room. I'm going to open the drapes. You two can enjoy the view as long as you stay awake. Just don't allow a ray of sunshine to hit you or you'll get burned. That's what happened to Glory before."

"We'll be careful." Jerry put his arm around me, and I could see the excitement in his eyes. We both waited until Rafe got the drapes open and the sheers closed to filter the sunshine. The sky was just beginning to lighten.

"Okay, all clear. Come closer." Rafe grinned. "Blade, don't press your nose on the glass. That's a little too close."

"Oh, man, would you look at that." Jerry laughed and hugged me, his eyes wide.

I looked. It was a beautiful sunrise. Even through sheer curtains and despite the fact that we weren't even facing east, the colors were incredible. Jerry and I held on to each other and watched, neither of us sleepy, as the beach came to life. We pulled up chairs and the hours flew by. Children built sand castles, their mothers gossiping with each other as they sat on towels and laid out picnics. It was so wonderfully ordinary. And the sun rose to shine down on all of it.

"I want Ma and Da to see this."

"Why *does* Mag hate me so? I know I'm common, but—"

"You're not common. Don't ever say that about yourself again." Jerry jumped up and paced around the room. Rafe had headed into the den hours before, and we could see him asleep on a couch through a doorway.

"Well, you can't tell me Mag doesn't think so. Otherwise, why did she hate me on sight?"

"Because I'd brought home another. Liza." Jerry ran his fingers through his hair, keeping a good distance between us.

"Liza?" Why had I never heard this name before?

"My wife."

"You've been *married?*" I jumped up, knocking over my chair.

Rafe, obviously a light sleeper, ran in with that stupid broken table leg in his hand. "Glory? Are the MacDonalds outside?"

"We're okay, Rafe. Go back to sleep. Please." I picked up the chair and sat again.

"I never told you about her, did I?" Jerry stared out at the beach instead of meeting my gaze.

"No, you didn't." And I thought *I* kept secrets.

"I was young. Fell in love. Her father was a simple tailor in the village. My mother declared her an unsuitable match for the heir, and so we ran away together. Came back married. This was long before I was made vampire, of course." He finally turned and looked at me.

"Of course." My mind was spinning. Jerry married. And Liza. I'd never heard one soul mention that name in the castle in all these years. Why?

"I can read your thoughts pretty clearly, Gloriana. I forbade anyone to mention her. That's why you never heard Liza spoken of in the castle." Jerry sat across from me. His hands were fists when he dropped them to his knees. He stared down at them. "She carried my child, Gloriana. Then one day I rode out on a raid against the MacDonalds. Heard they were on our land again, stealing cattle."

"That damned feud." My heart skipped a beat. I didn't want to hear this. "What . . . ?"

"This feud needs to end. Taking the heir won't end it. Only stir things up all over again. Make it ten times worse."

"Jerry, what happened to Liza and the baby?"

"The MacDonalds tricked us. While we were gone, they raided the village, burned some houses and killed the few lads left behind to defend the place." He punched his knees and laughed, a bitter sound. "We have a code, ye ken. They don't touch our women and children, and we abide by the same rule. I'll give them this: They fight fair. But fat lot of good that did Liza that day." Jerry scrubbed his hands over his face, but his eyes were dry.

I reached out and rubbed his knee. "Jerry?"

"It's been a long, long time, Gloriana, since I've let myself remember." He shook his head. "Nay, that's a lie. I remember every day. Wonder what my son would have looked like. Grown up to be." He covered my hand with his and squeezed hard. "Liza went into labor that day. It was too soon. She and the babe both died." Jerry turned his head to stare at the children playing on the beach. "My fault. Ma didn't want Liza to live in the castle, and I let her have her way. If Liza had been safely inside, she and the babe would have lived." His eyes met mine, the pain I saw there stealing my breath.

"Damn it, Gloriana, that's why when I brought you home, I made sure you were set up in the castle, pushed in my mother's face. I dared her to object. Ma knew she'd lose me for good if she didn't go along with it publicly. I'd not have another woman I loved risked because of Ma's pride." He looked down and realized he was about to crush my fingers. He loosened his hold. "Of course, I'm afraid she's done plenty to punish you when I'm not around. That slap the other night wasn't the first, was it?"

"Forget it, Jerry. I've learned to handle Mag." Including dodging a few of her attempts at staking me in the back in castle hallways. I touched his cheek with my fingertips. "I'm so very sorry, Jerry."

"No, *I'm* sorry, Gloriana. I set Ma straight after we left you. She'll treat you with respect from now on, by God, or I'll never see her again." He stood suddenly, as if all this talk and eye contact had been too much for him.

"That's a pretty heavy threat." I got up too and followed him to the windows. We were close enough to feel the warmth of the sun through the sheers, and we both watched a surfer ride a wave in.

"Make no mistake. I meant what I said to her. Ma understood that too." Jerry didn't look at me.

"What did you do after Liza's death?"

"I begged to be turned vampire right away. My first thought was to tear out some MacDonald throats. But I soon realized it was me and my own mother who held the most blame."

"You were mad with grief." I put my arms around Jerry's waist and leaned against him. I could only imagine how he'd felt. Yes, I'd lost my husband as well, but poverty had dulled the shine of my first love for a struggling actor long before he'd been killed in a freak accident. And then I'd had to scramble just to survive. I hadn't had time to indulge in tears or grieving. I'd been too terrified and too hungry.

"Yes, I guess I was a bit mad. But Da obliged me, turning me even though Ma wanted me to marry again and have more bairns first. I didn't have the heart for it and certainly wasn't going to do anything to please *her*. Not after the way she'd treated Liza." Jerry faced me and put his hands on my shoulders. "Once I found you, I held on tight, didn't I? Maybe too tight. I'll always protect you, Gloriana, no matter the cost. You needed me when I found you, and I guess I can't forget that. I'm sorry if that's no longer to your liking, but there it is. Maybe that's what's pushing you away now, seeing as how you've become so independent. I've tried to change, but I'm not sure I have it in me."

When he was right, he was right. I reached up and stroked his cheek. Did I want him to change? Of course I did. No way was I the same woman Jerry had fallen for more than four hundred years ago. But now wasn't the time to get into that. I noticed that Ian's drug was wearing off. Jerry suddenly looked exhausted.

"Thanks for telling me this, Jerry. I wish I'd known it years ago. It would have helped me understand a few things."

Like why my maker had continued to feel so responsible for me. Example: Valdez number whatever sleeping on the couch a few yards away.

Jerry yawned. "MacDonald's drug has made me loopy, or I probably wouldn't have spilled my guts now. It's not my way to trot out my pain, as you know. But if it makes you happy to know this, so be it." He pulled me to him and sighed against my hair. "I'm sorry, Gloriana, but I don't think I can stay on my feet much longer. How do *you* feel?"

"I'm still good for a few minutes more. For some reason, Ian's drugs don't work on me the same way they do on other vampires." I pulled his lips down to mine and kissed him. "I mean it, Jerry. Thank you for sharing so much. I know that was hard for you. I'm really sorry about Liza and . . . and the babe."

"It was a long time ago. And I can't lay the blame on the MacDonalds any more than I can on my own stubborn family. You're right. The feud must end. I'll tell Da that the daylight drug works. We'll use that as our excuse to end it." He gestured toward the beach. "This *was* a miracle. I'll be damned if I'll let the man who made it possible be sacrificed in the name of an ancient hatred that started over a stolen cow and a tumble in a hayloft with the wrong woman."

"Very sensible." I hid a smile. I knew how these Highlanders felt about their livestock and their women.

This time it was Jerry who dropped a kiss on my lips. "Now I've got to find a bed, or I'll hit the floor. Are you sure you're all right, Gloriana?"

"Fine. I'm going to stay here and enjoy the day." I smiled and watched him stop to hit Rafe's foot, then head down the hall.

Rafe stood and stretched. "He had a pretty good dose of daylight. Think this will really stop the feud?"

"Looks promising. Uh-oh." I realized I was sinking fast myself. "I thought I had more time, but now I think I may have run out." I yawned. "I've got to hit the sheets as well."

"This way." Rafe led me down the hall to what looked like the master bedroom.

"Thanks, Rafe." I yawned and stumbled after him.

"Watch your step." He smiled and took my arm when I bumped into the door.

"I'm swearing off those supplements. Too much weird stuff happens. Daylight was cool, though." I patted his cheek. "Thanks, pal." I smiled back at him, feeling some of that weirdness right then. Like maybe I wanted to kiss him. His human form was so totally hot, and I was more than a little miffed at Jerry for keeping such a huge secret from me for, oh, centuries. Nope, couldn't do that. Rafe *was* a pal. Besides, he'd think I was crazy.

"All part of the job, Glory. Now you'd better take off that beautiful dress. Don't want to wrinkle it." He steered me to a spot next to the empty bed.

"Where's Jerry?" I tried to reach my zipper but couldn't manage it.

"Down the hall, in another bedroom. Stretched out, still in his kilt. This bed is bigger. You'll be more comfortable here." He gently turned me around and unzipped my dress. "Wait till I leave the room before you drop that. Lay it over a chair."

I yawned again and smiled, holding the dress to my breasts. "Always taking care of me. Don't know what I'd do without you."

"You did look amazing tonight, my lady." He touched my cheek, then sketched an old-fashioned bow. "Perfect." He turned on his heel and walked out of the bedroom, shutting the door quietly behind him.

I put my hand on my cheek. Nice. Should've at least given him a hug. Oh, well. I let go of the dress, then realized I didn't have on anything underneath but a thong. I staggered to a chair, dragging the dress over it before I fell on the bed. I was out.

I woke to a most delicious feeling. Hands on my body, knowing hands that got it just right. Umm. I lifted my hips and then I was naked. Skin against skin. Rough against smooth. I explored a firm back and walked my fingers up through silky hair until I angled his head where I wanted it. I opened my mouth and kissed him, seeking his tongue and his taste. My eyes snapped open.

"Ray, where did you come from?"

"Surprise." Ray grinned and ran his hands over my bare bum.

"Jerry?"

"Is dead to the world in a bed down the hall."

I sat up, my heart in my throat. "You didn't—"

"Stake your lover in his sleep?" Ray grimaced. "Damn, why didn't I think of that?" He pulled me back under him. "But, no, he's safe and sound. I doubt Rafe would have let me at him anyway." He leaned down and drew his fangs along my throat.

"You're right. But we can't—" I realized my legs were wrapped around Ray's hips, sending a totally different message.

"Sure we can." He nibbled my lower lip and pulled my breasts against his chest. "Mmm. This has been too long coming. I need you so bad."

"I can feel that." Obviously Ray had taken one look and decided to strip so he could join the party. He felt amazing against me and tempting beyond belief. What was stopping me? A man who hadn't trusted me enough to share his past with me?

Ray kissed me, his thoughts wide-open. He'd reached his limit as far as watching me with Jerry was concerned. If I rejected him this time . . . And part of me ached to finally let go and have him love me like he wanted to.

But he was going to stay in L.A. I knew it. And I was leaving. I had no choice. My real life was in Austin. This rock-star fantasy was just that. I'd known when it started that it couldn't last. A one-night stand would just make our parting harder. It was already going to just about kill me.

He rolled me on top of him and gazed up at me. "Let me look at you. God, you're beautiful. No more of that diet shit.

I want to just fall into these breasts and forget breathing." He proceeded to bury his face between them, then kiss his way from one nipple to the other with the enthusiasm of a true believer. He explored every inch until I shivered and moaned and clutched his hair.

I tried to think. Tried to push him away and start a rational discussion of all the reasons why this wasn't going to happen. Then he slid me up and began to lick a path down my stomach. Oh, this was a bad idea. I grabbed the iron headboard when I meant to push him away. How had that happened? I couldn't let him . . . But he was strong and he had a goal and knew clever ways to get there. Oh, yeah. Touchdown. Or score. Or home run. Whatever. I gasped and bucked, so far gone I had to bite my lip to keep from keening and slamming my head into the wall behind the bed.

"Say my name," he whispered, his breath warm against my thigh.

"Ray." I barely managed it. "Ray, don't."

"Yes. Don't chicken out on me now, Glory. It would kill me."

I forced my eyes open and glimpsed the heavy drapes across the room. There, just at the edge, I could see a trace of light. The one thing that, for Ray, might rank above mind-blowing sex at this point. It was reason enough to shove him aside, leap off the bed and hopefully not infuriate him or break his heart. And mine.

"Ray, look! We're awake and it's still daylight outside." I stood next to the window.

"I know. Don't you love it? Ian's a friggin' genius for sure." He dragged his eyes from my naked body to the drapes where I pointed at that sliver of light.

I grabbed a pillow and held it in front of me. "Tell me how you managed to get here. In daylight."

"I took a double dose of Ian's drug at his place. Then I watched the beach through his tinted windows all day. It was totally cool, Glory." Ray lay back, all glorious naked male.

Why was I talking when I could be doing? No, I had a

list of reasons why that was a bad idea. I struggled to trot them out again. Ray grinned, doing a little mind reading. Then he climbed out of the bed.

"I did the same thing. Watched the beach with Jerry." I put out my hand to keep Ray from getting too close. "But how'd you get here?"

"I called Fred and had the limo pick me up. Tinted windows. Ian has a covered carport at his front door. So does this house. Sun's rays never hit me, and here I am." He moved in and tried to steal my pillow. "With my woman."

"But how did you find me?"

Ray grinned when I did a vamp leap across the bed and out of reach. "I'm in tight with Chip now, and who else is a vampire going to go to for a safe house? My new buddy was happy to help out when I told him you'd practically been abducted by the Campbells." He shook his head. "The Council isn't too happy about a feud on their turf. Blade didn't mention it to Chip when he rented this place. I told my boss I'd make sure the Campbells cleared out." Ray snatched at my pillow, but I dodged him.

"No problem. This was just temporary. When Jerry wakes up—" I gasped when Ray leaped and landed behind me, wrapping his arms around my waist.

"Gotcha." He nuzzled my neck, his desire hot, hard and very apparent against my backside.

"Ray." I snagged my thong with my toe and dragged it to me. "We can't—"

"Sure we can." Ray snatched the thong and tossed it at the door. "Not thinking of getting dressed, are you?"

"Come on, Ray." I dropped the pillow and turned in his arms. "We've got a sunset coming. You have any idea how rare that is for me? I don't want to miss it. Do you?"

He pushed me down to the bed and fell on top of me.

"Glory, Glory, Glory. Making love to you would be way better than any sunset, any sunrise. Stick with me, and I'll buy you a thousand sunsets." Ray licked the vein throbbing in my neck and I shivered.

Every inch of Ray pressed against me, and I knew he meant what he said. Which made this so much harder to do. But Jerry was down the hall. And now I understood him. Knew why . . . Then I felt a vibration. No, a hum. Ray had closed his eyes and held me close, his mouth against my throat where the blood pumped slowly to my heart. He rocked us gently to a beat only he could hear. It was a lovely tune, one I'd never heard before. He even sang a few words, his breath soft and sighing against my skin, and my eyes filled with tears. One dripped down my cheek and landed on his forehead.

"Not the reaction I was going for." He looked up and smiled sadly. "See how you inspire me?" He braced himself on both elbows and gazed down at me.

I felt his strength and saw his tenderness. God, I hated to deny him or myself. But I couldn't do this. He saw my answer and shook his head.

"Shit. This is going to be one of those 'crying in your beer' love songs, isn't it?"

"Afraid so, Ray." I pulled his head down and kissed his lips. "Let's go see that sunset."

"You sure? No sunset color will ever compare to the way your cheeks go pink when you're turned on, baby." He brushed his thumb along my cheekbone. "Or the way your eyes sparkle when you're happy. Like you were last night wearing that red dress and looking like a goddess."

"Ray." I swallowed. I wished . . . I finally shook my head.

He smiled sadly and eased off of me, then held out his hand. "Guess there's a sunset for us to see, then. Come on." He pulled me to the door.

"Put on your pants, Ray. Please?" I jumped between him and the door. No way was he going out there naked in front of Valdez. "I'll wear your shirt."

"What's the matter? Afraid Rafe will get jealous if he thinks you and I did the wild thing in here? Or report your infidelity to Blade?" Ray feinted right, then left, but I didn't fall for his tricks. I just stayed in front of the door.

"I'm serious, Ray. This is nonnegotiable. If I have to"—I grabbed a lamp—"bean you over the head, you're going to put on those pants."

Ray grinned and picked up a lamp of his own. "Dueling lamps. Let's go, baby. I'd love to see Blade lose his security deposit."

I just shook my head. I knew what Ray was doing. Playing to save his pride and maybe give me time to get over my urge to cry, which was pretty strong right now. I think I loved him more in that moment than I ever had. But having sex with him wasn't the right move here. Wrong place, wrong time. I wished for a shred of dignity. Forget it. Not while I was standing there naked, wearing nothing but a frown.

"Humor me. I refuse to flaunt my love life in front of the hired help." God, I hoped that hadn't carried into the den. I'd never thought of Rafe as just an employee. But whatever worked at this point. "We can waste time like this until the sun goes down and Jerry comes out of his bedroom. Don't think that's a threesome you'd enjoy. Blade would be wanting to kill you for being here. But it's your call."

"Shit." Ray grabbed his pants and stepped into them. "Now, move."

I smiled and did just that, then grabbed his shirt and slipped it and my thong on. They covered me enough for modesty, and I followed Ray. Twilight streamed into the living room through the sheers, and Ray stopped and stared for a moment. Then he was slapping Rafe on the back and talking a mile a minute.

"See that Jet Ski? I have one like that on the island. No, mine's got a larger engine." He leaned forward. "Fool's going to turn over." He laughed. "What did I tell you? Glory, check it out. Look what's coming down the sand. You ever see a dune buggy before?"

I joined him at the window. "Not until this morning. Funny how Ian's formula works differently on some of us. Guess Jerry is still dead to the world." I took Ray's hand. "And a double dose let you stay up all day."

He grinned. "Blade will be sorry he missed this. But I bet the Campbells stop feuding now that Blade's realized Ian's stuff is the real deal and he saw the sunrise this morning. He did see it, didn't he, Glory?"

"Sure did. He's all for ending the feud now. That's what he plans to tell his father."

"Guess he'll shift out of here when he wakes up." Ray turned to Valdez. "Rafe, call Fred and arrange to have the limo pick up Glory and me here after dark. You know, I want to buy a place on the beach. I wonder if this one is for sale." Ray couldn't quit smiling.

I saw Rafe pull out his cell phone. He just turned his back and hit speed dial. The hired help. Okay.

"Talk to Chip. If you're staying in L.A., he has several properties he's trying to sell. Check out all his listings." I turned back to the beach. A group of teenagers had gathered wood and looked ready to light a bonfire. What fun.

When I'd been sixteen, I'd already run away from home and married an actor. It had been a hard life and, after he'd died, worse than hard. My parents had decided it was better to pretend I was dead than admit I'd made such a foolish choice. So I'd had no support. No wonder Jerry had been so important to me and I'd jumped at the chance to be taken care of.

Of course I'd loved him and been dazzled by his power and sensuality. I'd never known a man like him before, a vampire. I'd been so grateful that he'd wanted me I'd been blinded to the complications my choice to join him for eternity brought with it. And every time I'd tried to think, to analyze why I might hesitate, he'd put his hands on me and I was lost. Damn. No wonder I had this simmering anger that had no place to go.

I turned to Ray. Not angry with him. But not going to take advantage of his gratitude either. I smiled.

"Do what you want, Ray. But no hasty decisions. That's my best advice."

"You're right, Glory. I'll take my time and do this right.

Rent first, then buy later. L.A. is where I need to be. Close to Ian and his miracles. And close to the music scene. Nate's told me that a time or two or six." Ray slipped his arm around me. "Stay. We can have a ball here."

I leaned against him. "I'm tempted, but no. I'm heading home tomorrow. I'll check into flights."

"The limo's not that far away. With traffic, it should be here in half an hour. Right after dark." Rafe walked up to stand beside me. "Nice evening. I get this is big for both of you. Guess MacDonald is something of a genius."

"You bet he is." Ray walked to the door. "It's almost dark. I'm going outside. If I freak or start frying, pull me in, Rafe."

I started to call him back, then realized it was too late, Ray was already out there. He was right. The sun was slipping below the horizon. In about ten minutes or so we would have been waking anyway. Ray stood, arms out like he was hugging the last bit of daylight. Thank God he didn't seem to be having any bad reaction to it. He grinned and waved me to come on out.

I ran to join him. So we stood there hand in hand and felt the magic. I tucked the memory away in my Israel Caine scrapbook. For once I wished for one of those damned paparazzi. A picture would have been nice. But, as the sun finally disappeared, I knew a photo wasn't necessary. The smell of wood smoke, the crash of the waves and the giggles of teenagers along with the feel of Ray's hand in mine were enough to make this a moment I'd never forget.

Nineteen

"You're not really leaving, are you, Glory?" Ray watched me carefully fold that beautiful red dress and place it in my suitcase.

"'Fraid so." I'd tried it on one last time. Snug. Of course. The reentry into Glory as usual had already begun. Actually going back to Austin would just make it official.

"I had Nate book you a first-class seat. Here." Ray stuck a packet into the side pocket of the case.

"I'm not taking money from you, Ray." I started to take it out, but he put his hand over mine.

"It's not money. It's a return ticket. So you can come back." He grinned and pulled me into his arms. "You know you're going to miss me." He had me up against him and I had to admit I missed him already.

"Of course I will. But you'll get busy and the women will be hitting on you, as usual. And"—I slid my hand along his jaw—"one of those hot female vamps we saw at that Masters' Club will initiate you like you deserve."

"I wanted it to be you, babe." He turned his head and teased my fingers with his teeth. "We'd have been great together."

"I know." I laid my head on his shoulder. "Give me some space, Ray. I'm too tangled up in this business with Jerry to get involved, really involved, with you."

"Yeah, I knew he'd be part of this." Ray kissed the top of my head. "He's in the living room. Surrounded by my guys from the band and looking like he wants to be anywhere but here. Too damned bad."

I leaned back. "I didn't even sense him come in."

"Maybe because he behaved himself for a change. Used the elevator, not the balcony, and actually knocked on the door." Ray put his hands on my shoulders. "You ready to see him? Is he going home with you?"

"Don't know about that, but, yeah, I need to talk to him." I smiled and pulled Ray's head down to kiss his lips. "Thanks for being so cool about this, Ray. I'll keep that ticket. And if you ever need me, I'm here for you."

"Good to know." His eyes glittered and he did what he always did, had to take this to another level. "If this is my kiss-off, Glory girl, it's got to be a good one." He pulled me to him, slid his hands down to my hips and snugged me as close as we could get with clothes between us.

I sighed and slid my arms up around his neck. I looked into his eyes and saw my reflection. I was Glory fangirl, Glory who melted when she heard the right song and Glory who knew a good man when she kissed him. I pulled his head down and let him know just how much he meant to me.

For a minute or more I thought I might not be able to go away after all. Oh, but he made me feel things. Then I heard the bedroom door open and the blast of music from the living room along with the shouts of the celebration still going on. Ray's Grammy win. A boon for him and his band. The guys had been all over him the minute we'd walked back into the hotel the night before.

Finally, Ray lifted his head and licked his lips. "I'm going to remember that. But it won't be enough."

I gently eased my hands from around his neck and stepped

back. I knew who was behind me. Now that he was in the room, I couldn't miss his scent or his disapproval. I wasn't about to turn around, though, and ruin this moment for Ray.

"Come visit if you get the chance." I touched my swollen lips. "And I'll remember that too." I blinked back sudden tears. "Take care of yourself. Promise?"

"Brittany's staying with me. She'll be my watchdog during the day." Ray glared at the man behind me. "He gives you any trouble, shout and I'll throw his ass off the balcony."

"You and what army, Caine?" Jerry's voice was a growl.

"I'll be fine. Go enjoy your win with your guests, Ray. I'm not leaving for another hour. I'll see you before I go."

"Right. Dismissed. I get it." He frowned and kissed me on the cheek, then strode out of the room.

I still didn't turn around, just picked up a stack of T-shirts and added them to the suitcase.

"Gloriana." He was right behind me. "Aren't you going to acknowledge me?"

"Oh, Jerry. Didn't know you were coming. Did I miss your call?" I made a show of picking up my cell phone. "No, guess not."

"I was tied up, but I'm here now." He turned me to face him. He was back in one of his new Rodeo Drive outfits, handsome in faded jeans and a burgundy silk shirt. "Why are you packing?"

"I'm going home. I've got a flight in a few hours. Can't leave too late or I won't beat the sun." I shook my head. "Oh, speaking of. What did Angus say when you told him how Ian's formula worked?"

"He could hardly believe it. Wondered if I'd been tricked somehow. He questioned me for hours. Centuries of distrust don't go away overnight. Now he's convinced we've got to keep an eye on MacDonald and let him keep making his brews." Jerry frowned. "He wants me to stay here and do that. Da will go home and start what he calls peace talks with the head of the MacDonalds."

"You'll be staying in Los Angeles." I sat on the side of the bed. Well, I'd always said I wanted to be independent. If both men in my life stayed here and I headed east, then I'd be truly on my own. I swallowed.

"It would be the smart thing to do. If I really want this feud to end. It's the first real incentive we've had to end it. You and Caine said your good-byes just now?" Jerry pushed the suitcase over and sat beside me.

"Yes. He's staying here too. The music scene is here. And he's hooked on Ian's formula. It was amazing, Jerry. Remember? Dune buggies and Jet Skis." I grabbed his sleeve. "We saw all of that after centuries in the dark. People going about their business in the daylight." I laughed. "Ian's brilliant. The Campbells *have* to let him do his thing in peace."

"Yes, obviously. Da is already trying to figure out how to buy some of Ian's formula through a third party so he can try it himself. He doesn't want MacDonald to know it's him doing the buying." Jerry smiled. "I do want to try it again, Glory. With you." He lost his smile. "But I sure as hell never again want to wake up after sunset to find you practically naked with Caine. Did you and Caine make love in that damned beach house with the sun shining outside?"

I didn't answer. Just stared at him. He hadn't even given me time to explain when he'd walked in on us at the beach house. He'd just taken one look at us standing on that deck, shifted and flown off in a rage.

Jerry flushed and stood. "What? I don't deserve to know?"

"I've given Ray back his ring. I never accepted yours. So, no, you'll not get an answer. I'm a woman who's free to love any man I wish, Jeremiah. Any man I wish. But I'm on my way back to Austin alone." I stood and put my hands on my hips. Hips that were wider tonight than they'd been the night before. Too damned bad.

"You don't have to go alone. I can get one of my brothers to take over here. If I knew you wanted me with you—"

I put my hand over his mouth. Want him? God help me, always. But have him?

"I've depended on you too much already, Jerry. I see that now." I drew my hand across his lips to caress his jaw. "I love you. Will always love you. But I need to do this. Go back and be totally on my own. While I figure out a few things."

"What's the rush to go back? Take a few days to think about *this*. Consider moving here. Look around Los Angeles without the Israel Caine circus going on. Stay with me in my hotel. I put my parents on their plane an hour ago. We can be alone." Jerry took my hand and pulled it to his lips.

I was actually tempted. What would a day or two hurt after I'd already been gone a week? I started to say as much when Jerry spoke again.

"You've not been yourself lately. I blame MacDonald's swill. I think I can persuade you to reconsider this mad plan."

"With sex?" I jerked my hand from his. "No, thank you. And just because I'm not melting in a puddle when you touch me doesn't mean I'm drugged or deranged." I turned my back on him and stuffed my precious pair of skinny jeans in the suitcase. I felt his hand on my waist and whirled around. "You think all you have to do is bed me and I'll cave. Well, get this, Jeremiah Campbell, Jeremy Blade or whatever the hell you chose to call yourself this century. I'm more than just a willing bedmate, that idiot who threw away her mortality for a dark and dangerous vampire lover centuries ago."

"I'm sorry if you regret that choice, Gloriana. But it's a little late—" Jerry reached for me again.

"Damn it. Do not touch me right now." I leaped over the bed to the other side. "I do *not* regret my decision. I love this century. Wouldn't have missed it for anything. I've learned so much since I met you. The main thing? Woo-hoo. I actually have a brain. I've built a successful business that needs me. People depend on me for their livelihood." It was true and something I was proud of.

"I always knew you were intelligent, Gloriana. Otherwise you would have bored me long ago." Jerry was pretty smart himself, staying on his side of the bed and jamming his hands in his pockets.

"Well, would it have killed you to have said something?" I wanted to throw a chair at him. "Never mind. Hear this. I *want* to go back, Jerry. I know you have no real ties to Austin. L.A. will be a good move for you. You'll enjoy the structure of the Council and it's important to keep an eye on Ian." I couldn't resist the wounded look in his eyes. My big bad vampire wasn't used to being dumped. Well, not dumped exactly. I was definitely leaving the door open for him. Couldn't imagine not having him back in my life sooner rather than later.

I walked around the bed and eased up in front of him. "Come on, Jerry. Surely you can see this is for the best. A little time apart. I'm not saying it's forever. We've done this before and survived it." I pulled his head down to kiss his cheeks, his chin, then his mouth. "Get to know Ian and the other members of the Council. Try the daylight drug again."

"I'd want to share it with you, Gloriana." He crushed me to him and stole my breath with a kiss that was part goodbye and part stay.

I twined my fingers in his thick hair and held on, tempted to give in to his persuasion. So many memories. I finally had to push him away before I ripped open his shirt and pants and knocked him to the floor. Damn me for a slut.

I stepped back from him. "I've made up my mind, Jerry. I'm going. Maybe not forever. Maybe I'll sell the shop or let someone else run it eventually and come back here to Los Angeles." I ran my hands through my hair, my mind so muddled I didn't know what I was saying. "But I'm getting on that plane. I have to."

"Then take this." He shoved a packet in my hand and took a step back. "Valdez told me what you were planning. Use it when you need to. Or want to. Call me and *I'll* come. Just don't forget who made you. Who loves you. Who is always going to be yours." He spun on his heel and slammed out of the room.

I stood there, still out of breath and off-kilter. I looked down and began to laugh. Yep, I had another first-class round-trip ticket from Austin to Los Angeles.

The flight attendant warned us that they were about to close the doors when a man slipped into the seat next to me. I'd been alternately crying and just staring out at the dark tarmac as the other first-class passengers boarded the plane. I'd left one piece of unfinished business that bothered me. Oh, come on, Glory. "Bothered"? Hell, I was beside myself. I'd wanted to talk to Rafe. Explain why I wasn't going to have a bodyguard anymore. But I hadn't been able to find him.

I'd talked to Brittany. Asked her to explain. She'd been happy to pass the word. Right. I could just imagine how that conversation would go. My Rafael Valdez deserved so much more than a secondhand kiss-off and the hastily scribbled note on hotel stationery I'd managed before the limo had picked me up to take me to the airport. I'd insisted Ray not see me off. The paparazzi would be rabid enough as it was. We planned to have Nate issue a statement in a few days about our engagement ending. But Flo had already called me to let me know that TMZ had reported that I wasn't wearing my engagement ring when I was spotted by a reporter as I was heading for the airport.

Oops, more tears. I turned away so the stranger couldn't see. Stupid. Tears did nothing but make my eyes red and swollen. A tissue suddenly appeared in front of me.

"Thanks." I grabbed it and dabbed at my wet cheeks.

"You'd better buckle your seat belt. We're getting ready to take off."

I knew that deep voice. I whipped around to make sure.

"Rafe! What are you doing here? I left you a note."

"Yeah. Saw it." He frowned and waved to the flight attendant.

"I'll take Jack Daniel's neat as soon as you get a chance. Thanks." He smiled at the woman, who looked only too happy to serve him anything he wanted, then he turned back to me. "You really going to do this thing all by yourself?"

"Yes." I didn't share the thought that I was scared spitless. Any vampire would worry about vulnerability during daylight and the death sleep. But my building was owned by Damian, a vampire who'd planned for those kinds of security issues. I just had to be careful. That's all.

"Fine." He leaned back and closed his eyes as the jet engines revved for takeoff.

"Fine? Then what are you doing here? You know I can't afford you. And I don't want a bodyguard now anyway. That's for rock stars and gangsters." I sat up and buckled my seat belt.

He just kept his eyes closed. "I get that."

"Answer me." I shook his arm. "What are you doing on this plane?"

"Going to Austin. Same as you." He opened one eye. "Relax. The plane's taking off. I'll talk to you after I get my drink. I haven't been getting a hell of a lot of sleep lately. Sit back and be quiet."

"Well!" I huffed, crossed my arms and plucked a magazine out of the seat back in front of me. Oh, great. One of the few I'd read this month. I stared at it anyway while the jet climbed and Rafe sat there with his eyes closed.

He looked different. Relaxed. Wow. Long lashes against his tanned skin. His black hair was growing out and curled against the collar of his white cotton shirt. His jeans were the kind of butt huggers that made me lick my lips. I quickly went back to my magazine and an article on designer shoes. I looked down. He wore black leather boots, the kind that went with Harleys. Did he own a motorcycle in his human form?

I had lots of questions for him. We really didn't know each other. Take that back. He knew *everything* about me. I knew next to nothing about him. Like what Jerry had on him that had put Rafe into a five-year contract to do the dog thing. And it hadn't been just about the money. They'd let that much drop.

"Here you go, Mr. Valdez." The flight attendant served Rafe a glass and fussed with his tray table. "May I get you something now, Ms. St. Clair?" She'd already tried to serve me before and I'd turned her down.

I shook my head. No synthetics on this flight and I didn't feel like dragging her into the bathroom and taking her down a pint. Oh, come on. Just a little sick vamp humor. I was enjoying a nice wallow in self-pity. Rafe took a swallow and smiled.

"Nice. Great to be off duty. Can't tell you how long it's been since I could just kick back and enjoy a drink." He took another sip. The flight attendant stopped on her way down the aisle and looked a question at him. "Keep 'em coming, sweetheart."

"You're not going to get drunk, are you, Rafe?" I could just see me trying to get him off the plane. I had vamp strength, but it would be awkward to say the least. Maybe I should call Flo and Richard to pick us up at the airport.

"No, I'll stop at three. I'll just be pleasantly relaxed, then I'll sleep the rest of the way." He glanced around the first-class cabin. "Not that I'm supposed to care, but I think you'll be okay if I actually sleep, right?"

"Sure. You read my note, didn't you?" I stuck the magazine back in with the others. "I'm not going to need your services. I e-mailed Jerry and told him the same thing. We're done. I'm on my own."

"Right. Got it." Rafe handed his empty glass to the attendant and took a fresh one, this obviously a double. He grinned at her. "You read my mind. Thanks." He took a sip. "Now, where were we? Oh, yeah. You were firing me."

"Not exactly. I can give you references if you need them. Jerry can too, I'm sure." I nibbled a fingernail, then jerked my hand back into my lap.

"No thanks. I've got my future all worked out. I've been

saving and plan to open a bar. I'm used to being up all night. Seems like the perfect fit." He smiled and tilted the glass to look at the liquid inside. "And you owe me a place to stay. Remember?"

"What?" I was still processing the bar thing.

"You told me I could have Flo's old room if I ever needed it. Since I'll be using all my money for this new business, I'm taking you up on that. The restaurant on the other side of the tattoo parlor next to your shop is folding, and it'll work for the bar. So your digs are a convenient location." He took another swallow. "We'll be roommates, Glory. But, sorry, no more dog body for me. You'll have to get used to my human form. I'll shift for emergencies, but that's it."

"Uh, wow." I leaned back in my seat. Rafael Valdez as roommate. Sharing the one bathroom. I sat up. "We need ground rules, Rafe."

"Sure. I get that." He grinned. "I'm really pretty easy to get along with. Same guy, just different"—he leaned closer when the flight attendant passed by—"exterior. This way you won't have to put me on a leash." He winked. "Unless that floats your boat."

My cheeks grew hot and I cleared my throat. "You know better than that. No running around in your underwear, Rafe."

"Fine. Don't own much anyway. But, Glory"—he drained his second glass and reached for his third—"feel free to run around in yours. I've always loved a woman with curves."

Read on for a special preview of
Gerry Bartlett's next novel

Real Vampires Have More to Love

Available December 2010 from Berkley Books!

"**Would** you quit walking around here naked?" I'd tolerated the smell of coffee and—much, much worse—baking cinnamon rolls, but I'd be damned if I'd watch my new roommate eat and drink wearing nothing more than a damp towel.

"Why, Glory? Is the sight of my bare chest getting to you?" Rafael Valdez licked white icing off one fingertip, and my fangs stabbed through my gums.

"Listen. I've put up with your marathon showers until there's no hot water left for mine. And your cooking smells." Oh, great. Tears. But was it fair? Rafe's a shape-shifter and seemed to have an insatiable appetite. He'd spent nearly five years stuck in dog form, acting as my bodyguard. Now he was staying all too human and was no longer at my mercy for his menu. Who knew he was a gourmet cook? Of course, popping open a can of sweet rolls may not be gourmet in some books, but I knew nirvana when I smelled it.

He polished off roll number six—yes, I'd been counting—then stood. I would *not* notice the towel flapping open. He strolled over—flap, flap—to lay a gentle hand on my shoulder. Someone in this apartment was making a trip to the nearest discount store to get jumbo beach towels tonight. Since Rafe obviously didn't care who ogled his family jewels, that "someone" would have to be me. Serve him right if I bought hot pink Hello Kitty. Let him strut his stuff in that.

"I'm sorry, Glory." He smiled, his dimples showing.

It was still a shock to see Valdez the human hunk. He'd been a cute dog, usually a Labradoodle with wavy black hair. He still had the thick, curly locks, with dark eyes to match, but now there was a whole Latin-lover thing going on, complete with those teasing dimples that were an absolute killer where the ladies were concerned.

Not me, of course. We were friends. Nothing more. V knew way too much about me. He'd been an up-close-and-personal witness to my love life, a tangled mess at the moment. And he'd listened to me wail ad nauseam about my issues. Which were numerous. I was even afraid he knew my deepest, darkest secret—the number when I stepped on a bathroom scale. I'd just been through a weight-loss experiment and had a feeling he'd peeked. I mean, wouldn't you if your best friend had been weighing in mere feet away?

"Forget it, V. I'm a mess. Doesn't take much to set me off these days." My voice cracked. Oops. Was another meltdown coming? Personally, I was sick of myself. Made some tough decisions lately and regretted at least one of them almost instantly.

"No, Glory, I've been an ass. I get it. Vampires can't eat. I know what it's like to crave what you can't have." He pulled me into his arms, and I felt weepy enough to actually lean into him. Damn those cinnamon rolls. Out of a can, but still.

"It's . . . it's just that they *smell* so good." And he looked so fine. And felt so warm and strong and . . . I sucked it up and pushed away. "We need to get some things straight here." I didn't have to glance down to know that, hello, part of him was already headed that direction under the stupid skimpy towel. Nice to know that Mr. Tall, Dark and Shifty wasn't immune to my dubious charms.

Oh, who was I kidding? I still had on my shapeless Snoopy nightshirt and hadn't combed my hair since yesterday. It was probably his breakfast Rafe was excited about.

"Yeah, well. It's your place. But I've got to eat." His dimples were showing again as he headed back to sit at the kitchen table. "I'll scarf these down, then spray some air freshener. Will that make you feel better?"

I sighed and collapsed on the couch. "What would make me feel better would be if you put on some clothes. Bought some underwear, for crying out loud."

"Whoa. Guess I *am* getting to you." He laughed. "Cut me a break. I spent years naked inside a dog body. No wardrobe necessary." He dragged a finger through a puddle of icing and licked it clean. "And I've never been too crazy about underwear. But for you, I'll deal. I just haven't had a chance to shop. I've been trying to get this nightclub off the ground."

"Yeah, how's that going?" I picked up my bottle of synthetic blood. Yawn. Not even my favorite type. Because my fave is expensive. And Glory St. Clair is always on a budget.

"Not great. Everything costs more than I'd thought it would. So today I finally caved and called an old friend. She has plenty of money and likes the club scene. Unfortunately, knowing Nadia, she won't be a silent partner." Rafe picked up his empty plate, rinsed it off and set it in the sink.

"Nadia? Is she a shifter too?" Even the name sounded exotic.

"Vampire. I worked for her back in the seventies. She's got bars and nightclubs all over the world. Austin will be a new scene for her, so she's coming tomorrow to scope it out. She wasn't about to invest just on my say-so. If she likes what she sees, we'll strike a deal." Rafe plopped into a chair across from me.

Oh, he did not just flash me. I stood and stalked into the kitchen to rinse out my glass bottle. We recycle.

"Good luck with that. Now I'm going down to the shop.

Up here we need some rules. You've got to shower during the day. While I'm conked out in my death sleep. The hot-water heater here has only one good shower a night in it, and I have a feeling you just took it." I strode over to the door leading to the bathroom, dreading what I'd get when I tried the water for my shower.

"Sorry. My body clock's still on vamp time. Work all night, sleep all day, but with one eye open. You know?" Rafe got up and sauntered over to face me.

"Right. You went way above and beyond what any pay-check required to protect me." I kept my eyes on his. Other-wise, I'd be checking out that truly great chest just inches from my nose. Didn't help that his scent was as familiar as my own. Hey, Valdez the dog had slept on the foot of my bed for *years*. One inhale and I felt safe and cared for.

"We're even. You saved my furry butt a time or two." He grinned. "Like from a crowd of energy-sucking psychos."

"We'll *never* be even." I couldn't smile at that memory. He'd almost been killed by a group of vampires who'd been trying to get to *me*. "I'll always be grateful to you. But you're off the payroll. And I've got to learn to deal without a body-guard now. We're friends. Roommates. So sleep with both eyes closed, buddy. You deserve that."

I admit that, while I was determined to be independent for the first time in my life, the concept freaked me out more than a little. But I'd told my overprotective maker and long-time lover, Jeremy Blade, to give me my space. That in-cluded no more freebies like the twenty-four/seven security he'd provided for the past, oh, four hundred years. Stupid me had even turned down the chance to stay in Hollywood and play house with amazing rock star Israel Caine.

Sure I'm insane. But that's me. Now I was out to prove that I could stand on my own two vampire feet. In cute shoes, of course. Me crying myself to sleep ever since I'd come back from Hollywood was just me being stupid.

"You deserve to be safe. How I sleep is my business, Glory. Don't stress about it." Rafe put his hands on my shoulders.

"And get this, lady." He stared down at me, suddenly serious. No sign of a dimple. "Yeah, I'm your friend, and I'll protect you if I see the need, with or without a paycheck."

"You shouldn't—" I blinked when he backed me up to the wall.

"I don't take orders from you anymore. Right?"

"Right. Rafe, what's the deal?" His body felt almost hot compared to my vamp subhuman temperature, and it was so close. I inhaled again, but this time, instead of "safe," I got a sizzle of something I hadn't expected.

"The deal is I've watched you with Blade and Caine, and I figure there's a reason you won't commit to either one of them." He moved his hands from my shoulders to my neck, his thumbs doing funny things to the skin behind my ears.

"Uh." I shivered, absolutely speechless for once.

His grin was slow and knowing. "Don't worry, Glory. I'm not going to rush you. But one of these nights I'm going to end up in your bed again, and it's not going to be lying at your feet."

He stepped back and headed down the hall, his towel hitting the floor as he walked into his bedroom and shut the door.

I was left with the image of his perfect, taut butt burned into my brain. Dimples there too. Damn.

"Glory, I'm glad you're here. Things have been crazy." Lacy Devereau, my day manager and right-hand girl in the shop, looked me over. "You okay?"

"Fine. V's been torturing me with his cooking again. That's all." I smiled at a customer who was heading toward a dressing room with a vintage dress over her arm. "Business good, then?"

"Okay, but that's not the crazy part. It's Flo. She's made this place into wedding central. You know I'm one of her bridesmaids." Lacy glanced behind her and lowered her voice. "You've got to stop her, Glory. She's talking about changing the dresses again. I don't care if she is paying. With the wedding only a few weeks away, they'll never get here on time."

"You're right. I'm on it." I picked up a pile of receipts. The daily take hadn't been too shabby. My vintage-clothing and antique store was on trendy Sixth Street, between Mugs and Muffins, a coffee shop owned by a fellow vamp, and a tattoo parlor. The location for Rafe's nightclub was a few blocks down. We weren't far from the University of Texas, and my shop had become a hangout for some of the students. Since I called my place Vintage Vamp's Emporium and my bud Florence da Vinci, the not-so-blushing bride, had painted a vampire mural on the wall, we were really popular with Goths and vampire wannabes. I'd tried to discourage that at first, then played along, even passing out fake fangs at Halloween.

"Where's Flo now? I'm not trying on any more brides-maid dresses." I'm maid of honor and had finally persuaded my former roomie to go with something black and slim-ming, with a bodice that would cover a double-D cup. Being a tiny size six herself, Flo really didn't get a full-figured gal's issues with some of the cute little numbers she liked.

"I'm right here, *cara*. Come see what I have in the back." Flo had thrown open the door to my storeroom and rushed forward to grab my hand. "You'll love this dress. Purple. Your color. It will look fabulous on you. Jeremiah will take one look at you and—boom!—he's yours again."

Jeremiah. Jeremy Blade. Whatever the hell he chose to call himself this week. We'd parted ways in Los Angeles. He was there; I was here. One of the reasons for my recent crying jags.

"Jerry won't be seeing me. He's not here, remember?" I didn't resist when Flo dragged me into the back room. She slammed the door. I hoped customers weren't scared off, but couldn't get worked up about it. Jerry. I missed him. But I'd told him we needed a break. So we were broken. Sniff.

"He'll be here. For the wedding. He's going to be Ricardo's best man." Flo hugged me. "You'll see. I fix everything for my BFF."

Ricardo, or Richard Mainwaring, was Flo's husband. They'd been married at one ceremony, but it hadn't been up to Flo's standards. She'd decided she wanted a big wedding and had turned into bridezilla with fangs. Her rich brother Damian was footing the bill, so this was guaranteed to be the wedding of several centuries.

"Jerry said yes? He'll stand up for Richard?" I sounded a little skeptical because even though the guys got along fine, Jerry is a hardheaded Scot and Richard is English through and through. I guess I thought Richard would bring over one of his old Vatican cronies for the occasion. Richard is a former priest. Long story.

"He was honored, of course." Flo flipped open a magazine and stabbed at a picture. "This dress. Cute? No?"

"What's with the manicure?" I couldn't help noticing that each nail wore a slightly different color. I lifted her finger to examine the dress under it. It *was* cute. Actually might work on my size-twelve figure if there was elastic involved. Forget puff sleeves. Make my arms look fat. But Jerry liked me in purple. And loved a plunging neckline. I had visions of him seeing me walk down the aisle and . . .

"Glory! I said I'm trying out colors for my wedding day." Flo held out her hand. "Which one do you like?"

I focused. Okay. The differences would probably not be apparent to the casual observer, but Flo and I compared the colors to the fabric swatch from her wedding dress until we finally settled on "Blush."

"*Perfetto! Grazie*, Glory." She hugged me again. "I knew you would help me. Now I have another favor. Did you see this?" She pulled a local newspaper out from under her magazine.

"What is it?" I glanced down and recognized the picture. "Ray? He's coming to town too?" Ray a.k.a. Israel Caine. The other man I'd left in L.A. Okay, I admit it. My heart, which barely beats anyway, gave a little jig of happiness.

Both my guys, hot vampires who I loved and had decided I should give up, were coming to town. Would either of them want to see me after the way I'd given them the brush-off?

Well, Jerry wouldn't have a choice, would he? And Ray? I grabbed the paper. He was singing at a venue at the South by Southwest Music Festival. The festival was held every spring in Austin to give music producers a chance to hear new talent. The article claimed that Ray was coming with the owner of his record label, another vampire, believe it or not. Maybe Ray would drop by the shop. I'd been his mentor, and it had only been a few weeks since Ray had claimed he loved me. But then I'd dumped him. Not an action guaranteed to keep his love light burning.

"Glory? Look at me." Flo fiddled with a bottle of nail-polish remover. "That favor?"

"What is it, Flo?" I threw down the paper. How pathetic. I'd been on my own for less than a month, and I was already imagining scenarios where both men in my life were begging for me to come back to them. And then there'd been Rafe's interesting behavior. I'd looked like hell. Surely he'd been playing me, hadn't really meant that he—

"Glory, would you quit ignoring me? And blocking your thoughts?" Flo frowned at me and shook my arm. "This is serious, *mia amica*."

I hid my smile. Didn't everything to do with my friend's wedding rank right up there with the desire for world peace and half-price sales? "Okay, Flo, I'm riveted. What's up?"

"Ray. Israel Caine. He'll be in Austin right before my wedding, *sì?*"

"Yes." I didn't like the calculating look on Flo's face. She was blocking her thoughts too. But then, she always blocked her thoughts. Not that I usually tried to pry into them anyway. But this was an emergency. "What do you want, Flo?"

"I want Israel Caine to sing at my wedding, Glory. You must ask him for me. Please. He'll do it for you. You saved his life. *Sì?*"

"He's done a lot for me too, Flo. We're even." I frowned

down at that purple dress. Six to eight weeks for delivery. But Flo would figure out a way around that minor technicality, probably by throwing money at it.

The major issue? Ray and Jerry at Flo's wedding. Sounded like a recipe for disaster to me. The two men hated each other. Because I loved both of them. And Rafe would be there, of course. I'd ask him to be my date. He'd love to jump into a brawl with my name on it. I smiled. The future looked positively Glory-ous. (Sorry. Couldn't resist.)